Smoke Wagon

A MORGAN CLYDE WESTERN

SMOKE WAGON

WITHDRAWN

BRETT COGBURN

FIVE STAR
A part of Gale, Cengage Learning

GALE
CENGAGE Learning·

Farmington Hills, Mich • San Francisco • New York • Waterville, Maine
Meriden, Conn • Mason, Ohio • Chicago

GALE
CENGAGE Learning®

LIBRARY OF CONGRESS CATALOGING-IN-PUBLICATION DATA

Names: Cogburn, Brett, author.
Title: Smoke wagon / Brett Cogburn.
Description: First edition. | Waterville : Five Star Publishing, [2017] | Series: A
    Morgan Clyde western ; book 1
Identifiers: LCCN 2016041611| ISBN 9781432831929 (hardcover) | ISBN
    1432831925 (hardcover)
Subjects: | BISAC: FICTION / Action & Adventure. | FICTION / Westerns. | GSAFD:
    Adventure fiction. | Western stories.
Classification: LCC PS3603.O3255 S63 2017 | DDC 813/.6—dc23
LC record available at https://lccn.loc.gov/2016041611

First Edition. First Printing: March 2017
Find us on Facebook— https://www.facebook.com/FiveStarCengage
Visit our website— http://www.gale.cengage.com/fivestar/
Contact Five Star™ Publishing at FiveStar@cengage.com

Printed in the United States of America
1 2 3 4 5 6 7 21 20 19 18 17

SMOKE WAGON

CHAPTER ONE

Morgan Clyde stepped out of the door of the passenger car and paused on the steps, apparently unaware of, or simply not giving a damn about, the other people lined up behind him who were wishing he would move so that they could get off the train. The locomotive up the line hissed as the engineer bled off the boiler pressure, and the late winter breeze blew a cloud of steam, cinders, and coal smoke down the depot decking. Morgan squinted through the haze while he shoved a cigar in the corner of his mouth below his black mustache. His left hand flipped the tail of his black frock coat behind the Remington and Beal revolver holstered high on that hip at a cross draw, and he struck a match on the butt of the pistol and cupped it before his face, coolly studying the sprawling tent city before him over the flame.

The first thing that struck him was the noise of so many people moving about the camp: men shouting to each other or cursing wagon teams, the pound of hammers and the rasp of saws where a crew was working to raise the frame on the new depot house, and someone banging away on an out-of-tune piano down the street.

The second thing that hit him was the smell—the smell and the filth.

It had rained recently, and the one so-called street was nothing more than a mud lane running straight as a Cherokee arrow through the tents and false-fronted, canvas-roofed businesses lining either side of it. Water stood in the low places and in every hoof divot and wagon rut. And it wasn't only mud and rainwater. Horse and mule manure, dog feces, emptied chamber pots, and trash all mixed freely into the viscous soup that the street had become, until the whole camp looked and smelled like a hog pen.

The letter he had received claimed that there were, at last count, three hundred souls in the construction camp, but here it was a little past midday, and with most of the railroad crews still out working, the street was teeming with people, wading and cursing their way across or along the street. Wagon wheels sank to the hubs in bottomless ruts, and the mule teams pulling them worked hock deep with their ears flattened and their backs humped against the strain of the mud sucking everything down, down, down. Their trace chains popped each time the mules lunged forward, and the drivers shouted at pedestrians to get the hell out of the way before their wagons stalled out and became stuck.

Boards had been laid as walkways in places, but most of the boards had already sunk below the surface. Staying even reasonably clean was impossible in the shin-deep quagmire. Everyone in sight was muddy from the knees down, and some worse.

A drunk came out of one of the tent saloons and sank to his knees in an especially deep hole. The suction of the mud took hold of one of his legs, and he windmilled his arms wildly to catch his balance until he fell face first in the street. He was soon up on his feet again, coated from head to toe in good old Indian Nations mud, and looking for the boot that had been pulled off his trapped foot. A wagonload of logs was about on top of him, and he lunged away just as the lead mules trampled whatever chance he had of ever recovering the lost boot. The wagon's driver and the drunk exchanged loud insults, but the wagon inched on toward the tracks.

Morgan took it all in with his face as hard and still and

expressionless as an Indian's, his ice-blue eyes gauging the scene before him like an undertaker measuring a man for a coffin. He shook out the match and flipped it to the ground in a smoking arc.

Somebody shouted near the bare-bones frame of the new depot house, followed by catcalls and boisterous laughter from several more men near the train. A pistol cracked, and out of instinct and reflex, Morgan's hand took hold of the Remington's grip. The people behind Morgan in the doorway of the passenger car flinched and ran into each other trying to get back inside. It only took Morgan an instant to spot the culprits. A young black man dressed like a cowboy in tall-topped boots and a red silk neckerchief, and two Indians dressed much the same, had their pistols out and were shooting them into the air. They paraded up and down the depot platform like strutting roosters.

At least fifty people were gathered alongside the newly arrived train, either as passengers or gawkers from the camp. The first pistol shot quieted the crowd, and then they scattered like quail flushed from the tall grass when all three of the drunken cowboys fired a second volley. A buggy mare spooked so badly that she kicked one of her buggy shafts in two, and fell on her side and became tangled in her harness.

"Welcome to the Indian Nations, you train-riding sons a bitches!" the black cowboy shouted and took off his broad-brimmed hat and waved it in a circle above his head.

One of his companions whooped beside him, and then leaned back his head and did his best imitation of a coyote yipping at the moon. He had a pint bottle of whiskey in one hand, and his pistol in the other. "Gonna scalp me a tenderfoot before today's over."

One of the carpenters up in the rafters of the depot house flung his hammer at the black cowboy, nearly striking him in the skull. The black cowboy popped off a shot at the hammerflinger, but the carpenter was nimble and smart enough to dodge amongst the rafters. The shot went wild, and it didn't help the black cowboy's aim that he was sloppy drunk and reeling on his boot heels. He was still peering up in the rafters with his pistol cocked and hoping for another shot at the carpenter when one of his Indian companions hissed a warning at him.

It looked like one of the railroad crews was coming up the street with its attention on the trio causing the ruckus. Every one of those railroad workers was carrying a club or a sledgehammer or some other kind of bludgeoning instrument to adjust the behavior of the men doing all the hell raising. The black cowboy forgot about the hammer-flinging carpenter, and he and his comrades began to slip away through the crowd, trying to put distance between themselves and the railroad gang coming their way. The whole episode ended as quickly as it had begun.

"You've got to be kidding," the woman behind Morgan said.

She was middle-aged, portly, and wearing a little bonnet as prim and sour as the look on her freckled, big-nosed face. Her husband, two inches shorter than her and half her weight, stood behind her in the passenger car door with a pipe clenched in one corner of his mouth. A mass of curly hair red hair stuck out from under the wool cap he wore.

"It'll be all right, Mother," her husband said.

"Where's the law?" She gave an indignant huff.

"There ain't no law in Ironhead Station, Mother. None at all."

"Lord, help us."

"They say there ain't no church west of St. Louis, and no God west of Fort Smith, neither," the husband added.

"Shame on you. Take that blasphemy back right now." The woman immediately slapped him hard on the shoulder.

Morgan let go of his pistol and continued to listen to the

pair's conversation while his eyes followed the trio of hellions' retreat down the street. Apparently, to hear him talk, the woman's husband had been in the camp before.

"They've appointed two marshals: one a former Yankee officer, and the other a Texan. But neither of them lasted longer 'n the time it takes to spit," the husband said. "First one turned in his badge his first day on the job and caught the next train north. Had his fill of it, and was glad he didn't ride out of here lying on his back. The second one, that Texan, wasn't so smart, but he had more guts than a slaughterhouse. Lasted a whole three days before Texas George picked a fight with him and shot him dead."

"Sodom and Gomorrah is what I see. We should've have stayed in Carthage," the wife said.

"We've already talked about this a hundred times if we've talked about it once. If you want to go back to Missouri, you can. It ain't like I didn't try to tell how it was going to be."

The wife shook her head. "No, we'll stick. Can't be a family with us back home and you down here. We'll have to find a way to get by, that's what we'll have to do."

"They're always like this," Morgan said, almost as if talking to himself.

It took the man and woman a bit to realize that it was he who had spoken, so quietly had he stood before.

"Begging your pardon?" the husband asked.

Morgan exhaled a cloud of cigar smoke and turned to them. "I said, these end-of-the-tracks construction camps are always like this."

"Yep, but this one's way worse than most, and it's gonna be wild for a while," the husband answered. "That trestle across the South Canadian has things held up. They bridged the North Canadian without a problem, but this one is a whole 'nother animal. The first one they built on the south fork of the river collapsed on them, and then some of the local badmen tried to burn down their next attempt. This railroad ain't never going to get across the Territory if they don't get that bridge built, and there's more and more men packing into Ironhead Station every day—most of them the kind that you'd rather not see around."

"Is that what they're calling it?" Morgan asked. "Ironhead?"

"For now, until it catches fire, or somebody comes up with a better name." The husband chewed on his pipe stem and made a clicking sound in his cheek. "The railroad's laid off more than half its men until the bridge gets built and they can start laying track again. Most of those they laid off are still hanging around with too much whiskey and too much time on their hands, and word's gone out across the Territory that the company is stalled out here. Every holdup artist, tinhorn gambler, whiskey peddler, and pimp and sporting woman in the Nations is either here, or on their way here to get in on the action."

"Hank!" the wife said. "Watch your talk."

The husband gave a fake grimace that was meant as an apology, but continued, regardless. "I've only been gone a week, but I already see another tent saloon that wasn't here when I left and about twice as many people."

"I know it sounds bad of me, but the Lord ought to strike this whole place down." The wife interrupted Morgan's thoughts. "Turn the whole thing to nothing but a pillar of salt and then wash it clean with a flood."

"Please don't mind the Missus. My Lottie is a God-fearing woman, but she just ain't used to all this." The husband set down an armload of luggage, and held out his right hand to Morgan. "Name's Henry Bickford. Everyone calls me Hank."

Morgan shook with him, surprised at the hard strength in the little man's calloused grip. "Morgan Clyde."

Hank Bickford pumped Morgan's hand, but leaned back as if to get a better look up at him upon hearing his name. There was a measuring and cautious look on his face, and he gathered his words carefully before he spoke again. "Pleased to meet you, Mr. Clyde."

"My Hank is a horseshoer and blacksmith for the line. What brings you here, Mr. Clyde? What line of work are you in?" the wife asked, oblivious to the warning look on her husband's face.

Morgan reached down and picked up his single little leather valise and the bedroll he had left on the deck while lighting his cigar. Hank Bickford noticed that the bedroll was wrapped around a suede leather rifle case.

"You might say I'm a troubleshooter." Morgan smiled around the cigar, as if it took an effort for the muscles of his face, and as if it were an unnatural expression for him.

"Troubleshooter?" the wife asked. "What kind of job is that? Are you here to get the bridge built?"

"You might say that. Good day." Morgan tucked his belongings under one arm, tipped his hat to them, and started down the steps.

Hank Bickford waited until Morgan was off the train and several yards away before he picked up their luggage again.

"Seemed like a nice man for a Yankee," she said. "Although, that was kind of rude for him to walk off like that without answering my question."

Hank didn't reply to her, still watching Morgan's tall form winding its way through the crowd of people headed for the company headquarters. Lottie tightened her shawl about her neck and shoulders and stiffened beside him when she noticed a pair of prostitutes standing alongside the tracks with nothing but skimpy wraps over their underclothes, and calling out ribald jokes and loud, lewd innuendos to a group of men at work unloading equipment off a flatcar.

"Those girls sure must be hot natured to go with so little clothes," Hank said.

Lottie elbowed him in the ribs and pulled her children close to her, hugging them to either side of her broad hips like little chicks underneath a mother hen. "This is the devil's playground if ever there was such a thing."

Hank gave her a half-hearted, worried smile, and then nodded his head at Morgan's back. "Maybe so, Mother, but the devil didn't show up until today."

"Him?"

"Yes, him. You might say hell's come to breakfast, sure enough."

"If you won't mind your talk in front of me, then remember our children."

"Sorry, Mother, but that's the pure truth." Hank's attention turned to the construction crew still chasing after the trio that had been hoorahing and threatening the train's arrival. He shook his head somberly and almost regretfully while looking over the camp, as if standing over a friend's grave at a funeral and mourning his passing. "And these poor amateurs don't even know what's coming. But they will soon enough. You wait and see. Won't be long until word gets out all through this hell-on-wheels that Morgan Clyde has come to town."

CHAPTER TWO

The railroad company had its office at the end of the platform alongside the depot house under construction, and on the corner facing the head of what passed for a main street. It was a single-story, two-room frame affair with a canvas wagon tarp for a temporary roof, and green-sawn yellow pine planks still oozing sap for siding. But however hurriedly and shoddily it was built, it did have the only boardwalk in town in front of it, consisting of a narrow ribbon of small logs laid side by side in a corduroy fashion, and a man could at least keep his feet dry. Morgan glanced at the sign over the front door. *MK&T RAILROAD OFFICE, IRONHEAD STATION, INDIAN TERRITORY.* Two tough-looking men sat in chairs to either side of the door, and both of them had shotguns laid across their laps.

He weaved his way through the crowd on the boardwalk, and nodded at the two guards. Neither of them spoke to him, but they didn't stop him from going inside, either. The front room consisted of a table piled with all kinds of ledgers and various other clerical papers, and a single chair behind it. Apparently, the clerk was gone on other business, but Morgan heard voices coming from an interior doorway to the rear of the office.

Three men stopped their conversation and looked his way when he stepped into the back room. One of them was a short, stocky, bulldog of a man, a tick past middle-age, and dressed in a tailored suit. He sat at the back of the room, reared back in his office chair with his fingers laced together over the belly of his paisley vest and his feet propped up on one corner of his office desk. Both of his jaws were covered in mutton-chop whiskers, combed and waxed and sticking out like wings, and his hair was oiled and parted with perfect precision down the middle of his skull. His blue-gray eyes were like glass when he glanced at Morgan in the doorway, and an impatient frown crinkled his mouth.

Another man stood at a large set of plans and draftsman drawings of the river bridge pinned to the wall. He was young, and unlike the man at the desk, he was dressed in rough work clothes with his sleeves rolled up to his elbows and his thumbs hooked in his suspenders. His lower body, from his canvas work pants to his lace-up boots, was covered in a thick layer of dried mud.

The third man sat in a chair at one end of the desk. He was tall and scarecrow thin, with a stoop to his narrow shoulders and a hump in his back to match a young buffalo's. Like the man behind the desk, he was dressed in a suit; however his wasn't nearly so expensive or neat. Everything about him was wrinkled and haphazard, from his threadbare jacket, to his untied string tie, to the crooked way his eyeglasses sat on the bridge of his beak of a nose.

"If you're looking to hire on, you need to come back when the clerk is in," the man behind the desk said in a tone of dismissal. He turned his attention back to the drawing on the wall, as if he had forgotten Morgan's presence already.

Morgan set his belongings down, leaning the end of the rifle case against the wall, and reached in his vest pocket and pulled forth an envelope. He crossed the room and pitched the envelope on the desk in front of the man.

"Your letter said you'd pay me fifty dollars for coming down here and looking things over, and I've looked it over," Morgan said.

16

"See here, we're holding an important meeting," the stooped man at the end of the desk said.

The man behind the desk held up a hand to quiet him, while he eyed the letter and then stared at Morgan as if seeing him for the first time. "Hold on, Euless. I did send for this man."

The one called Euless gave Morgan an expectant look, as if waiting for a name. Morgan ignored him and focused his attention on the man behind the desk.

"Your answering letter said you would be here a week ago." The man behind the desk had a midwest accent that Morgan couldn't quite place—maybe Illinois, or Indiana.

"I was busy," Morgan replied. "Are you Superintendent Duvall?"

"That I am." The man behind the desk reached into a shipping crate behind his desk that served as a temporary cabinet, and pulled out a bottle of whiskey and several glasses. He set them on the desk. "Willis G. Duvall, MK&T Railroad, at your service. This man to my left is the agent for the Creek Indian tribe, Euless Pickins."

The Indian agent nodded at Morgan. He was the odd one in the room—nervous and restless and continually shifting positions in his chair. Morgan noted how the man stared at the floor and rarely made eye contact, and how he picked at a scab on the back of one of his hands.

"And this Scotsman is my head construction engineer and foreman." Superintendent Duvall pointed at the man in work clothes standing before the bridge plans on the wall. "Hope McDaniels, meet Morgan Clyde. Mr. Clyde is going to be our new chief of police."

"Morgan Clyde!" the Indian agent blurted out before the engineer could reply. He made no attempt to hide his distaste at hearing Morgan's name.

"Care for a toddy?" Superintendent Duvall tried to smooth

over the embarrassing gaff by gesturing at one of the whiskey glasses on the desk.

"Business first," Morgan replied.

"Have a seat then." Duvall pointed at a spare chair.

"I believe I'll stand."

"Are you always so disagreeable?"

"No sense wasting any of our time."

"Suit yourself." Duvall poured himself a drink and pitched a tin badge on the table before he leaned back in his chair again. "You start today."

Morgan didn't even look at the badge, much less pick it up. "We need to sort out a few things first."

"Go ahead." There was impatience in the superintendent's voice.

"One hundred and fifty dollars a month," Morgan said.

"You never told me you were trying to hire this man," Agent Pickins interrupted them again.

Superintendent Duvall made another dismissive wave of his hand at the Indian agent. "Let's hear the man out, Euless."

"I hire my own deputies, and you'll pay them seventy-five a month," Morgan said as if it were only he and the railroad superintendent in the room. "I won't hire more than two of them."

"Your price is too steep. That's half again what you quoted me in your reply to my letter."

"You get what you pay for," Morgan said. "And I quoted you that first price before I had a chance to look this camp over. I've seen it now, and I think it calls for a premium on my services."

"I suppose this is negotiable?"

"Those are my terms, take them or leave them," Morgan said. "Normally I get a cut of the fines, too, but this place won't be here long enough to set that up."

"This is preposterous. You've no right to hire a marshal,"

18

Agent Pickins said. "This isn't a real town, nor will it be according to the terms the railroad has promised the Indian tribes."

Superintendent Duvall pulled a folder from his file cabinet while the Indian agent was talking. He slapped the file down on the desk and thumbed it open, donning a pair of spectacles so that he could inspect the documents within it. "Morgan Clyde: Two years as a New York policeman. Quit at the start of the war to join up with Company A, 1st United States Sharpshooters, Berdan's regiment. Decorated for valor at Malvern Hill and Gettysburg. Marshal of various cow towns: Sedalia and Baxter Springs. Last known job, U.S. Deputy Marshal for Judge Story's federal court out of Van Buren, Arkansas."

"I don't need your report to know of this man's reputation . . ." Agent Pickins tried again, but wasn't allowed to finish.

"Euless, I'll remind you that we're all gentlemen here, and that there's little that you can add about this man that I don't already know." Duvall gave the Indian agent a sharp look and then closed the folder and slapped it with the palm of his hand like a judge's gavel in a final verdict. "The Pinkerton Detective Agency put this dossier together for me as a favor."

Morgan leaned over and rubbed his cigar out in the tin ashtray on one corner of the desk. "What else does that file of yours say?"

Duvall laced his hands together over his belly again and met Morgan's hard look. "Among other things, it says you killed two men in Baxter Springs, and then another while you were working for Story's court. Says you're a damned hard man who's too quick to shoot to suit the tastes of most of your employers. I heard myself that Judge Story fired you for shooting and wounding a prisoner who claimed his hands were shackled at the time of the incident."

Morgan ground the cigar more firmly into the ashtray,

unaware that he was crushing the stub of it. "Somebody's a damned liar."

"Maybe, but if I didn't believe most of this report on you wasn't accurate, I wouldn't have sent for you. My job is to get this railroad to Texas, and yours will be to see that none of these secesh sons of bitches and renegade trash that have been holding up my trestle job get in my way again." Duvall leaned forward until his face was closer to Morgan's over the desk. "You can sweet talk them, kiss them, rock them in a baby cradle, or you can shoot every last living one of them between the eyes for all I care. This line has got to make it into Texas by the first of the year, and I want some by God law and order in this camp."

"You should have discussed this with me first," Agent Pickins said.

Duvall held Morgan's stare a brief instant longer and then turned to the Indian agent. "It's my company's money that's going to pay this man, and what do you care if I hire a railroad policeman to handle my camp?"

"Your line runs on Indian land, and as a duly appointed agent to the Creek tribe . . ."

"My line runs on a right of way granted to me by the federal government." Superintendent Duvall turned to the engineer at the bridge drawing. "What do you think, Hope? It's your bridge."

"Something has to be done." The engineer already seemed to have lost interest in the conversation and he was studying the diagrams again.

"There you go, Euless," Superintendent Duvall said. "Two votes to one. You've now been consulted with."

"I agree we need a peacekeeper, but this man's little better than an outlaw himself," Agent Pickins said.

"You be careful before you go any farther with that line,"

Morgan said quietly.

"I will not be bullied by the likes of you." The Indian agent looked defiantly at Morgan, quickly adjusting the wire-rimmed eyeglasses on the bridge of his nose, but only managing to leave them more askew than they had been before. "We have no need for another ruffian in this camp."

"I'll not warn you again." Morgan turned slowly to face the Indian agent, and the tone of his voice had changed.

Superintendent Duvall cleared his throat. "I don't think striking a federal Indian agent and a man of the cloth will help your reputation any, Clyde."

Morgan frowned at the Indian agent, as if reassessing the man. "Him?"

"I'm an ordained Methodist minister," the Indian agent said, straightening a bit in his chair.

"Euless used to run the Ashbury Mission school for the Indian children, and he was appointed agent to the Creeks not long ago," Duvall added. "He and his Indians have been howling to Washington about my right of way being granted without their approval."

Morgan grunted. "You've heard my terms. Agree to them, or give me my fifty dollars for coming all the way down here."

"And here's my final offer," Duvall answered. "Seventy-five dollars a month for you, and fifty dollars a month for your deputies. Have we got a deal?"

"Pay me my fifty dollars, and I'll be gone." Morgan turned to McDaniels, the engineer, while Duvall opened the safe behind his desk. "That's quite a bridge you're building."

McDaniels nodded absentmindedly, and it took a bit to pull his attention from whatever he was thinking on. "Yes, yes, it's a real corker. We made a good start on it once, but the first design was all wrong and the pylons didn't hold and the whole bloody thing collapsed. And now we've got other problems."

"Such as?"

The engineer shared a look with his superintendent, and only continued when Duvall nodded at him. "It seems some of the rough element in camp don't want the railroad to progress past here. Somebody tried to burn the bridge down two weeks ago."

"They're fine with making their profit right here, aren't they? And I'm guessing you've got a few saloon owners and a bunch of others that like having all the sheep they can fleece congregated in one herd."

Again, a look was passed between the superintendent and the engineer, but like before, the superintendent showed his agreement with a simple nod of his chin. "There's a bad mob of outlaws down in the thickets along the river. Not only do they cause problems in camp, but they robbed one of our wagon trains coming overland with supplies from Fort Smith two weeks ago. And the worst thing might not be all the criminal sorts, but the fact that I'm having problems getting all of my men to show up for work because they're drunk and laid up in one of those tent saloons."

Duvall held out Morgan's money. "My offer still stands."

"No deal." Morgan took the mix of paper money and coins and counted them before shoving them inside his pocket. He pointed at the safe behind the desk. "Is that why you've got the guards out front?"

"Rented Pinkerton agents. I keep a little money on hand, but we wait to bring in the payroll from Kansas City each month."

"Must be worse than I thought."

"You aren't the only peace officer for hire."

"No, but I'm the only one that's here." Morgan gave a curt tip of the brim of his hat and turned and went out the door.

"Abrupt, isn't he?" the engineer said when Morgan was gone.

"A difficult bastard, for sure." Superintendent Duvall scowled at the door.

"You should count yourself lucky that he didn't take your offer," the Indian agent said after Morgan left.

Duvall didn't answer him, and swirled his whiskey around in its glass and continued to stare at the door.

Agent Pickins knocked a bit of grass off of his rumpled coat and took up his hat from the rack on the wall. "Mr. Duvall, if you don't get this camp under control, I will be forced to take action. You know that the sale of intoxicating spirits in the Indian Territory is against the law, as well as the fact that you are basically setting up a town here, rather than the station you originally promised."

"My right of way grants me the roadbed and every alternate section of land alongside it."

The Indian agent scoffed. "Save that for those that don't read the newspapers. News travels fast, even way out here, Duvall. No matter what you say, Congress has revoked all but your roadbed rights. You know it and I know it. Much of your so-called grant has been deemed unconstitutional and illegal, and was never agreed to by the tribes."

"It is still being discussed. Damned lawyers." Duvall threw down the last of his drink and poured himself another one. "Shysters and crooks and liars, every one of them."

"Unless Congress changes its mind, your authority extends nowhere beyond the narrow strip surveyed to lay your tracks."

"Say what you mean, Euless," Duvall said with color flushing his face. "Don't beat around the bush if you are going to threaten me."

Agent Pickins willed himself to lift his eyes from the floor and meet the superintendent's hard look head on. "I'll go to the Board of Indian Commissioners, or Office of Indian Affairs if I must. My brother . . ."

"Yes, we know all about your brother, the great senator from the state of Vermont, and how you got your job. You've thrown his name around more than enough."

Agent Pickins shoved his hat on his head so hard that he dented the crown, and stormed out of the room.

"That Clyde is an independent, surly devil isn't he?" Duvall said to the engineer when the Indian agent was gone.

McDaniels chuckled. "I think that's putting it mildly. Kind of reminds me of someone else I know."

Duvall propped his feet up on the desk and poured himself another glass of whiskey. "That's a shame. I think he might have been mean enough to pull it off."

"We need that man. You should have paid his price."

"I'll be damned if I'll be held up by an overpriced badge packer with too high of an opinion of himself. No, he can work for what I've offered, or I'll find us another man for the job."

"And then what? What happens while we wait for you to find someone else? The camp's getting worse every day," the engineer said. "From what I hear of Clyde, he's a fair man, even if he has a reputation for being a little too willing to use his gun."

"To hell with Clyde. We don't need him."

"That was some of Texas George Kingman's mob out there shooting things up. He's supposed to have more men coming in any day. Most of his men are secesh, and they're talking it up big that no bloody Yankee railroad is going to come through their country."

"I said I'll hire us someone else. Maybe get the Lighthorse down here like Useless Pickins has been suggesting."

The engineer was too serious to laugh at Duvall's nickname for Agent Pickins, and the superintendent had said it too many times in the past for it to have any humor left, even on a better day. "The tribal courts don't have any jurisdiction over white men, and those Lighthorsemen won't bother themselves with mixing in our business. Not with Story's crooked court ruling against the tribes every time they go to trial. You know this."

Duvall downed his whiskey and threw the glass across the room, busting it against the far wall. "First, I've got the board members, politicians, and every bondholder breathing down my neck, and now I'm hearing it from you. Build your damned bridge, and leave the rest of it to me."

The engineer put his back to his boss, acting like he was studying his drawing again. He kept his back to him when he spoke again. "You didn't tell Clyde that Bill Tuck was in camp," the engineer said. "I hear Clyde killed Tuck's brother-in-law up in Baxter Springs."

"Let him and Bill Tuck kill each other if they want to. We've got a railroad to build."

CHAPTER THREE

What some were calling Ironhead Station was named after the large warehouse alongside the tracks that was used to store iron rails and other railroad construction equipment and supplies. The camp proper lay on the other side of the railroad tracks, running perpendicular to it. Some enterprising soul had built a sled of flattened logs with peeled-pole handrails, and was charging five cents to haul passengers up and down the muddy street. Morgan paid the man his fare and stepped up on the contraption, grasping desperately at one of the handrails when the driver shouted and cracked a buggy whip, and the single, skinny mule lunged against its harness.

That long row of tents flanking either side of the street had two tent saloons, and Morgan had the driver stop in front of the first one they came to. A hand-painted sign was staked beside the open flap of the door. *BULLHORN PALACE; WHISKEY, BEER, & GAMES OF CHANCE.*

Morgan grunted with irony, for there was nothing palatial about the establishment. It was a boar's nest if he had ever seen one, slung together as haphazardly and temporary as the rest of the camp. The whole thing could have been torn down and moved on in the matter of an hour—exactly what it was meant to do when the camp moved further down the line.

He stepped off the sled and trudged through the mud to the open door flap. A long oak plank laid atop three barrels served as a bar, and the tent roof sagged so low that the tobacco smoke

26

hung at head level. The floor of the tent was nothing but bare ground with the grass long since beaten away. The damp ground, spilled beer, chewing tobacco spit, and other miscellaneous discharges left a slick slime on the surface that was treacherous to anything but the most cautious step.

But that didn't seem to matter to anyone present; not to the railroad crews fresh off a long day of work, or to the other riffraff who came from hell and half creation there to try and steal their wages. The plank bar was lined elbow to elbow with men sampling its offerings, and nobody was complaining about the liquor, whether they were drinking cheap trade whiskey flavored and colored with burnt sugar and plug tobacco, and with a tiny dose of strychnine to give it a little kick, or for the big spenders, the two-bit shots of Old Crow, Thistle Dew, Hermitage, Old Forester, or Jameson Irish Whiskey. Soiled doves, or what the railroad boys called "girls of the line," intermingled with the crowd, rubbing up against the men provocatively and asking for a drink or suggesting other things. Two faro layouts, a roulette wheel, and a Mexican monte game were at the back of the tent, and there were plenty of players at each.

Morgan recognized one of the faro dealers as a man he had run out of Baxter Springs three or four years earlier. They called him Charlie Six Fingers, or something like that, and he was a known cheat and card case artist. And behind him, drinking a beer and pretending like he was watching the game, was another one that Morgan recognized from other places. He couldn't put a name to the man, but it was obvious that he was working as a bouncer or hired muscle for whoever was running the saloon. Many of the construction workers were single men apt to play as hard as they worked, and having a thumper or two around to handle them when they got too rowdy was a standard practice. The problem was that some of the more dishonest proprietors employed such men to keep an eye out for drunks with a little money who might be taken out back and rolled. The big man standing behind the faro table had that look about him, all thick skull and muscle with a hard, callous face.

Around the room, he saw several others that he didn't know, but still recognized their kind—the kind to come running when news of a boom camp spread: gamblers, whores, pimps, whiskey men, and other shady sorts, flocking to the next hell-on-wheels like crows to carrion. In any such place there was plenty of meat to pick off the bone, and easy money to be made. More than one pair of eyes was on Morgan, suspicious and wary of any stranger.

Morgan had seen it all before, and it was an ancient game that was being played. He surveyed the room for a seat to be had. There were several tables, but every chair was full. When he saw a break in the line at the bar he took the opportunity to slide in between two men, sitting his belongings at his feet and turning his back to the bar where he could keep an eye on the room. There were two bartenders working steadily, but he paid little attention to them until he felt one of them standing behind him.

"What are you having?" The voice that said it was one from the past, but not one that Morgan had forgotten.

Morgan turned slowly and faced the bartender. The man's shaved skull glistened under the lamplight as much as the gold watch chain draped across his silk vest, or the nickel-plated pocket pistol sticking out of one vest pocket. The bartender smiled and the front teeth below his waxed handlebar mustache were as white as piano keys. But there was nothing friendly in his smile, nor in the hard glint of his blue eyes.

"Long time, no see, Tuck," Morgan said. "I'll have a double shot of Old Reserve."

The bartender continued to stand with both palms flat on

the bar plank, and the muscles of his heavy arms bulging above his gartered sleeves. "You here in an official capacity? I heard the railroad's looking to hire a lawman, but I don't see a badge on you."

Morgan tried to smile back, but couldn't summon the effort—not for a man like the one he was talking to. The two of them continued to stare at each other, and to anyone who had taken the time to watch, the dislike between them was obvious.

"No, I'm only another civilian looking for a drink," Morgan answered.

"Clyde, you've got a lot of nerve coming in here after what you did to Harvey."

Morgan kept watch on the bartender's hands and the Smith & Wesson pocket pistol in his vest pocket. "Harvey got what he was asking for."

"Some don't see it that way."

"Meaning you?"

"Meaning me. Harvey was family."

"Harvey never was as tough as he thought he was. He was just mean."

"True, but that doesn't change things. Doesn't change you coming in here and rubbing my nose in it."

"This your place?"

Tuck nodded. "Lock, stock, and barrel."

"Are you going to bring me a whiskey, or do I have to get it myself?"

Bill Tuck's expression changed in an instant, as if the tension between them had never existed. He took down a bottle from behind the bar and poured a double shot for Morgan. "Just like old times, huh? This camp's booming."

A fight was breaking out at the back of the tent, between Charlie Six Fingers and one of the men he was dealing to. The disgruntled player was already up out of his chair and cursing the dealer. The rest of the tent had gone suddenly quiet, and many of them were scooting away and making room for the bloodbath they thought was about to happen.

Morgan tilted the drink back, his eyes never leaving the bartender. He set the empty glass down on the plank with a thump. "Yeah, like old times."

"That isn't any of your business," Tuck said. "You aren't the law here."

"Right, none of my business." Morgan shoved the empty glass toward him with one pointer finger. "Give me another one."

Tuck looked to the back of the tent and waited until he had the attention of the big man behind the faro table. When their eyes met, Tuck gave a nod. Charlie Six Fingers had produced a knife from somewhere on his person or from a sheath rigged under the table, and he was holding it low down with the cutting edge up and ready to gut the man who was cursing him and accusing him of cheating.

"Damn a sore loser," Tuck said. "Nobody forces them to play, and they still complain."

The man cursing Charlie Six Fingers wasn't a little man himself. He had the kind of shoulders that a man only gets swinging a sledgehammer on the rail crew, and towered over the smallish faro dealer. Knife pointed his way or not, he wasn't backing down, and he had both fists cocked and ready to fight. The bouncer moved around the table and stepped between the two of them. Two other men that Morgan hadn't noticed moved in from the sides.

The railroad worker threatening Charlie gave the bouncers an appraising, rebellious look, as if daring them to lay hand to him. He shook his head as if to clear and focus his drunken vision, then said something defiant to the big bouncer in front of him. Morgan couldn't make the words out, but barely had the man finished what he had to say before the big bouncer produced a short club from behind his back and struck him over the top of the head. The solid crack of the hardwood club on bone could be heard even at the bar. The other two bouncers caught the falling man by his armpits and skidded him towards the door with his limp legs and boot heels leaving snake marks in the slimy mud of the tent floor. The railroad man was out cold, and maybe even dead.

"See? No trouble at all," Tuck said. "My boys know how to handle such things."

Morgan took up his second drink, but paused with the glass halfway to his mouth. "And maybe they'll go through his pockets a little before they dump him in the street, hmmm?"

Tuck's former, hateful look came over him again briefly, and he took a deep breath as if willing himself to patience. "I run an honest operation."

Morgan downed the second whiskey so that he didn't have to answer. Tuck gave a nod to the piano player, the same as he had earlier to the bouncers. The piano player immediately started pounding on his keys again, and the room went back to its former, ribald self. The drinkers went back to their drinks, and conversations that had ceased at the outbreak of the difficulties between Charlie Six Fingers and his player took back up where they had left off, as if a man getting his skull cracked with a club was apparently old hat in the Bullhorn.

The three bouncers coming back inside made a beeline for Morgan, and he knew that Tuck had given them some kind of signal when he wasn't looking. He shifted slightly to watch the bouncers and Tuck at the same time. His left hand flipped his coat behind his pistol butt.

"You should leave camp," Tuck said.

The bouncers stopped at arm's length from Morgan, standing shoulder to shoulder with the confident air of schoolyard, backstreet bullies. They obviously enjoyed their work, and made no attempt to hide the fact that all they were waiting for was word from their boss.

"You don't have a badge to hide behind here," Tuck added. "I heard that Judge Story fired you."

"You'll not be getting that pistol out before we lay hands to you," one of the bouncers said.

"You take one step closer and we're going to see," Morgan said without raising his voice.

"Morgan Clyde!" A new voice, a female's voice, rose above the din. "How long has it been?"

A buxom redhead in a green dress shoved past the bouncers and to Morgan's side. She was maybe on the hard side of middle age, a little fleshier than she had been when Morgan had last seen her, and with all the years and miles of her profession written on her face, even though she tried to hide the road marks and wrinkles with a heavy coating of powder and rouge.

"Don't act like you don't remember me." She took Morgan by the arm and pressed one of her large breasts against his elbow.

"Afternoon, Molly," Morgan said.

"You boys will have to pardon us. Me and the marshal here have some catching up to do." She gave Tuck and the bouncers a big, red-lipped smile and a lurid wink of her eye before she led Morgan off with a swish of her wide hips.

"You've got some nerve waltzing right into Bill Tuck's saloon," she said when they were out of hearing distance of the bar.

"Didn't know it was his when I came in here."

"And you wouldn't have given a damn if you had known, would you?"

A man at one of the tables reached out and tried to pat her on the bottom as they passed, and without giving him so much as a look she lifted one leg and kicked him in the chest. The man was so drunk that he toppled from his chair and landed flat on his back. The men at the table with him laughed and cheered.

"What say you fellows let me and an old friend have this table?" she asked the group.

"And what do we get if we do?" one of them asked.

"Joe, since you're so sweet, the next time you come calling I won't laugh at you when you pull out that puny little thing you call your manhood."

Instead of being angry, the men seemed to find that even funnier than their other friend being knocked down by a sassy whore. The one she insulted staggered to his feet and started fumbling at his pants. "Let me show you what kind of tool a railroad man works with."

Molly let go of Morgan's elbow and put both hands on her hips, waiting as if half bored. "What have you got to show me, Joe Nelson, that I haven't seen twice as much of on most men? You go find Rat Tooth. She isn't as picky about her customers as I am, and she'll hump you for four bits."

The man gave up fumbling at his trousers. "You're a hell of a woman, Red Molly."

"And don't you forget it. Now give a lady your seat."

The men helped their friend up from the floor, shoving him toward the bar when he wanted to hang around and make an issue of her kicking him. Morgan picked up the overturned chair and seated her in it before he sat down, all the while frowning at the backs of the men who had left the table.

She saw the look on Morgan's face. "Damnation, but I've missed you, you stubborn, wonderful man. You're still the same—always have to play the gentleman. How long has it been since Baxter Springs?"

"A man ought to mind his manners, drunk or not."

"Talking polite before you kill a man or bending a pistol barrel over his head doesn't make you a saint or something," she said. "Fancy Dan ways or not, you aren't a gentleman, not by a long shot. No more than I'm a lady."

"Molly, you pulled my fat out of the fire once, and I won't forget that."

"I'm a whore, Morgan, and I'm not ashamed of it. Not one bit. I've done what I had to do. I survived. Some of these girls complain about having to work on their back and what brought them to such a life, but not me. I like men, and I like how they like me."

"Working a room like you and the other girls are doing causes trouble. You need to tone things down."

"Is this your camp now?"

"I turned down the job."

"I don't know if even you could handle this one," she said. "And a good thing, too. You would have us all dressing like nuns and hiding inside until the sun went down. Or paying a license fee and having that old drunk of a doctor, Chillingsworth, looking up our love boxes once a week and signing some certificate to say we didn't have the clap."

"It makes less trouble for everyone if you operate with a little more on the quiet," he said. "Three things cause most of the trouble in a camp like this: whiskey, women, and gambling."

"Me cause trouble among the men?" she said innocently, but her eyes batted a message otherwise. "And, like you said. This isn't your town, and I don't need you telling me how to run my business."

The body heat from so many men packed into the tent raised the temperature considerably compared to the outside. She dabbed at the beads of sweat in the crease of her breasts with one hand while she fanned herself with her other hand. "Winter's hardly over and it's already hot in here. What say you buy us a bottle, and we go to my tent and get some of these clothes off?"

"Is Tuck running things here?"

"Didn't you hear me? I'm practically throwing myself at you. There isn't a randy goat in this entire camp that wouldn't take me up on my offer."

"What about Tuck?"

"There are only two saloons, as of this morning—Irish Dave's Bucket of Blood, and Tuck's Bullhorn."

"Irish Dave is here?"

"Dave's behind the game. Tuck's already the big man in camp. Dave's got his reputation to go on, but Tuck's got the muscle."

"Are you working for Tuck? I wouldn't have thought you would, considering how everyone believed it was him that did for your husband."

"Marty, that pimp of a no-good, so-called husband? That's all he was. I don't miss the black eyes when he had a bad night at the cards, or him taking everything I made. Good riddance, I say, and if it was Tuck that killed him, so be it. Marty was probably cheating or stealing from him like he did everybody else. Maybe I ought to thank Tuck." Her words didn't come off with the flippancy she intended.

"You don't mean that. Say what you want to, but I still don't see how you could work for him."

"I don't work for him. I help sell a few extra drinks in here and give him a little cut of my action so I can work in his place."

"What about the rest of the doves in camp? Are they working for him?"

"All but Sugar Alice's girls and a few that Irish Dave brought with him, and I think Alice is paying Tuck protection money."

"How's he playing it so far? The camp, I mean."

"Quiet. There's too much easy money right now to have to

play it any different. You know him," she said. "But he isn't who's stirring things up in camp. It's Texas George and his boys making all the noise. I don't know how many men he's got out in the brush, but he's cutting a wide swath in these parts."

"I had papers on George once, but he was always too good of a judge of fast horseflesh to catch him."

"Well, he's still running free, and he's been swearing to anybody that will listen that there won't be any law in Ironhead Station."

"He didn't used to crow so much."

"He didn't have so many riding with him then. It's said he was the one that hit the bank up in Olathe. The Kansas City newspaper said that was a five thousand dollar haul, although you know how the banks always lie. No matter, George's a little full of himself since then, and there are plenty of outlaws that want to ride with a man that has a little success on his record. There's that robbery, and the fact that he was the one that ended the second marshal we had here, Frank Lester. You might remember him."

"Frank? Hate to hear that. Frank was a steady man and ran a quiet town."

"Well, Frank won't be hearing anything but quiet now, because he's six foot under. Texas George called him out and shot him dead right out there in the street. Didn't know that, did you? George had his brothers waiting with him, and they cut poor Frank to ribbons."

"George has got brothers?"

"Yep," she said, nodding. "And they're every bit as bad as he is."

"What about Superintendent Duvall?"

Red Molly looked surprised. "What would I know? He doesn't come down here. He's always in his office, at the bridge site, or in that private car of his they've got parked on the siding. What are you so interested for? This place will be gone as soon as the tracks move on, and I thought you turned down the job."

"Call it professional curiosity."

"When are you leaving?" She toyed with one of her earrings and watched him closely, as if she felt she could read more into him than what he said.

"Thought I would catch a ride north on the train in the morning."

"We've got time then."

"I'm flattered, Molly. Really, I am, but I believe I'll save my money."

"Don't you think I'm pretty anymore?"

"Not tonight, Molly."

Her mouth parted, revealing a smear of red lipstick on her front teeth. "Suit yourself. Sleep out in the brush if you want to, for you'll play hell finding a bunk to rent in this camp, nor a soft body to rest your head on. You were always a restless sleeper, anyways."

"I thought you would have given up this sort of place a long time ago," he said. "Figured you would be running your own house by now, somewhere more civilized."

"Are you implying that I'm getting too old for this? That I can't cut the mustard anymore?" She tried to fake a frown, but couldn't hold it. The sassy smile that she gave him seemed to take ten years off her face, if only for the flash of a defiant instant. "No, I've still got what it takes, Morgan Clyde. I might be a little more woman than I once was, but I'd trade what I know now for my old girlish figure anytime. Most of the chippies here are nothing but crib whores, drunks, and opium addicts, and a nice dress and a clean cunt sticks out like a Christmas bow amongst the likes of them. I'll make good money while this camp lasts. You ask anyone who's the belle of Ironhead Station, and they'll tell you that Red Molly shines like a diamond."

"You're a lot less likable when you're play acting like you're the toughest wench on the line."

She smiled again, but faintly, the defiant glow giving way to a sort of weariness. "You always were a good sort. Hard as a preacher's prick, but fair and dependable. I can't say that for most of your sex."

"So long, Molly. Maybe I'll see you again sometime." He stood and gave the brim of his hat a slight bend to her.

"Did you ever find that wife of yours?" she asked before he could leave.

"I found her." He tipped the brim of his hat again and walked away.

Red Molly watched Morgan pass by the bouncers with the same tip of his hat and his hand on that Remington pistol on his hip, and then she noticed Bill Tuck still standing with both palms on the bar as he had been earlier. If his burning eyes had been gun barrels, Morgan's body would have been shot full of holes. Bill Tuck hated Morgan Clyde, and maybe not only because Morgan had killed Tuck's brother-in-law. You couldn't have two such strong men on opposite sides of the law in the same place and them not hate each other.

"You remember what I said, Clyde," Tuck called out to Morgan as he neared. "Harvey was soft, but I ain't."

"I heard you the first time." Morgan bent and picked up his gear and went out the door without looking back at Tuck.

Red Molly went over to a man she saw standing alone at the bar, noting the small stack of coins he had stacked on the bar top before him. She adjusted her cleavage to a higher location with a firm shove from both hands and tried to work up her best smile. It was too early for the saloon to be really packed, but there was no reason she couldn't make a few dollars before then. Regardless, she stopped and paused to watch Morgan's tall, broad-shouldered frame disappear out the door. Instead of the bright smile she planned for her next victim, a wistful, half sad and thoughtful hint of something moved her red lips and faded as softly as it had begun. She whispered something to herself.

"What did you say?" Bill Tuck had moved down the bar near to her.

"You better leave him alone, Tuck. You think you're tough, but you cross Morgan Clyde and he'll drink your blood for breakfast."

"What's that, you stupid slut?" Tuck leaned closer over the bar.

"Nothing, sweetie." She gave Tuck a flippant grin and pressed her body close to the railroad man standing alone. "I was going to ask this handsome devil if he would buy a lonesome girl far from home a drink."

Tuck ran the waxed tip of one end of his mustache between a thumb and pointer finger to sharpen it while he scowled at the redheaded prostitute. Then he gave the empty doorway one last look before he waved at his bouncers to follow him to the back of the saloon. Red Molly saw it all, and knew that they were going to have a meeting about how to kill Morgan Clyde before he left the camp. Bill Tuck wasn't one to forget a wrong, perceived or otherwise, and it wouldn't be a fair fight that Morgan got from him.

And it was all over that worthless, no-good gambler, Harvey Wayt. Morgan arrested Harvey one night for drunk and disorderly and discharging his pistol at a stray dog passing along the street. Harvey didn't like everyone knowing that Morgan had manhandled him, and he spent the next two days telling everyone who would listen how the next time Morgan so much as looked at him there was going to be a fight.

Well, it wasn't long before Harvey had too much to drink again, and he decided he couldn't wait for Morgan to look at him wrong. So, he went out onto the street and called Morgan every foul name that he could think of, a coward being the least of them. Of course, Morgan heard him and went to meet him. He tried to talk Harvey down, but everyone was watching by then, and Harvey was a prideful man. He should have known not to go for his gun, but worse than Harvey's pride was the fact that he was never as good with a gun as he thought he was. In the blink of an eye, Baxter Springs was relieved of one of its tinhorn gamblers, and Tuck was short one brother-in-law. And a grudge was started between Tuck and Morgan that wouldn't go away until one of them was dead.

Molly was about to ask the man beside her again to buy her a drink, when a gunshot sounded from the street, followed by more gunshots. Like everyone else in the saloon, her spine stiffened ramrod straight and her heart flinched and skipped a beat. Bill Tuck hadn't waited long, but then again, he was an impatient man and as cold-blooded and ruthless as they came. She hated knowing that Morgan Clyde was likely dead right then and that he had fallen to the schemes of a son of a bitch like Tuck.

Poor Morgan, but he'd had a long run when many of his kind didn't last long at all. His problem was that he was a man without any give to him. Live by the sword, die by the sword, wasn't that what they said? And never had a man lived by the sword more than Morgan Clyde.

No matter, no one lasted forever. You lived a little and got what you could, some things you didn't deserve and some things you did. And then you died hard. It was as simple as that, and let the softies and the weak souls think it was any different. At least Morgan wouldn't whimper when they put him down, and neither would she.

She ran one hand under the bar top and gave her new man's crotch a playful squeeze. "Want to stick that in something besides your fist?"

She didn't so much as flinch when another gunshot sounded from the street, but if the man she was teasing hadn't been too busy trying to keep from humping her fist under the bar he might have noticed that same weary, wistful smile she bore for what it was.

"Let's go out back," the man she was fondling said in a broken, raspy rush of air. "I got two dollars left."

"Buy me another drink first. Today's my birthday." She let go of his crotch and threw an arm around his shoulders.

"How old are you?" the man asked while he motioned to the bartender for another round.

She shoved him away from her and waited for the drink to come. "You never ask a lady her age."

"Begging your pardon."

"I'm thirty-five today, and old enough to be your mother," she said, taking up the fresh glass of whiskey.

The man looked disappointed. Not because of her age, but because he noted the change in her tone and probably thought he was all worked up and about to lose his chance at doing something about it. "I meant no offense."

"Oh, shut up. I'm still more woman than you'll likely ever get ahold of, and I can still screw the legs of any man in this camp."

"Yes, ma'am." His hand reached tentatively to her waist, and then drifted down to her buttocks.

"Say that again," she said to him.

"Yes, ma'am."

"There now, that's better. It's best you remember that." She sighed and lifted her glass, and her voice raised high and clear. "Let's all raise a glass and drink a toast to Morgan Clyde."

41

Nobody in the room was listening except for the man with his hand on her ass. They had all gone to door to see who had shot Morgan Clyde.

CHAPTER FOUR

Morgan was halfway back to the train tracks when the shooting started. Two men ran out of a gap between a tent and several parked freight wagons on the far side of the street from him. The man in the lead was the carpenter who had flung the hammer from the top of the depot house earlier, and the man chasing him was the black cowboy he had flung the hammer at. Neither man was making very good time in the mud, and they ran with comical, high-kneed lunges. The black cowboy was tugging at the holstered pistol on his hip and trying to get it into play, and the fact that the carpenter was unarmed made him a determined and motivated runner.

The black cowboy's first shot went wild, notwithstanding that there wasn't ten yards between them. Both men were panting and heaving from exertion, and maybe that foiled the pursuer's aim. The carpenter quickly ducked behind one of the freight wagons briefly before another bullet knocked splinters from the wagon box near him. Now that he had the carpenter at bay, the black cowboy began walking in a wide arc towards the center of the street, trying to flank his victim and to get in a killing shot.

People in camp scampered to whatever cover they could find, or peered out of tent doorways as if canvas walls would stop a bullet. Some of the onlookers shook their heads disapprovingly at what was happening, but not a one offered to help the carpenter. And more than a few that Morgan noticed seemed to view the whole thing as some kind of entertainment put on for their benefit.

Morgan kept walking, and met Superintendent Duvall and Agent Pickins on the end of the boardwalk in front of the railroad office.

"Somebody needs to stop this," Agent Pickins said to Duvall.

The black cowboy cracked off another shot, but the carpenter was dodging around the wagon and was hard to hit.

"Hold still and take it like a man!" the black cowboy shouted.

Duvall scowled down the street at the scene playing out. He looked at Morgan. "Are you going to let this happen?"

"None of my business." Morgan backhanded his pistol halfway out of his holster with his left hand, as if offering it to either of them. "You want to stop it, go do it yourself."

Duvall reached inside his coat and pulled the same tin badge that he had offered Morgan earlier from his vest pocket. He pitched it to Morgan. "You're hired. Now tend to this."

Duvall looked at Agent Pickins as if he dared him to complain about the hiring, but the Indian agent didn't say a word. Morgan offered his pistol again to Agent Pickins. "Sure you don't want to show me how a good man would handle this?"

The Indian agent looked down at the boardwalk and shook his head.

"I figured as much." Morgan set his belongings down on the boardwalk and slowly pinned the badge to the breast of the wool vest underneath his black frock coat. Then he shrugged out of the coat and folded it neatly and laid it on top of his valise and bedroll. He turned around and slid his pistol from its holster and flipped the loading gate open to double-check the loads in it while he watched the would-be murderer firing off more shots at the carpenter.

"For goodness sake, hurry!" Agent Pickins said. His face was flushed with excitement.

Morgan continued to check his pistol. The 1858 Remington

Army was one of the recent ones that the company had converted to shoot .46 Short cartridges from its original design as a roll-your-own, cap-and-ball percussion revolver. The bright ends of five brass rimfire cartridges shone in each chamber, spinning like slots on a roulette wheel as he rolled the cylinder down the length of his left forearm.

He snapped the loading gate shut on the pistol and started down the street, calling back to Duvall as he stepped off the boardwalk into the mud, "Give my things to Red Molly if I don't come back."

The carpenter was moving frantically from cover to cover among the wagons, and trying desperately not to show enough of himself to get shot. The black cowboy had climbed into the bed of one of the freight wagons trying to gain some elevation for a clear view of his prey. He was standing up in that wagon and reloading his pistol when he noticed Morgan coming and turned to face him.

"What the hell do you want?" he shouted at Morgan.

Morgan was still fifty yards away, but he stopped in the middle of the street. The Remington hung at the end of his right arm, and he tapped the badge on his vest with his other hand. "I'm the law now. I run this camp."

"Ain't no law in Ironhead." Only the cowboy's head and torso showed above the high sides of the freight wagon, and his gun hand was hidden from sight.

"Put that gun down. I won't tell you but once," Morgan said. "Throw it down and come along peacefully."

"You can kiss my black ass, you Yankee talking sumbitch!" The outlaw laughed again and raised his pistol above the wagon boards.

The Remington lifted almost methodically in Morgan's own hand, the revolver held at arm's length, and his body turned sideways to his adversary like a duelist standing on a dueling ground, narrowing his profile and making himself a smaller target. He took long enough to aim that the black cowboy's first shot skimmed by him and knocked a chunk out of a hitching post beyond him. Another bullet burped up a splash of muddy water in front of Morgan before the Remington bucked in his hand. The black cowboy staggered and clutched at his chest with only the side of the wagon holding him up. Morgan fired again and the outlaw tumbled over and came to rest with the upper half of his body draped limply over the side of the wagon.

"That was a sixty-yard pistol shot if I ever saw one," someone said from the crowd of onlookers lining the street.

Morgan kept his gun pointed in the direction of the body as he started wading towards it. Before he was halfway there, the carpenter appeared around the wagon end and lifted the black cowboy's head by its hair so that he could survey the damage.

"Where did he hit him?" another voice called out from the onlookers who were slowly filtering out into the open.

"Straight through the heart," the carpenter called back.

Morgan reached the carpenter. "Are you hit?"

"No, I'm fine, but he ain't." The carpenter lifted the body off the wagon boards by its head again.

His victim was younger than Morgan first supposed, maybe twenty. The same grin that he had borne when he was laughing at Morgan was frozen on his death mask, as if he were still laughing, but fading like he had realized in the last seconds of his doom that all the fun had gone out of the joke. Morgan stared back at the gruesome leer of the dead man with a tight-lipped expression.

As the carpenter had said, Morgan's first bullet had taken the man directly in the center of the breastbone. The second bullet had struck about two inches to the right of the first. Both bullet wounds were marked by bloody circles on the man's yellow shirt, slowly creeping into the fabric, expanding and losing their shape as they did so.

Morgan heard someone splashing through the mud behind him, and whirled with his gun ready. The man coming his way didn't notice the Remington briefly pointed at him, and continued to take over-exaggerated and long strides through the deep mud, counting with every step.

". . . fifty-eight, fifty-nine, sixty, sixty-one, sixty-two," the man said as he reached the body. He turned to the onlookers on one side of the street. "Sixty-two paces, and two bullets in the chest not half a hand apart!"

A few in the crowd let out a ragged cheer, and some of those standing outside the saloons held up beer glasses in toast.

"Who was he?" Morgan asked the carpenter.

"Don't know his real name, but I heard someone call him Strawdaddy."

"Strawdaddy, that was it," the other man who had stepped off the distance chimed in.

"You saved my life, and don't think I'm one to be forgetting that," the carpenter said, offering his hand.

Morgan ejected the spent hulls out of the Remington's cylinder and removed two fresh cartridges out of a small leather box on his left hip. He thumbed them into the empty chambers before he looked up at the carpenter, and even then he ignored the offered hand. "Is there a gravedigger in camp?"

"Gravedigger?" the other man interrupted again. "Only rule here in Ironhead is that you bury 'em if you shoot 'em. That or you can wait for the hogs and the buzzards to clean 'em up."

"Shut up, Jim. You're drunk," said the carpenter.

The other man huffed indignantly as he started across the street to the Bullhorn, but he couldn't resist throwing one last bit over his shoulder. "While you're burying Strawdaddy, you might want to dig a grave for yourself before old Texas George hears about this. Him and George were friends."

Morgan holstered the Remington, gazing up and down both sides of the street at the crowd watching him. "You men go back to your business. Nothing to see here."

"Me and some of the boys will take care of the body," the carpenter said. "That's the least I owe you."

Morgan picked up the pistol that the dead man had dropped over the side of the wagon into the mud. He shoved it behind his belt buckle. "Did this man have any next of kin that you know of?"

"I don't know him from Adam, except for what I already told you," the carpenter answered.

Morgan started to leave, but hesitated. "Make sure you bury him deep, and put some kind of marker over his grave in case some of his family shows up looking for him."

"We've already got a graveyard started. Deacon Fischer was here for a while this winter right about the time the first trestle collapsed, and when all the hard cases started showing up from everywhere."

"Fischer's here?"

"Was until he left. Stayed long enough to shoot a disrespectful Indian and give us a start on a graveyard."

Morgan nodded thoughtfully and started towards the depot house, aware of all the attention on him from tent doorways and from those who hadn't paid any heed to his orders to clear the street. The weak sun was going down in the gray sky to the west, and he could see the silhouettes of Duvall and the Indian agent waiting for him on the boardwalk.

"Is he dead?" Duvall asked when Morgan neared to within earshot.

"I made a good outlaw out of him." Morgan stomped and scraped the worst of the mud off his boots on the edge of the boardwalk and took up his frock coat and shouldered into it.

"You didn't even try to talk him down. Not really," Agent

Pickins said.

"I warned him once."

"You stare at me all you want, Marshal," Agent Pickins said, taking an unconscious step backwards. "I won't be intimidated by you, nor will I hold my tongue."

"Shut up, Euless. That man down there was one of them that tried to burn my bridge," Duvall said.

Morgan turned his attention to Duvall. "I expect my month's wages in advance."

Duvall nodded. "See my clerk and tell him I said to pay you."

"There's a few things I need to talk to you about," Morgan added. "We need to be all on the same page when it comes to the rules of this camp. Since this isn't a real town, we will have to make up our own ordinances."

"What gives you the right to make up the law?" Pickins asked. "Who do you think you are?"

Morgan tapped his badge again. "I'm the man that wears this. I'm the man that's going to walk down that street everyday worrying who's going to try to put a knife in my back."

"Don't be so melodramatic."

"This camp will only get worse before it gets better, and the bunch you want run out of here plays rough." Morgan's voice grew a notch louder, and he took an unconscious step towards Pickins.

"Clyde," Duvall warned.

Morgan stopped, but continued to glare at Pickins. "Oh, I'm not going to hit him. I thought about it some, but it wouldn't do any good."

"God have mercy on your soul," Agent Pickins said.

"I've asked him for that more than once," Morgan said. "You go ahead and ask again in case he'll listen to you."

"You're right, we need to lay down some rules," Duvall

49

interjected, trying to ease the tension and dislike between the two men.

"Take their guns away," Pickins said. "Make it against the law to have guns in camp. Put up signs."

"That's a thought," Duvall said. "Anybody coming into camp could turn their guns over to you and get them back when they left."

Morgan shook his head. "I won't have any part of that."

"What just happened is the very reason we shouldn't have armed men in camp," Pickins said.

Morgan snorted softly through his nose. "Bad guys don't play by the rules, last time I checked. I won't have any part in disarming good men, and fact is, there might come a time when we need a few good men with guns."

"That's a preposterous argument," Pickins said.

"I wouldn't give up my guns to any man, and I'll not ask of others what I'm unwilling to abide by myself."

"Gentlemen." Duvall held out a hand to each man, palms out as a peacemaking gesture.

Morgan nodded at Duvall and then took up his bag and bedroll. "I've got work to do."

"You get this camp under control, Clyde," Duvall said.

"Know where I might find a bed?" Morgan asked.

"There's a boarding tent up the street."

"I'd like something a little more private."

"I'll have the men set you up a tent tomorrow." Duvall waited until Morgan disappeared into the railroad office before he turned to Pickins. "Euless, you're either part of the solution or part of the problem."

"You saw it. He gunned that man down in cold blood," Pickins said. "It was like he wanted that man to try him."

Duvall nodded. "I would guess that it didn't exactly break his heart to shoot that fellow."

Pickins couldn't hide his surprise or his shock. "What? You sound like you approve of what he did."

"I don't pretend to know Clyde's business, but if I had his certain set of skills then that's how I would do it."

"What are you talking about?"

"He made an example of that outlaw. Sent a message to the rest of the toughs in camp."

"He's little better than those you want run out. Pinning a badge on him is the same as backing a killer."

"You're damned right he's a killer," Duvall said. "That's what I was counting on when I hired him."

"You don't mean that."

"That's absolutely what I mean—a stone-cold killer with a badge on his chest is what Ironhead Station needs . . . exactly what I need."

"You're as bad as him. Why . . . why . . . you would do anything to get your railroad built."

"Now you're getting it, Euless. Now you're getting it."

CHAPTER FIVE

Morgan woke up before daylight and sat in the open doorway of the boxcar with his legs dangling over the edge and his coat tucked tight about him. He exhaled and watched his smoky breath float away. The temperature had plummeted during the night, and it was cold for an early March morning and the frost glistened on the ground in the false dawn like the whole world was made of tiny bits of crystal.

The railroad boxcar had been wrecked sometime in the recent past, and although the box was intact, it had been shunted over to a siding along with a few other miscellaneous cars. It had been too late in the evening to get one of Duvall's crews to put up a tent, and he had had no wish to sleep shoulder to shoulder with strangers in the overcrowded boarding tent some entrepreneurial spirit had opened in camp. He had spied the empty boxcar sitting alone across the tracks on the opposite side from the camp right before dark. It was parked alongside the big rail warehouse that had given the camp its name, and he had immediately chosen it for his temporary domicile. The car was relatively clean, except for some dust and a little straw and sawdust littering the floor. The only problem was that one of the sliding doors was too bent to close, and the north wind that had brought the cold whipped around so much that he might as well have been sleeping outside.

Regardless of the airy confines of the boxcar, he wouldn't have slept well, anyway. The old dreams and the old memories had come again like ghoulish, long-lost friends—as real as they had ever been, despite the years. And wakefulness wasn't enough to escape the feelings that the dream left behind. Those feelings were so slow to leave that they made made him shiver as much as the chilly morning.

He tried to shake off the unsteadiness and studied the camp and his surroundings revealed in the gray morning light. It would be a green land with the coming of spring, most of it covered in post oaks and other short hardwoods with dotted clearings of grass in-between, gradually opening up more and more to tall grass prairie to the west or the farther north one went towards Kansas. The camp itself lay in a fertile river bottom, hemmed in between a low mountain to the north and the river and another low mountain to the south. Larger trees and denser vegetation marked the belt of the South Canadian River: sycamores, elms, sweet gums, cottonwoods, and water oaks, interwoven with a mesh of sumac, grapevines, green briars, and switch cane breaks in places.

And it was no wonder that so many people had found Iron-head Station in such a hurry, for the construction camp sat near a crossroads of two emigrant trails. The MK&T was laying its tracks almost on top of the Texas Road that had been the main thoroughfare from Missouri to Texas for fifty years. During the war and right after it, the very same trace had been known as the Shawnee Trail by a few Texas cattlemen driving herds to eastern Kansas, Missouri, or points in the Midwest. And the California Trail, the central route to the goldfields back in the days of '49, passed through the camp, following the river east to west and providing a good trail from Fort Smith, Arkansas.

Plenty of timber for building things and water everywhere, but despite the beauty of the land, Morgan's mind shifted to other things—the very same problems that brought him there.

The Indian Territory had been formed when most of the

Indian tribes in the Southeast were forced from their original homes and moved west in the 1830s. The Territory was broken up into individual nations according to each tribe's allotment, and the whole vast chunk of landscape was set up basically like one giant reservation. Accordingly, the whites were to leave it alone, but it didn't work that way.

There wasn't any law in the Indian Nations, other than tribal law, and those laws didn't apply to white men. According to the Great White Father in Washington, Indians were to govern Indians, and white men were to govern white men. The way it was, it didn't take long for white renegades to figure out that that there weren't enough federal lawmen in such a wide swath of country, and the Indians weren't allowed to do anything about them. When a white man was said to be gone to the Indian Nations, it was the same as saying he was an outlaw.

The ring of a shop hammer pounding against an anvil was the first sign that the camp was coming to life. Morgan hopped down from the boxcar and followed the sound to a set of livestock corrals on the same side of the track. A man was already at work shoeing a mule in front of the open-faced pole lean-to that served as a blacksmith shop. Two other farriers were working on their own mules nearby.

Once he got closer, he noticed that the first man was none other than the Hank fellow he had met on the train the day before.

"Good morning." Hank Bickford rested his hammer atop the shoe he was shaping and wiped his other hand on his leather apron. "You look like you feel awful."

"Didn't get much sleep."

"Heard about your trouble with Strawdaddy. Don't reckon I would have slept much either after that."

"How's the family?"

"Getting by. We got us a surplus Sibley tent I bought back in

Missouri. Set it up outside camp," Hank said. "There ain't but two other families here. It'll take the Missus a while to settle in and get used to this life, but she's already planning to put in a bakery or maybe take in some laundry to do for the men."

"Tell her to be careful in camp for a while."

Hank gave him a knowing look. "You ain't telling me nothing. I was here before you were."

"Might be worse for a while."

"You didn't come over here to chew the fat."

"No, I've got a chore for you."

Hank turned the glowing red mule shoe atop the anvil with a pair of tongs and gave it another couple of licks until the metal began to cool, then placed it in the burning coals in his forge bin to reheat. "I'm on the railroad payroll and don't work for the general public."

"This job will be for the railroad." Morgan lifted back one lapel of his coat to reveal his badge. Plainly written on it was *RAILROAD POLICE, MK&T,* and a little pendant hanging under the tin shield was marked *CHIEF.*

"Well, Chief, what can I do for you?"

Morgan explained what he wanted.

When he was through, Hank nodded. "Might take me awhile to get that done, and I'll have to fit it in between my other stuff. We've got sixteen mules to shoe today, and some new coupling pins and bridge plates to make."

"I need them by tomorrow. Let one of the other farriers handle those mules for you."

"I don't want to get in trouble with the foreman."

"You won't get in trouble. I'll let Duvall know I put you to task," Morgan said. "Take them over to the railroad office or leave them in that boxcar there when you're finished."

"Have it your way," Hank said. "I'll get on it as soon as I finish this mule."

"Thanks." Morgan started away.

"Can't say as I ever made anything like what you're asking for," Hank called after him.

Morgan didn't reply and crossed the tracks to the railroad office. The clerk was already at his table in the front room, and had a fire burning in the coal stove beside him. Morgan borrowed a stack of paper and a pen and inkwell from him and started for the back room.

"You can't go in there. That's Superintendent Duvall's office," the clerk said.

Morgan shut the door behind him and took a seat at Duvall's desk. It took him half an hour to write what he wanted and to make five copies. He met Duvall coming into the room as he was going out.

Duvall eyed the papers in Morgan's hand. "What are you up to?"

"Getting a start on what you're paying me for."

Morgan shoved past him and went out onto the depot platform. He borrowed a hammer and a few nails from a carpenter's box he found lying inside the unfinished depot house and tacked up his posting on the wall of the railroad office facing the tracks. He took a step back to admire his handiwork once he was finished.

WELCOME TO IRONHEAD STATION.

1. *No firing off guns in camp.*
2. *No running horses, mules, or other saddle stock or wagon stock through camp.*
3. *Saloons or other establishments selling liquor or ardent spirits will not open before noon and will close no later than 2 o'clock in the morning.*

4. *All games of chance will be run honestly, and such games and the establishments housing them shall be inspected at will by the railroad police or other authorities.*
5. *Anyone found to be loitering, wandering, or loafing about the saloons with no visible means of employment will be deemed a vagrant.*
6. *All persons will go fully clothed while in camp.*
7. *Those not employed by the MK&T will not follow the construction crews to construction sites, or otherwise distract or hinder those employees from their work.*
8. *Trash or dead animals must be buried or hauled out of camp by the responsible party.*
9. *No destruction of MK&T property.*
10. *All other applicable rules and laws of the MK&T Railroad, the Indian Territory, and the United States of America will be enforced.*

Posted by Morgan Clyde, MK&T Chief of Railroad Police, Ironhead Station

Duvall walked up behind him and read the posting. "There's a lot that aren't going to like that. You better be ready for trouble."

"There's no sense beating around the bush." Morgan strode away, looking for other places to hang his ordinances.

The night must have been colder than he thought, for the muddy street had frozen into a rough, rock-hard crust that made passing along it more difficult than it had been before. His fourth stop was in front of the Bullhorn Palace.

The place was dead quiet except for the sound of someone snoring from inside. Whoever it was must have been drunk or worn out from the previous night's revelry, for the pounding hammer didn't wake him when Morgan tacked one of his signs on the post beneath the Bullhorn's own sign. The thought of how Bill Tuck was going to take seeing it gave Morgan a chuckle.

Finished with his morning chores, Morgan found the cook tent. Most of the construction gangs were already filtering out of the tent and headed out for a day's work, and he had the tent almost to himself. One of the railroad cooks, a short, wiry black man in a stained white apron, grinned at him when he came through the door.

"Mornin', Chief," the cook said.

Morgan's badge was hidden by his coat, but the cook recognized him anyway. Word had spread fast.

"Good morning. Can't say that I know you," Morgan said.

"Saul's my name. We ain't never met, but everybody was talkin' about you at breakfast," the cook said while he slopped a plateful of hominy grits, pork sausage, and scrambled eggs on Morgan's plate.

"Is that a fact?"

" 'Tis, surely. Bill Tuck's gamblers down at the Bullhorn are already givin' three to one odds that you won't last till tomorrow at sundown. One of his fellows was in here this mornin' making the rounds of the men and taking their bets."

"Which way were most of them betting?"

"Didn't see many that wasn't takin' those three to one odds. Most thinks that you ain't nothin' but a walkin' dead man."

"What about you, Saul? Are you taking any of that easy money betting against me?"

The cook grinned again. "No, sir. I likes to keep my money 'stead of giving it to the likes of Bill Tuck. Man like him always gots an angle, and the Katy don't pay me enough to be playin' with my money."

"The Katy?"

"That's what we calls this railroad. MKT, you know, Katy," Saul the cook said. "And castin' lots ain't Christian, no how. My old mammy would roll over in her grave if I was to turn gamblin' man."

"Thanks for the breakfast."

"You come earlier next time before the eggs get cold and soggy. Man ought to eat good before he dies."

Morgan started away, but stopped when the cook said that. But Saul was already carrying a panful of dirty dishes out of the tent. Morgan grunted humorously. Three to one that he wouldn't make it two more days—the gamblers in Baxter Springs had only given two to one, and for whether or not he would last a week, at that.

He took his food and a cup of coffee to one of the empty tables against the wall where he could see the doors in both ends of the tent. Nobody spoke to him and nobody bothered him while he ate. The dishwashers and cooks cleaning up or preparing for the next meal gave him wide berth, and the remaining construction men at the other tables made a point not to get caught looking his way, either.

By the time he came out of the cook tent there were already small crowds gathered around his ordinance posting at each of the saloons. Morgan stopped to watch. The conversation about the ordinances seemed to be worthy of lengthy, heated debate, if the men's gestures and antics were any sign. One of the men in the group at the Bucket of Blood noticed him standing at the cook tent and pointed in his direction. A lot of hateful looks were thrown his way before they all went back inside the saloon.

Morgan shifted his cigar to the other side of his mouth. *Your move, boys.*

CHAPTER SIX

Morgan pulled up on the lip of the riverbank and sat the horse he had borrowed from the railroad stock pens. It was a short, two-mile trip to the site where the men were building the bridge over the South Canadian. The wide bed of the river was at least a hundred and fifty yards wide, and the heavy spring rains had it running from bank to bank.

He glanced at the skeletal timber frame of the high trestle extending a third of the way across the river, like the fossil bones of some colossal and ancient dragon revealed and eroded from the sandy riverbank. Scores of men climbed among the bridge timbers above the brown current, pinning and plating new beams into place. A steam-powered crane suspended an especially large timber, and the heavy load swung wildly over the heads of the crew in the stiff wind.

Morgan rode over to the tracks at the near end of the trestle, weaving his way in and out of the men. Hope McDaniels, the foreman and project engineer that he had met the day before, was standing with his hands on his hips, studying the trestle as if his eyes were surveyor's instruments.

"Wouldn't have thought to see you out here," the engineer said when he noticed Morgan.

"What did the officers call it during the war? A tactical assessment of the battlefield?"

"I would think your battlefield would be in camp."

"Thought I would see what has things held up and is causing

all the trouble on the home front," Morgan said and then pointed at the bridge in progress. "You've got quite a task there."

"I could say the same for you."

Morgan couldn't help but smile. The young engineer got straight to the point, but it was plain that he meant nothing by it. Morgan already liked him. You always knew where you stood with such a man.

Morgan could see railroad tracks across the river, running straight as a string and out of sight to the south.

The engineer noticed what he was looking at. "There's five miles of tracks already laid over there. We were hauling materials and equipment across by the old ferry for a while, but it was too much of a fight and we can't move materials fast enough to keep the crews busy. We ought to be over yonder, as we speak, grading new roadbed and laying track, but now there's nothing to do but wait until we get this trestle built."

"I don't see but maybe forty men working here," Morgan said. "I got the impression that a lot more of the men in camp were working for your railroad."

"They were, and that's half your trouble. Duvall laid all but the bridge crew off, but most of them are still hanging around camp and drinking up their last wages while they wait for us to get going again. And we don't say anything, because we're going to need them when this bridge is finished and we fire back up."

Morgan pointed at the charred bridge pylons just above the surface of the water beneath them. "Who did that?"

The engineer shrugged. "Who knows? It was dark when they did it. Duvall had four Pinkerton detectives standing night guard, but there were a lot more of the bad guys. They came out of the brush carrying coal oil and torches, and shot off the guards and did their best to get a hot fire going before we could get men from camp down here."

"What happened to the Pinkerton men? I saw those two at Duvall's office, but I haven't come across any others."

"You sound like you don't care for the Pinkerton Detective Agency."

"You might say I have an old beef with them."

McDaniels nodded. "Two of them were wounded the night the bridge caught fire, and Duvall sent the rest of them back where they came from. He said he had no use for men that couldn't do their job."

"He strikes me as man who is used to getting his way."

The engineer laughed. "You don't know the half of it."

"Have you worked for him long?"

"Long enough. You'll have to pardon me, but I've got work to do. I suggest you do the same. If this bridge isn't built by the end of the month, Duvall will put you and me both out of a job."

"Good luck." Morgan lifted a hand as he rode off.

Shortly after noon he was back in camp. After a quick lunch at the mess tent, he crossed the tracks to a stack of railroad ties. The eight-feet-long sections of log were flat hewn on two sides and still green and oozing sap. He took off his coat and stood one of the crossties on end and managed to heft it on his shoulder. The green wood was heavy, and he struggled to a place in front of the door to the boxcar he had slept in. Dropping the tie, he went back to the stack and carried over two more, one at a time.

He found a small tool room in one corner of the warehouse, and came out carrying a long pry bar and a pair of posthole diggers. Thus equipped, he rolled up his sleeves and went to work. The day had warmed enough to thaw the ground, and the digging was easy and relatively rock free. He had the first posthole dug by the time the group of riders rode up.

There were five of them, all Indians in white man clothes and packing guns, and they were leading three unsaddled horses behind them. They spread out before him, saying nothing and seemingly content to watch him work. He hefted one of the crossties and dropped one end of it into the hole he had dug.

"You boys can lend a hand if you want to." Morgan raked a little dirt back into the hole around the tie and began to tamp it in with the pry bar, working one-handed and holding the tie plumb with the other hand.

One of them, an older man, laughed. "We came to see the new marshal."

"Now you've seen me, so what do you think?"

"I think your post is set crooked, and I don't recall seeing a lawman work as hard as you are."

Morgan gave the tie a firm shake and decided it was set tight enough. He brushed the dirt off his hands and squinted into the sunlight at the Indians. Every one of them was wearing a badge.

"What are you building?" the Indian who had laughed asked.

"A jail."

"Better build it big."

Morgan walked over to him and offered a handshake. "Morgan Clyde, chief of the MK&T railroad police here in Ironhead."

"Sergeant Jim Harjo, at your service, Creek Lighthorse." The Indian leaned down from his saddle and shook Morgan's hand.

The other tribal policemen kept their faces blank, as only an Indian could. None of them spoke, staring at him with their dark eyes like coal dots in their sockets. Morgan stared back at them, trying to match their stoicism.

"Never seen an Indian before?" Sergeant Harjo crossed his arms and rested them on the butt of the rifle sticking out of the leather boot beside his saddle swells.

"Oh, I have, but not one that talked so much," Morgan replied.

"We've heard of you. Weren't you the marshal of Baxter Springs for a while?"

"That's the rumor."

"The Cherokee say you're a fair man."

"Be careful what you believe."

The sergeant laughed so hard his body shook, and his saddle creaked beneath him. "We don't believe a word a Cherokee tells us. We were passing through, and when we heard the railroad had hired you, we thought we would ride over and have a look for ourselves."

"You speak good English."

"Four years in a boarding school and a mother that's white will do that to you, but these full-bloods with me don't hold it against me too much." The sergeant's joke finally caused a couple of his men to grin.

"Just passing through, huh?" Morgan asked.

"Yep. Rode over from North Fork to take a gander at things."

"North Fork?"

"It's downstream a few miles where the river forks. There's a trading post there, a few houses and farms, but not much else," the sergeant said. "We come through there regular-like looking for whiskey peddlers. Whiskey's bad for Indians."

"How come you men haven't taken ahold on this camp?" Morgan asked. "I don't imagine you care too much for having this in your backyard."

The Lighthorsemen exchanged glances before the sergeant spoke again. "No, we don't like this place, but our council agreed to having the railroad. What you white people do is none of our business, as long as you keep it here."

"We've got two saloons running full bore, and there's enough whiskey in camp to float an iron-sided gunboat."

The sergeant looked back at the camp across the tracks with no love at all on his face. "Don't get me wrong. I suggested to the council that we burn this place to the ground. Arrest every-one that looked at us crossways and haul them to Fort Smith and hand them over to the court."

"Your council seems more tolerant than you."

"They don't want any trouble with your government. Somehow, every time there's a problem between a white man and an Indian, the Indian gets the short end of it."

"How many men do you have?"

"There's twenty of us wearing badges, but I can get more," the sergeant said. "You keep your troubles here and we'll turn our heads. But the first time one of these men here causes our people trouble, we'll come running. I promise you, if we come like that, your railroad won't like it."

"Fair enough."

"Thought you might like to know that there was a camp on the river above the trestle you're working on. White men."

"Somebody I need to pay attention to?"

"My guess was that it was Texas George's boys."

"And?"

"George and his friends have got themselves a horse-moving business. You know, holding other people's horses in the brush until they cool off, and then moving them on to new country."

"How come you haven't tended to that?"

"We rode through there this morning, but nobody was home. Burned his cabin, and a few brush huts and a pole corral." Harjo jerked a thumb back over his shoulder at the loose horses behind him. "Took these horses back."

"I saw that finger of smoke to the west this morning and wondered what it was," Morgan said.

"That isn't all. There's a new bunch come down from the north. One of my men was riding to Webbers Falls two days ago and got a look at them when they crossed Elk Creek."

"Anybody I might know?"

"He saw one of them wearing a butternut shirt like those Missouri bushwhackers used to wear during the war."

"Was Deacon Fischer with them?"

"My man was too far away to tell, but it wouldn't surprise me. That bunch was the kind that Deacon used to favor."

"I was just thinking out loud."

"Pessimist, aren't you?"

"I've got a worried mind."

Sergeant Harjo shifted in the saddle. "And you're thinking Deacon used to ride with some of the old Clements Gang back before Little Arch Clements got himself shot to doll rags, and there's the rumor that he rides with the James–Younger Gang time to time since."

"Maybe."

"I heard he was too crazy to suit Cole Younger, and that even Frank and that squirrely eyed brother of his, Jesse, walked careful around him. Some say they ousted him because of it."

"That's what they say, if you believe it. Those James boys and the Youngers know this country, and so do the Millers and the rest of them that used to ride with Quantrill and Bloody Bill. I understand they used to come through here on their way to Texas to get a break from the war."

"I never said it was the James Gang. I was just making conversation. Last I heard, they were keeping their work up north, and they've lain low since they robbed that Iowa bank last summer," Harjo said. "They might get all the attention in the papers, but they aren't the only ones. It could be anyone my man saw, but he had the feeling that they were up to no good and riding like they were on the scout."

"That's all I need right now."

"Your trouble, not mine. I've got my hands full with horse thieves and whiskey peddlers, and I'll leave the worrying about Missouri bank robbers and train wreckers to you. So long." The sergeant tapped two fingers to the brim of his hat in salute, and turned his horse. His men lined in behind him, two by two.

Morgan went back to work, driving the diggers into the ground while he thought about what the sergeant had told him. It was almost sundown by the time he finished the third post. There was a water tank next to the tracks for topping off the boiler on a locomotive, and a livestock trough at the foot of its stand. He rinsed off the worst of the grime on him with the icy cold water, finger-combed his hair, and put his coat back on before crossing the tracks and heading for the mess tent.

This time, several of the men he had met while touring the bridge site nodded at him or muttered brief greetings. Normally, such hard work as he had put in setting the crossties in the ground would have given him an appetite, but he didn't feel much like eating. He stood at the door of the tent facing the street and watching the sun go down, while he absentmindedly nibbled at a half piece of cold cornbread slathered in butter and a cup of spring water to wash it down. By the time he was finished with his snack, lantern and lamplight was already shining on the water standing in the street.

"You be careful out there tonight," Saul the cook said from behind him.

Morgan hadn't heard the cook come up behind him. "I try to make a habit of being careful in my line of business."

"You better be. Somethin's gonna happen tonight."

"What did you hear?"

"Nothin', but I can tell when somethin's up. Mostly, by this time of day things have done got loud in camp. Listen. Don't you hear that quiet?"

Indeed, the camp was quieter than the evening before. Morgan lit a cigar and puffed on it thoughtfully.

"I tell you somethin' is up, and that somethin' probably has to do with you," Saul said.

"Thanks."

"Think nothin' of it. I'd just as soon there ain't no shootin'. Those bullets don't care where they fly, and I don't want none flyin' in here. I gets hoppy when the bullets is poppin' around me."

He left Saul and went outside and edged down the side of the street headed for the Bullhorn. Navigating the muddy mess was difficult in the broad daylight, much less traversing it at night. He stepped in an especially deep hole, and muddy water flooded over his boot top, soaking his sock to the point that it squished when he walked.

He passed the heads of several horses tied to a hitching rail in front of the Bullhorn, and stopped in front of his sign, slightly surprised that Tuck hadn't already torn it down. He went inside the saloon and took a stand at the near end of the bar. One of the bartenders behind the bar started to come his way, but Bill Tuck turned him away and came to Morgan himself.

"What'll it be tonight, Marshal. Or is it Chief?" Tuck asked.

"Two fingers of Old Reserve."

Tuck took down a bottle from behind the bar and poured a glass for each of them. "I got to hand it to you. Nobody ever said you didn't have plenty of nerve."

Morgan took a sip of the whiskey. "Makes me nervous when you start sweet talking me, Tuck."

"You're rubbing it in a little, aren't you, putting that sign on my place?" Tuck didn't take up his own drink.

"Figured you needed to know how things stand now. Have you got a complaint?"

"You're going to cost me a lot of business cutting down my hours of operation like that."

"The railroad needs their men working, and not laid up in here. Are you going to give me problems, or are you going to play nice?"

Tuck forced a pleasant smile and took up his drink. He held it up to Morgan before he threw it down his gullet in one swallow. He waited for the liquor to hit bottom and then grimaced and shook off the effects. "Trouble between us isn't good business for either of us."

"There will be no favors from my end."

"I don't expect any, but don't you ride me too hard, either."

Morgan finished his whiskey and straightened at the bar and brushed a few flecks of mud from the front of his coat. "Run a square place. That's all I ask."

"I will, and I do. You figure that out and maybe I won't have to see you in here too much."

"That suits both of us, but I need to have a word with one of your dealers."

Morgan drifted away and through the crowd until he reached Charlie Six Fingers's faro table. The gambler had three men playing his game, and was studying those players and the layout so intently that he didn't notice Morgan until the lawman was almost on top of him.

"What do you want?" Charlie growled.

All three of the faro players scooted back their chairs and stood clear.

Morgan leaned over the table with both palms flat on its top. His face was only inches from the dealer's. "You're tinhorn and a card cheat, Charlie. Everybody knows it."

"You . . ." Charlie Six Fingers shoved himself back from the table, one hand darting under it.

"Don't try for that knife, Charlie, or it'll be the last thing you ever do."

The gambler glanced quickly around the room out of the corner of his eyes, seeing that the whole tent was watching how he handled himself. Either pride or stubbornness seemed to get the best of him.

"You're riding me hard, Clyde."

"You set a fair game, Charlie, or I'm going to run you out of camp like I did in Baxter Springs." Morgan leaned his face a little closer. "No rigged decks. No funny dealing."

"Are you saying I cheat?"

"I've said that twice now. Are you hard of hearing?"

"I'll . . ."

"You'll what, Charlie? You'll what? Don't look around. You look right at me. Nobody's going to help you. I run this camp, and it's me you have to please."

Charlie's whole body was shaking with anger.

"Call me Chief, Charlie. Say it where everyone can hear you."

"You can go straight to hell."

"Say it."

Charlie went for the knife under the table, but he was too slow. Morgan grabbed the Remington around the cylinder frame left-handed, drew it, and busted the gambler across the top of the head with the butt of it. Charlie groaned and then groaned again when his chin thumped on the table while his eyes rolled back in his head with nothing but the whites showing.

Morgan holstered his pistol while he looked around the tent. Nobody seemed inclined to make any trouble over Charlie, and there were a few that were nodding as if they were pleased to see the faro dealer get buffaloed.

Morgan turned to the bar, his attention on Tuck. "When he comes to, you put him on a horse or on the train and get him out of here. I'm going to take it personal if I see him in Iron-head again."

Tuck waited a full ten seconds before answering him, with his face turned as red as if he were holding his breath. "I'll tell him."

Morgan looked around the tent again, giving Charlie's lookout and casekeeper extra attention. "And that goes for any of the rest of you running games. Keep it honest."

Morgan went outside, and Red Molly followed him out. She stood at his side, staring across the street at the lights of the Bucket of Blood. Neither of them spoke for a bit.

"You need to quit, Morgan," she finally said. "It's turning you mean."

"You think I enjoyed that back there?"

"You didn't used to, but, yes, I think you did."

"That's the only thing Tuck and his kind understand. You've got to make an example of a few of them; cow them down before they work themselves up to run over you. Lay down the rules, and lay them down hard."

"What did you show them? That you're as mean as they are?" Her voice remained soft and husky. "There's a fine line that isn't always so easy to see, and I'd hate for you to cross it. Most don't go back once they do."

He realized that he was breathing hard, and didn't know where the anger raised in him had come from. "Molly, you of all people ought to know the kind of men I'm dealing with."

"And what's the difference between you and them?"

"This." Morgan put his hand on his badge.

"That cheap piece of tin? You're better than this, Morgan. Don't let it drag you down. Get out and go somewhere else before it's too late for you. You're on the edge and you don't even know it."

"You don't know what you're talking about."

"You mean how dare a whore like me lecture you?"

"I didn't say that."

"I know how hard it is to get back across that line, Morgan. Believe me, I know it."

He splashed into the street and left her alone and watching him from the lit doorway of the saloon. The harmonica and banjo music coming from inside the Bucket of Blood guided

71

him. It was time he paid them a visit and laid down the law as he had in the Bullhorn. Molly was a decent sort, but she didn't understand. No one did, unless they had pinned that cheap piece of tin to their chest and strapped a gun on their hip.

His right foot was still squishing and sloshing inside his wet boot, distracting him and making it hard to think. When he was on the far side of the street he found a spot of firm ground that was relatively dry compared to everything else. He cursed and leaned over to tug off the boot and pour some of the water out of it. The instant he did, a gun flamed from an alley between two tents, and he felt the bullet pass right over his head.

Whoever was laying for him was shooting in the pitch dark, and their second shot came no closer than the first. Morgan staggered backwards, temporarily blinded by the gun flash, and pinned himself against the canvas wall of the tent nearest him. He drew the Remington and waited for some sound from whoever had tried to kill him. An old Indian fighter had once told him that the first man to move in a stalking fight was likely the first one to be killed, and with those words in mind he willed himself to hold his ground and to see whose patience gave first. He rubbed at his spotty eyes and tried to clear them while he waited.

It didn't take long, for he soon heard splashing, running footsteps going away from him. He cocked his pistol and dashed around the corner of the tent into the alley. The fleeing assassin was only a dim shadow, but Morgan fired a snapshot from the hip down the gap between the tents. It might have been his imagination, but he thought he saw the running man falter before he disappeared in the dark.

Morgan moved forward cautiously, ready for another ambush, but found nothing after going all the way to the edge of camp. Whoever it was could have darted into a tent, or been hiding in the brush waiting him out. Nothing was to be gained by risking his neck bumbling around in the dark, and he made his way back through camp, headed for the boxcar and his bedroll. On his way there he saw several men gathered in doorways, their forms outlined by the lamps glowing behind them. He wondered how many of them had known that someone was lying for him, and not a single soul had so much as warned him if they had.

Saul was the last person he passed. The cook had come out of the mess tent in nothing but his long underwear and was holding up a lantern head high and peering down the street.

"Is that you, Chief? I done thought they did for you when I heard that shootin'."

"That's day one, Saul, and I'm still standing," Morgan said without stopping. "Three to one odds and only one more day to go. I must be lucky."

"No, I think you's just stubborn, Chief."

CHAPTER SEVEN

"You're a sound sleeper," Hank Bickford said.

The clank of metal and the blacksmith's voice startled Morgan from his sleep. He lifted his hat brim and cocked one eye open to see Bickford standing outlined in the open boxcar door.

"I finished your order." Hank gestured at the tangle of chains and black steel he had thrown down at his feet.

Morgan threw back his blanket and propped himself up on one elbow. It was barely past sunup.

"You ought to get you a cot in here if you're calling this place home now," Hank said. "Dress it up a little, you know. Me and you might get this door to close with a little work. It won't be like Duvall's fancy private car, but it might do."

Morgan got his legs under him and stood. He belted his Remington around his hips while he waited for his foggy mind to come fully awake.

"You put that gun on like most men have their first cup of coffee of a morning," Hand observed.

"Do you always wake up this chipper?"

"Always been an early riser. Thought I might help you finish your jail."

Morgan noticed the blacksmith's examining gaze. "Maybe, but I think you came to look me over after last night."

Hank smiled. "I heard about the shooting this morning. Thought I might come around and see how many holes they put in you."

Morgan held his arms out wide and turned a circle. "I'm as right as rain."

"Who tried to kill you?"

"Don't know, but I aim to find out."

Morgan picked up a length of heavy chain with a set of manacles at its end. Hank had hammered a hot length of rod steel into flat bands, and then bent them around a mandrel in the shape of handcuffs. The dimples of his hammer marks showed in the dull, soot black of the metal. Morgan had never seen irons made anything like them. The handcuffs worked like a small set of stocks, a single top piece curved to fit a pair of wrists, hinged on one end, and fastening on the other with a small, but stout, padlock. Morgan hadn't been specific about his order, other than the shackles work, and the design was solely of Hank's imagination.

"They don't look like much. I had to hurry, but they ought to work," Hank said.

"They'll do fine. Thanks."

"I tell you what, why don't me and the kids fasten these irons to those posts you set yesterday while you go find yourself a shave and a bath? You look like death, and you smell like a litter of pigs."

Morgan only then noticed the other two faces revealed barely above the floor of the boxcar through the open door. The boy and the girl were both looking up at him with big eyes, especially the boy.

"Thought I would let them help me a little this morning. Don't get to spend much time with them," Hank said.

"Morning, kids," Morgan said.

The girl looked away bashfully, but the boy, the younger of the two, didn't. He pointed at the cased rifle leaning against the boxcar wall. "Is that a rifle?"

"It is."

"Can I see it?"

"Clarence, you watch your manners," Hank said. "Don't mind the boy, Mr. Clyde. He's always full of questions."

"I had a boy myself and know how they are."

"You've got a boy, mister?" Clarence asked, looking down at the ground and scuffing the dirt with the toe of one shoe.

"He was about your size the last time I saw him, but I guess he's about grown by now."

"How come you ain't seen him?"

"Clarence." Hank's tone was scolding.

"Maybe his son's back home like we used to wait for Daddy while he was off working on the railroad," the girl said.

Morgan smiled again at her. She was a thin little wisp of a girl, maybe fourteen or so, with pale blond hair and pair of large blue eyes. It was already easy to see that she would one day be a beautiful woman, and Morgan wondered how such a picture of girl came out of a homely woman like Lottie Bickford and a redheaded, pug-nosed, sawed-off bull of a blacksmith like Hank. It only went to show that you never could tell.

"What kind of rifle is that?" Clarence asked, oblivious to his father's warnings.

Hank leapt down from the boxcar and took the boy by the arm and grabbed up the wad of shackles at the same time. "That's enough questions for now. You kids come help me."

Morgan watched the blacksmith lead the kids over to the posts he had set in the ground, and the three of them bantered playfully while Hank wrapped one of the chains around a post.

Morgan ran his hands through the black whiskers on his jaw, and then glanced down at his muddy clothes. Leaving the Bickfords, he took his valise across the tracks and headed for the bathhouse.

It wasn't really a bathhouse, being only another tent like all the others in camp. A German fellow ran it, and he had two teenaged Indian girls to tend the water in a pair of oak stave tubs set on raised pallets above the tent floor. One of the Indian girls in a flour sack dress guided Morgan to a tub, and he eyed the water critically.

"It's hot," she said.

Morgan could see bits of grass and other offal floating on the dingy water. "Hot, maybe, but how many times has that bathwater been used?"

The Indian girl shrugged.

"How about pouring me some fresh water?"

"That will cost you twenty cents extra."

Morgan waited while the two girls drained the tub and carried in fresh water. They had a fire built beneath a large steel tank behind the tent, and they filled their buckets from a spigot tapped into its side. They worked silently, carrying a bucket in each hand while the German stood in the doorway watching the street and occasionally scowling at Morgan as if he thought he was too much trouble. Morgan couldn't tell if the young Indian girls only worked for the German, or if they were his daughters or his wives.

One of the Indian girls handed him a clean towel and a bar of lye soap when the tub was filled, and then went to sit in a chair a little ways off with her back to him. The German made him pay his twenty cents for the bath in advance, and then he and the other girl left the tent.

Morgan stripped down and climbed in the tub, letting the hot water soak into his muscles all the way to the bone, and liking the steam rising up around him. He washed his hair and scrubbed himself with a long-handled brush he found hanging on the side of the tub. Finished, he leaned back and closed his eyes. The bath felt so good that he must have dozed off. It was Bill Tuck walking into the tent that woke him.

The saloonkeeper was carrying a fancy walking cane with a

silver knob on it, and he glanced at Morgan for an instant before he went to the other tub and tapped it twice on the rim with that cane. Morgan glanced at his Remington lying on top of his coat beside his own tub, making sure it was within easy reach. Tuck noticed that and smirked.

The Indian girl rose from her chair and brought Tuck a towel and some soap of his own. Tuck didn't wait for her to leave, and immediately removed his clothes. He climbed in the tub, then reached over the side and pulled his nickel-plated pocket pistol from his vest pocket. When he straightened he saw that Morgan had reached out and put a hand on his own gun.

Tuck laughed and laid the Smith nearby on the pile of his clothes and let it go. He slid under the water and came up wiping his face and sputtering.

"Heard you had a bit of trouble over at the Bucket of Blood last night," Tuck said as if he were discussing the weather or some equally trivial topic.

"You didn't have anything to do with that, did you?"

"Clyde, from the way you sound, a person wouldn't know what a law and order man I am."

"What about Charlie Six Fingers?"

"He got on a horse this morning and lit a shuck," Tuck said. "I'm short one faro dealer, thanks to you."

"I gave Charlie a fair chance."

"You make a lot of enemies when you don't have to."

Morgan stood, toweled himself dry, and took out a fresh pair of clothes from his valise. The shirt and the pants were badly wrinkled, but at least they were clean. He frowned at the pile of filthy clothes he was replacing while he dressed.

"Did you get that scar in the war, or since?" Tuck asked.

Morgan glanced down at the puckered scar that grooved his left ribs before he pulled his shirt over his head and covered it. "It's only a scar."

"Whoever shot you wasn't playing around," Tuck said. "Looks like a chunk of shrapnel or maybe a big bullet did that."

"Yeah." Morgan tucked his shirt in and took the scrub brush and tried to use it to brush his frock coat clean.

"I can't imagine anyone wanting to shoot a likable fellow like you," Tuck added.

Morgan belted his gun on and went out back where the proprietor had a wash pan on a table at the foot of a tree. A little mirror was nailed to the tree trunk. He took the wash pan and dipped it full of water from one of the warming tubs by the fire, and then went back to the tree and took out an ivory-handled straight razor from his valise and a bottle of shaving cream. He hung his hat on a nail in the tree beside the mirror and studied his reflection with a slight frown upon his face.

He was still lathering his whiskers when he saw the two horsemen pass behind him in the mirror. Turning, he got a quick look at two men riding down the street. Both of them were on big horses, and the nearest one to him was wearing a Confederate greatcoat and had a brace of pistols strapped to his saddle swells. They both twisted their heads and looked at him during the brief moment they were visible through the alley between the bath tent and the next one beside it.

Morgan finished shaving, combed his hair to suit him, packed his things, and donned his hat and went back into the bath tent to get his dirty clothes. Tuck was smoking a cigar with his head leaned back over the edge of the tub and watching smoke rings float above him.

"Care for a good Havana?" he asked. "I don't know how you smoke those cheap things you smoke."

Morgan passed out of the open tent flap onto the street. The sun was already brighter and warmer than it had been the day before, and the wind had swapped until it blew out of the south. The warmer temperatures and the sun felt good on his clean-shaven face.

"You won't believe who I just saw passing by," Tuck called to him. "I thought both of those Kingman brothers were still down in Texas. George must have fetched them up here."

"Can't say I ever met them."

Tuck laughed again. "Oh, I imagine you will, seeing as how people are saying that was Texas George you winged last night. Story is, you shot off one of his fingers. Shot it off right down to nothing but a nubbin."

Morgan turned around and looked back through the doorway. "Do tell."

"Oh, nothing. Only a rumor, but they say that those Kingman boys are a tight bunch. I don't imagine they will take kindly to you maiming their brother."

Morgan walked away, drifting aimlessly while he thought on what Tuck had said. He was still thinking about it when he found himself at the edge of camp. Someone had cut the underbrush away from beneath a large hickory tree and set up one of those tepee-looking Sibley army tents beneath it. Lottie Bickford came out of the tent. She had a wicker basket under one arm, and when she saw that Morgan was carrying his laundry she nodded her head at it.

"I'll take those down to the creek with me and wash them for you for a nickel," she said. "Ten cents if you want them ironed."

Morgan went to her and handed her his dirty clothes. "That's fair enough for me."

She stuffed his clothes in her basket. "You haven't seen my children, have you?"

"They were with their father an hour or so ago, over by his shop."

She sighed. "Glad to hear it. My Suzy is a pretty girl, but a little headstrong like her father. I don't like how some of the men in this camp look at her, and she's still too young to know that they're looking and what some might be thinking."

Morgan turned back, following the edge of the woods on the north side of camp. Before long he came close to the point where his ambusher from the night before had fired from. The muddy ground was chewed up with the tracks of numerous people, but he examined it anyway, starting there and working his way in the direction the man had fled. The only thing he found was what looked like a single smear of dried blood where someone might have rubbed against a wagon's side. It might not have been blood at all, or it might have nothing to do with what happened the previous night. It was a rough country, and could bleed a man in more ways than one.

He made his way back to the street and passed in front of the Bucket of Blood, only pausing to study the two big sorrel horses tied in front of the Bullhorn across the street. They were the horses the Kingman brothers were riding earlier, and that Confederate greatcoat was hanging from one of the saddle horns.

When he arrived back at the abandoned boxcar he'd claimed, he was surprised to find that someone had fixed the door enough so that it was closed and would slide open with a little effort. He opened it, and saw that there was now a cot, a rug on the floor beside it, a wicker-bottomed chair, and a coal oil lamp sitting atop a little night table beside the cot.

"Home, sweet home," he said to himself, and took a quick glance to make sure his rifle was still leaning in the corner.

He closed the door and went to what would serve as his new jail. Hank Bickford had wrapped a shackle chain tightly around each upright crosstie about four feet above the ground, and riveted it back into itself with a hammered cold shut link. Then he had driven several railroad spikes through various links in the chain to keep it from sliding up and down the post. Morgan grabbed one of the chains and gave it some experimental tugs.

Short of digging one of the posts out of the ground with their bare hands, nobody secured with the shackles was getting loose, and if they did, they weren't going far dragging a hundred-pound railroad tie.

"Chief Clyde!" someone shouted.

Hope McDaniels, the construction foreman, was riding a horse toward Morgan with two other riders following him, and a man between them bound and leading on the end of a rope from both of their saddle horns.

"Got a prisoner for you," McDaniels said when he neared.

They stopped their horses and the man they were leading staggered forward. He wore a Johnny Reb forage cap sitting crooked on his head, and his face was battered and swollen on one side.

"What's he done?" Morgan asked.

"This is the second time he was fighting with his crew instead of working," McDaniels said.

"Them Yankees were razzing me," the prisoner drawled and held up his bound hands before him. "You let me loose."

"He knocked some teeth out of my crane mechanic, and may have broken the boiler tender's arm," McDaniels added.

Morgan studied the prisoner for a second time. He was tall, even with him standing slouched like he was. Tall maybe, but also as thin as a gutted snowbird; a long, lanky sort if ever there was such a man. A lock of dark hair dangled out from under his cap and across his forehead, and he kept trying to shake it out of his eyes.

Morgan went to the first post he'd set and took his keys from his vest pocket and opened the shackles. "Bring him over here."

The two men leading the prisoner dismounted and shoved him towards Morgan. The man in the Rebel cap staggered forward, but tried to head butt the first of his escorts that got near him and kicked at the other.

Morgan drew his pistol and shoved its cold barrel against the prisoner's temple. "I suggest you hold still."

The prisoner grinned and strained his eyes in their sockets, trying to see the pistol held to his head. "Now, that's some way to treat a stranger, Chief."

The two men guarding him untied the rope around his wrists and replaced it with the manacles. Morgan handed them the lock, and they snapped it closed.

Morgan holstered his pistol and stepped back. The prisoner tugged against his new bindings experimentally and then tested how far the chain would let him get from the post. They all watched while he started walking a half circle at the end of the chain, reversing his course and going back over the same arc like a mad bull pacing a fence.

"What are you going to do with me?" he finally asked after two or three times back and forth.

"I don't want him back on my line. All he wants to do is fight," McDaniels said.

"You sure make me sound like a desperate man." The prisoner talked tough, but the humor in his voice was plain enough to cut the edge off anything he said, as if he thought it was all fun and games.

"I'm spread too thin to take him to Fort Smith, so that leaves two things. We could form a camp court and let his peers decide what to do with him, or I can put him on the next supply train headed north," Morgan said.

"Court sounds good to me," the prisoner said. "There's plenty of good Southern men left in this camp, and they won't stand for this."

"You're the lawman. I'll let you figure it out." McDaniels waited until his men were mounted and turned his horse and rode away.

"Hey," the prisoner said to Morgan's back, "I won't forget

you holding that pistol to my head. I owe you one."

Morgan paused long enough to frown at him, but started walking towards the tracks.

"Hey, you aren't going to leave me here out in the open, are you? What if it rains again?" The prisoner called after him. "Ought not arrest a man if you don't have a proper jail. Who in the hell do you think you are? I'm telling you, law dog, you're trying my patience."

"Don't worry, I'll grow on you. Especially if you want some supper."

CHAPTER EIGHT

Morgan brought his prisoner a plate of beans and a stale chunk of sourdough bread right before nightfall. He handed over the food and squatted a little distance away to watch the man eat.

The prisoner bowed his head and said grace over his food, and then looked up at Morgan with a sour expression on his face. "You're probably one of those pointy-hatted, cross-yourself types like all these damned potato-eating, mick Irish bastards in camp. I'm Baptist myself, and proud of it."

Morgan gestured at the man's hat. "Did you fight in the war?"

The prisoner nodded and said between mouthfuls of beans, "Got the lobe of my ear shot off at the Peach Orchard, and then took a bullet in the ankle trying to help Hood's boys pry those sumbitches off Little Round Top. Did you do any fighting yourself?"

"I was one of those *sumbitches* you were trying to pry off Little Round Top."

The prisoner shook his head. "You Maine boys came screaming down that hill at us with nothing but your bayonets, and us shooting the hell out of you until our skirmish line lost its nerve and broke and fell back. Never seen anything like it for sheer nerve."

"I wasn't with the 20th Maine," Morgan said. "You boys ganged up on my sharpshooters on the road to Gettysburg and then down in the Peach Orchard, and what was left of us was sent to help out on Little Round Top."

"You weren't one of those pot shooters wearing green, were you? There were regiments that paid a bounty for tipping one of you over."

Morgan nodded.

"I gotta admit, you boys shot pretty good for Yankees."

"Where were you after Gettysburg?" Morgan asked.

"Nowhere. The surgeons wanted to cut my foot off, so I mustered myself out of the army without asking anyone's leave and went back to Alabama before I was missing any of my favorite parts. That's the unofficial version, of course." The prisoner grinned around a mouthful of food and winked at Morgan. "What about you?"

"Invalided out and sent home."

"Did you get it on the hill that day?"

"No, I got it the next day on Cemetery Ridge."

"How about some more of these beans?"

"That's the last of them."

"That figures. Ain't never had enough to eat since my mama weaned me. My name's Shelby Rayburn, but my friends call me Dixie."

"Morgan Clyde."

"Heard of you. Not much of it was any good."

"I could say the same about you."

Dixie grinned again. "My older brother and me served in the same company during the war. They called him Big Dixie and me Little Dixie."

"Is your brother here with you?"

"He didn't make it."

Morgan stood and took Dixie's empty plate. "Sorry to hear that. A lot of good men on both sides didn't get to go back home."

"That's a fair thing to say, but there are those that don't think that way. What's it been, six, seven years? And there are still a lot of hard feelings left over." Dixie wiped his mouth with the back of one shirtsleeve and looked up at him. "Ol' Texas George must figure you're some shakes with that hog leg on your hip for him to have laid for you like he did. George usually shoots his men looking at him so he can brag a little."

"I never got a good enough look to see who shot at me."

"Oh, it was George all right."

"Are you chummy with George?"

"Far from it. He ain't my kind by a long shot." Dixie pointed at Morgan's badge. "Believe it or not, I used to wear one of those."

"Back in Alabama?"

"No, I worked for Boss Ichord as a deputy down in Denton, Texas right after the war."

"How's Boss? I met him once when I was working for the U.S. Marshal's office out of Van Buren."

"Boss is dead. He went to serve a subpoena and got blown out of his saddle before he knew what hit him," Dixie said. "Never thought it would be some farmer with a shotgun that got him."

"It can happen," Morgan replied. "You're sure it was Texas George that shot at me last night?"

"That's what they're saying. I heard you clipped off one of his nose pickers, and that he's laying up over at North Fork nursing his wounds."

"Do you know anything about his brothers?"

"Not much. I was drinking one night with some Texas cowboys holding a herd on the prairie west of here. The way they told it, all those Kingmans rode for some Texas cavalry outfit, and George was their captain. The story goes that they all went to Mexico right after the war, or some such like that."

Morgan was still contemplating that when gunshots sounded from camp. Both of them looked in the direction of the gunfire.

First it was one shot, and then several other guns joined in. The firing was totally random, mixed in with wild yells and catcalls.

"Sounds like somebody's doing a little celebrating," Dixie said. "If we were sharp, we'd go into the ammunition business, considering how much shooting goes on in this camp."

Morgan stood and flipped his coattail behind the butt of his Remington.

"That could be nothing but some drunks shooting up in the air, or it could be a setup, you know," Dixie added. "Wouldn't take a real smart man to figure that a little ruckus will bring you running, especially since it wasn't but this morning that you posted your new camp rules. And there are some that didn't take kindly to you giving Charlie Six Fingers the rough treatment. In case you don't know it, you ain't the most popular man in camp."

Morgan hesitated, already thinking the same thing. "What caused your trouble today?"

Dixie shrugged. "A lot of those Irish and Yankee boys on the line don't have any use for a secesh like me. That mechanic was riding me pretty hard all morning, and things were said that I won't take from anyone. I'll clean his clock when I see him again. You can put that in your pipe and smoke it."

"And I suppose you didn't do anything to help bring it on?"

A sheepish grin spread across Dixie's face while he stretched his legs in front of him to a more comfortable position. "It might be that I questioned the motherhood of that mechanic, although I don't rightly remember if this is for the official record."

"Are you wanted for anything?"

"No, I ain't on the scout."

"Have you got a gun?"

Dixie knuckled the bill of his cap farther back on his head. "That mechanic is a brass-plated bastard, but, no, I don't intend on shooting him if that's what you're asking. A couple more licks upside his head ought to fix him good enough to suit me."

"How about you come to work for me? I'm short a man to watch my back."

Dixie rubbed his chin with a mischievous look. "I don't know what to make of this. Do you generally ask criminals to work for you?"

"Not generally, but if Boss Ichord hired you once, that's good enough for me in a pinch. Let's say I'm offering you a job on a trial basis, and we'll see how it works out."

"Some might say your hiring practices are a little foolish, or you must be a man that trusts his hunches."

"I'm a man in a hurry." Morgan pointed in the direction of the gunfire.

"I'd say you're desperate."

"It means I let you loose, and you get seventy-five dollars a month to get shot at like I do. And nobody, especially me, is going to say thank you."

"You expect a secesh like me to work for a blue-belly like you? It wasn't too long ago that we might have been swapping shots at each other."

"I'm offering you a chance to get off that chain, and enough trouble to keep even a knot-headed scrapper like you happy."

"You must be a man with few friends to come to this."

"How about it?"

"Are you expecting me to go down that street with you?"

"A man that went up Little Round Top ought to think this a stroll in the park."

"I hate getting shot at, but I hate being chained up worse." Dixie held up his shackled wrists. "I'm your fool."

Morgan unlocked his wrists and waited for him to stand. They stood eye to eye for a long moment.

"You don't know me from Adam," Dixie said. "I could slug

you on the ear right now and not feel a lick of guilt about it for you putting that pistol to my head."

"I'll give you five minutes to get yourself heeled and get back here ready to work," Morgan said. "Or I can whip your ass right here and shackle you back to that post. Your choice, Dixie Rayburn."

"By golly, but if I don't think you believe you could do it."

"Try me."

"Don't believe I will. That's a poor way to start a working relationship."

Morgan watched him trot towards the railroad tracks, and then waited, listening to the noise from camp and periodically straining in the fading light to check the face of his pocket watch and wondering if Dixie would come back.

Four minutes had passed and it was long into dusk before Dixie returned wearing a brass-framed Confederate Navy at a cross draw on one hip and carrying a Spencer carbine in his hands.

"Are you ready?" Morgan asked.

"Ready as I'll ever be." Dixie hung the Spencer in the crook of one elbow and took a plug of chewing tobacco out and tore off a chunk with a tug of his jaw teeth. "I saw them when I went to fetch my guns. There's a whole bunch of them down in front of Irish Dave's saloon."

"Let's get to it, then. There's no sense dragging things out."

"There's no sense hurrying to our graves either," Dixie said. "One of my sergeants used to say that there are two kinds of fools in battle. There's the fool that runs to fight, and there's the fool that runs after him because he said so."

"Do you always talk so much?"

"Only when I'm awake."

"Come on." Morgan started towards camp with long, purposeful strides.

Dixie wallowed the chew around in his cheek until it was comfortable and spit a thick stream of juice on the ground before he set out after Morgan. "Right, Chief."

CHAPTER NINE

It had grown dark by the time they crossed the tracks and reached the head of the street, and they could see the group of men gathered in front of the Bucket of Blood and standing in the pool of dim lamplight spilling out of the open flaps of the tent door. A stab of flame flashed every time one of them let off his pistol at the sky.

"How do you want to play this?" Dixie asked.

"Are you any good with that Spencer?"

"Night shooting is spotty business at best."

"Don't let the nerves make you hair-triggered. We handle it easy if they'll let us."

"Right, Chief."

They worked their way slowly down the same side of the street as the saloon lay on, walking side by side.

"Watch the far side of the street," Morgan said.

"Got it."

They neared to within fifty yards of the Bucket of Blood. Someone must have spotted them, for the group of rowdies had gone back inside.

"That's a setup if I ever saw one," Dixie whispered.

"What are you whispering for? They saw us coming."

Dixie shrugged. "Picky sort, aren't you?"

"You keep watching the other side of the street."

"You're taking this awful calmly. Have many times have you done this?"

"Some. Keep an eye on that wagon over there."

"You bet."

They stopped at the edge of the lamplight and studied the entrance to the saloon.

"You go around and come through the back way," Morgan said.

Dixie took three steps and then stopped and turned back. "How do I know what to do? I'd hate to get off on the wrong foot with you my first evening on the job."

"You shoot anyone that looks like they're going to shoot me."

"Easy enough."

Morgan heard Dixie stumble and curse, and knew that his new policeman had tripped over one of the tent ropes or a stake in the dark. He waited long enough to give him time to make it to the far end of the saloon. Like the Bullhorn Palace, the Bucket of Blood was a large, canvas wall tent, maybe sixty feet long, with five-foot sidewalls and the peak of the roof supported by a peeled pine ridgepole.

Morgan stepped through the front doorway and the room went dead quiet except for the hiss of one lamp flame whipping in the wind coming through the open doorway. He motioned to the men to either side of him, and they went deeper into the tent where he could see them all. Every face was turned to him, and he knew that they had been waiting for him to show up. There must have been twenty or thirty men in the saloon, but it didn't take him long to spot the threat. The nasty little setup someone had rigged for Morgan was so obvious it was almost childish.

There was a man in a flop-brimmed, leather hat and a wolf hide vest seated with his back to the wall in the shadows to his right, and he was alone and leaned over and intently watching Morgan with a shotgun laid across the table in front of him. He wasn't at all good at masking his intentions. The one hand he had on the side lock of the shotgun was fidgeting nervously, as was one of his knees, which Morgan could make out under the table.

The other two who caught Morgan's eye were both at the bar on the other side of the saloon and directly opposite the first man. Irish Dave O'Malley himself stood behind the bar, grinning like the little, pint-sized demon he was. Morgan had never worked a town out west where Irish Dave ran one of his operations, but knew of him from his days back in New York. Dave was run out of the Five Points during the draft riots in '63, and after that he followed the Union Pacific west as it built tracks from Council Bluffs to Promontory Summit, Utah, setting up his hog wallows every time a new end-of-the-tracks sin city sprung into being. He had to have been well into his sixties, but he was as lean and hard as a man half his age. And Morgan didn't let his leprechaun looks fool him. Irish Dave was credited with killing six men since he had come west, with gun and knife, or his bare fists or whatever else was easy to hand.

Hands—both of Irish Dave's were out of sight, and Morgan guessed he had a gun hidden behind the bar.

The third of them was a curly-headed, half-breed Indian kid with a pockmarked face and with his hat hanging on a string from his neck and resting between his shoulder blades. He was known as Seminole Bob around camp, and was proud of the name. Everything about him was cocksure and inflated, and he stood not far from Irish Dave at the end of the bar with his back to it and both arms outstretched and resting along it, one boot crossed over the other. Two ivory-handled six-guns stuck out of his open coat, butts forward, and it was obvious that he wanted Morgan to see his guns.

Morgan guessed how it was meant to play out. The kid would purposely pick a fight with him, and the man at the table on the other side of the room would give it to him in the back. Irish

Dave would be the insurance and mop-up man. Even if he didn't have to pull a trigger, Dave would want everyone to know he caused it all to happen. Men like Dave made a business of fear and violent reputation.

Three men and maybe more that he hadn't spotted, and one of the first things he noticed when he stepped into the saloon was that it didn't have a back door for Dixie to come through. Morgan was weighing the odds and trying to figure out how best not to get killed when a slit in the back end of the tent ripped open, and Dixie's head appeared through it. The next thing that came through was the barrel of his Spencer carbine.

"Evening, fellows," Dixie said as he put one leg through the hole he'd cut with his knife and followed it with his other. "And ladies." He sheathed his knife and bent the bill of his cap to the soiled dove sitting on a man's lap nearby and gave her a rakish smile.

Smile or not, the dark bore of the Spencer carbine meant nothing but business, and the crowd in the back made room for him. He took a stand under the ridgepole, and Irish Dave scowled his way, knowing that he had lost his edge. Only the half-breed kid at the bar didn't seem to care.

"Which ones of you were doing the shooting?" Morgan asked. "I gave you boys fair notice that there wasn't to be any pistol popping in camp."

"Skunks," the kid said.

"What's that?" Morgan asked.

The kid dropped his arms off the bar slowly and straightened his slumped, nonchalant posture. "I said we were shooting at a skunk. Those skunks can be hydrophoby, you know."

"You tell him, Bob," someone in the crowd said, and someone else snickered, egging the kid on.

Morgan's attention didn't waver from the kid. "You pull those shooters out of their holsters real slow and lay them on the bar," Morgan said.

"You got to take them from me if you want them." The kid was obviously enjoying being the center of attention, and he held his coat front wide open with both hands on the lapels, revealing his pistols plainly. "Come on, Clyde. You come right on. They say you're tough, but I ain't seen any of your grave-yards."

Morgan took a quick glance at the man at the table with the shotgun. Handling the kid was going to put his back to that shotgun—exactly the way Irish Dave wanted it.

"I got the jasper by the wall." Dixie's voice rang clear and plain in the saloon's tight confines, as if he had read Morgan's mind.

The man in the leather hat with the shotgun on his table looked nervously from Dixie to Irish Dave.

"He so much as flinches, and I'll put one through him deep and wide," Dixie added.

Morgan shifted his attention to Irish Dave. "I'd appreciate it, Dave, if you would let me see your hands."

Irish Dave didn't budge at first, and Morgan's right hand moved slowly to his belt buckle and closer to the butt of the Remington on his left hip. His other hand took hold of the end of his holster to keep it from moving if he had to draw. "You got something to show me, Dave?"

Slowly, Irish Dave lifted his hands and inched down the bar away from where he had been standing. "Nothing but me mitts, Chief."

"Why don't you try me?" the kid asked, not liking being ignored.

"Kid, I won't tell you again to hand over those pistols," Mor-gan said.

"Call me kid again. Go ahead." The kid's voice had a whine to it. "You know who I am?"

He was about to remind everyone that he was the one and only Seminole Bob, but Morgan started for him in long, quick strides, cutting him off. The kid's hands dropped and took hold of his Colt revolvers, but Morgan kept coming, rapidly closing the distance between them and making no move for his own gun. The kid was wound so tight that he was shaking, but his pistols stayed in their holsters as if he couldn't make his arms work.

"You stop!" the kid shouted, and his voice cracked and quavered, trying to shout himself to bravery.

Morgan lunged forward and grabbed him by the shirtfront, and only then did the kid manage a feeble attempt to jerk out his pistols. But it was already too late. The time it had taken him to talk himself into some courage was that much too long, and Morgan butted him in the nose with the top of his forehead and crumpled him against the bar. He was still struggling weakly when Morgan punched him hard in the gut and followed that with an uppercut to his chin. The bar patrons in the far end of the tent heard the kid's teeth clack together like a steel trap snapping shut. He was out cold before he hit the floor.

Morgan picked up his hat, which had fallen from his head in the scuffle, knocking out the dent in the crown that the kid's face had put in it, and then turned to the rest of the room. "Who else was shooting at skunks?"

Nobody answered him, and the room had grown so quiet that he could hear his own breathing. The man across the room with the shotgun had scooted away from his table, distancing himself from his gun and eyeing Dixie's Spencer like it was the plague. Morgan nodded at Dixie, and then bent and tugged the Navy Colts out of the kid's holsters and shoved them behind his own gun belt.

Dixie followed his example and went to the man at the table and stuck the barrel of the cocked Spencer in his belly. "You lay that pistol of yours on the table, and that gut knife in your boot top, too."

The man did as he was told and then stood with his back to the tent wall and his hands high and wide. "I wasn't causing no trouble."

"To hell you weren't. You've got a guilty look about you if I ever saw one," Dixie said.

"A guilty look ain't against the law."

"Save it for the good Lord or your judge." Dixie gave Morgan a fretful look. "You about ready to get out of here? This ain't the friendliest place I ever sashayed through."

"Not yet."

Morgan was looking at Irish Dave when he said it. He stepped around the end of the bar and went behind it, and Irish Dave turned to him with his thumbs hooked in his belt and his bowler hat cocked on his head at a rakish, jaunty angle. Morgan reached under the bar and found a double-barreled shotgun there. He hooked his thumb over both hammers and held it one-handed, aimed at Dave's belly with the butt resting against his hip.

"What's this, Dave?" Morgan's voice sounded as if he were scolding a child. Mocking. "Were you planning on jumping in?"

"Nah, Clyde. That's me scattergun for holdup men and other pikers who might want to take me till," Irish Dave said.

"I think you're lying. I think that same smug look would have been on your face if this two-bit kid had managed what you put him up to."

"I was only standing here minding me own business."

"Don't beg. It isn't becoming on a man of your reputation."

"What are the charges?"

"Maybe I'll think of something, or maybe not. But what matters is that you're going to carry that kid across the tracks for me. You're going to do it with everyone watching."

"Piss off, copper."

Morgan slashed out with the shotgun, striking Irish Dave across the temple and staggering him. Irish Dave caught himself against a beer keg, clutching it for a moment until he got his wits about him. He came back at Morgan with a knife in his hand, and made a wild, lunging backhand swing. Morgan blocked the blade of the knife with the forearm of the shotgun and then butt-stroked Dave under the chin. The knife clattered from Irish Dave's hand and his knees sagged and he clung to the bar with both hands, fighting to keep from going down in front of everyone. He glared at Morgan with a trickle of blood already running down the side of his face when he managed to get his legs under him again.

"You might want to rethink things, Dave. I'm fresh out of patience."

"I'll kill you for this."

"Get moving."

The two of them came out from behind the bar with Morgan following and keeping the shotgun inches away from the back of Irish Dave's head. Dave bent over and wrestled with trying to get the kid up off the floor and into a fashion where he could carry him, but it was a losing, embarrassing proposition for a man of Irish Dave's reputation. And a man like Dave didn't have anything going for him but his reputation as a hard man.

"Drag him if you have to." The contempt in Morgan's voice cut like a knife.

"Don't do it, Dave," somebody in the saloon said.

Irish Dave jutted out his jaw and shook his head, as if the voice in the crowd had given him new determination. "I won't."

Morgan lifted the shotgun in both hands, reversed it, and drove the butt of it hard enough between Dave's shoulder blades to knock him to one knee. "Keep talking, Dave, and I'll break you to pieces."

"That's enough!" A woman's voice broke the quiet of the room.

Morgan twisted so that he could keep watch on Dave out of the corner of his eye, and still see who had spoken. A large woman—a very large woman—in a tall-topped man's hat with a turkey feather stuck in the sweatband and a pair of size thirteen lace-up work boots on her feet had stepped to the front of the crowd. She was three inches over six feet tall, and twice as wide as any man in the room. She wore a striped Mexican skirt and little else above the waist other than some kind of scanty camisole. The sweat-stained undergarment barely contained her enormous, sagging breasts.

Somewhere, sometime, some sweet gent had put out Fat Sally's right eye and knocked out half her front teeth. She breathed heavily through her mouth, and that bad white eye glared at Morgan like a wet marble.

"You got no call to do him like that," Fat Sally said.

Something about her face reminded Morgan of a bulldog—a dumb, fat, mean bulldog. He put his hand back on his pistol. Fat Sally and Irish Dave had been partners ever since the two of them came west, and if anything, she might have been the worst of the pair. She was volatile, to say the least.

There was a Dragoon pistol stuffed behind the broad leather belt she wore to cinch in some of her girth, and the fringed and beaded Indian purse she wore on one hip and slung from her shoulder had a knife sheath built into the flap of it. An ivory-handled Arkansas Toothpick's handle showed from it. She had made quite a name for herself with that knife among the Mississippi flatboatmen, and often bragged when drunk that she was more than a match for any man with fist or a blade.

"Leave him be!" She took another step closer.

Morgan drew his pistol. "Fat Sally, don't you take another step. You know I mean it."

Her jowls were trembling, and he could tell she wasn't going to listen.

"Don't you do it!" Morgan threatened.

Her hand darted for the Colt's Dragoon, and she charged toward him with a wild screech, so high-pitched that it was in no way in keeping with her size. Morgan leveled the Remington, hesitating for as long as he could, but thinking for sure he was going to have to kill her. Dixie came in from the side and clipped her in the back of the head with the butt of his carbine. He must have hit her harder than it looked, for she fell on her face at Morgan's feet and lie there groaning and writhing in pain on the dirt floor.

"Never buffaloed a woman before," Dixie said, standing over her.

"Fat Sally said that she'd give it for free to any man that could best her," someone in the back hooted, and the whole room joined in nervous laughter.

The man in the leather hat over by the tent wall must have made a suspicious move, for Dixie stepped toward him and shoved the barrel of the Spencer against his forehead. "Where are you going?"

The man in the leather hat crossed his eyes so that he could look at the rifle barrel pressed into the flesh of his brow line. "I wasn't moving. I wasn't moving."

"You son of a bitch." Irish Dave was back on his feet, swaying and staring at Fat Sally.

"Pick him up." Morgan pointed with his pistol at Seminole Bob.

Irish Dave bent over and grabbed the kid by both heels and started dragging him across the floor. The kid was skinny, but for a man of Dave's slight stature it was all he could do to move him. The veins in his face stood out like tiny ropes under the strain.

"What do you want me to do with this one?" Dixie pushed the carbine harder into his prisoner's forehead and then nodded at Fat Sally on the floor. "And her."

"Leave them." Morgan glanced at the man in the leather hat, his eyes still crossed and looking upwards as if he were hypnotized. "Fellow, you'd best get out of this line of business. I don't think you have the disposition for it."

Dixie eased off with the Spencer so that the man could look down at his own feet and at the pool of urine forming where it trickled out of one pants leg. The others in the room noticed it for the first time, and snickers and jokes were passed among them. Dixie took up the man's weapons from the tabletop and backed towards the door. Morgan heard the splash when Dixie pitched the confiscated items into the muddy street.

Irish Dave went next, dragging Seminole Bob, and Morgan followed last, backing out the door with the bartender's shotgun covering the saloon and daring anybody to make a play.

Out on the street, Irish Dave was soon up to his shins in mud, and he fell twice in his struggle. The third time he fell he refused to rise, sitting with his shoulders slumped and his head hung. He had lost his bowler hat, and the single patch of hair on the front of his balding head hung lankly, dripping with mud. The street was soon lined on either side with people appearing out of the night to see the show. The patrons of the Bucket of Blood slowly filed out of the saloon, keeping plenty of distance between themselves and the shotgun in Morgan's hands but refusing to leave.

"Get up, Dave," Morgan said.

"I can't go any farther."

Morgan took his eyes off the saloon crowd long enough to gauge the distance to the train tracks. They were still fifty yards away.

"Get up and take hold," Morgan repeated.

Irish Dave slung the worst of the mud off his hands and got to his feet. He tugged once and almost fell again when one of Seminole Bob's boots slipped off. Dave flung the boot away, and his temper gave him a last surge of strength. He managed a few more yards before he stalled out again. His chest heaved and his lungs gasped for air while he stared around him at the shadows of people watching him.

"Look at them, Dave," Morgan said. "Every one of them is seeing what you really are—nothing but a little Irish thug. You aren't anything, and they all see it now."

"I'll carve you up like a side of meat," Irish Dave gasped.

"You had your chance." Morgan freed one hand from the shotgun and gave Irish Dave a shove.

Irish Dave fell face first in the mud and stayed there, broken and too exhausted to move.

"Get up, tough man, or stay down there in the mud where you belong."

Irish Dave lifted his head feebly out of the muck, but Morgan's boot shoved it down again. Seminole Bob was moaning and coming to, squirming beside Irish Dave like a wet maggot wriggling in a muddy wound.

Morgan turned a circle, straining to make out who was in the crowd around him. He had long since passed through the last pool of lamplight spilling from the tents along the row, and the closer they got to the tracks, the darker it became, until there was only the light of the half-moon overhead, glowing through the smoky clouds and casting the world in half-tones and shadows. He recognized the shapes of men, but not their faces. If it happened, he would probably never see who shot him. The shotgun in his hands swung in a wicked arc from one imagined threat to another. Seminole Bob was on his hands and knees by then, cursing and choking.

"We need to move," Dixie said.

"Help him up," Morgan said to the kid.

Seminole Bob was groggy but somehow he understood what was being asked of him. He sloshed to his feet and tugged at Irish Dave until both of them were standing. Holding on to each other, the two of them started for the tracks. Dixie followed behind them with his rifle at their backs, and Morgan took up the rear, crabbing sideways so that he could keep watch behind them. A single light glowed ahead of them.

The group reached the train tracks, and Morgan saw that the light was two lanterns hanging from one end of Superintendent Duvall's private car. The shadowed form of Duvall stood there on the rear deck of the car sipping a glass of something and holding a decanter in his other hand. He lifted the glass to Morgan as if in toast before throwing the liquor down his throat and disappearing back inside.

They crossed the tracks, and Dixie stopped in front of the three posts that served as Morgan's jail. Irish Dave and Seminole Bob fell to the ground.

"Chain them up." Morgan handed Dixie the padlock keys for the shackles.

Dixie let Morgan hold his Spencer and, in short order, had both prisoners secured. Morgan stared at the tracks and the street beyond them.

"At least none of them followed us," Dixie said. "Looks like they're going to take it."

"For now." Morgan said.

"I'll stand the first watch," Dixie said. "You get some sleep."

Morgan didn't argue with that, and handed the Spencer back to him. He couldn't say why he suddenly felt so tired. It was always like that after he was keyed up and wound tight, as if the adrenaline and emotions drained him as surely as if he had run two miles at a sprint.

He went to readjust his hat and felt something wet on his

forehead. He rubbed whatever it was between two fingers and found it warm and turning slightly sticky to the touch. Even without being able to see it, he knew it was blood. He first assumed it was Seminole Bob's blood, but gentle probing with his fingers revealed a growing knot and a cut in his skin all the way through to the bone. He had apparently split his scalp head-butting the kid.

"You ever kill a woman?" Dixie asked before Morgan could walk away.

"I haven't."

"Well you about had to pull the trigger on one back there. I'd tackle three of Irish Dave before I tackled her."

"I hear you."

"What about Seminole Bob? How'd you know he wasn't going to pull on you?"

"He was all talk."

"You could have been wrong."

"Yeah, I could have been."

"Being wrong can get you killed."

"Everything about this job can get you killed."

CHAPTER TEN

Dixie woke with a start when he realized he had slept so long. Morgan had let him use the cot in the boxcar when it came time to swap the guard. The sun was already shining into the open door, and he went to it and looked out with one hand shading his eyes. Seminole Bob was curled up on his side, but Irish Dave was awake and on his feet. He stood at the end of his length of chain as if he had been up all night. Dried mud coated him from head to toe, and he twisted his body mechanically when he heard Dixie moving to the open door of the boxcar.

"You let me loose and ride out of here, Reb, and I'll forget you helped Clyde," Irish Dave said.

Seminole Bob sat up with his back against the post he was chained to. His nose was swollen terribly and smashed almost flat against his broad face. Both his eyes were bruised to the point that he only had slits to see out of. "I'm going to kill that Clyde for this."

"Shut your piehole," Irish Dave said. "You had your chance. All that blarney, and you didn't do a thing."

"Don't talk to me like that," the kid muttered. "You were supposed to back me."

Irish Dave jutted a pointer finger at Dixie. "I bet a man like you could use a little spare coin, couldn't you? And you can't tell me you like working for a man that wore the blue like Clyde."

"What side were you on, Dave?" Dixie asked.

"I'm a loyal Union man."

Dixie sat down in the doorway of the boxcar with his legs dangling and his Spencer rested across his thighs. He gave Irish Dave a smart-ass smirk and then began to sing in a deep, rich, baritone, "O, I'm a good old Rebel, now that's just what I am, For this 'Fair Land of Freedom' I do not care at all; I'm glad I fit against it, I only wish we'd won. And I don't want no pardon for anything I done."

"You piece of secesh trash," Irish Dave sneered. "You keep taunting me, bucko, but we'll see who gets the last laugh. I'm going to hang that shitty gray hat of yours behind my bar for a trophy when I'm through with you."

Dixie feigned a perplexed frown. "Where you from, Dave? New York, ain't it? Or are you American at all?"

"Go to hell."

"Well I'll tell you, I'm from Alabama. Alabama, you know where that is, you runt potato digger?"

Irish Dave started pacing at the end of his chain around the post that it was fastened to, cursing Dixie and cursing his predicament. "You don't have a friend in this whole camp. We'll get you, you wait and see."

"I bet you didn't take up a flag for either side, Dave. Chief Clyde tells me the Yankee recruiters paid you a bounty for every mick you signed up for them right off the boats. Made a living sending better and braver men than you off to fight."

Dave said nothing.

Dixie began to sing again. "And I don't want no pardon for what I was and am, and I won't be reconstructed and I do not care a damn."

Morgan came around the end of the boxcar carrying a bucket of food in one hand and some dinner plates in his other. Dixie hopped down and traded Morgan his rifle for the food, and then went over and set a plate on the ground before each man and ladled out a pile of grits and a single piece of bacon.

"You don't slop me like a dog." Irish Dave kicked the plate away.

"Suit yourself." Dixie picked up the plate, grimacing and shaking his head. "You're trying me sorely, Irishman."

At that time Superintendent Duvall and his two hired Pinkerton bodyguards came across the tracks in a buckboard wagon. One of the Pinkertons was driving, and the other was riding in the back with a Winchester Yellow Boy carbine resting across one shoulder. They pulled the buckboard team up beside Morgan.

"Good morning," Duvall said.

"What's good about it?" Irish Dave answered before anyone else could.

Duvall studied the two prisoners before he spoke to Morgan again. "You had quite a time last night."

"I've had worse," Morgan said.

"What are you going to do with these men?"

Morgan frowned at Irish Dave. "I know he put the kid up to it, but I've got nothing on him."

"The kid?"

Morgan nodded in the direction of Seminole Bob. "I think the best thing is to put him on the next train and leave him as far up the line as possible."

"You won't . . ." the kid started.

Morgan cut him off. "Count yourself lucky you're getting off so easy."

"What about the federal court at Fort Smith?" Duvall asked.

"That's an eighty-mile ride, one way."

"You should have killed him," the Pinkerton on the seat beside Duvall said. "I hear he tried to pull on you. Any man that pulls on me gets nothing but a short ride to the bone orchard."

Morgan looked from one Pinkerton to the other. He'd seen their kind before—maybe not bad men, but toughs in every sense of the word. The Pinkerton National Detective Agency had agents that specialized in investigative work, and others that were little more than bone crackers that could be hired out as company security. The two in the buckboard looked to be of the latter kind.

"Easy for you to say, tough man. I didn't see you helping us last night," Dixie threw in, making no attempt to hide his disdain.

"You hear this secesh trash?" the Pinkerton on the wagon seat said to the one in back.

"He's working for me," Morgan said coolly.

"That inbred cotton picker? That's what you're calling a policeman?" The Pinkerton gave an ugly laugh. He was a hairy, unshaven sort in a cheap suit, a hat too small for his head, and tobacco stains on his lips and the front of his white shirt.

"What did that man call me?" Dixie moved forward to stand by Morgan.

"Let it be," Morgan said.

"No, sir. What did he call me?"

"I think he said something about inbred cotton pickers."

"That's what I thought he said." Dixie flexed his fists and started for the wagon, but Morgan caught him by one shirt-sleeve.

"Sid, tone it down," Duvall warned his hired man beside him.

"You must not think much of the Pinkerton Detective Agency," the other Pinkerton in the back of the buckboard said to Morgan.

Morgan didn't answer, instead only staring at the two agents. The one in the back looked much the same as the one on the wagon seat.

"Damned Union spies," Dixie muttered. He had left Irish Dave and was stalking his way closer to the buggy. "The eye that never sleeps, my ass," he said, referring to the notorious slogan that the agency used and the large eye displayed prominently in all of their advertising.

"I shot a wagonload of Reb trash like you in the war," the Pinkerton on the wagon seat said.

"Sid!" Duvall's voice lashed out. "I won't tell you again. You say anything else and you can draw your pay."

The Pinkerton beside him looked fit to be tied, but he kept quiet. Duvall watched him to make sure the message was clear, and then turned back to Morgan. "Last night leads me to believe we ought to rethink this. You come with a pretty big reputation, but I don't know if you can handle this camp alone."

"Is that you talking, or your hired men there?" Morgan asked. "I understand it was Pinkertons on watch when your bridge was almost burned down."

The Pinkerton beside Duvall whipped his head around to glare at Morgan, but he held his tongue.

"I fired those men," Duvall said. "Sid and Mike here were handpicked and sent to me as a personal apology for the failure of the men I fired."

"I can handle my business without your hired guns," Morgan said.

"Hired guns? If that's what these men are, then what does that make you?" Duvall tried to keep the sting out of what he said by keeping his voice purposely mild and even.

"I police the camp, you run your railroad," Morgan said. "That's the deal."

Duvall sat quiet for a long moment and then made a wave of his hand. "Sid, take me to the trestle."

The Pinkerton beside him gathered his reins, but hesitated long enough to give Dixie and Morgan one last nasty look.

Then he slapped the ribbons across the team's backs and wheeled the wagon around in a half circle and left them at a high trot.

Dixie stood where he was, watching them leave, while Morgan went over to Irish Dave and unlocked his wrist shackles.

"Dave, I'll hang you from the new trestle over the river the next time I get so much as a whiff that you're trying to cross me."

Irish Dave rubbed his wrists and stared straight at Morgan's chin, unblinking and trembling with rage.

"Do you hear me?" Morgan asked.

"I hear you."

"Good."

Irish Dave started back to camp without looking back once.

Seminole Bob watched him go, and slapped at the dried mud on one pants leg and sniffled through his broken nose. "Dave'll get you."

"So he's said." Morgan unlocked the kid's wrists and shoved him toward the tracks.

Dixie followed them as Morgan walked the kid to the train. The train wasn't set to leave until the supplies on it were offloaded, but Morgan sat the kid on the cowcatcher at the front of the locomotive and fastened his wrists to it with a pair of handcuffs he took from his coat pocket.

The engineer crawled down from the cab and looked askance at the prisoner perched on the front of his engine. Morgan pitched him a key to the handcuffs.

"What do you want me to do with this?" the engineer asked.

"Are you going all the way back to Kansas City?" Morgan asked.

"Sedalia."

Morgan pointed at the kid. "Don't turn him loose until you get there."

"That's a long ride, and he's going to get awful uncomfortable perched there like that. What if he falls off?"

Morgan glanced at the kid. Truly, there was only a little flat place above the grill of the sloping nose of the cowcatcher, and barely enough room for the kid to perch there.

"Drag him."

"What?" the engineer asked.

"I'm going to come back here and shove one of those Colts up your ass and pull the trigger," the kid said.

Dixie laughed at him. "Best thing you can do, kid, is to hang up those guns and take up mumblety-peg or something that won't get you killed."

"You bring me back those handcuffs on your next run," Morgan said to the engineer. He started at a brisk walk towards the livestock pens down the tracks.

"Where are you going?" Dixie asked.

Morgan stopped and looked back at him. "No *me* to it, Dixie. *We.* I'm going to get us some horses."

"And where are *we* going?" Dixie had to hustle to catch up to him.

"We're going to ride over to North Fork and see if we can find Texas George."

"Shit, I should've known it would be something like that."

CHAPTER ELEVEN

The horses Morgan borrowed from the railroad pens were thin and hard used, and Morgan set a leisurely pace because of it. The railroad crews were going to work, either walking towards the river or riding on a flatcar pushed by a little pony engine. Morgan and Dixie passed through them, only stopping once near the head of a tent row next to the tracks where a snake oil man was standing in front of his garishly painted "herb" wagon and barking in a powerful voice. A skinny woman with smallpox scars on her face and two black front teeth stood near a crate of bottled medicine, ready to hand out the goods to any purchasers. She nodded her head at everything the man beside her said.

"Come one, come all, and I'll tell you about this powerful elixir," the man in the swallow-tailed coat and tall hat said. His Adam's apple bobbed in his stringy neck with every word, and his gray, bushy eyebrows worked like caterpillars on his brow. "One spoonful of this nostrum, morning and night, will cure the ills of men and beasts!"

Morgan leaned over his saddle horn and waited for the hawker to notice him.

"Got the croup or colic? Are you experiencing the trots, feverish, or suffering from the ague? Try this patent original . . ." The snake oil man stopped in mid-sentence when he noticed Morgan watching him. "Didn't know you were working this camp, Marshal."

"It's Chief here, Sam. Chief of the railroad police," Morgan said. "You aren't going to cause me any trouble, are you?"

"No, sir, not at all." The snake oil man held up a flat pint bottle to Morgan. "How about one on the house to show my appreciation for your staunch concern for law and order?"

Morgan warded away the offered bottle with an upheld palm. "I believe I'll pass."

Dixie took the bottle and held it up to the morning sunlight. "What's in it?"

"Various exotic medicinal ingredients gleaned from my lifelong study of pharmacopeia and my tireless travels around the world to improve the well-being of my fellow man," the snake oil man said. "For instance, the oil of the African baobab tree was shown to me by a witch doctor deep in the heart of that dark continent. The pulp of the spiny cactus has long been known by desert *curanderas* in Old Mexico, and the . . ."

"What he means is a pinch of red pepper, a dash of opium, and the rest of it cheap booze," Morgan said.

The snake oil man tried to look offended while Dixie pulled the cork with his teeth and took a quick slug from the bottle. He grimaced and leaned over to spit out the bitter concoction. "You'd have to tell me it would make me bulletproof before I would drink any more of that."

The snake oil man shrugged. "There are those that take extra doses who might claim such."

Morgan reined his horse around, pointing it down the street. He did his best to keep a straight face when he spoke to Dixie. "Now that you've tried Sam's medicine, maybe you want to try Etta's magic mattress in the back of that wagon."

The pock-faced woman grinned up at Dixie. "I've worked the kinks out of many a man with a bad back."

Dixie stoppered the medicine bottle and pitched it back to the snake oil man. He tipped his hat to the woman and kicked his horse down the street.

"You know that man?" he asked when he caught up to Morgan.

"The city fathers had me run him out of Baxter Springs right before they ran me off," Morgan said. "Seems like Sam's medicine was making people shaky, and Etta's mattress was giving them the clap."

"Strange friends you have. Not exactly the upper crust of society."

"That's the high-toned life of a frontier lawman. Get used to it."

"What did you do before the war?" Dixie asked.

"Same as now," Morgan said. "I was a policeman in New York City."

"And before that?"

Morgan gave him an irritated look, obviously bothered that he had answered Dixie at all. Before Dixie could ask more questions they neared the edge of camp and came across two men putting up a good-sized tent. Lottie Bickford was supervising their work.

"Hello, Lottie," Morgan said. "Expanding the household?"

Lottie rested a hand on each hip and smiled. "Going into business for myself, Mr. Clyde. Putting in a laundry."

"Businesswoman, huh?"

"My Hank's got his strong arms and a shop hammer, and you . . . well you do what you do," she said. "Me, I know how to wash and I know how to work hard. I figure there's plenty of these bachelors around here with some clothes that could use a good scrubbing and delousing."

"What about that Chinaman up the street?" Morgan asked. "His laundry has the jump on yours."

Lottie hissed, intending the sound to serve as a profanity she was unwilling to voice. "Him? He does his business laundry in that muddy creek, and he couldn't sew a patch or mend a tear

115

to save his life."

Morgan smiled at the Bickford boy shooting a bean flip at an empty can out from the new tent. The boy's sister was nowhere to be seen, and Lottie must have seen him looking for her.

"Don't know where my Suzy's at," she said. "That girl beats all. Always wandering about with her head in the clouds. Yesterday, I didn't see her for the whole afternoon, and when she comes back she tells me she was down on the creek taking a walk. Sometimes I think I ought to tan her for running off like that, but she's a good girl, only scatter-minded sometimes."

"You and Hank have fine children, Mrs. Bickford," Morgan said.

"I haven't got 'em raised yet. Not by a long shot," she said. "You and your deputy ought to come to church tonight."

"Church?" Morgan asked.

"There's a preacher riding over tonight, and I told him he could hold service in my tent. You're welcome to come if you're back in time from wherever it is you're gallivanting off to."

"Thanks for the invite."

"Deacon Fischer held a Bible reading two nights ago, and preached a few of us a short sermon," she added. "And I must say, he sure is a man on fire for the Lord."

"Deacon Fischer?" Morgan asked.

"You know him?" She seemed pleased or incredulous that Morgan knew of her evangelist.

Morgan and Dixie shared a comical look, but kept what they knew to themselves.

"Know him?" Dixie said in a strained voice. "Sure we do. I always said that myself about the deacon. Now there's a man who's likely to end up on fire, that's what I always said."

Lottie gave Dixie a perplexed look, sure she was missing something, and twice as sure that she wouldn't like it if she knew what he was thinking. "Might do both of you some good to hear a bit of the gospel. This whole camp needs to hear Deacon Fischer bringing the good word."

"Oh, the deacon has given the good word to more than one man," Dixie said, almost tittering with glee.

Morgan tipped his hat to Lottie and rode off before she could totally figure out that they were funning with her, and weren't much impressed with her newfound holy man. Dixie soon caught up with him.

"Can you believe that? Deacon Fischer?" he asked.

"Wouldn't do any good to tell her different," Morgan replied. "I guess she'll figure it out in time."

Dixie let out a low, long whistle. "They say he carries a Bible in one hand and a pistol in the other. He'll either preach you out of hell with one hand, or send you there with the other. I hear when he was still riding with the bushwhackers during the war that he used to sit and read scripture to their prisoners all night before he shot them in the head the next morning."

They rode on east along the road to Webbers Falls, Van Buren, and Fort Smith. The wagon track wound through the timber, climbing over a low hill, and occasionally breaking into a clearing or a flat stretch of prairie. Clouds were building to the west, and it looked like it was going to rain again.

"The weather in the Nations doesn't ever stay the same two days straight," Dixie said. He kept casting sideways glances at Morgan, obviously hoping to stir some conversation.

Morgan glanced at the clouds, but didn't say anything.

"I saw you watching that boy back there, and could tell you like children," Dixie prodded.

"Are you going to talk all the way?"

"It helps pass the time."

"I had a son and a daughter," Morgan replied after a silence of several minutes.

"Had?"

"I haven't seen my son since before the war."

"What happened?"

"Things."

"How old is he?"

"Seventeen. He wasn't but seven or eight the last time I saw him before I joined up."

"And his mother?"

"Things between us got off kilter. I haven't seen her since I last saw the boy."

"That's tough. Did she remarry?"

"I couldn't tell you."

"Don't you and the boy write each other? I'd think he would want to know his daddy," Dixie said. "Surely, she wouldn't begrudge you that."

"You don't know her. Helvina isn't one to let go of things." Morgan kicked his horse ahead.

Dixie was quick to catch up. "What about your daughter?"

"Lost her to the Scarlet fever while I was off to the war." Morgan made a show of looking off in the distance while he gathered his words. "I got a letter from my wife the first year telling me how good she was doing. Then there was one more letter while I was in an army field hospital. It said that our baby girl was dead, and there was a set of divorce papers with the letter."

Morgan put his horse to a lope, going ahead. Dixie regretted prying into Morgan's business. Folks were full of sad old things, and talking about them was like picking scabs off the wounds. His mother back in Alabama had always said he talked too much, but he couldn't seem to break the habit. Miffed, he loafed behind, thinking as much on what Morgan hadn't said as what he had said, and whistling snatches of several tunes and playing with the tail of his bridle reins out of boredom.

Before long, not three miles along the trail, they broke out into a wide clearing between the forks of the North and South Canadian. A thin wisp of fog hung above the ground as if the ground were steaming. Woodsmoke lifted from the chimneys of five or six log or frame homes scattered over the open ground, and the brown winter grass was dotted with fenced off fields that had already been plowed in preparation for planting later in the spring.

In the center of the clearing was the settlement called North Fork Town. During the gold rush of '49, and a decade later during the Pikes Peak rush, it had been a busy place, lying like it was on a good crossing of the North Canadian and at the crossroads of the Texas Road and the California Trail. But its glory years were long since past. The war had left the Indian Territory all but vacated for several years, as the civilized Indian tribes took up the sword against each other like their white counterparts. Once-prosperous farms were burned, and families and whole settlements fled the fighting for Texas or Kansas, depending on whether they sided with the Union or the Confederacy. The tribes and a few white settlers had returned since then, but it was going to take a long time to rebuild.

Morgan could see where more farmhouses had once stood, marked by the soot-black outlines of their stone foundations and the remains of charred timbers protruding from the ashes. What remained standing of the town itself was nothing but seven or eight rotting log buildings lining either side of the trail, a set of corrals made of quartered oak rails, and a large, leaning hay barn on the west end with half of its roof gone. Under the gray, overcast sky, the weather-beaten settlement looked like a lazy, slow ghost that might fade out of sight at any moment.

"I've seen graveyards livelier than that," Dixie said.

They rode around a small herd of cattle driven by two Indian boys with short-cropped hair and big cowboy hats on their heads. The boys waved at them.

"Friendly enough," Dixie observed.

As soon as he said it, a gun went off ahead of them, and they both pulled up their horses.

"Yeah, real friendly," Morgan said.

"Damned if this ain't the shootin'est country I've ever seen," Dixie added, casting a quick glance over his shoulder and behind them as if he would much rather ride back the way they had come. "If that's Texas George up there, he'll pick us off pretty easy if he's any kind of a rifle shot at all."

"That shooting wasn't aimed at us." No matter how Morgan assured Dixie, his voice was still tight and tense. There was a lot of open ground between them and the settlement.

They followed the wagon ruts before them and soon rode slowly down the single street. A store, a post office, and a saloon seemed to be the only going businesses. The rest of the buildings didn't look to have anything occupying them other than pack rats and the cobwebs visible through the gaping sockets of busted windowpanes staring at them from both sides of the thoroughfare. The gunfire had them both on edge, but they soon saw that Morgan had been right about the shooting not being aimed at them.

The single saloon still open for business had a long porch across the front of it with a swaybacked, sagging roof with most of its shake shingles blown off, and a man with a pistol was sitting in a rocking chair in its shadows. A white bulldog with a bobbed tail and one ring eye was sitting on its haunches in the middle of the street in front of the man with a mason jar balanced on its head.

The man on the porch edge must have been drunk, for his pistol wobbled greatly as he aimed at the jar on the dog's head. After long deliberation, the gun bellowed and the glass jar shattered. The inebriated marksman whooped in delight, although the dog never flinched or moved a muscle, obedient and cowed in place. The canine wagged its tail feebly, a pool of urine spreading beneath it.

Morgan and Dixie dismounted in front of the saloon and tied their horses at the hitching rail. The jar shooter only glanced at them once before he took up another jar from the porch and went to set it on the dog's head. He was a scrawny, shirtless man with the pair of suspenders over his shoulders framing his pale potbelly. The porch recesses were heavily shadowed, and Morgan only then noticed the two other white men standing in the open doorway of the saloon. Both of them held brown bottles of beer in their hands, and both of them were wearing pistols. The way they were looking at the two policemen marked them for men on the scout, or very distrusting sorts, at the least.

"A beer would hit the spot," Dixie said. "You never gave me a chance to get breakfast."

"You stay here and keep an eye on things," Morgan said.

Dixie loosened the cinch on his horse, and kept it between him and the door of the saloon. He waited until Morgan was up on the porch before he slid his Spencer out of its boot and rested it across the seat of his saddle.

The men in the doorway had drifted back inside the bar by the time Morgan arrived. Surprisingly, despite the rundown appearance of the outside of the saloon, the inside was tidy and spoke of better times. The bar was made of swirly grained walnut with a brass footrest and a big mirror behind it, and ran across the width of the back end of the room. An old man with neatly trimmed white whiskers stood behind the bar. There was a welcoming smile on his face, but Morgan noted the uneasiness behind it and the way he kept glancing at the two men at one end of the bar.

Morgan ordered a beer and turned a hip against the bar where he could see both of the other customers. It was then that he noticed Deacon Fischer sitting in the shadows in one corner, and he chided himself for bumbling in without casing the room first. A tiny window spilled weak sunlight onto the floor and the front half of Deacon's table. A pistol and a bottle of whiskey lay on the tabletop in front of him, surrounded by dust motes dancing and floating on the beam of sunlight.

The outlaw gunman marked his place in the Bible he was reading with one thumb and raised his head until the flat brim of his hat was tilted back enough for him to see Morgan at the bar.

Morgan looked into the coldest face that he had ever had the misfortune to meet, and one not easily forgotten. Deacon's skin was as white as fine China, as if it had never seen the sun, and the hands and the frame bones of him were slim and almost feminine, as were the rest of his features. There was nothing strong about him except for the sense that hung about him. A dangerous, slim, pale, killing machine—you knew it at first glance, and you felt it like electricity in the air.

"I didn't expect to see you again, Clyde." Deacon's voice always shocked those who heard it for the first time. It was as low as the bottom of a well, crackly, yet surprisingly gentle. His accent was Deep South, and despite his calm, there was a hint of some kind of fervor and of barely suppressed madness behind his words.

"I could say the same for you," Morgan said. "Men in our line of work don't often last long."

"That's a fact." Deacon took another sip of whiskey and set the glass down and laid his hand beside his pistol on the tabletop. The gun was one of the new Smith & Wesson No. 3 Americans. Its nickel plating gleamed in the weak pool of sunlight.

Morgan took up his beer in his left hand. "I thought it might rain this morning, but it looks to be clearing off."

"You looking for me?" Deacon asked.

Morgan looked away from Deacon to the men at the other end of the bar. "No, I'm looking for Texas George."

Both of the men at the bar cast a quick look at him and then went back to studying their beer bottles as if the glassware had become the most interesting thing in the world.

The jar shooter's pistol cracked outside again, and Deacon's eye's flickered to the open front door.

"That's a good dog," Morgan said. "That man out there ought to be horsewhipped."

"Ah, that's the thing about the Indian Nations," Deacon said. "A righteous man can run himself ragged trying to cure what ails it."

The two men at the end of the bar finished their beers and left the saloon, casting a last glance at Morgan as they went out the door.

"Have you seen Texas George?" Morgan asked Deacon.

"Do you think I would tell you if I knew?"

"You wouldn't run with an amateur like George."

Deacon smiled, taking it as a compliment. "You won't find George here. He's laid up at Tom Starr's cabin down the river. I wouldn't advise you going there."

"Is Tom riding with George?"

"You know better than that. If they were partnered it would be the other way around."

"Who else is hiding out at Tom's?"

"Don't insult me, Clyde. The only reason I gave you what little I have is that George crossed me not too far back. I'll kill him myself when I get around to it."

Morgan took a sip of the lukewarm beer, and found that it didn't set well on his stomach. The barkeep had made a point of taking himself to the other end of the bar, acting like he needed to wash out some empty beer bottles, but plainly wanting to get out of the line of fire.

Deacon gestured slowly at the pistol on Morgan's hip. "They say you put two bullets in Strawdaddy at better than sixty paces."

"Believe half of what you hear."

"Strawdaddy wasn't so tough, but still, there's not many men that could have made that kind of shot on him with a short gun."

"It was a lucky shot."

"You have a knack for coming out on the lucky side of a fight. Some men are blessed or cursed that way." Deacon swirled the whiskey around in his glass. "The word's gone out that there's a price on your head. Three hundred to the man that gets you."

"Is that why you're hanging around?"

"I haven't decided yet."

"I'd hate for us to get cross."

"That's a lot of money to pass up."

Morgan was keenly aware of the pistol lying so near Deacon's right hand. "There are easier ways to earn your money, Deacon."

Deacon nodded and then held up his gun hand. "You see this hand? When I was a small boy the local minister tried to baptize me down on the creek with all the church congregation standing on the banks and looking on to see my sins washed away. But the love of Jesus hadn't taken hold of my heart yet, and I was scared of him dunking my head under that water and holding me down and not letting me up. I'm sure that was Satan whispering in my ear and filling me with doubt. His snake hissing is more powerful than most know."

Morgan took a careful sip of his beer, never taking his eyes off Deacon for an instant.

Deacon plainly expected a question or a comment from Morgan, but continued his story when he didn't get it. "The Lord found me wanting that morning, verily he did. No matter how hard I tried, I couldn't quit thinking about that minister hold-ing me down under that water and not letting me up for air. So I fought and I fought, with that preacher holding me like he was wresting Lucifer himself. We fought until the only thing that was dunked in that water was this hand before I tore loose from him and ran back home."

Morgan watched as Deacon held up his thin-fingered right hand, spread wide as if it were meant as some kind of strange symbol or sign language that the Deacon falsely assumed he should understand.

"Know what this is?" Deacon asked.

"You tell me."

"Iniquity, that's what it is. When I was still a boy I thought this hand might be the only part of me that was clean and pure and washed in the cleansing blood of the Lamb. There were times later when I thought maybe this hand of mine was anointed to slay the sinners that vexed and tried me." Deacon turned the hand before his eyes, as if seeing it for the first time. "Dunked and baptized and blessed up to my wrist, only it's not pure, nor is it anointed. Do you know how many men I've killed with this hand?"

"I know what they say about you."

"Twenty-three men, Clyde. Twenty-three men smote with this backsliding, blasphemous hand. Were you to look at it through God's eyes you would see the flesh not white, but black as sin. A black hand, same as that which hangs on the end of your own gun arm."

The more Deacon talked, the surer Morgan became that the man was crazy. Morgan was also sure that he wasn't leaving the saloon without one of them dead.

"We ought to cut off these hands of ours, Clyde. Cut them off before they can offend the Almighty more," Deacon continued. "It's sacrilege that we carry, but we are not the brave men we portray ourselves to be, are we? We would cure ourselves if we were."

"You're drunk."

Deacon used that same gun hand to tap the Bible in his other hand. "David himself was a hunted man, living with outlaws and beset by his enemies on all sides. King Saul put a price on his head."

"You're talking in riddles, Deacon."

"You're no David, Clyde. The best thing you can do is to get out of the Nations before they run you down. Go somewhere else and get right with the Lord."

"Why the warning?"

Deacon gave an almost imperceptible shrug of his shoulders. "Call it professional courtesy, if you will, one shootist to another."

"I've never quit a job I started."

"Neither have I. Isn't pride a terrible sin?"

"Are you saying you've taken the job?"

It was Deacon's turn not to answer, only staring at Morgan with that mad light burning in his eyes.

Morgan set aside his unfinished beer and went outside, keeping a careful watch on Deacon as he passed him in the room. Deacon was known as an odd man wherever he went, operating by his own code. But Morgan wasn't about to put any trust in the gunman warning him of what was at play, especially not a crazy like him. The man had as much as said that he might buy into the game, and only his warped sense of honor led him to tell Morgan that much.

Morgan put him out of his mind as best he could as soon as he went out the door. Deacon might shoot him for the three-hundred-dollar bounty, but he wouldn't do it in the back. Whatever they said about Deacon Fischer, all his victims took it in the front.

Morgan drew in a deep breath and tried to fight down the anger building in him. His first guess was that Bill Tuck had put the price on his head, and it was his own fault that he hadn't run the backbiting saloonkeeper out of camp already. But Tuck was crafty, and hard to catch with his hands dirty.

The jar shooter was trying to reload his pistol and doing a poor job of it. The dog looked at the man with sad, loyal eyes.

"Get out of here!" Morgan shouted at the dog and waved his arms.

The jar shooter looked up, and his drunken eyes fought to focus on Morgan standing on the porch. "What the hell are you doing?"

The dog ignored Morgan and continued to sit where it was. Morgan tried to shoo it off again, but it only hunkered its head lower.

"You leave my dog alone," the drunk said.

Morgan reached down and yanked the pistol out of the man's hand and flung it in the weeds on the far side of the street. He was about to go to his horse when he heard Deacon step onto the porch behind him. He turned to face him, and saw that the gunman already had his Smith in his hand and hanging beside his thigh.

"That dog is either too loyal or too blind to know when it ought to run," Deacon said.

Morgan didn't answer, only squaring himself to face Deacon and his left hand taking hold of the bottom of his holster to hold it in place should he have to draw. He could feel his own heartbeats in his ears.

Deacon looked at the dog again, and then at Dixie down the street standing behind his horse with the Spencer resting over his saddle. He went back inside, and Morgan couldn't tell whether he had come outside at the sound of the commotion or because he intended to finish their little talk.

"Who was that in the door?" Dixie asked when they rode out of the settlement.

"Deacon Fischer."

Dixie twisted in the saddle and looked back, as if he could see through the saloon walls and get another look at Deacon. "What happened in there?"

"He told me that there's a price on my head."

"He said it just like that?"

"Just like that."

"What else did he say?"

"Not much else, but he's a hard man to follow. I think he either told me that I was as good as dead, or that if I keep hanging around with outlaws, that I'm going to be a king."

Dixie gave him an odd look and let out one of his low whistles. "Is he sticking around?"

"I imagine he will."

"Well, look on the bright side," Dixie said. "After running across him, your day ain't liable to get any worse."

They rode on and were soon back in Ironhead, riding side by side down the single street. Two men were standing in front of a stack of cordwood, both of them intensely watching the lawmen pass by. Morgan noticed the two big sorrels tied to the cordwood stack—one of them with the Confederate greatcoat still hanging by the saddle horn. Even if it hadn't been for that, he would have known the Kingman brothers in an instant, for something in the cold, hard, meanness of their oxlike eyes gave them away for killers.

The two brothers could have passed for twins, so closely did they resemble each other. Both of them were big, burly men, with long beards that started right beneath their eyes and ended at the top of their bellies. Both wore a Colt Army on their hip, and the one on the right had another Pocket Model in a shoulder rig underneath his left armpit and a Bowie knife in his hand, whittling on a fat, sycamore stick. The white, curled shavings peeled away effortlessly before the razor-sharp edge of the Bowie and fell at his feet like flower petals. He leaned over and spat a stream of tobacco juice onto his shavings pile when he and Morgan locked eyes.

Morgan rode on. Passing near the Kingmans felt like lying down to sleep with snakes, and everything in him told him not to turn his back on them. He resisted the urge to turn in the saddle and take one more look back down the street at them. Those two men hadn't come to Ironhead Station on a whim; they were there for one thing and one thing only, and he could almost feel the hate radiating off of them.

"Those who I think they are?" Dixie was turned in the saddle and looking back at the Kingman brothers with a twitchy, nervousness to his usually relaxed drawl.

"I'm pretty sure that was the other two Kingman brothers," Morgan said.

Dixie let out a low whistle between his front teeth. "First, Deacon Fischer, and now them. No offense, Chief, but it sure is hell to be you."

CHAPTER TWELVE

It was a quiet evening in Ironhead, and Morgan and Dixie gathered in the boxcar that had become their headquarters. The MK&T had been generous enough to supply them with another cot, and Dixie was reclined on his, making studious but slow work of a book he had propped up on one raised knee.

"Where in the tarnation is Gaul?" Dixie asked. "I suspect it's a long ways off across the water."

Morgan looked up from a copy of a Kansas City newspaper he was reading. "It's what the Romans used to call France and parts of Western Europe."

"There's all kinds of places in this book that I can't even pronounce, much less ever been to," Dixie said.

Morgan eyed the battered copy of Julius Caesar's *Conquest of Gaul* in Dixie's hands. "What do you think of that book?"

Dixie shrugged noncommittally. "I admit, that Caesar was a crafty one, and not one you wanted to cross. And those ancients weren't much different than us. Lots of fighting and killing, and Caesar conquering one tribe or another," Dixie said.

"Some things never change."

"Don't you laugh at me for making such slow work of this. My reading ain't what it should be. I was working by the time I was big enough to tote a cotton sack or a weeding hoe. Nigh wore my feet out walking in a furrow behind a mule."

"I won't laugh at any man trying to educate or better himself," Morgan said.

Dixie sat aside the book. "It's no wonder why I'm where I'm at, but you? You're obviously an educated man. You talk fancy and you've got a bag full of books. Yet, here you are just like me. Did you like the war? Some did. When it was over they couldn't go back to the normal life. Too tame for them."

Morgan put aside his newspaper, strapped on his pistol, and studied his blanket coat hanging from a nail on the wall. It was made of a red wool trade blanket with a beaver fur collar and cuffs, and bone buttons down the front to fasten it. A wide leather belt with a big brass buckle was made into the waist.

"That's a fine coat," Dixie said when he realized Morgan wasn't going to answer his first question.

"It's a fine coat if it's coming a blizzard, but too hot otherwise."

"Maybe so, but you decide you don't want that coat, you let me know. I'd give ten dollars for it, promise I would. Hell, there were times back in the war when I would have given my eyeteeth to have a coat like that, or shoes, either one."

"The trader in Baxter Springs I bought it from claimed an Osage woman sewed it for him." Morgan debated on taking the coat off the wall. The evening was too cool for his frock coat and too hot for the heavy wool coat, and there was nothing he could do about it except to decide whether to freeze or sweat. He shunned the heavy coat and pulled into his black frock coat. "I'm going to make a walk through camp."

"Want me to come with you?" Dixie asked, getting to his feet.

"Come if you want."

It was almost sundown when Morgan and Dixie crossed the tracks. The threatening storm clouds had only been a bluff, and not a single drop of rain had fallen. The street was slowly drying out, and was almost passable in places—almost, at least until it rained again. Morgan promised himself that the next chance he got he was going to by some tall-topped India rubber boots.

They paused at the corner of the depot, surveying the length of the street in the fading light. The street was all but empty except for a few horses tied at the hitching rails in front of the two saloons, and the only sound was the faint tinkle of a piano from inside the Bullhorn.

"Damned quiet," Morgan said.

Dixie leaned against the corner of the railroad office and pulled his pouch of chewing tobacco from his coat pocket. "Did you know that the railroad payroll is almost a week late?"

Morgan nodded. "Duvall gave a speech while we were gone yesterday morning. Apparently, he explained what was holding up the payroll to the satisfaction of his crews, or at least the grumbling has quieted some."

"Good. Men that don't get paid tend to get angry real quick, and there was a rumor starting to go around that the railroad was flat broke."

Morgan had seen what late payrolls could do to a camp, and all Ironhead Station needed was an excuse for trouble. The camp had quieted a little since the law had been laid down, but there were still too many toughs around ready and willing to stir things up at the slightest excuse.

The two of them crossed over to the company store and moved down the north side of the street. A little dun horse was tied to the hind wheel of a parked freight wagon in front of them.

It had zebra stripes crossing its legs, and probably didn't weigh much more than the heavy saddle and the other gear strapped on its back—a runty, thirty-dollar Texas pony so common as to not be worth mentioning. He couldn't say what had drawn his attention to it. He walked close and rubbed a hand across the lightning bolt brand on the horse's right shoulder, ruffling its long winter hair to make sure that was what the mark was intended to be.

"Odd brand," Dixie said as he came up behind Morgan.

Morgan nodded. He was no thirty-dollar a month cowboy that could name every brand from the Gulf Coast to Kansas, but the brand did strike him as unusual and not one he recognized from the Indian Nations or elsewhere. It was then he spied the buttstock of the rifle sticking up on the far side of the saddle behind the cantle. He walked around to the other side of the horse to look at it.

The rifle was of a kind Morgan hadn't seen since the war, and rarely then. It was tied off with saddle strings against the skirt and slung under the stirrup leather, long as a freight train, with three steel bands to secure the heavy target barrel to the stock, which reached almost to the end of the gun. A thin-tubed telescopic sight was mounted oddly off to one side of the barrel, its mounts attached to the stock rather than the barrel.

"What kind of shooter is that?" Dixie asked.

"Whitworth."

"Heard of them, but never saw one. Britisher gun, ain't it? Shoot a man all the way into next week with one of those."

Morgan only nodded again. British-made in actuality, but there were Union troops in the war who swore that Lucifer himself must have forged the barrels of the Whitworths in the fires of Hades, so spitefully and wickedly accurate were they in the hands of the Confederate sharpshooters. The images and memories the rifle brought forth were strong, and for an unbidden instant he could hear guns crack on far battlefields and the scream of men dying or begging to die, and the smell of black powder smoke and raw, burned flesh everywhere. The simultaneous and conflicting urges to run or fight almost overcame him. He threw out a hand and braced it against the horse to steady himself.

"You all right?" Dixie asked.

Morgan cast an embarrassed glance at Dixie. He straightened himself, willing a steadiness into his body and glancing up and down the street to locate himself in the actual moment, rather than the past.

Without thinking, and as if compelled to do so, he slipped the tip of his pointer finger inside the .45-caliber bore and could feel the odd flats inside it. Not round and smooth and spiraled with rifling like most gun bores, but six-sided. A cold chill crawled up his spine, and he remembered the clink of a heavy hexagonal bullet from such a gun clanking into a metal wash pan beside his bed when the field surgeon dug it from the muscles of his side and let go of it with the forceps. And the blood everywhere—his blood mingled with the blood of hundreds more, and the smell of entrails and vomit and feverish sweat so thick he couldn't breathe, and the orderlies pushing wheelbarrows of amputated limbs amongst the wounded like reapers come to take a price from the living.

He stepped back from the horse and grounded himself in the present again, instantly ashamed to have handled another man's gun without asking, and angered by the weakness that briefly overcame him. He took a quick look around to try and spot the owner of the horse and the gun, lest he be watching.

Dixie noticed the pale, strained expression on Morgan's face. "I'd say you're either coming down sick or that you just saw a ghost."

"No ghost. Nothing but a gun." Morgan glanced again at the rifle under the stirrup leather. There were all kinds of guns left over from the war, and it should come as no shock that he had come across a Whitworth, no matter how rare.

"You're having a spell, aren't you?" Dixie asked.

"What?" Morgan asked.

"I asked if you are having a spell. I've known other soldiers that did. Maybe it messed us all up a little, but it hits some worse. Those I've seen might get the shakes for no reason, like they had the fever, or get a look on their face like they were alone when there might be friends all around them. Wound up tight and all messed up and apt to take off running at some harmless noise, or to go on the fight for no reason."

"I'm all right."

"Maybe, but there ain't no shame in it if sometimes things get a little confused," Dixie said. "I remember I got the soldier's heart one time in the middle of a fight. Our officer called for us to advance, and I couldn't go anywhere. Couldn't move, couldn't breathe, and my heart was beating crazy until it felt like I was dying. Some buck lieutenant saw me like that, and was going to write me up later for what he called, 'moral turpitude' and cowardice when the doctors couldn't find anything wrong with me. He'd have had me up in front of a firing squad if he could have had his way, but my sergeant, he told them I had my knapsack straps too tight and that was what made me where I couldn't breathe."

Morgan had turned his back to Dixie, but Dixie saw that he was still listening to him, whether he acted like it or not.

"Funny thing was," Dixie continued. "I wasn't any more scared than I ever was with the cannon shot whistling over my head. I'd been in several fights and two battles before that and made a good showing, but something in me broke for a little bit that day. You know, got off-kilter. I think some men can get off-kilter a little bit with all the bad things they saw. Not anything a doctor can find, but not right inside."

"I said there's nothing wrong with me." There was anger and a threat in Morgan's voice.

"You holler out in your sleep sometimes," Dixie said more quietly. "You know that, don't you?"

"I know it." Morgan said more calmly.

"Bad dreams?"

"Some."

"I still have a dream or two like that, but they come less often than they used to. Is it the same dream or a different one?"

"Usually the same one."

Morgan walked away, continuing down the street, but it didn't take Dixie long to catch up to him.

"Talking about it might help," Dixie said after a few silent steps.

"I never saw that it helped anything."

"I don't know how you figure that. Prying anything about yourself out of you is like pulling teeth."

"You do enough talking for the both of us." Morgan sped up and was soon two steps ahead of Dixie.

The Bucket of Blood was open, and Morgan led them to there. The sun was down by the time they reached it, and the sky was like tarnished silver with the evening star hanging off to one side of the moon. Shadows crawled across the street when Morgan turned back for one last look at the scrubby little horse and the gun tied to it. But the horse was gone.

The crowd in the saloon was lighter than usual, but there were still at least twenty men inside. Both lawmen halfway expected trouble, but Irish Dave was nowhere in sight. Fat Sally was in the saloon, though, playing a hand of poker at a back table. She stared pure hate at the two lawmen, but said nothing.

"Keep an eye on her," Morgan said.

"Damn, that's a big woman." Dixie took a stand alongside one of the faro layouts, trying to appear nonchalant, but doing a poor job of hiding the fact that he wasn't going to take his attention off of Fat Sally for a second. "She don't seem to like us, do she?"

"You're the one that hit her."

"Thanks for reminding me." Dixie rubbed the whisker stubble on his jaw. "Problem with fighting a woman is that you whip her and somebody says you're a woman beater, and if you lose, well, nobody is ever going to let you live that down."

More than a few in the room were whispering about them, and the looks thrown their way were sullen and hostile. But nobody seemed primed to make an issue of the events of the previous night. Even Fat Sally seemed unwilling to do any more than make ugly faces at them.

"This is a real happy bunch," Dixie said. "I've been to funerals where the mood was better."

Morgan sensed the mood of the men in the room, also, and it wasn't only their presence causing it. "We're showing face, Dixie. Nothing more. Calm and cool."

They sauntered through the saloon, nodding to those who were semi-friendly, making small talk where possible, and ending their visit by making a show of checking out the play at the roulette wheel.

The two left the Bucket of Blood and crossed the street to the Bullhorn, slipping inside the door flap and surveying the room as carefully as they had the previous saloon. The MK&T had contracted for a small herd of cattle to provide beef for its workers, and the trail crew had arrived with it the day before, holding their stock on a little prairie six miles west of Ironhead. In addition to the usual crowd of toughs and railroad men, some of the trail crew was enjoying a little unrest and relaxation, courtesy of the Bullhorn's whiskey, and they were the loudest faction in the saloon. The cowboys, five of them, were already drunk by the time Morgan and Dixie arrived. Four of them were gathered around one of the faro tables, advising and cheering on the other of their crew currently betting on the game. The three-man team running the faro table—dealer, casekeeper, and lookout—were obviously annoyed by the loud-talking Texans, and the large stack of coins and greenbacks heaped on the U-shaped table didn't help their mood. The cowboy seated before that pile of money was obviously well ahead of the house.

The crew of loud-talking, pistol-packing Texans in their big hats also had Tuck's bouncers standing nearby ready for trouble. Tuck himself was at the bar and so focused on the status of the game that he didn't notice the lawmen had come into his saloon.

Red Molly motioned to Morgan from the table where she sat alone, and he left Dixie and went to sit with her. He immediately noticed that she looked under the weather.

"Feeling poorly?" he asked.

Molly smiled at him, but the smile was a little more faint than she intended, and her eyes were slightly bloodshot and her skin had a pallor that wasn't only the white powder of her makeup. "Just a touch of a cold."

Morgan nodded at the cowboys. "How long have they been in here?"

Molly coughed into a handkerchief before she answered. "An hour or so. Long enough to get a thousand dollars ahead of Tuck's faro layout."

Morgan glanced at the bar. "Tuck can't like that."

"No."

Morgan turned his attention back to her. "You ought to turn in tonight. Get some rest."

Molly shook her head. "I'll be fine."

"As right as rain, my dear Molly! Fine, fine, indeed," said a short man with a belly too big to button his vest and a sack coat with one torn elbow as he approached their table. He took a seat with them without asking, and nodded at Morgan. "Our new marshal, I presume?"

Molly nodded at the new arrival to their table. "Morgan Clyde, meet Doctor Beauregard Chillingsworth."

Doctor Chillingsworth's eyes were glassy and his skin yellow and jaundiced and dry as old ivory. He caught one of the bartenders' attention and called for him to bring a bottle.

"Doctor?" Morgan asked.

Chillingsworth answered with a chuckle. "The people of this burg have labeled me so." He waved a hand around the room, as if the gesture encompassed all. "I learned the surgeon's trade in the late war, though that should hardly qualify me as one of Hippocrates's own anywhere but here."

"You're still the only game in town," Molly said. "Drunk or sober."

Doc Chillingsworth gave an indignant huff and adjusted his narrow-brimmed hat before it fell off his balding head. He held his glass up in toast. "To the good life."

"To the good life." Molly raised her own glass.

"And to the siren charms of corn liquor and women such as sweet Molly here," Chillingsworth quickly added before he downed his drink and wiped at his mouth with the back of his hand. "They've been the ruin of many a man."

Molly frowned at him while she took a sip from her own glass.

"I understand you too are a veteran," the doctor said to Morgan. "The right side I presume?"

"That would depend on what side you were on," Morgan replied without looking at him.

The clipped remark didn't go unnoticed by the doctor. He gave another indignant huff and poured himself a second drink. "From your accent, I would say you are an upstate man like myself. And I see that you are still in one piece, so I presume that I never had cause to work on you during that altercation."

Morgan threw an irritated glance at the doctor.

"I wouldn't grow too partial to my limbs, were I in your line of work," Chillingsworth said. "War or not, I've sawn off two legs and one arm since I've been in camp. One man crushed by a falling bridge timber, one with his knee shattered by a kicking horse, and one shot in the shinbone with a pistol. Counting the war and since, I suspect that, should I keep count, I've cut off enough body parts in my career to outfit an entire regiment of whole men."

"Don't mind Doc. He talks to himself when nobody will talk to him," Molly said with a boredom that told Morgan she had heard the doctor say that very line more than once.

"Friendly banter is a quality your friend here seems to lack," Chillingsworth said good-naturedly.

To Morgan, the cowboys at the faro table looked like trouble in the making, and he hardly heard any of the conversation between Molly and the doctor. He saw Dixie near the bar watching them, too. It wasn't until Molly coughed again that Morgan broke away from the faro game long enough to glance her way.

"Turn in for the night before you catch pneumonia," he said.

"And what do you care?" she asked flatly.

"You know better, Molly."

"Pour me another drink," Molly slid her empty glass across the table to the doctor.

Morgan looked to Chillingsworth. "Doctor, in your professional opinion do you think she should be drinking?"

She spoke before Chillingsworth could. "No, and I shouldn't be humping nor dancing neither, but I do both of them just to spite the devil." She laughed at him and threw the whiskey down her throat.

Tough talk—Molly was full of tough talk, but Morgan knew her well enough to sense something else behind it. That something else was fear, although she would never admit that. It was a thing that hadn't been there when he had first known her, but it was there now in her weary tone, her worried eyes, the set of her mouth, and hinted at in the things she occasionally said. And the fear was starting to eat at her, like he had seen it do before in other women who survived the way she did. Worse, on a night like this when she was tired and off her game.

He had no clue how old Molly was, but he guessed her in her mid-thirties—not old at all except in her profession—and maybe starting to think about things that the young and carefree don't pause to think about. Scared of getting older and uglier in a flesh game of diminishing returns; scared of being alone; scared of all the things everyone was scared of. A woman like Molly was only a single turn of bad luck or few years or a few steps away from the grave or working on her back in some filthy crib or dark alley for whoever would pay her and for whatever they would pay her. The second one was a worse kind of dying, and the way so many of her kind ended up when fortune, age, or their health turned against them.

"You look after Molly," Morgan said to the doctor. "She saved my hide once."

Molly laughed again. "The cholera almost got you, sure enough. Those Kansas doctors had already given you up for dead and were ready to carry you out in a wheelbarrow. I didn't know if you were going to make it myself, but you hung in there—shriveled up to nothing more than a skeleton and turned so blue that the whole time I sat with you I kept leaning over to make sure you were still breathing."

"Like I said, I owe you."

"Quit that, and quit looking so somber. A man being nice to me always throws me off."

The cowboys at the faro table were getting louder, and Morgan stood and headed for them, wanting to be closer if trouble should break out. One of them had said something that the dealer didn't like. The drunken cowboys were so busy celebrating their buddy's latest win that they didn't seem to notice Tuck's bouncers ringing them and edging closer. Morgan rose and was halfway to them when the night watchman from the stock pens burst through the tent flaps. He scanned the room and quickly spotted Morgan.

"Come quick," he said. "Somebody's stole a set of horses from the corrals."

Morgan caught Tuck's attention, and then jerked his head in the direction of the cowboys. "Keep on the square, and no trouble."

Tuck said nothing, but he nodded after a short delay.

It was the night watchman who had brought the news of the stolen horses, and Morgan followed him outside with Dixie quick on their heels. Molly and Doc Chillingsworth remained at their tables. Doc was studying the whiskey in the glass he had filled again, and she was staring at nothing.

"You love him, don't you?" Doc finally asked.

Red Molly coughed in her handkerchief and shoved her empty glass to him. "What do you know about anything? Shut up and pour."

Doc gave her an odd smile, more than a bit of pity in it. "I see the way you look at him. Tell me I'm wrong."

She jerked the bottle from his hand, but didn't immediately pour her drink. Instead, she sighed and looked to the doorway where Morgan had gone. "God help me, I do. And he doesn't even know it, and it wouldn't do me any good if he did."

CHAPTER THIRTEEN

Morgan and Dixie went with the night watchman to the company corrals, and stood to either side of him while he lit a lantern and held it above the fence planks of one of the pens. There was barely enough light to make out several horses standing sleepily inside the enclosure.

"Why didn't they take the rest of the horses and mules?" Dixie asked. "There must be fifty, sixty head."

"Probably figured they couldn't slip out of camp driving a whole herd without being noticed," the watchman said.

"Well, they damned sure took four head without you catching them."

"Six head," the watchman said. "Six big matching grays that the company uses to pull their dirt-moving slip."

"And where were you?" Morgan asked. "I understand there is supposed to be a stock tender on duty at all times."

"I had to go to the outhouse. They must have been watching and waiting for a chance, and took the horses while I was gone." The watchman's face was hidden in the darkness, but his voice gave away that he was a poor liar.

"I hear that you're sweet on one of Fat Sally's girls," Dixie said. "Were you over at the Bucket of Blood sparking her instead of doing your job?"

"Honest, no, it wasn't that," the watchman said. "It was just that I got cold and thought maybe it wouldn't hurt to go inside my shack and take a little time by the stove."

"And you didn't hear anything?" Morgan asked.

"Nothing."

"How much did they pay you to be in there by that stove while they took the horses?" Morgan asked.

"That ain't true," the watchman said.

"Matched team of big horses like that would sell real good to the farmers up in Kansas or down in that cotton country on the Red," Dixie said. "Quick, easy money."

"Saddle a horse and ride down to the river. See if that ferryman saw those horses cross," Morgan said to Dixie. "I'll ask around here to see if anyone else might have seen them leave camp."

The night watchman, glad that their attention had moved on from him, grabbed up a halter and lead rope hanging on the fence and went through the gate to catch Dixie a horse. Dixie remained where he was.

"Damned I hate chasing horse thieves," he said. "They never do travel slow, and considering horse thieving is a hanging offense, they ain't likely to give up peacefully if you can run them down."

It took Morgan and Dixie until daylight to determine that the stolen horses had gone east instead of up or down the Texas Road. A farmer bringing in a load of dried feed corn had met two mounted men leading six gray draft horses on the trail the other side of North Fork.

Morgan and Dixie were saddling up company horses at the corrals when Sergeant Harjo and two other Lighthorsemen rode up. They had come south from the Creek capital at Okmulgee on general patrol, and Sergeant Harjo volunteered their services after he had a few words with Morgan to get the straight of the matter.

"Thought you stayed out of white man business," Morgan said.

"I do, but this isn't only white man business," Harjo said. "These brush outlaws around here aren't picky about what color your skin is when they decide to steal your stock. Creek man up the road had a good chestnut gelding stolen two nights ago. Might be this is the same bunch we burned out a few days ago, and if we run them down we might can get that gelding back."

Morgan wasn't about to argue with having some men along who could track and who knew the country. They were still determining their strategy for pursuit when Superintendent Duvall pulled up in his wagon with his usual Pinkerton bodyguards. He motioned to Morgan to come over with the impatient, confident air of a man who was used to people doing what he commanded.

"McDaniels tells me that my slip horses are missing," Duvall said when Morgan walked over. "Those horses cost the company better than a thousand dollars."

"We're about to leave to see if we can get your horses back."

Superintendent Duvall put his pipe in the side of his mouth and leaned forward to the lit match that the Pinkerton on the seat beside him held cupped in his hands. He puffed the tobacco in the pipe bowl to life and waited through two more clouds of smoke before he spoke again.

His voice grew quieter, as if he didn't want anyone to overhear what he was about to say. "I've got a payroll headed here in two days."

"There will be a lot of your men that are happy to hear that," Dixie said.

Duvall acted like he hadn't heard him. "I want you on the train to Kansas City. You will personally see to the loading of the payroll and escort it back here. These Pinkerton men will go with you."

"Dixie or I will come back if this horse business keeps us gone too long."

Duvall puffed on his pipe again, his face expressionless except for the suck of his cheeks on the pipe stem. "You make sure you're back by Friday. Both of you."

Morgan went past Duvall's buckboard, headed back to the corral. When he came past Duvall again he was riding a long-legged, high-headed sorrel that looked fast and tough, if more than a bit on the flighty side.

Morgan, Dixie, and the Creek Lighthorsemen were barely out of camp when Deacon Fischer caught up to them astride a big bay that looked like it could run all day and all night. The quality of the horse didn't surprise Morgan, for an outlaw didn't usually live long if he couldn't pick a good piece of horseflesh.

"You don't mind if I come along, do you?" Deacon never so much as nodded at the other men, but kept his attention on Morgan.

"Since when did you get so concerned over other people's livestock?" Morgan asked. "Got civic-minded all of a sudden?"

Deacon gave a thin smile, and that gesture was out of place on his cadaverous face. "Thought I might see what the other end of one of these chases look like."

Morgan couldn't help but chuckle at the man's audacity. "Could it be that you want to keep an eye on me and make sure that nobody else plugs me before you decide to take a whirl at that bounty on my head?"

"Such a cynic you are."

"I tell it like it is."

Deacon nodded. "Say what you want, but it wouldn't hurt you to have another gun along. And you know I'm good."

"Come along if you're of a mind to."

Morgan wasn't sure why he had agreed to let Deacon go with them, but he did enjoy the sight of Dixie's mouth hanging open in shock.

Harjo and his Indian policemen took the lead and Dixie cut in behind them. Morgan and Deacon were left sitting their horses in the middle of the trail. The borrowed sorrel Morgan rode was restless and ill-broke, stamping and walking in place.

Morgan gave a sweep of his hand towards the trail ahead in the direction the rest of the posse had gone. "After you."

The strained attempt at a smile was gone from Deacon's mouth, and his lips were pressed tight and thin. "If I ever come for you, you can rest assured it will be face to face."

It was Morgan's turn to give a half smile. "As you say, I'm a bit of a cynic. If you don't mind, I'll ride easier with you in front of me."

Deacon kicked his horse forward and put it to a lope to catch up to the men ahead, and Morgan was thoughtful and slow in letting his horse go after him.

The posse pushed hard, stopping only three times along the trail: once at North Fork, another time at the Ashbury Mission school to the north of that settlement, and the last at some Indian farmer's cabin at the rocky crossing on the North Canadian above where the two rivers joined. Nobody they talked to had seen the stolen gray horses, and apparently the thieves had ridden hard trying to put as much distance between them and any pursuit as they could before daylight. To make things more difficult, the trail was so heavily traveled that deciphering anything from the muddy mix of tracks was almost impossible, but the Creek trackers somehow were sure that the thieves were sticking to the main trail.

Once across the North Canadian, the posse kept their horses to a long lope, hoping to gain some ground. Two miles downstream of the fork in the river they passed a giant finger of rock sticking up out of the middle of the channel. While the other two Lighthorsemen worked ahead searching for sign on a sandy stretch of the trail, the rest of them stopped to let their horses blow.

Sergeant Harjo pointed at the finger of rock. "Folks hereabouts call that Standing Rock. It's got all kinds of markings and drawings on it."

"Markings?" Dixie asked. "Do you mean Indian markings?"

"Some Indian, maybe, but made before my people and the other Civilized Tribes came west. Old marks. My uncle thinks some of them were put there by Spanish conquistadores, and that they show the way to hidden treasures if you can figure out how to read them."

"Treasure. Now you're talking," Dixie said. "Beats saddle sores and chasing horse thieves for two-fifty a day."

After the Creeks had a chance to study the tracks in the sandy trail they came back sure that the thieves were still headed east along the trail. The bad news was that they were a good three or four hours ahead of the posse.

The posse moved on, holding their horses to a long trot to save them, and leaving the rock landmark with its strange hieroglyphs behind. The trail hugged close to the north bank of the river, and to either side of the trail was a dense forest of giant hardwoods and sycamores and elms, under laced with cedars and other shorter brush. In places the green briars and grapevines were so intertwined with the trunks of the trees that it would have been impossible to leave the trail. Not far downstream the river made a big bend where it ran around the south end of Hi Early Mountain and then turned almost due north up the west side of another low mountain beyond it. A broad curve of sandy riverbed and a few farm fields lay between the two mountains.

Morgan glanced at the sun, measuring its progress across the sky since he had last checked it. His guess was that they had three more hours of daylight. He checked his pocket watch to make sure. Three o'clock. They had ridden hard, but had gained little on the horse thieves. He knew their best hope was to catch them quickly, and that there was very little chance after that if their quarry decided to leave the trail and hit the rugged, mountainous country to the south. He told himself that he would ask Sergeant Harjo and the Lighthorsemen to go on ahead alone to look for the horses and spread the word about them if they hadn't caught the thieves by morning. He and Dixie would go back to Ironhead for payroll duty.

"Shame there isn't a telegraph wire to send a message ahead to Fort Smith," Dixie said.

"I sent one to Fort Gibson before we left, and asked them to forward it on to Fort Smith and Van Buren so the law there could be on the lookout," Morgan answered.

"My guess is that they'll cross the river when they get to Hoyt," Harjo said. "There's supposed to be some kind of outlaw hideout not far south of there. Regular robbers' roost."

"The caves," Deacon said.

They all looked at him. It was the first thing he had said since they left Ironhead.

"What's that?" Harjo asked.

"I said the caves. That's what they call them," Deacon answered. "It's about half a day's ride south of here in the Choctaw Nation, maybe less."

"I take it you've been there," Morgan said.

"It's nothing but a big rock pile on the side of a mountain. There's a brush horse corral and a cave to sleep in, nothing more."

"Could you take us there if it came to that?" Morgan asked.

"You don't want to go there."

"Might be we do," Dixie challenged.

"That's rough country, and there's a reason that place is used for a hideout," Deacon said. "A couple of men could fight off a whole posse from those rocks, and it's too easy for a man hiding out there to shoot you up and then slip out without you seeing him. We'd be risking your necks for nothing but a chance to get our heads shot off."

The Creek Lighthorsemen led them to a fork in the road where one branch óf the trail turned south, crossing a shallow stretch of the river and passing through the middle of some farm fields until its trace disappeared in the distance. A cable was stretched across the river, and a flat-decked ferryboat was moored on the far side with a mule-drawn windlass beside it to power the craft from one bank to the other. The ferryman saw them, and paddled over to them in a skiff, making slow work of it. His helper remained on the far bank, shading his eyes and watching them with a rifle in his hands.

The ferryman was a short, stout Choctaw. He was some put out to have paddled over only to find that the posse didn't need to be ferried across the river once he informed them that he hadn't seen anyone pass his place since the day before.

"They aren't headed to those caves if they didn't cross the river here," Harjo said.

Morgan watched the Indian ferryman paddling back across the river, and studied the cluster of cabins about a half-mile from the river's southern bank. "That ferryman's house is quite a ways from the river, and with the river down, they could have swam those horses across in the night without him knowing it."

"He said there weren't any tracks on his side of the river," Harjo added.

"Think he's telling the truth?" Morgan asked. "A lot of people in the Territory don't mind lying to a peace officer."

"No, he's honest. If he says they didn't come through his place, they didn't."

Morgan frowned as he studied the trail to the east.

"That ferryman keeps a few trader horses up at his place. We could ride over there and swap out for some fresh ponies and make a hard push for the crossing at Webbers Falls," Harjo added.

"We'd be running blind in the dark before long and gambling they stick to the trail," Morgan replied. "Our horses are fresh enough, and if we haven't caught them by dark we probably won't catch them anyway."

They returned to the main trail and once again headed east at a fast pace. In another mile or so they rounded the northern end of the easternmost mountain, and in a clearing they found a recent campsite. The two horse thieves alone hadn't made the camp, for there were the fresh remains of three campfires and the ground was beaten bare between several trees where a large number of horses had been tied on a picket line, military style.

"Maybe twenty men," one of the Lighthorsemen said after he had time to look around.

Sergeant Harjo squatted by one of the fire rings and placed a palm to the ashes. "Still a little warmth to them. They haven't been gone long. Headed north off the trail. Could be that bunch of bushwhackers my man spotted a few days ago."

"Could be."

"You worrying about what I think you're worrying about?"

"The payroll? How do you know about that?"

"Who doesn't know about it? The gossip in Ironhead hasn't talked about much else since it was overdue. Maybe I didn't know the how or when, but it's only a matter of time before Duvall has to pay up or he's going to lose every worker he has."

"That's a lot of men to be camped out in the brush for no good reason."

Harjo nodded. "Maybe waiting for a big payroll coming down the tracks to Ironhead."

The Creek trackers continued to scout around the camp, and it was soon apparent to their keen eyes that those who had made use of the abandoned campsite didn't leave as a single group, but divided up in small parties, avoiding the more open country to the northeast and sticking to the timber. What's more, the horses thieves the posse was following had either joined up with the new group, or had intentionally turned in behind them to cover their trail. The Creeks could read sign where Morgan's eyes saw nothing, but even they were having a hard time of it. Morgan, Dixie, and Deacon remained at the campsite while Sergeant Harjo and his men tried to work out the trail.

Morgan glanced at Deacon. "You know anything about this camp that you want to say?"

Deacon's burning eyes encircled in the dark sockets of his gaunt face peered at Morgan from under the shadow of his hat brim. "You ride in the land of the Canaanites, Clyde, beset by troubles on all sides. What would it change if you knew their names?"

"Tell me one thing. Is it the James Gang?"

"It isn't."

"They say you ride with them from time to time."

"Not since Little Arch ran things, and that was a long time ago. I never did cotton to that Jesse. He's too crazy to suit me."

Dixie laughed, but the look Deacon gave him cut him short.

"Is that all you're going to tell me, Deacon?" Morgan asked.

"The most I'll say is that a Yankee lawman like you might want to ride careful. Those that were camped here aren't partial to you, nor the railroad you work for."

"Do they intend to hit the Katy payroll?"

That question gave Deacon pause, as if he were weighing how much he was willing to say, if anything at all. When he finally did speak it was in the form of a question instead of an answer. "If you were eighteen men strong, didn't give a damn for the law, and wanted all the money you could get and to cripple the railroad at the same time, what would you do?"

Morgan soaked that in, understanding that Deacon had as same as told him that the gang that had been camped there were intending to hit the payroll. Deacon, perhaps thinking he had said too much, rode his horse into the timber after the trackers, leaving Morgan and Dixie behind.

"You know that Deacon's not right in the head. You know that, don't you?" Dixie asked when Deacon was out of hearing range.

"He's a strange one."

"No, not strange. He's pure crazy as a mad dog, and he's put his mark on you. I could see it plain as day," Dixie said.

"I'm keeping watch on him."

"Won't do you any good." Sergeant Harjo rode out of the timber and alongside them. "They say you're good with a gun, Clyde, but you haven't seen the day when you can beat Deacon head-on."

"Have you got any more good news to share with me?" Morgan asked.

"Yeah, I've got more news." Sergeant Harjo took off his hat and wiped the sweat from his forehead with the back of his forearm. He looked back the way he had come with a grimace. "We've lost the trail of those horse thieves."

CHAPTER FOURTEEN

Morgan and Dixie returned to Ironhead the afternoon of their second day gone. Both men were weary to the bone, and the horses they rode no better. Deacon Fischer was with them, but he stopped off at the Bullhorn when they rode in front of it.

Superintendent Duvall met his two policemen in the street in front of his office. "I see you don't have my slip horses."

Morgan looked back to the east.

"We rode west as far as Webbers Falls before we turned back. Sergeant Harjo and his men are still on the trail," Morgan said.

"You look tired, Clyde."

Morgan looked at Duvall again, and thought he could have said the same for the superintendent. Usually an immaculate and fastidious man, he wasn't his usual sharp-dressed self. His coat was as wrinkled as if he had slept in it, his string tie hung loose and untied, and there was a coffee stain on the front of his white shirt. Along with the disarray of his clothes, his eyes were bloodshot as if he too hadn't slept in a while or as if he had been on a drunk.

"Nothing a bath and a bed won't fix," Morgan said. "A bed might not hurt you, either. You look like you've been on the trail two days yourself."

Duvall ignored the remark aimed at his appearance. "I expect that you'll be rested and ready to take the train to Kansas City tomorrow evening."

"How much money is this payroll?" Morgan asked as if

payrolls and guard duty were the last things he wanted to consider at the moment.

"A month's wages for better than a hundred men, plus fees owed to various small contractors here in camp."

"You didn't answer my question. How much?"

"Thirty thousand dollars."

Morgan looked at Dixie, and Dixie let out a low, long whistle.

"Delay things for a day, or maybe two," Morgan said. "We ran across an abandoned camp yesterday. We think it belonged to a bushwhacker bunch intent on robbing your payroll."

"That's not an option."

"If the men in that camp we found are the sort I think they are, they would charge hell with a bucket of water for a chance at thirty thousand dollars."

"I said there will be no delays. Apparently, you aren't aware of recent conditions within the camp. My bridge crew walked off the job at lunch today and refuses to return to work until they are paid. Right now they are down there in the saloons drinking and getting angrier and less reasonable by the minute."

"Afraid they're going to come hang their boss by the heels?" The look on Dixie's face told that he immediately regretted saying it.

Duvall stiffened. "I have promised them that the money will be here no later than day after tomorrow. Do you understand that?"

"I understand," Morgan answered, and understood Duvall's haggard appearance and the worry in his voice. No doubt, whatever Duvall's difficulties with the payroll were, those troubles had cost him some sleepless nights.

"Very well, then," Duvall continued. "Ten more Pinkerton guards will meet you at Kansas City, and the army is sending some infantrymen to ride the train."

"Soldiers, huh?" Morgan asked.

"I'll remind you that there are some very important and powerful men who want to see this railroad completed. I'll get the whole U.S. Army down here if I have to. Things have been difficult enough of late, and I won't have my project hindered by Missouri border scum."

Morgan turned his horse around and headed back the way he had come, his hat brim pulled low down and the collar of his frock coat turned up against the wind.

"Where are you going?" Dixie asked. "I thought we were going to catch some shut-eye?"

Morgan didn't answer, and they watched him pull his horse up in front of the Bucket of Blood and dismount.

"What's eating him?" Duvall asked.

"He's a worrier sometimes," Dixie answered. "Don't think anything of it. He'll be ready to ride with your payroll when it comes time."

Duvall nodded as if he understood. "I'm a worrier myself."

Two hours later Morgan was still seated at a table in a far corner of the saloon, alone except for a full bottle of Old Reserve standing on the table before him like a bullet.

It was sometime in the wee hours of the morning when Red Molly called it a night. She stepped out the back door of the Bullhorn and trudged along the short, muddy path to the little tent behind the saloon that she called home. The night air was cold enough to fog her breath, and she tucked her shawl tight about her against the chill. She had only taken a few steps when she noticed the lamplight glowing through the canvas walls of her tent, although she hadn't left the lamp lit.

Cautiously folding back one flap of the door, she saw Morgan sitting slumped in a chair beside her bed with his black hat resting on the nightstand beside him and an empty bottle of whiskey dangling at the end of one arm. He didn't say anything while she tied the door flaps shut, but when she turned to him she recognized what she saw in the sad, somber set to his face. She recognized the lonely emptiness in him, for she had that feeling herself—had it more and more often of late, like a little sickness in the hollow of her belly.

She gently took the bottle from him and leaned over the bedside lamp and blew it out. Her hand found his, and she guided him to her bed.

"I . . ." he started.

"Sshh. You don't have to say anything. It's too cold and dark to be alone tonight."

They made love in virtual silence, with the only sound the whisper of their breathing and faint yip of coyotes somewhere off in the distance. She held him long after he fell asleep, pressing her naked body against his, and the fingers of one free hand twining a lock of his hair. She didn't want to fall asleep and lose the moment, but she did.

It was his stamping into his boots that woke her. She propped herself up on one elbow and watched him finish dressing, liking the sight of the hard crease of his spine and the flex of the lean muscles in his shoulders, his skin still shining with a thin sheen of sweat, despite the chill of the room.

She had come to know much about men, at least their ways if not their hearts. A cowboy might have put on his hat first, but he took up his gun belt and slung it around his hips with practiced ease. The hat and then the frock coat came last, and never once did he turn to look at her, keeping his back to her the whole time as if he were ashamed to have come to her. That hurt her, but pride was something hard to afford and easily spent, and in quiet desperation she purposely let the blanket and sheet stay at her waist, hoping that the sight of her naked flesh would keep him a little longer if he should look her way.

He started for the door without so much as a single glance at her.

"You called me by her name," she said before he could pass out her door.

She thought she saw him hunch slightly, and imagined a brief falter to his steps. "You called out her name twice last night."

He left without answering her, and she rolled onto her back and pulled her covers to her chin. She lay like that for a long while, staring at the ceiling. The wind lifted the flaps of the tent door where he had gone, and she dabbed at her eyes with the edge of the blanket.

"Damn you, Morgan Clyde."

CHAPTER FIFTEEN

"Good morning, Charlie. You're a mighty sound sleeper."

That voice was what started Charlie Six Fingers awake. He propped himself up on one elbow under his blankets, rubbed the sleep out of his eyes, and blinked a few times. Bill Tuck squatted on his heels on the far side of the smoking ashes of the night's campfire with one bridle rein laid across his thighs to hold his horse, which was picking at the dead winter grass behind him. What's more, Charlie's holstered pistol was missing from beside his bedroll and hanging from Tuck's saddle horn.

"Doesn't act like he expected us for breakfast, does he?" Tuck lit a cigar with a twig he had been holding in the coals, and then twisted his head around to look to his side and farther behind him.

Charlie swept back the cowlicked strand of hair that hung down over his face and shaded his eyes against the rising sun. It took him a moment to focus on the form of Deacon Fischer, Texas George, and the other two Kingman brothers sitting their horses farther back from the fire.

"Hello, boys." Charlie tried to smile like he didn't have a care in the world, but his eyes darted from Tuck to the men with him. "I don't have anything but a little chunk of side meat in my saddlebags, but I could cook that for you."

"We aren't hungry, Charlie. Breakfast was just a figure of speech," Tuck said. "You never were too bright."

Charlie started to flip back his blankets, but the sound of a cocking pistol stopped him in mid-motion. Texas George had his Colt out and cocked and pointing at him.

"Go easy there, Charlie," Tuck said. "You wouldn't want to make George nervous. George gets shooty when he's nervous."

Charlie folded his blankets back slowly, holding one edge high to show that he had no weapons hidden under there. Slowly, he rose to a sitting position while Tuck puffed a few times on his cigar and watched him.

"Charlie, I'm pretty displeased with you," Tuck said. "Fact is, I'm purely peeved."

"With me?"

Tuck ignored the question and looked to where Charlie's horse was tied to a nearby blackjack oak. Another horse, a good palomino gelding with a bald face and two white socks on its hind legs, was tied with it, and a second saddle and bedroll lay not far from where Charle had lain down for the night.

"Who else is with you?" Tuck asked.

"Joe Luke."

"Where's that Indian at?"

Charlie's camp was in a stand of timber, and he gave his surrounding a baffled look. "Can't say."

Tuck looked at the men with him, and Texas George's brothers immediately spurred their horses into the woods, one going one way and the other circling the camp in the opposite direction.

"That Joe Luke must have heard us coming and slipped off," Texas George said. "Injuns are slippery like that."

"When did you and Joe Luke start keeping company?" Tuck asked.

"Met him on the road and we thought we would throw in together," Charlie answered. "Thought we would go down to Dallas and see how things were there. You know, do a little gambling."

"Gambling with my money. That's what you mean, don't you, Charlie?"

"I don't know what you're talking about."

Charlie could hear the Kingmans busting through the brush in the near distance and looking for his traveling companion. Deacon Fischer stayed beside Texas George, saying nothing and with an almost bored look on his face.

Tuck rose, dropped his horse's rein, and took a step towards Charlie's saddle, standing nose down beside the fire. "Come to think of it, I could use something to eat. How about I get that side meat out of your saddlebags and fry it up like you said?"

Charlie stood and held out a hand to stop Tuck. "Let me do that, Bill."

Texas George stretched the pistol in his fist to the end of his arm, staring down it at Charlie's gut. "You better not take one more step."

"What's the matter, Charlie? Is there something in your saddlebags you don't want me to see?" Tuck chided, and then bent over and opened first one bag and then the other, throwing the cloth-wrapped bundle of bacon and other miscellaneous things on the ground until he straightened back up and held his empty hands out to Charlie. "Where'd you put the money?"

"What money?"

"The four hundred dollars you shorted your bank when you turned it back in to me your last night dealing."

"I didn't short you any money, Bill."

"Where's the money, Charlie? I won't ask again."

Charlie's shoulders slumped and he wouldn't meet Tuck eye to eye. "I spent it."

"Say that louder."

"I spent it, but I'm going to pay you back."

"Spent it on what?"

Charlie shrugged. "Whores and whiskey and such, I guess.

161

My head hurts something awful since that damned Clyde buffaloed me. Can't remember like I should."

"You're a poor liar, Charlie, and I hate that almost as bad as I hate a man that steals from me."

"Bill . . ."

Tuck cut him off. "It's going to hurt a lot worse if you don't give me that money."

Charlie never looked up, but pulled a roll of greenbacks from his vest pocket, doing it slowly and gingerly lest Texas George or one of the others think he was going for a hideout gun. Tuck came closer and took the money.

"It's all there, Bill. Count it if you want to."

Tuck pocketed the money without much more than a glance at it, picked up his bridle rein, and stepped up on his horse and looked at Deacon and Texas George. "Tend to this."

Deacon Fischer and Texas George remained where they were when he rode away. Charlie looked at them and the sharp knot of his Adam's apple flexed convulsively. Texas George leaned over the front of his saddle with one forearm resting on his saddle horn and the other arm laid across it with his pistol nonchalantly pointed in Charlie's direction. He grinned while he cocked and uncocked his pistol, over and over again, like the sound of it was the funniest thing in the world.

"You've got to be the worst thief I ever saw, Charlie," George said. "Deacon, have you ever seen the likes of him?"

Deacon's only reaction was to keep staring at Charlie with that still, lifeless expression on his pale face.

"How's that?" Charlie asked.

"What kind of fool steals Tuck's money and then camps right beside the road?" George laughed.

"You don't have to do this. I never did anything to you boys," Charlie pleaded.

"Sorry, Charlie. Nothing personal, but Tuck's paying me a

little extra for a horse swap he and I made if I tack your hide to a tree."

"I needed a stake to get me on down the road. You know how it is."

Texas George laughed again. "What say you, Deacon. Feel sorry for him?"

"The wages of sin is death," Deacon said. "And ye shall reap what ye sow."

"I never did like you all that much, no how, Charlie," Texas George said.

Charlie let out a slow, quiet sigh. "How about you let me have my breakfast? You can at least do that."

Texas George raised his pistol, aiming it at Charlie's head, but lowered it thoughtfully after a moment's hesitation and glanced at Deacon. "Be kind of like a last supper, wouldn't it?"

Deacon blinked once, slowly, and then shrugged.

Charlie let out a sigh and set his hat on his head gingerly. The knot at the top of his forehead left by Morgan Clyde's pistol-whipping left the hat setting at an awkward angle. He hobbled to his saddlebags in his socked feet and picked up the package of bacon off the ground and a little black cast-iron skillet with the bottom side stained white with ashes and flame. He heard the creak of Texas George's saddle on his way back to the fire, and the sound made him flinch.

He gave them a squeamish, embarrassed smile. "Thought I was already a goner there for a second."

Neither man watching him said anything while he knelt down and went about raking the ashes until he had found enough coals to light the sticks he laid on top of them. He set the skillet on the flames after a while, and sliced the bacon into strips with a little mother of pearl–handled pocketknife. He remained kneeling and hovering over the cooking bacon, and once or twice looked over at his horse tied to a blackjack oak a few steps away. There was only the sound of sizzling pork and the occasional stamp of the horses.

Sometime later, Charlie set the skillet off the fire. He stared at the sky and made no attempt to eat. "I never thought it would come to this."

"Eat your breakfast," Texas George said.

Charlie's hand was shaking when he picked up a piece of bacon, tore off a tiny piece of it, and dropped the rest back in the skillet. He nibbled delicately at the tiny remnant he held, making a show of how hot it was. Finishing the bacon, his attention drifted to his pair of boots over by his bedroll, and then he looked down at his feet and wiggled one big toe out of a hole in that sock.

"Don't that beat all?" he asked, and was quick to continue talking when neither outlaw answered him. "You got any family, Deacon? I got a sister that lives in Missouri. Not two days' ride up that road yonder, and I ain't seen her in three years. She ain't like me. Pretty, sweet thing. Took after our mama in that respect. Wouldn't think a man like me could have a sister like that, would you?"

Charlie reached for another piece of bacon, careful to keep the tips of his fingers from getting burned by the hot grease, and blowing on the piece he chose to cool it. He made as if to take a bite from it, but seemed to think better of it and held the bacon aside. "I wonder what she's doing right now? Probably milking time."

Texas George's pistol cracked and the bullet struck Charlie in the forehead and his body went limp and he fell on his face with the uneaten bacon at the end of his outstretched arm. Deacon rode his horse closer.

"You told him he could finish his breakfast," Deacon said.

Texas George rode his own horse over, and looked down at the bloody mess that he had made of the back of Charlie's head. "Son of a bitch eats too slow."

Deacon kept his horse where it was while Texas George dismounted and rolled the body over and began to search Charlie's coat pockets. The search resulted in a couple of coins and a sack of Watson & McGill cigarette tobacco. Texas George held the offerings in his open palm for Deacon to see and grunted his disdain.

"Two dollars and change. Can you believe that?" He stuffed both the money and the tobacco sack in his own coat pocket and took a piece of bacon from the skillet. "I wish they would hurry up and find that Indian so we can get out of here."

"You told him that he could finish his breakfast," Deacon repeated. "You could have done that much for him."

George wolfed down the piece of bacon and sucked at his greasy fingers. "What's it matter? He was dead one way or another. You don't steal from Tuck and think he ain't going to come after you. Especially, when you've got a day's head start and you don't get no further than twenty miles down the trail. Charlie always was a dumbass."

"I don't like you, George."

Texas George twisted on his heels where he squatted beside the fire, and gave Deacon a cautious, measuring look. "I hate to hear that, Deacon."

He licked his lips and gave Deacon one more look before he reached down and drew Charlie's knife from the dead man's belt. "How many men do you think Charlie gutted with this pig sticker?"

Deacon didn't answer.

"Give me a pistol every time." George speared another piece of bacon from the skillet with the knife and was about to eat it before he cocked his head towards the sounds of his brothers' horses cracking limbs and underbrush close by. "I wish they would hurry up and find that Injun. There ain't no profit and damned little fun in running errands for Tuck."

"Joe Luke didn't steal Tuck's money," Deacon observed.

"Maybe so, but those brothers of mine don't cotton to In-juns. Old Joe better light a fire under his heels and hit the high country." Texas George shook his head. "Besides, I always did take a shine to that yellow horse of Joe's."

Charlie noticed for the first time that Deacon's coat was flipped back on one side behind the butt of his pistol. It hadn't been that way before.

"We ain't cross, are we, Deacon? Hell, if I had known you wanted to drag things out . . ."

"You don't have any pride in your work, George, and your word doesn't mean anything. That's the problem with you."

"Listen here." George shifted uneasily, not liking the look that Deacon was giving him.

In that same instant a man broke from the timber not twenty yards from the fire. He was in a dead run and closing fast on them. Texas George barely had time to recognize the Indian aiming a shotgun at him from the hip before the weapon bel-lowed and a splattering of lead shot stung the ground beside him, scattering dirt and bits of grass and leaves everywhere. George cursed and dove to the side and rolled over twice to avoid being trampled by Deacon's frightened, dancing horse.

The Indian slid to a stop ten yards away and swung the gun towards Deacon, but never got a chance to pull his trigger again, for Deacon's pistol appeared as if by magic and the bark of it when he fired was sharp and loud in the still morning air. The first shot struck the Indian high in the chest, half turning him, and the second bullet hit him in the side of the head. Both gunshots came in almost one breath.

The Indian dropped the shotgun from his lifeless hands, but remained on his feet for a long instant, his head tilted back on his neck as if on a broken hinge, and staring at the sky before his body went limp and he folded into the ground. The other Kingman brothers charged their horses from the timber behind the body with their rifles in their hands.

Texas George got to his feet, staring first at the dead Indian and then at Deacon. One of George's brothers got down off his horse and gave the Indian's body a kick.

"That's some shooting, Deacon," he called out. "Second one took him right in the earhole."

Deacon had calmed his frightened mount and had his Smith broken open and was thumbing two fresh cartridges in it. He didn't look at the pistol while he reloaded it, keeping his attention on Texas George instead.

"You're quick with that shooter, Deacon." Texas George took a couple of steps backward as he spoke. It was only then that he realized that he was still holding the knife with the slice of bacon speared on the end of it. That was the most ridiculous and helpless feeling in the world with the way Deacon was looking at him.

Deacon snapped his pistol closed, and Texas George flinched at the sound. "Finish your bacon, George, but don't eat too slow."

Deacon's face was as bland and expressionless as always, but there might have been a slight hint of a tight-lipped smirk to go with the odd look in his eyes.

CHAPTER SIXTEEN

The train rattled and clacked over the roadbed with a rhythm of its own. The only sunlight coming inside the express car was through the narrow slits high in the two sliding doors, or through the single barred window on the far wall. Morgan paced the floor, pausing occasionally to stare out one of those limited vantage points, and not liking not being able to see outside any better than he could. Dixie sat on a stool against the wall opposite the doors. He and two soldiers were playing pitch and using the strongbox for a card table. The two other troopers in the car had found places on the floor and gone to sleep when the train was barely south of Kansas City.

Morgan glanced at the strongbox—not a safe, but a simple steel box with two hasps and big padlocks holding it closed. Morgan debated kicking the sleeping soldiers awake, but instead he reached for a Winchester carbine he had stuck in one of the shelving pigeonholes usually reserved for express mail.

"Where you going?" Dixie looked up from his card hand.

"Checking things out."

"Going smooth as a baby's bottom so far."

"That's what worries me."

Morgan went out the door in the end of the express car and closed it behind him. He stood on the platform surveying the flatcar hooked between the express car and the tender car and locomotive. On the flatcar were stacks of bridge timbers, metal beams, and other iron meant for the bridge construction on the

South Canadian, all secured with long, heavy chains and booms. On one side of that cargo along the edges of the flatcar deck, the sergeant commanding the troops had set up a gun pit of waist-high sandbags. In the middle of that gun pit was a Gatling rapid-fire battery gun mounted on an artillery carriage with its wheels chocked. Morgan had heard about such guns, but never seen one. Supposedly capable of firing seven hundred .50-70 rounds per minute, the Gatling gun consisted of six revolving barrels fed by a box magazine inserted vertically above, and powered by a hand crank on the side. A four-man team manned each gun, and the brass fittings and bolt housing glinted in the morning sunlight like angel swords.

The rest of the infantrymen sat on the other side of the chained-down stack of building supplies with their Springfield rifles propped on their thighs, squinting at the countryside flying past. The Pinkertons were scattered among the soldiers, and a couple of them were riding in the locomotive with the engineer or on top of the firewood stack of the tender. Although armed with whatever their personal tastes led them to, not a man among the Pinkertons wasn't carrying a rifle or a shotgun and at least one pistol on his person. They were a mixed bunch, but had a tough, seasoned edge about them—professionals and paid fighting men that wouldn't flinch if it came to a scrap.

Morgan went back inside the express car. He and Dixie, along with Duvall's two Pinkerton bodyguards, Sid and the other one, had climbed on the train in Ironhead Station the evening of the day before and ridden it north through the night. They crossed the brand-new Hannibal Bridge over the Missouri River not long before daylight, and the train had barely rolled into the station before the new force of Pinkerton guards and the army escort was loading the strongbox into the express car.

Hours later, they were on a downhill run from the Neosho River on the Kansas/Indian Territory line, and the boiler tender wasn't sparing any firewood and the engineer wasn't sparing any throttle. The company surveyors had chosen a route that followed a peninsula of prairie and rolling hills that ran between the Arkansas and Neosho rivers, and the going was straight and smooth. The countryside flew away and there wasn't so much as a hint of any of the bushwhackers. Morgan checked another point off his list after each successful passing of a prospective sharp bend, steep, slow grade, or other prospective site where the tracks might be torn up or barricaded.

They took on water at Downingsville, less than two hours above Ironhead, and it was the first time they had stopped the train since leaving Kansas City. The train station was nothing more than a water tank, a construction supply yard, three or four log cabins, and a trading post scattered west from the tracks. A handful of tents belonging to a crew pouring concrete pylons for a more permanent bridge across one of the creeks lay on the other side of the tracks.

The soldiers in the gun pit manned their Gatling gun, while the rest of the soldiers on the flatcar fanned out to either side of the train, standing guard. The Pinkertons took high positions atop the cab of the locomotive and express car, lying on their bellies with their rifles ready. The denizens of the sleepy settlement kept their distance, but watched the drama of the guard's security precautions with interest.

"Looks quiet enough," Dixie said, peering out the tiny window in one of the express doors.

"Don't sound so disappointed." Morgan looked out the same window. "It isn't over until we reach Ironhead."

"The only thing that will disappoint me is if I get shot guarding this payroll."

"They couldn't know where we would stop to take on water. We might have passed them at any of the normal stops we went by this morning."

"Or we could have been worried over nothing."

"Yes, there's that."

The boiler tank was topped off and the train was soon moving again. The men in the express car relaxed a little, all of them having been on edge while the train was parked in Downingsville. Only Morgan remained on his feet, slowly marching up and down the length of the express car deep in thought and periodically looking out the window. He was at the tail end of the car when one of Duvall's Pinkerton bodyguards came through the other door from the flatcar. It was the one called Sid.

Sid glanced at Morgan, then looked away and went to the coffee pot warming on the kerosene burner. He poured himself a mug of coffee and stood with his back to Morgan.

"Hello, cotton picker," Sid said to Dixie.

Dixie took a deep breath and laid down his cards and started to rise, but before the matter could go farther the sound of Morgan sliding the express door open drew everyone's attention. He didn't say why he did it, but stood quietly in the open door with the wind tugging at him.

"Not a bad idea," said one of the soldiers. "We could use some fresh air."

Sid glanced at Morgan, but Morgan seemed to be ignoring the situation, as if he had gone deaf and had eyes only for the passing countryside. Morgan's apparent disinterest in the situation emboldened Sid, and he couldn't resist picking at Dixie more.

"Secesh trash," Sid said where only Dixie and the soldiers playing cards could hear. "Me and you started an argument that I'm going to finish one of these days."

"Dixie!" Morgan said before Dixie could respond.

Dixie's fists were clinched on top of the strongbox, but he stayed seated. "What do you want, Chief?"

Morgan leaned against the frame of the open door with the Winchester cradled to him in the bend of one elbow. "Sid, that's what they call you, isn't it?"

"That's right." Sid turned up his coffee and watched Morgan over the lip of his mug.

"Why don't you come over here, and we have a talk," Morgan said.

Sid put down his mug and gave Dixie one last hateful leer. "You got to hide behind his skirts, do ya?"

"I said come over here," Morgan repeated.

Sid sauntered over, making a show of nonchalance. Morgan kept staring out the open door. No matter how carefree and fearless he acted, Sid made sure to stop with plenty of space in between them.

"What do you want?" he asked.

"How are things on the flatcar?" Morgan asked.

"The men are sharp," Sid said, relaxing a little. "Anybody would be a fool to tackle so many guns, much less trying to stop a train going this fast."

"We are going at a pretty good clip, aren't we?"

Sid looked down at the ground rolling away beneath him, grinning and relaxing even more. "One of those bushwhacker ponies would have to grow wings to run this train down."

Morgan looked over Sid's shoulder and past him to where Dixie sat.

"I'm thinking that Sid here isn't ever going to learn to play nice," Morgan said.

"Might be I could change his disposition if you'd let me." Dixie stood and cracked the knuckles of his right hand in the other. "I'd purely enjoy the chance."

Morgan shook his head. "No, I don't think there's any help for him."

"Maybe so. He seems like a knuckleheaded sort."

Sid gave Morgan a hard look. "You won't buffalo me with your tough talk. I don't like that secesh piece of trash you've got working for you, and I don't care what you think about it."

"Well, then, I guess all I can say is that you're fired."

"You can't fire me. I work for Mr. Duvall."

Morgan reached carefully into his coat pocket and produced a California twenty-dollar piece. He held the coin before Sid long enough to make sure he saw what it was.

"This ought to square things up between you and him," Morgan said.

Sid was about to say something just as Morgan flipped the coin high and out the door. Sid was poised for a fight, but the sight of the coin flipping through the air made him hesitate and he inadvertently leaned forward to watch it fly out the door. And in that brief moment he was slightly off balance when he shouldn't have been.

Morgan grabbed him by the coat front with one hand and heaved him towards the open door with one quick jerk. Sid's arms flailed the air wildly before he hit the ground, and then he tumbled and rolled like a ragdoll. Morgan leaned out the door to watch, and Dixie and the soldiers were soon beside him. The last they saw, Sid was on his feet clutching one arm to chest gingerly, and hobbling in a circle on a bad leg.

"I reckon that must have smarted some," one of the soldiers said.

Morgan left the open door and stashed the Winchester back into one of the mail pigeonholes and poured a mug of coffee. Dixie followed him to the coffee pot, watching him closely.

"You really don't like Pinkertons, do you?" Dixie asked. "Maybe someday you'll tell me about that."

Morgan took a sip of his coffee with an innocent look on his face. "A man ought to be careful standing in front of an open door like that. Get to running his mouth and not paying attention, and there's no telling when he might lose his balance and fall."

"Anybody ever tell you that you're a hard man, Chief?"

"So they say, deputy. So they say."

CHAPTER SEVENTEEN

They crossed the wide channel of Arkansas with the throttle wide open, and the boiler pressure gauge needle tilting towards the red, as the tender continued to shovel the coal to the furnace at a prodigious rate until the safety valves hissed steam, and the locomotive's coal stack poured black smoke and brimstone that bent backward over the train in a long, billowing cloud. The trunnion-connected rods on the drive wheels churned and pumped so hard that the bridge trestle shook and quivered beneath the train's speeding weight. A small herd of cattle grazed along the tracks on the far side of the river; the engineer yanked on the chain dangling from overhead in his cab, and the steam whistle shrilled low and loud, scattering the animals in flight and out of the way while the train roared past.

Not far beyond the Arkansas the train encountered a barricade of logs and rocks piled on the track on the far side of a sharp-combed ridge where the tracks made a tight curve through a thick stand of timber and between two cut banks. The engineer shoved his cap bill lower down on his brow against the bright sun while he leaned his head out of the cab window and slowed the train to a crawl. The men on the flatcar immediately shouldered their rifles and looked sharp, expecting gunfire to pour down on them at any second from the cut banks above. Morgan and the others in the express car locked the doors from the inside, readied firearms for a fight, and peered cautiously out of the little windows.

But whoever had stacked the barricade must have changed their minds, for no outlaws appeared. Regardless, and for good measure or simply out of nervous unrest, the crew on the Gatling gun cranked out a couple of bursts into the woods, shredding limbs and leaves and sending bark and earth flying. The noise of the battery gun letting off rounds was mind-numbing, and it took the sergeant's curses and shouted threats to get the soldiers to cease firing.

Without coming to a complete stop and only slowing to a crawl, the engineer eased the locomotive's cowcatcher into the barricade and shoved it off the track. Within minutes, the train was flying down a straight stretch again. Any outlaw that might have remained behind and seen the firepower demonstration was probably glad the heist had been called off. The men on the train guarding the payroll were no less enthused at the avoidance of a fight, except perhaps for the Gatling crew who seemed overly fond of playing with their rapid-fire toy and a tad on the hair-triggered, jittery side.

At half past one the three-car train crossed over the bridge on the North Canadian with Morgan standing once again in the open door of the express car. On a high-wide stretch of rolling prairie to the west of the tracks he spied a long line of horsemen skylined atop a hill some hundred yards from the tracks with the afternoon soon burning lazily and directly behind them. Eighteen men, as Deacon had warned, and all watching the train pass below them like barn cats watching a mouse titter by in reach of their paws.

Their rifles were silhouetted like black sticks where they rested the stocks on their thighs with the barrels pointed up at the blue sky. The distance wasn't so great that Morgan didn't recognize them for what they were. He would have known them for bushwhackers from the way they sat their horses and the calm, almost languid feeling of death about them that floated towards the train like the wispy strings of cotton-thread clouds overhead.

Partisan rangers, guerrilla fighters, or whatever you called them, they were all much the same—the kind that took the Old Testament adage of an eye for an eye and tooth for a tooth to its farthest extremes, full of hate and a maddening desire to see their enemies suffer more than they. Both sides of the recent war had their own raiders riding the countryside. Other parts of the country suffered from night riding and killing and burning, but nowhere was it as bad as in eastern Kansas and western Missouri. Whole towns were burned, stock stolen, murders committed. Old animosities escalated until things were done that no civilized man could excuse or fathom.

Kansas had Hoyt's Red Legs, Doc Jennison's jayhawkers, and the free-state raiders led by the Grim Chieftain, Senator Jim Lane. And if you asked one of their supporters they would tell you that those boys were fighting against the slaveholding, thieving Missouri trash.

But nowhere did they grow them rougher than Missouri. Bushwhackers they came to be called, mostly fighting on the run, they were dead shots with the profuse array of cap-and-ball and pinfire revolvers strapped on their persons or saddles. As stealthy at ambush and mayhem as the Indians that taught them many of their fighting ways, they were as cruel and merciless to their enemies as the ancient barbarians of old.

Many Southern sympathizers insisted that the Missouri bushwhackers rode for a cause, to right the wrongs done by raiding jayhawkers and wild-eyed abolitionists, but to Morgan's mind, neither the bushwhackers claiming loyalty to the Southern cause, nor the jayhawkers claiming fealty to the Stars and Stripes, were anything other than outlaws using the cover of war to rape and pillage, or to quench their thirst for revenge, crazy with bloodlust and forgetting whatever taste of the milk of human kindness they had ever known.

In the latter years of the war the army had hunted some of the bushwhackers down, but not all, although they depopulated most of southwestern Missouri and turned it to ashes in the attempt. Bloody Bill Anderson, horse thief turned Missouri guerrilla, barn burner, rapist, and man killer, was shot in the head at Glasgow, Missouri in a wild charge against Union forces pursuing him. His body was displayed at the local courthouse, minus one finger that a souvenir hunter had hacked off for the ring it bore, and the soldiers that brought him in claimed that they had found a string on his person with fifty-three knots, one for every man he killed.

Little Arch Clements was cornered by militiamen in a saloon in Lexington, Missouri after treeing the town, and like all of his kind, he went for his guns instead of surrendering. Shot to pieces and dying in the street, he tried to cock his pistol with his teeth so that he could take one more with him.

Former schoolteacher William Quantrill, infamous for his raid and massacre at Lawrence, Kansas where his bushwhacker force executed 183 men and boys, was finally run to ground and shot dead by soldiers in western Kentucky after bragging he was on his way east to personally assassinate President Lincoln. Major Tom Livingston trapped a small group of Union soldiers in a courthouse in Stockton, Missouri and took a bullet in the head trying to charge his horse through the barricaded front doors. John Nichols was hauled to his hanging scaffold in Jefferson City, Missouri in the back of a wagon and sitting atop the casket he was about to reside in.

George Todd, William Stuart, Riley Crawford, Joe Hart—one by one, gone under in a hail of gunfire. But not all. Some were simply too good at running and fighting and hiding to be cornered, and the worst of them were too tough to die easy. The Youngers, the James boys, and other leftovers were still kicking and raising Cain, and turning hard-won skills into a new trade—robbing banks and trains, or anything else that would produce a dollar at the end of a pistol.

Those were the kind of men sitting their horses on the hill watching the train go past, and Morgan watched them walk their horses down to the tracks and turn into it and follow it south, slowly receding from view until they disappeared.

Dixie came to stand beside him and looked back along the tracks at the bushwhackers turning in behind the speeding train. "Think they'll ride into Ironhead?"

"Are you thinking on quitting me?"

"No, I was thinking on what I wanted put in my last will and testament. You got any particular wishes in that regard?"

CHAPTER EIGHTEEN

The train rolled into Ironhead Station in the late afternoon, and half the camp came to meet them at the depot. The other half of the population was soon on hand when word spread that the payroll had finally arrived. The Gatling crew stayed on their gun, and kept a close watch over the crowd while the rest of the soldiers forced a lane from the express car to the Katy office. The blue uniformed troops stood with their Long Tom Springfield rifles at port arms with bayonets mounted, spaced evenly apart and facing outward towards the crowd along the opening they had created. The express car was opened, and Morgan and one of the Pinkertons carried the strongbox to the office with Dixie leading the way with a cocked rifle in each hand. The other Pinkertons immediately followed and took up guard positions outside the office when the money was inside.

Superintendent Duvall took charge of his money in the front room, and soon he and his clerk had the open strongbox sitting on a desk. The clerk broke out his ledgers, sharpened a pencil, and donned a pair of spectacles. Duvall took a seat beside him and behind the desk to supervise the proceedings. Soon, the long line of men waiting outside to be paid were filing into the office, admitted one at a time by the guards.

Many of the men had little coming to them, despite putting in more than a month's work. The clerk weighed the wages owed to each man against any debt rang up against the company. Nothing was cheap in Ironhead, and especially not in the mercantile run by the Katy. There were two tent stores in camp, but only the one owned by the railroad was well stocked. A man needing clothes, boots, and the other necessities of life could little avoid giving a part of his wages back to the company that employed him. And there was a rumor going around that the store wasn't actually owned by the Katy, but rather Duvall himself. More than one worker frowned at the lean stack of coins or greenbacks in his palm and then at Duvall, but Morgan and Dixie stood against the wall with shotguns in their hands. Some of the hotheads were ready and willing to argue the situation with the Katy, but nobody in their right mind was going to argue with two double-barreled ten gauges.

Morgan didn't find the company's practice admirable, but it was little different than the way other large companies acted. He'd seen the same thing in mining towns and lumber camps. And it wasn't as if the hardworking fools could have held onto their money anyway. The majority of them made a beeline to one of the watering holes or brothels as soon as they were paid, ready to let off a little steam one way or another. In preparation for payday, Bill Tuck had brought in a new load of bottled beer from Fort Smith. And following that freight over the trail, on the very evening of the payday, came a garishly painted six-seater surrey with a fancy tasseled top and loaded with bawdy house doves who had come over from Fort Smith and Van Buren. Business in Arkansas was a little slow, and they had heard Ironhead was wide open and booming. The men of camp, some of them already drunk by then, gathered on the sides of the street to greet the new arrivals, smiling and waving and passing ribald greetings. The women leaned from the surrey and blew harlot kisses and flashed flesh and smiled back at the men with mouths painted as red as the surrey's wheels. By nightfall, all of the crews were paid, the whiskey taps might as well have been left wide open, and Ironhead Station was running wild.

Morgan and Dixie returned the shotguns back to the rack on the wall in the rear room, and Morgan watched Duvall transferring the leftover money from the strongbox to the safe behind his desk, noting that it appeared that little of the original funds had been spent.

"That's a lot of money to have to worry about," Morgan said.

Duvall shut the safe door, turned the dead bolt lever before he stood, and straightened the front of his coat. "I'm going to keep these Pinkertons around from here on out."

"Is that so?"

"And the army has promised to stay for a few more days. You'll stay in charge of policing the camp, but don't think about arguing against my decision."

Morgan never got a chance to argue, for at that moment a whore known as Rat Tooth Alice came charging into the room. Rat Tooth always looked sickly and spent, but she must have come in a run, for she was panting heavily. She took a moment with her hands on her hips, bent over at the waist slightly, and her two buck teeth hanging out over her bottom lip.

"Red Molly said for you to come," Rat Tooth finally managed to gasp.

"Is she all right?"

"She's fine, but she said to come quick."

Morgan gave the Pinkertons orders to break up in shifts and to keep at least half of them in the office or outside the door at all times. Some of them seemed to want to talk to him about what had happened to Sid, but he ignored their hard looks for later.

Dixie followed him at a trot down the street to a tent behind the Bullhorn Palace, and they found Doc Chillingsworth standing inside the door. Red Molly was sitting on a stool beside her bed where lay a younger woman covered to her chin with a sheet. The young whore's face made it plain to see that she was in pitiful shape and had been beaten badly. One eye was swollen into a blue plum, the other eye bloodshot, and her lips were split so deep they could have been cut with a knife. She stared out of that one open eye at the ceiling, and Morgan couldn't tell if she knew they were in the room.

"What happened to her?" he asked.

"One of Ruby Ann's customers got rough with her, but she won't say who did it," Molly said while she took up a wet rag and bathed the woman's face.

"When did it happen?"

"Last night, I guess. Some of the railroad men found her lying in the woods on the way to work this morning. The poor thing must have lain out there suffering all night."

"Who was she with last night?"

"I talked to the rest of the girls and they said she left the saloon alone about midnight, and the talk in camp for the last week was about her wearing a new dress and sporting a fancy necklace," Molly said. "Seems she has found a special customer. Candy man."

"How bad is she hurt?"

Molly rolled down the sheet far enough for a bit of the beaten woman's bare collarbones and the crease of her breasts to show. Two little red circles of raw flesh dotted her skin.

"Burns," Molly said. "The bastard burned her with his cigar."

"She has a broken arm, maybe some busted ribs, and her . . . well her . . . her female parts . . ." Chillingsworth said.

"He means her quim is all torn up," Molly said.

The beaten whore's right arm was folded against her chest in a makeshift sling, but her other hand dangled out from under the sheet. Morgan lifted it gently and studied the rope burn marks encircling it.

"Tied her up," Chillingsworth added.

"Isn't Ruby Ann one of Tuck's girls?" Morgan asked.

Red Molly shook her head. "No, she works for Sugar Alice. I know what you're thinking, but Tuck wouldn't hurt his merchandise, even if she were his. He might rough her up for holding out on him, or such like, but not like this. Alice is the same. Whoever did this is pure evil."

Morgan stood and looked out the door into the street.

"Morgan," Molly said before he could go. "You get this bastard."

Dixie was waiting for Morgan outside, having remained there peering into the tent and listening to the conversation. "This country sure is hell on women."

Morgan rubbed the whisker stubble on one cheek. "Ask around about who Ruby Ann has been seen with."

"Will do. And maybe she'll talk after she's had time to think on it."

"Have you asked yourself why she hasn't said who it is?"

"Shock, maybe. I don't know."

"Maybe, or maybe she's afraid to talk."

"Afraid? Half the camp would line up and fight over who got to put the noose over the son of a bitch's head for doing that to her. There ain't many women to go around, and Ruby Ann was a good sort."

"Why didn't he kill her?" Morgan asked. "He's taking an awful risk doing that to her and letting her live."

"You're right. That's something to think on."

Morgan took the stub of a cigar and shoved it angrily in the corner of his mouth. He tried to strike a match on the tent pole, but only succeeded in breaking it in two. A second match resulted in the same failure. He threw the second broken match away and left the cigar unlit, chewing on it methodically and staring down the street.

"You look like you want to cuss," Dixie said. "It's always

been my opinion that a man that won't cuss is liable to explode holding down what's inside him. Cussing's the best tonic in the world when you feel like you want to bite a railroad iron in two."

"They say Ruby Ann had a special customer. Who in this town sells dresses or women's jewelry?" Morgan finally asked after a long moment of silence.

"Nobody," Dixie answered.

Morgan went back inside the tent and soon returned with a thin silver chain with a single pearl pendant belonging to Ruby Ann clutched in his hand. He tucked the necklace in his vest pocket. "Let's go ask around."

They walked side by side, and hadn't gone far when Dixie jerked a thumb at the far side of the street. "You see what I see?"

It took Morgan a moment to pick out what Dixie was referring to, but he followed the direction of Dixie's gaze to the big oak east of the Bullhorn Palace that served as the spit-and-whittle gathering point in camp. A long bench and a few stools and chairs were always left under that tree for anyone wanting to swap stories of an evening or for the less industrious sorts to while part of an afternoon away.

Bill Tuck and one of Texas George's two brothers were sitting under the tree, and the other Kingman brother was up on his feet talking to two strangers on horses. Both mounted men were wearing pale canvas dusters that covered them from their necks to their calves. One of them had a short-barreled shotgun laid across his lap and was keeping a careful watch on his surroundings—a man on the dodge if Morgan had ever seen one.

"Recognize those two men on the horses?" Morgan asked.

"No, but not many honest men ride around with three or four pistols tied on their saddle swells," Dixie said.

"What do you make of it?"

Dixie worked his chaw around to the other side of his cheek, spat a long, thick stream of tobacco juice, and squinted at the men under the tree like he was sighting a rifle. "I'd say they're having themselves a meeting, and that the Kingman brothers and Tuck might be making some kind of deal with those fellows."

CHAPTER NINETEEN

Morgan wiped the worst of the mud from his boots and stepped into Duvall's private train car, closing the door behind him. The lower walls of the modified passenger car were wainscoted with raised mahogany panels and everything above that covered in pale blue, diamond-checked wallpaper. The long row of windows along each side of the car were framed by burnt red curtains with gold tassels dangling from their edges, giving the room the feeling of a French parlor. Duvall sat waiting on a couch at the far end of the room with one leg crossed over the other and holding a glass of brandy, the closed door of his sleeping quarters directly behind him.

"What do you think of my little home away from home?" Duvall swirled the glass of brandy under his nose while he watched Morgan take in the room.

"You seem to be a man who likes the comforts of life," Morgan said.

Duvall gestured at the decanter of brandy and a set of crystal glasses on the desk between him and Morgan in the center of the room. "Pour yourself a drink and have a seat. We need to talk."

Morgan ignored the liquor and went past the desk and took a seat in a high-backed chair facing the superintendent. He rested one ankle atop the knee of his other leg and removed his hat and laid it in his lap. A glob of mud from his upheld boot fell onto the carpet.

"You sent for me," Morgan said.

"Straight to business, as always." Duvall set his half-finished brandy on the end table beside him, as if the removal of such social niceties marked the beginning of serious conversation. "My foreman assures me that the river will be spanned by the end of the next week at the latest."

"You didn't bring me here to tell me what I already know."

"No, I brought you here to tell you that there will soon be several very important visitors to this camp. Nine days from now, to be exact."

"What kind of visitors?"

"The Secretary of the Interior for one, various politicians, members of the press, along with a group of shareholders," Duvall said. "They come to christen the bridge upon its completion, and to get a feel for the progress of the railroad in general."

"I'm sure they'll be impressed." Morgan flexed his foot in the boot propped atop his knee, and another flake of mud fell on the carpet.

Duvall cleared his throat before speaking again. "Perhaps you don't understand the situation we're in. We have incurred unexpected difficulties lately that have, let us say, displeased certain people."

"You're behind schedule with construction, and Congress has taken away those alternate sections of right of way. Your projected profits are way down without the potential land sales, building costs are more than expected, and the shareholders are breathing down your neck."

"That would be an indelicate and blunt way of putting it, but yes."

"And if you don't get this railroad across the river, those very same shareholders are going to replace you with another superintendent."

"You seem informed."

"I'm only repeating what the newspapers are saying, and the same thing that is being bandied about all over this camp."

Duvall stood and went to a map laid out across the desk. Morgan followed him there and looked down to where the superintendent traced a pointer finger over the line of tracks laid thus far.

"We were laying two and a half miles of track a day, and three on a good day," Duvall said. "Until we stalled out here."

Morgan rethought his earlier reluctance to partake of Duvall's brandy, and poured himself a glass. "And time is money."

"Exactly." Duvall hit the desktop with the same finger. "I'm only a fifteen percent shareholder, Mr. Clyde. There is a certain faction within the MK&T board of directors that would gladly see me go, and several men who would like to have my job."

"I don't have a thing to do with laying your tracks," Morgan said.

"But it's your job to see to it that this camp is peaceful and industrious to all appearances when my guests arrive."

"I'm doing my best." Morgan turned up the brandy and finished it in a single swallow.

"That brandy is meant to be savored and enjoyed, and not downed like common tavern swill."

Morgan raked back his hair with his fingers and settled his hat on his head. He poured another glass and made a slight salute with the glass to Duvall. "One for the road."

He downed the second glass of brandy as he had the first, and set the empty glass carefully on the desk.

"I think you have been too long out here on the frontier, Mr. Clyde. It has made a boor of you." Duvall took a delicate sip of his own brandy. "But nevertheless, I did not hire you for your social graces. A tribal delegation will arrive at about the same time as our other guests. Along with the Creeks, there will be representatives from the Choctaws, whose land we will be crossing from the South Canadian all the way to the Red. While I am highly concerned with keeping the Choctaws happy, especially given the rumors of viable coal fields in the heart of their reservation, I am more concerned with the payment owed them and the Creeks currently residing in my office safe."

"Wondered why you were keeping so much extra money on hand," Morgan said. "There was more than thirty thousand in that payroll shipment we brought in, wasn't there?"

"A lot more. In addition to the payroll, there was another fifty thousand dollars meant for the Choctaws and Creeks. In order to gain the tribes' approval for construction and the right of way grant, we contracted with them and with certain of their leaders to supply ties and firewood for our engines, and horses and mules and food for my workers."

"Bought off the Indians, and gave bribes and kickbacks to those among them that wouldn't sell cheap."

Duvall frowned, but continued. "The payment for those services has yet to be made. Failure to make that payment would be most injurious to my railroad's cause."

"You should have made payment in Kansas City or elsewhere, and not brought that much money here."

"The Indians wanted it delivered in coin. They were most stubborn about that, much to my chagrin, as you can imagine."

"We need to strengthen the guard on that money."

Duvall gave a dismissive wave of his hand. "Make what preparations you feel you must."

Morgan went to the door, but stopped with his hand upon it. He turned and pulled Ruby Ann's necklace from his vest pocket. He held it dangling at eye level where Duvall could get a good look at it.

Duvall gave the jewelry a peremptory glance, as if unimpressed, his expression showing nothing other than disdain and boredom. "What's that?"

"It belongs to Ruby Ann, one of Tuck's girls. Somebody beat her badly night before last."

"I hope you catch the scoundrel. I surmise that such travesties are heartrending but common occurrence for a woman in her trade, but that makes it no less sad."

"The rumor is, Ruby Ann had herself a man she was seeing on the side. He bought her this."

Duvall straightened and his face went cold. "Up until this point, Mr. Clyde, I'll give you the benefit of the doubt that you are only doing your duty as a policeman, and that you have been asking everyone else in camp the same questions."

"I've asked around."

"Very well then, I'm telling you without question that I have never met Miss Ruby Ann, nor if I were to associate with such a woman of ill repute would it be with the haggard, homely dregs of womanhood that satisfy the men of this camp."

"It's fake," Morgan said.

"What?"

"The pearl isn't real," Morgan said. "Just a cheap trinket made to look like something expensive and to impress a girl that might not know the difference."

"So?"

Morgan shrugged. "Selling fake gems and jewelry is an old con of Dr. Sam's to supplement his snake oil profits. He said it was one of your men that he sold it to."

"Which of my men?"

"Your grading foreman, the one they call Tubbs. That's why I'm showing you this. Thought you might know his whereabouts."

"I let Tubbs go when we suspended construction south of the river until the bridge was done," Duvall replied. "I haven't seen him in a good while."

Morgan nodded. "Nobody else has seen him, either. Not for

at least a week. This Tubbs, how did he strike you?"

"Do you mean is he the kind to beat a whore? He's a most disagreeable man, and with a penchant for the bottle. I was already considering firing him before our recent construction delays."

"Let me know if you get wind of where he's at."

"I assure you I will. Hanging is almost too good for him if he is indeed the guilty party."

Morgan tucked the necklace back in his pocket and went out the door, closing it gently behind him. Dixie was waiting at the foot of the steps.

"What did he want?" Dixie asked.

"Good news and bad news."

"Give me the good news first."

"There's fifty thousand dollars left in that office safe meant for payment to the Indians. He expects us to make sure nobody gets off with his loot before the Indians show up to take it."

"I can hardly wait to hear what you call the bad news," Dixie said. "Shoot it to me straight and don't hold back. I can take it, no matter how bad it gets."

"A trainload of politicians and government men are coming here."

Dixie unpinned the badge on his shirt and offered it to Morgan, unable to keep a grin from spreading. "That's it, I quit."

CHAPTER TWENTY

Morgan had the Gatling gun set up in a sandbag position to one side of the office door, and the soldiers split into three eight-hour guard shifts. Two Pinkertons were posted inside in the office with the safe, while the rest of the hired security took up residence in a tent across the tracks in order to be ready at hand should they be needed.

"What do you think of the setup?" Morgan asked Dixie from where they stood in front of the office.

Dixie studied the Gatling gun behind the waist-high sandbag wall. "You're certainly going whole hog, but I don't know what use that coffee grinder will be in a camp full of bystanders."

"Coffee grinder?"

"You know . . ." Dixie pointed to the Gatling and made a cranking motion with one hand to indicate the crank-handle firing mechanism.

"That Gatling is more for show, and to let anybody with bad intentions know we're serious."

"When are Duvall's guests supposed to arrive?"

"Eight days from now, next Thursday."

Dixie pointed to the white canvas of a large tent that had only been raised an hour earlier by some MK&T workers. "Duvall's going all out. I saw those boys carrying fancy furniture and some oriental rugs inside that tent a bit ago. Imagine a tent outfitted like that."

"Like I said, it's politicians and government sorts. Duvall

probably figures they won't be used to roughing it."

"Politicians," Dixie scoffed. "Well, we've got killers, thieves, and women beaters in camp. Some politicians should round things out."

"Anything new on who Ruby Ann might have been seeing?" Morgan asked.

"Whoever she was seeing, she did a good job of doing it on the quiet."

"How was she keeping it a secret in a camp this size?"

"They found her in the woods. Maybe that was where she was meeting him."

"Maybe. Any word on the Tubbs fellow?"

"Nobody has seen him. They say he hung around here for a good while after Duvall let him go, but the general assumption is that he must have finally run out of money and lit out for other parts."

"How about the girls? Any of them have dealings with him?"

"What do you think? He likes girls, but no more than most of this camp."

"Any of the girls say he got rough with them?"

"Nothing out of the ordinary." Dixie pointed across the tracks. "Speaking of women."

Morgan watched Lottie Bickford coming their way. She walked fast for a heavy woman, and her pace always made it appear that she was charging forth on some kind of mission. She lifted her long dress enough to cross the tracks and soon stopped in front of them, breathing a little heavily. She took in the security preparations going on around the railroad office with a disapproving scowl. "Mr. Clyde, I was wondering if you could help me."

"What can I do for you?"

"It's my Hank." She paused, mincing over her words as if she was reluctant to say what she needed to say. "He didn't come home last night."

"Did you two have a fight?"

"No, not at all."

Morgan rubbed his chin thoughtfully, surmising that there was more to the story than she had as yet said. "Have you been to the blacksmith shop?"

"I'm told that he is in the Bullhorn Palace, and has been there since last night." She cleared her throat and stood a little straighter. "My Hank is a good man, but he is occasionally given to imbibing intoxicating spirits."

"You're telling me he has fallen off the wagon?"

"His weakness for such is a cross to bear handed down to him by his late father, who was a drunken sot and a sorry excuse for a Christian man if there ever lived one. Hank's bouts with the tonic don't come often, but he can be days on one of his binges. I would greatly appreciate it if you would save me the embarrassment of going into such a place myself to retrieve him."

"I'll talk to him."

"I'd appreciate it. Tell him that his wife and children need him home." Lottie gathered her dress and left, going at the same pace as she had arrived, with her head bowed as if to a headwind and her broad hips swaying like a caboose.

Morgan turned to Dixie when she was gone. "I'll try to find Hank. Why don't you sashay down to the horse pens and make sure those watchmen are on the job, so that we don't end up chasing more horse thieves."

"Will do, Chief."

"You ought to think about buying yourself a new hat. That cap of yours looks like something the dogs drug up."

Dixie touched the Johnny Reb forage cap on his head and tried to feign insult and shock, and his answer was performed in a stuffy imitation of an effeminate southern gentleman with a lisp. "Why, is it this fine gentleman's cap that you're referring to? Surely, sir, you must jest. I wouldn't think of ridding myself of the latest in fashionable, gentleman's headwear. And besides, it's pure imitation wool, bought on government contract with strict demands as to quality from the cheapest contract bidder by the late, great Confederate States of America."

"Suit yourself."

"I will, sir." Dixie cocked the cap to one side of his head at a jaunty angle, and headed for the stock corrals, nodding at everyone he met on his way in a dapper fashion as if he were some kind of gent out for an afternoon stroll.

Morgan laughed and headed in the opposite direction. He was at the door to the Bullhorn Palace when he noticed that the same puny zebra dun horse that he had seen earlier in the week was tied in front of Irish Dave's saloon across the street. The Whitworth rifle was still lashed under a saddle fender. He took a last glance at the horse before he went inside the Bullhorn.

He found Hank Bickford slumped over an empty beer mug at the bar. Bill Tuck was at the far end of the bar talking to a pair of men, but he noticed Morgan's entrance and nodded at Hank and shook his head as if to say someone needed to get him out of the saloon.

"Hello, Hank." Morgan settled in beside the little blacksmith at the bar.

"What do you want?" Hank's breath reeked of alcohol, and his eyes were bloodshot and he had trouble focusing.

"Lottie needs you home."

Hank shoved the empty mug away and gestured to Tuck for another one.

Tuck stayed where he was. "I've told you twice today that there won't be any more drinks on credit. Go home like Chief Clyde says."

Hank gave Tuck a dirty look, but turned his attention back to

Morgan with a friendly grin on his drunken face.

"Let's you and me get us a bottle and go down to the river and catch us a catfish," Hank said. "All that rain lately ought to have them biting." Hank gave Morgan a conspiratorial wink.

"You're not making any sense, Hank. Let's get you out of here."

Morgan put a gentle hand on Hank's shoulder, but Hank shook him off.

"I ain't going nowhere with you. That Lottie put you up to this, didn't she? Never will let a man have any fun."

"She's only worried about you. How long has it been since you went to work?"

Hank's face sobered a little bit. "A day, or maybe two."

"I'll talk to McDaniels about it. You're a good blacksmith, and I bet he'll cut you some slack."

"I don't need your help."

"You're sloppy drunk, Hank. It's time you go home and sleep it off." Morgan took hold of Hank's arm and gently got him to his feet.

"Laughing at me, ain't you?" Hank slurred.

"I'm not laughing."

Hank let Morgan guide him out the door. "You wouldn't be laughing if you knew what I know."

"What's that?" It was all Morgan could do to keep the staggering man on his feet and moving down the edge of the street.

"I had to go down to the trestle to do some work for Mc-Daniels. Saw a man with a rifle on that grassy hill at the foot of the mountain across the river. Looked like he was watching the trail and waiting for someone to come by so he could kill them."

"That's the way," Morgan said. "Keep walking. It isn't far to your tent now."

"You don't believe me?" Hank slurred and tried to jerk free of Morgan's grasp. In doing so he almost fell, and they had to stop to get him righted again. "You think I'm talking foolishness."

"I think you're tired. That's all."

Hank glared up at Morgan. "I've seen that man on the hill before, up in Missouri."

Morgan decided that the only way to get Hank moving again was to act interested in his ravings. "Who was he?"

"Don't know his name, but I know what folks call him. It was the Arkansas Traveler."

"You're drunk."

"I wasn't drunk when I saw him."

"Are you sure it was him?"

Hank, dead drunk or not, recognized the sharpness in Morgan's voice and the immediate interest where formerly there had been none. "Got your attention, now, don't I?"

"I asked if you were sure."

"Somebody wants someone dead in a bad way if they've hired the Traveler," Hank said.

"What kind of horse was he riding?"

Hank shoved free of Morgan and staggered the last several yards to his tent. Lottie met him at the door and took ahold of him, casting a grateful but embarrassed glance at Morgan before she turned away.

Hank seemed to have forgotten about the story he was telling, but at the last moment as she led him inside the tent he twisted and said over his shoulder, "He rides a zebra dun."

Morgan headed up the street in the direction of the Bucket of Blood. But when he got there the dun horse was gone.

CHAPTER TWENTY-ONE

A storm front blew up right after sundown; the wind whipping through the cracks in the boxcar door made the lantern in the middle of the table between them flicker, and the tiny flame hissed as if it were whispering stories of its own. Morgan leaned back in his chair and waited for Dixie to reply to what he had told him.

"How could he be sure it was the Traveler?" Dixie asked.

"Hank wasn't making much sense, but he swore it was him."

Dixie reached for the whiskey bottle beside the flickering lantern, as if he needed another belt upon hearing the news. "They say he notched his rifle for two Yankee generals and a captain at Gettysburg alone. I don't know if it was true, but us Southern boys believed the story about General Meade himself offering five hundred dollars to the man that could take down the Traveler."

"Old Death," Morgan said absentmindedly.

"What?"

"Old Death, that's what we called him."

The gaze Morgan put on Dixie was more than a little glassy with the whiskey he had consumed since they sat down together. The rain outside was coming down in bucketsful, beating on the roof of the boxcar like a drum.

"I guess a man like that might get hooked on hunting men for sport," Dixie added. "A thousand dollars a head, that's what he's supposed to get if you hire him to kill a man."

"There's a lot of talk around a man like him. Hard to tell truth from made-up stories."

"You don't seem too awful excited about a known drygulcher for hire being seen outside camp." Dixie raised his voice as if he needed to wake Morgan up.

"It doesn't change anything." Morgan straightened in his chair and tapped the rim of the whiskey glass with a forefinger thoughtfully.

"You know how you can tell when the Arkansas Traveler does a killing?" Dixie asked. "He sticks a feather up the nose of every one of his victims. Always works from long range with a rifle. Moves like an Indian. Sets up an ambush, does the deed, and then he's gone."

"What's he look like?"

"What's a damned ghost look like?" Dixie asked. "Some say he's short and bald, and some that he's tall with long yellow hair that he braids like an Indian. The only thing all the stories agree on is that the Traveler is an Arkansawyer, and that he can shoot like no man alive."

"I think I'll catch some shut-eye." Morgan went to his cot.

"You're awful damned calm, considering how many enemies you have, and now the Traveler might be wanting your hide pinned up on a barn door. If I didn't know better I would think you didn't care if you were dead or alive."

Morgan lay down and pulled the blanket over him. "Been that before."

"You've been what?"

Morgan rolled over with his back to Dixie and his face against the wall. He mumbled something that was said too quiet to hear or that was muffled by the blankets.

"What's that? You've been what?"

"Dead."

The sound of Morgan's deep, slow breathing said that he was asleep before Dixie could ask anything else.

When Dixie awoke the next morning Morgan was sitting at the table again working on a rifle. Beside the gun was the leather case that was usually propped in the corner of the boxcar next to Morgan's cot. Dixie rose up on one elbow on his cot, curious about the rifle. He had never seen it out of the case before, yet something about the way Morgan always checked to make sure it was still there upon returning to the boxcar made him think that it was dear to the man.

The rifle wasn't one of the new cartridge guns like a Spencer or a Henry, nor was it even a breechloader like a Sharps or a Remington. It was an old-fashioned muzzleloader, but like no muzzleloader Dixie had seen before. It was obviously some kind of target rifle, for the octagonal barrel was so fat that there was room only for a thin slab of a forearm beneath it, and so heavy that no man would have chosen to carry it very far. Mounted atop the barrel and running the length of it was a steel-tubed telescopic sight with adjusters built into the mounting rings, and the buttstock was made of burled walnut oiled to a dark, rich sheen.

"What kind of rifle is that?" Dixie asked.

Morgan looked up from where he was rubbing gun oil into the rust-browned steel. "It's a R.R. Moore bench rifle."

"Looks expensive."

"It was."

"What do you use it for?"

"I bought it for target shooting."

"Target shooting?"

"Some of my associates and I used to shoot for prizes. I bought the gun for those competitions."

"Associates? You weren't always a poor lawman, were you?"

"They'll tell you that money's hard to come by, but what they forget to tell you is that it can be just as hard to hang on to." Morgan unthreaded the nipple cap above the side lock and held it up to the lamplight to look through it and to check it for corrosion or obstructions. "One of the deals when Colonel Berdan was first recruiting sharpshooters was that a man brought his own rifle to try out. There were more than a few of us that shot competitively or were noted sportsmen."

"Was it true that you had to put ten offhand shots into a five-inch circle at two hundred yards to qualify for his regiment?"

"Not offhand. A man could take whatever position he wanted, and we took men into the companies later that didn't have to pass the qualifying test."

"I've never shot a gun with one of those telescopic sights on it," Dixie said.

Morgan handed the rifle to him, and Dixie went to the door and opened it a crack where he could sight the rifle out it into the morning light. He hefted the heavy rifle, snuggled the curled, target-style, Schuetzen buttplate against his shoulder, and peered through the sight tube. A hair-fine set of crosshairs bracketed whatever he aimed at, and the magnification surprised him.

"That's a twenty-power Malcolm sight," Morgan said, seeing his reaction.

"Got to get your cheek just right on the stock to get it in focus, don't you?"

"Yes, and there's a focusing ring on the tube."

"How far did you ever shoot with this and hit anything?"

"I haven't shot it since the war, but a lot of craftsmanship went into the making of it. Maybe that's why I've kept it."

"Some things are hard to let go of." Dixie's tone implied more than he said, and he watched Morgan closely to see how he would take that.

Morgan began to put the rifle's cleaning supplies and accessories back in the case. "Sounds like the rain has let up."

Dixie took another glance out the door, frowning. "Yep, but it's sleeting now."

Morgan took the rifle from him and cased it, then placed it in its usual corner beside his bed. He tugged into his red wool coat, turned up the collar, and tugged his hat far down on his head. "Think I'll go make a round."

"I surely do admire that coat," Dixie said.

Morgan opened the boxcar door farther, but hesitated as if dreading going out into the chilly morning. The temperature had plunged overnight and was obviously hovering around the freezing mark. The precipitation was a mix of drizzling rain and sleet. The outside of the boxcar was coated in a thin sheet of ice, and the tiny ice pellets stung Morgan's exposed skin.

"Does your taking out that rifle got anything to do with the Traveler's appearance?" Dixie said before Morgan could leave.

"Maybe. He brings back a lot of memories I'd as soon as forget." Morgan stepped to the ground and slid the boxcar door shut. His footsteps crunching over the sleet-covered ground slowly faded out of hearing.

CHAPTER TWENTY-TWO

Morgan caught a ride on a flatcar load of workers headed out to the bridge site. The mixed weather had turned to pure blowing sleet, but that didn't stop the work. He hunched alongside the other men, nobody saying anything and keeping their chins tucked into their collars against the cold. Hope McDaniels, the engineer, was already on the job, standing on the north bank in front of his bridge. When he saw Morgan climb off the flatcar he pointed proudly at his almost completed trestle rising above the river waters.

"Give me five more days, and you'll see the first engine roll across her," McDaniels said.

Morgan eyed the sky, squinting against the sleet. "Better hope the river doesn't get up again."

The engineer frowned at the same sky. "This weather here, I've never seen anything like it since I left Scotland. One day it's hot and the next day it's freezing. Yesterday I was counting the new buds on the trees and admiring a bit of green here and there, and now I'm standing in this."

Morgan plucked a bit of sleet from his mustache. "I'm ready for this weather to break, myself."

"You didn't come all the way down here to talk to me about the weather."

"I'm looking for a man named Tubbs. I understand he was the grading foreman for a while."

"He was until this river held us up."

"How come he wasn't put on your bridge crew? I would think the railroad would want to keep around a man they thought enough of to make a foreman."

"Not on my crew. I can tell you never met Tubbs. A most disagreeable man. I never did see what Mr. Duvall saw in him. An odd pair if you ask me."

"I want to question him about a girl that was beaten."

"I heard about that. Tubbs was hanging around camp the last time I saw him, and keeping himself in pocket money by running errands and doing odds job for Mr. Duvall."

"He seems to have left camp since then."

"Well, if he did, he's come back. I saw him early this morning riding his horse along the river."

Morgan walked the tracks back to camp. It was a cold walk, and the soldiers in the gun pit nodded at Morgan begrudgingly as he passed by them and went into the office, no doubt wishing it were them going inside to a hot stove. The six Pinkertons lounging in the front room said nothing to him.

Duvall was at his desk in the back room and he looked up from his paperwork at the sound of Morgan's boots on the floor, first at Morgan, and then through the open door into the front room at the Pinkertons glaring at Morgan's back. "You didn't tell me what you did to Sid."

"You didn't ask," Morgan said.

"That man was in my employ."

"That man was a troublemaker."

"You pushed him off a going train."

"I pushed him gently, if that helps you."

Duvall seemed about to explode, but took a deep breath and changed the subject. "McDaniels tells me that one of his best workers was injured in a knife fight last night."

"That's partially true," Morgan replied.

"What have you done about that?"

"He was the one that pulled the knife. He and one of the Italians got too much whiskey in them and hooked up pretty good, but I broke them up and sent them to their tents. Nobody got cut."

"Well, Hope's man didn't make it to work this morning."

"He was probably too hung over to work."

"I expect you to get this camp under control. You're spread too thin. I want you to take some of the Pinkertons on patrol tonight."

"If that's the way you want to play it."

Duvall was shocked that Morgan agreed so easily, but he quickly recovered. "I'm glad you've changed your mind about some help, and I trust you won't throw any more of them off a train."

Morgan returned to the front room. He studied the Pinkertons around him, and then pointed out four of them. "Come with me."

"We work for the superintendent." The one that spoke was a broad man in a beaver coat and a chin like the end of a two-by-four. A wool cap was cocked over at a rakish angle on his square head, the cocky set of it matching the man's demeanor. His Dublin accent was thick and hard to understand.

"You work for Chief Clyde now," Duvall called through the doorway.

"Maybe he's yer man, but this poxy maggot gobsmacked Sid and threw him off the train, and Sid was me sham," the Irish Pinkerton said. "Me and my blokes here are more 'n a bit langered about that bit o' business, and would give him a puck or two upside the noggin and put the toes of our Wellies to his rib bones before we would work for him."

Morgan noticed the scars on the man's eyebrows and cheekbones, and the crooked knot of a nose that had been broken more than once. He probably wasn't long off a ship from the old country. New York, Boston, and many other ports on the eastern seaboard were full of such men. The most brutal of them found jobs working as strong arms for the bosses and crooks who ran one racket or another and needed men who weren't afraid to hurt people. He was two inches shorter than Morgan, but a good twenty pounds heavier. And he carried himself with the confidence of a man that had won many a fight.

Dixie came through the door, ducking in out of the wind and closing it quickly behind him. He took quick measure of the room and the way the Pinkertons were looking at Morgan and leaned back against the front wall with his Spencer tucked under one armpit and resting his forearm.

"Trouble, Chief?"

Morgan looked at Dixie, and then at the Pinkerton standing before him. "No trouble."

The Pinkerton smiled, revealing a missing front tooth. "Bend your stalk up your own arse and go feck yourself."

"Are you the toughest?" Morgan asked quietly.

The Pinkerton cocked his head. "Eh?"

"I asked are you the toughest one of these men. I'm assuming that you are."

The Irishman made a charge at Morgan, but Morgan took up the cast-iron firewood poker from the ash bucket beside the potbellied stove beside him. He swung the poker in what appeared an almost negligent backhand stroke, and the end of it clipped the Irishman on the point of the chin and knocked him staggering. A curse of rage and pain gusted from the Irishman's lungs, but Morgan was already bringing the heavy poker down like a tomahawk for a second lick. The improvised weapon met the crown of the Pinkerton's skull, and he dropped in a heap at Morgan's feet.

Morgan made a few air strokes and then a flashy, quick

riposte with the poker as if it were a sword and then brought it to his chest in some kind of formal salute. He gave Dixie a quick glance and shrug of his shoulders. "Fencing Club, Yale class of '52."

"Oh, you dashing, manly devil," Dixie said in his most bland and stuffy imitation of an affluent, New England gentleman.

Morgan set the improvised weapon back in the ash bucket. "Anybody else a friend of Sid's?"

Apparently, none of the other Pinkertons had been fond of Sid, or if they were, nobody was going to say it. Instead, they made a show of watching the trickle of blood oozing out of their fallen comrade's head and leaking onto the floor to mix with the drool running out of one corner of his slack mouth.

"My God," Duvall said from his office. "You, sir, are out of control. Simply because you represent the law does not make you above the law."

Morgan pointed at the other Pinkertons lining the wall. "Any man of you that can't see fit to work for me can draw his pay right now. I don't think much of your damned agency, but Dixie and I could use some help."

The other Pinkertons continued to stare at the Irishman on the floor.

"All right, now that that's settled, let's be about our business." Morgan beckoned the other three men he had originally picked. "The rest of you haul this man over to Doc Chillingsworth and tell him that he bumped his head. Then you get back here on guard."

Three of the Pinkertons followed Morgan and Dixie out of the office, while those remaining tried to get the fallen Irishman to his feet. Once outside, Morgan crossed the head of the street to the company store and led them inside to the hardware section at the back end of the tent. He pointed at a barrel containing axe, sledge, and pick handles.

"Get one." Morgan drew out a pick handle, and stood patting the pale white hardwood stick in one palm while he watched each of the men in turn choose their own clubs. "You men know the rules, and if you don't, make them up as best you can or come find me. The number of people in camp has doubled in the last two days, and we know that most of them have nothing to do with the railroad. Some of them are just innocent men passing through or looking for work. The rest of them? Well, there's our trouble."

The men around Morgan nodded grimly.

"We go easy where we can. Take them quietly if they'll let you, but if any man bucks the law he gets Old Hickory upside his head. You understand that? No guns unless you have to. Know the difference between a harmless drunk and a man looking for trouble. Be courteous but firm."

All three of the Pinkertons mumbled their understanding.

"Good. I want two of you to take this side of the street with Dixie. You there, I'll take you with me and work the Bullhorn's side of the street. Any questions?"

There were none. Morgan went out of the tent, saying nothing to the storekeeper chasing after them wanting payment for the handles the men had taken. Two of the Pinkertons stopped to face the storekeeper.

"Police business," one of them said. "Chief Clyde's orders."

The storekeeper appeared very upset at his goods being taken, but he wasn't dumb, nor was he foolishly brave. He quickly decided that he had business elsewhere in the store. Outside, Dixie started a slow walk down that side of the street with his force, while Morgan crossed to the far side trailed by the single Pinkerton he had chosen. People were quick to take notice of the clubs the men were carrying, and gave them wider berth and right of way than usual as they passed. But Morgan smiled at them as if nothing was out of the normal.

The Bullhorn wasn't open for business yet, but Morgan went inside anyway. One of Tuck's bouncers sat on a stool right inside the door, and was the only one in the tent other than a swamper cleaning up the mess from the night before. Morgan was about to turn and leave when Bill Tuck came in through the back door carrying two wooden cases of beer bottles on one shoulder. The saloonkeeper sat the load down with ease on the end of the bar while he took stock of the clubs Morgan and the Pinkerton were carrying.

Tuck wiped his hands with a bar towel and pointed at the pick handle in Morgan's hand. "What's that for?"

"Keeping the peace," Morgan said.

"Funny, with that shillelagh in your hand, you don't look much different from those of us you're supposed to be keeping a lid on," Tuck said. "Maybe the only thing different about you is that you've got that badge to make you official."

Morgan dropped one end of his club to the ground and leaned on it for a rest. "There's going to be more men in camp tomorrow. Duvall's got crews coming for when the bridge is finished and he can start laying track again."

"You didn't come in here to tell me that."

"This railroad is going to move on, whether you want it to or not."

Tuck's face was slowly turning red, but he kept his anger in check. Morgan had to give him that. Tuck was a man of quick temper, but willpower, also—a dangerous combination.

"You didn't used to make so many threats." Tuck's voice held only a slight hint of the strain he was under.

Morgan straightened and hefted the pick handle one-handed again as if weighing it or checking its balance. "Walk the line, Tuck. We're going to bring law and order to this camp if we have to drag it here kicking and screaming."

Morgan and the Pinkerton with him went out the door and

made a slow round down their side of the street and back to stand in front of the Bullhorn again. Morgan hadn't really expected any trouble. The railroad crews were still at work, and the rowdies were recovering from the previous night's celebration. It would be dark before the camp came fully awake again, but it wouldn't hurt for those out and about to see the latest show of force so that they could spread the word.

Dixie waved from the far side of the street. Morgan gave a slow lift of his hand to recognize the signal that all was well, and then turned to the Pinkerton beside him.

"You go tell Dixie that you boys can loaf the rest of the afternoon, but that I want you three at the head of the street and ready to go to work right at sundown," he said. "We'll put one man in each of the saloons, and it might not be a bad idea if we could find some whistles to let each other know if there's trouble."

The Pinkerton nodded his understanding, but made it only halfway across the ice-crusted street before a long line of horsemen came riding two-by-two over the hill to the west. There must have been twenty of them. The soldiers guarding the railroad office were already manning the Gatling gun or taking cover behind their sandbags with their Springfield rifles at ready.

Morgan walked rapidly in the direction of the approaching riders. Dixie and the Pinkertons took the same course, falling in behind Morgan as he reached the train tracks. The riders were almost upon them, and the Pinkerton beside Morgan drew his pistol.

Morgan reached and blocked the man from lifting the gun. "Put that away. Those aren't bushwhackers."

Morgan called to the soldiers and the rest of the Pinkertons to hold off, knowing how on edge they were, and then went out to meet the riders alone. Sergeant Harjo was in the lead of the new arrivals, and when he pulled up his horse in front of Morgan the rest of the party behind him did likewise. Morgan stepped wide of Harjo's horse so that he could get a closer look at the men riding with him. They were all Indians, some young, some not, but all tough-looking men on sound horses and with every man of them with a good rifle in a saddle boot and pistol hung on his hip. All Indians, except for Agent Pickins. Morgan spotted him halfway back in the line sitting on a shaggy white mule.

Harjo did his own appraisal of the guards Morgan had put in place around Duvall's car, and especially at the Gatling gun. "You don't take many chances."

"Some of my men thought you might be marauders," Morgan replied.

Harjo pointed at the man beside him. "This is Colonel Samuel Checote, chief of the Muscogee Creek Nation."

Morgan took in the tall man in a Confederate uniform coat and a broad-brimmed white hat. His dark hair, streaked with gray, was worn shoulder-length, and a wispy-thin mustache and goatee adorned his face above the string tie knotted around his celluloid shirt collar.

Morgan reached up and shook the man's hand. "Morgan Clyde, chief of the railroad police here in Ironhead."

Chief Checote pointed at the soldiers. "Are they guarding our money?"

"Yes," Morgan replied.

Agent Pickins and his white mule pushed their way through the Creek guards and pulled up beside the chief. He didn't so much as nod at Morgan in greeting. Duvall and his clerk arrived on foot, and Duvall immediately invited the chief and Agent Pickins into the railroad office.

One by one, the Creek men at arms began to dismount. From the way they stamped their feet and stretched the kinks out of their muscles once on the ground, Morgan could tell that they had been long in the saddle.

Sergeant Harjo saw Morgan studying the Creek guards. "Councilmen and Lighthorse, all come to help guard our money back to our capital."

"I'll see if I can get a tent put up for you," Morgan said.

Sergeant Harjo shook him off. "No need. We won't be staying. We ride back to Okmulgee as soon as the railroad pays us."

"The weather looks like it might turn bad again. Best wait until this blows over."

"Still worried about those bushwhackers?"

"You ought to be, too." Morgan went on to tell the sergeant of the gang he had seen north of the camp while bringing the payroll south on the train.

Sergeant Harjo looked back at the dismounted men behind him. "Those are the best guns in the whole territory, and we've got more men that are supposed to meet us on our way back. I think we can keep our money safe."

"It still seems a chancy thing to be hauling so much money overland with times being what they are."

Harjo gave a fatalistic shrug. It dawned on Morgan that Sergeant Harjo didn't like it any more than he did, but was only doing as he was told.

"There will be no waiting," Harjo said. "There are many who want to get the money to our council house so that they can argue how it will be spent."

"Bureaucrats arguing over somebody else's money. Sounds familiar."

"We've got our problems, just like you. Colonel Checote used to be chief only of the lower Creeks and he commanded the Creek Mounted Rifles for the Confederacy. Some don't like him becoming the chief of all our people, mostly the Union men, like myself. Some that ride with us are only here because they don't trust him with the money."

"You fought in the war?"

"The war was bad on us. In my grandfather's time we fought other tribes, but it seems the white men have taught us to fight each other. The bad blood left over will be a long time going."

"You keep a sharp lookout on your way back home," Morgan said.

"We'll be all right."

"How's a cup of coffee sound?" Morgan asked.

Sergeant Harjo didn't get to answer, for Colonel Checote came out of Duvall's car and motioned for his men. The Creek tribal council had requested that their payment be made in coin, not trusting to paper money, and Duvall's clerk and four of the soldiers brought over two head-sized cloth bags sagging with the weight of silver and gold coinage from the depot house. The money was transferred to Checote's saddlebags, and the whole Creek party remounted as quickly and quietly as they had arrived, forming up again two-by-two with outriders riding the flanks and with the chief in the middle of the line. Agent Pickins spurred his mule forward and took a place beside Colonel Checote when the party rode off. Sergeant Harjo tipped his hat at Morgan and then wheeled his horse and took a place at the rear of the line.

Morgan headed for his boxcar, and halfway there it started to sleet again. He took one last look at the Creek party and could barely make out the figure of Sergeant Harjo waving at him through the gray haze of the storm.

CHAPTER TWENTY-THREE

It was the next afternoon when Agent Pickins lashed his lathered and spent mule into Ironhead Station and relayed the news that a gang of bushwhackers had attacked the Creek party not fifteen miles outside the camp and stolen the railroad payment. The outlaws had sprung their ambush in a narrow pass between two hills, and several of the Creek guards went down on the first rifle volley from the brush. The bushwhackers then made a wild charge among the Indians, and it was all pistol fighting and hand to hand after that. Agent Pickins was unsure about the details of the fight, but he thought he saw Colonel Checote's horse shot out from under him and one of the Lighthorsemen swoop in and pull him up in the saddle behind him for a getaway. Nor did Pickins know how many of the Creeks survived or if the payroll was saved, and counted it as a major miracle that he had been able to escape the bloodbath unscathed on his slow mule.

Duvall ordered his clerk to send a telegraph north to Fort Gibson informing the troops there of the robbery and requesting assistance to guard his camp. Two hours later he received a reply from the commanding officer that a partial cavalry company would be sent to Ironhead, but that they would be a day or two departing, as they had only recently returned from a long patrol and needed time to outfit and rest their horses.

Duvall called a meeting with Morgan, Agent Pickins, and his engineer, Hope McDaniels, in his private car. A scowling Duvall

215

greeted them one by one as they arrived, pacing the room and only pausing to refill his brandy glass. The rest of them took seats, but Morgan remained standing near the door.

"The Secretary of the Interior will be here in seven days." Duvall stopped his pacing and loosened his string tie and unbuttoned his celluloid collar while he looked from man to man as if daring one of them to contradict the news he delivered.

"The Choctaw payment should be safe with the security measures we have here," McDaniels said.

Duvall whirled on Morgan. "How many people are in camp, not counting my employees?"

"Maybe a hundred, or maybe more."

"That's a hundred men that can make me look like a fool when my guests arrive. And we know that there are more camped out in the brush."

"Camp's been quiet the last few days," Morgan answered.

"I rode by your improvised jail this morning and saw two new men chained up."

"One case of disturbing the peace, and the other man revealed himself to your storekeeper's wife on the street," Morgan said.

"What of the shots fired at my bridge crew this morning?"

"I'm checking into that. It would be like some of the toughs around here to leave camp with a few under their belts and think it funny to pop off their pistols just to see your men scramble."

"I lost two hours of work today because of that shooting."

Morgan struck a match to his cigar, waiting to exhale a cloud of smoke before he answered. "I sent three of the Pinkertons to the bridge to keep an eye on things. They'll camp there around the clock."

Duvall thumped his fist on the desktop before him, and his brandy slopped over the rim of its glass when he jabbed with it for emphasis. "Clyde, I want you to run every saloonkeeper, whore, cardsharp, and the rest of the vagrant rabble out of Ironhead."

"That wouldn't help. You can't stop them from setting up their operations close by," Morgan answered.

"Run them out. If they set up too close by, we'll burn them out. Wait for that cavalry company out of Fort Gibson to back you up if you want to, but get it done." Duvall turned to his engineer. "Hope, how long until my bridge is finished?"

"Two days, or maybe three."

"Perfect. I want our guests nothing but impressed by our industrious achievements, and I'll expect you to be prepared to elaborate to them on what a massive undertaking such a project has been."

"I'll make this railroad sound like building one of the pharaoh's pyramids."

"Good." Duvall turned his back on the room, gazing out an open window at the camp as if studying a battle plan. "I'm sure the newspapers will soon get hold of the news that the Creeks were robbed of their payment."

"You made the payment," McDaniels said.

"Bad press is bad press. In case you haven't noticed, there are several railroad companies that are angry because they weren't the ones to get permission to build across Indian Territory. You don't think they are bending every ear and twisting every event into a so-called failure in an attempt to have the MK&T lose its contract?" Duvall paced half the length of the room again and then back to the desk. "Damned this river and damned your bridge, McDaniels. If you had built right the first time we wouldn't still be here."

McDaniels said nothing, but held Duvall's hard stare without flinching. It was Agent Pickins who finally spoke up.

"When are the Choctaws supposed to show up?" Pickins asked.

"They should be here at about the same time as Secretary Cox and his entourage," Duvall answered. "I suppose you will report to your superiors how fairly I have treated the tribes."

"Fairly?"

Morgan was shocked to see the bold look on Pickins's face, and to hear him challenge the superintendent so. In fact, Pickins was surprisingly snappy and seemed no worse for the wear, considering what he had been through.

"Fairly." Duvall repeated. He turned his back on them again, staring out the open window once more. After a long, awkward wait he said, "That's all. You may leave."

Morgan was the first to go, but McDaniels called out for him before he made it too far.

"A word with you, Mr. Clyde."

Morgan waited for him, not at all liking the concern written all over McDaniels. Whatever it was he was about to tell him, it was bound to be bad news.

"I thought you should know that we're missing three cases of dynamite," McDaniels said when he neared.

"Are you sure you haven't simply misplaced them?"

"Three cases? A man might misplace his pocket watch, but not three cases of dynamite," McDaniels said. "I needed a stick or two to blow a beaver's dam this morning, but couldn't find even that much. We've double-checked the warehouse against the clerk's ledgers, and there is no explanation for the missing explosives, other than that someone has stolen them."

"Have you told Duvall?"

"No. He has enough troubles on his mind without bothering him with such petty problems as missing supplies. As chief of police, I thought I should report thefts to you."

Morgan gave McDaniels a wry smirk. "You don't think this is

a petty problem, or you wouldn't be acting the way you are. And I'm supposing you don't want to be the one to tell Duvall about this."

McDaniels returned a similar wry look. "I couldn't help but ask myself what anyone would want with three cases of dynamite."

"Maybe somebody who would want to blow up a bridge or a safe."

"Unfortunately, that's what I'm thinking," McDaniels said. "It's more than the shady element wanting the camp to stay where it is and for the Territory to stay lawless. A lot of the secesh sorts here see this railroad as nothing but another corrupt, Reconstruction project intended to make a bunch of carpetbagger Yankees rich, and there are those that keep that feeling stirred up. Bill Tuck supposedly bought a round for everyone in the house last night and swore over a toast that it would be a cold day in hell before the Katy makes one more inch of track across the Territory."

"I'll double the Pinkerton guards on the bridge," Morgan replied.

"I'd appreciate that."

Morgan left McDaniels, going over in his mind what the young engineer had told him. It could have simply been someone stealing the dynamite to sell elsewhere, or some of the crew had misplaced it or left it out and didn't want to admit they did. But he didn't really believe that. Things had been too quiet, and he couldn't help the feeling that the whole place was about to explode—explode like three cases of dynamite.

He was still lost in his thoughts when he arrived at his boxcar as the sun was setting. The failing sunlight and his state of mind almost made him miss the piece of white paper stuck between two planks in the sliding door.

Lighting the lamp on the table, he took a seat and unfolded

the piece of paper. The note was written on a badly wrinkled scrap of newspaper, and the penmanship was little more than a childish scrawl with the faint pencil marks hard to decipher amongst the newspaper print.

I did not remember you until I seen you yesterday with my spyglass. You weren't wearing your green uniform coat. Come when you are ready to finish old business.

The Traveler

Morgan refolded the paper and put it in his pocket. *Old business? It couldn't be. After all the years gone by.* His hand unconsciously went to the old wound in his side, and then his head turned towards his rifle leaning in the corner.

CHAPTER TWENTY-FOUR

Dixie found Morgan in the mess tent the next morning barely after daybreak.

"Aren't you going to eat?" Morgan asked between bites of his breakfast.

Dixie shook his head. "Later. You know those Italians that McDaniels has working for him?"

"Don't tell me they're fighting with the Irish again."

"No, one of them came to me a bit ago claiming someone had stolen a ring off his finger."

"We'll check into it." Morgan took a deep breath and exhaled. Petty theft and pickpocket work were becoming all too common in the camp. "I imagine it was a big gold ring with a diamond the size of a bean, according to that Italian."

Dixie laughed. "Why of course, if you believe him. Worth a king's ransom and handed down by his dearest relative. He couldn't understand why I didn't deputize the whole camp and go hunt for his ring right then."

Morgan gave Dixie a measuring look. "Something besides a stolen ring has you stirred up this morning."

Dixie gave him a look back that told he hadn't said all. "Do you remember Sergeant Harjo saying that one of his people had a good chestnut horse stolen not long before we lost those grays?"

"I remember."

"Well, when that Italian quit complaining about his missing

ring he told me the crew saw a man ride past the trestle on the south bank on a good-looking chestnut horse. He also said that that man made camp not far off the tracks on that side of the river."

"Our job is to police this camp and to protect Katy property. As bad as I hate a thief, we've got our hands full here."

"True, but if that's the chestnut Harjo was talking about, the man riding it might have an idea who might have stolen the grays or where they're at. Slim odds, but maybe worth a shot."

"Take a couple of the Pinkertons with you, and be careful."

"Careful is my middle name."

Morgan took his coffee and went to the door of the mess tent facing the street. He leaned against the tent pole there for a long while after Dixie was gone, nursing that coffee and watching the camp. The fog was beginning to lift, and only a few smoky tendrils rose like steam from the muddy street. A flock of ducks flew high overhead, a "V" of faint black dots against the gray sky, and their calls were faint and forlorn in the still morning air.

"I always like this time of mornin'." Saul the cook had come up behind him without him knowing it. "Kind of peaceful, don't you think?"

"Peaceful?" Morgan took a last swallow of coffee and slung the cold dregs at the bottom of his mug into the street. He straightened and adjusted the Remington on his hip and squinted down the street as if he were staring at an old foe, rather than a stretch of mud and a confused jumbled of tents and haphazard structures. "Saul, have you ever seen a den of snakes in wintertime, all sluggish and sleepy so that you would never guess you could get bitten? No? Well give it time, my friend, and she'll show you her fangs."

★ ★ ★ ★ ★

Red Molly glanced both ways down the corridor between the tents behind the Bullhorn Palace to see if she was observed before she wrapped her shawl more tightly about her and took the last few hurried steps to Bill Tuck's tent.

"Are you in there, Bill?" she asked as she stood in place, stamping her feet to keep some warmth in them.

"Don't stand out there in the cold like a fool." Tuck's voice came to her from inside.

She pushed her way through the tent flaps in time to see Tuck uncock the pistol he held and set it aside. He was in his underwear and didn't get up from his cot, but bent over and picked up a piece of firewood on the floor and opened the stove door and shoved it in.

"What do you want?" he asked when he straightened.

"You know what I want." She held out some coins in her closed fist.

"It bothers you to have to come to me, doesn't it?" He didn't take the money she offered.

"What bothers me is how much satisfaction you take in that." She opened her hand to reveal the money.

He looked closely at the hand she stretched out to him, rather than the money it held. "Already got the shakes, don't you? I figured you would be asking me a day or two ago. Trying to cut back?"

"I don't have to buy from you." She closed her fingers around the money again and made as if to draw her hand back.

He grabbed her around the wrist. "And who's going to feed that nasty little habit of yours? Are you going to fake a headache or your monthly female problems and get Doc Chillingsworth to sell you a bottle of laudanum, or maybe hit up that snake oil man? Oh, no, Molly, your hunger has gone long beyond that. Like your stuff straight, don't you?"

Brett Cogburn

"You son of a bitch." She tugged to free her hand, but her effort was half-hearted.

Tuck kept hold of her, but reached under his cot and drug out a small leather satchel. From it he pulled a small, square glass bottle with a cork stopper and held it up to the sunlight spilling through the crack in the tent flaps. He swirled the clear liquid in the bottle before her eyes.

"The stuff of magic, isn't it?" he said.

She snatched at the bottle, and he let her take it from him on the second try. She made as if to hide the bottle behind her shawl, but he pointed at the coffee pot on the stove top.

"Go ahead and mix yourself of cup of morning tonic. You're looking kind of rough, Molly, and it isn't as if I don't know about your little secret."

She pitched the money on his cot, glaring at him. "One of these days you're going to know what it's like to crawl."

He chuckled at that and looked her up and down slowly from head to toe. "What I miss are the days when you weren't so prosperous. There were times when I enjoyed trading my product out for . . . shall we say your wares? Maybe I haven't been charging you enough."

She was halfway out the door when he said, "Use that carefully, dear Molly. Not too much. They say that Chinese flower petal is addictive, and we wouldn't want you forming a nasty habit, would we? I'd hate to see a sweet girl like you turn into a dope whore."

Molly fled away from Tuck's tent faster than she had come, only slowing when she was inside her own tent with the flaps tied shut. She immediately poured herself three fingers of whiskey in a tin cup and added a quick dash of opium from the little square bottle. Her hands were still shaking when she added another dash, and there were tears in her eyes when she lifted the cup with a shaking hand and put it to her lips.

★ ★ ★ ★ ★

Morgan was making a round through the soldiers guarding the depot at lunchtime when he heard someone shouting for him from camp. He rounded the corner at the railroad office and saw a group of men ganged around a saddled horse. When he got closer he saw that it was the shaggy blue roan that Dixie was partial to riding. Immediately little bells began to go off inside his head. The crowd parted and Morgan stepped close to the roan, not wanting to see the blood caking one side of the saddle, but seeing it regardless.

"Come behind me with a wagon," Morgan said as he swung up on the roan.

He left camp in a spray of mud and in a dead run, following the railroad tracks and headed south towards the river. People on the street scattered before him to keep from being run down and wondering why their chief of police had suddenly gone crazy.

The blue roan was lathered and blowing after the long run to the South Canadian, and Morgan pulled up to give him a rest a quarter of a mile upriver from the trestle. He had paused only long enough at the bridge sight for the bridge crew to inform him that they had seen Dixie go upriver instead of downstream towards the ferry. What's more, all of them had heard a rifle shot not long after Dixie went out of sight.

The riverbed was four hundred yards wide west of the bridge site, and most of it nothing but sand dotted here and there with scattered thickets of cedars and willows and sparse dead grass. In the middle of that expanse the river ran in its normal course, almost a hundred yards across and deep.

Cattle going to the river to drink had beaten out a cut in the flood bank, and erosion had widened it. The hoofmarks of Dixie's horse were plain in the bottom of that steep gully leading down to the flat along the water's edge. Morgan nudged his horse down the trail and was halfway down the slope when he spotted Dixie's body lying in the grass downstream of a clump of willows not fifty yards away. It was Morgan's red coat that he was wearing that stuck out in the buckskin-colored grass. Heedless of the steep slope and the tangle of green briars and overhanging branches, Morgan lashed his horse with the tail of his reins and charged down the wash in a spray of sliding dirt. He pulled the running horse hard onto its hindquarters, and bailed from the saddle.

Dixie was lying facedown with one arm stretched before him and the other curled up underneath him. From the drag marks on the ground and the handful of sand clutched in the clawed contraction of his outstretched hand, Morgan could tell that he had crawled several feet before succumbing to his wound. The skid marks where he had drug his body along on his belly were streaked with blood, and the same blood darkened the back of the red coat.

Gently, he rolled Dixie out of the coat and lifted his shirt, noting how the bullet had struck him right below the juncture of his collarbones and exited below the left shoulder blade, leaving a nasty exit wound. Whoever had shot Dixie had done so from a higher elevation. Morgan's eyes immediately went to the flood bank behind him and then to the timber-sided mountain in the distance across the river, wondering if the shooter was even then watching him or aiming at him.

Dixie groaned ever so faintly, and Morgan put one ear close to him. A weak, ragged gasp escaped Dixie's lungs, and his body spasmed.

"I didn't even see him." Bloody froth bubbled between Dixie's lips.

"Who?"

"You know who."

"You damned fool, you were wearing my coat." Morgan

pressed Dixie's shirt hard against the wound front and back, trying to stop the blood steadily percolating out of the bullet holes.

"It's a good coat," was the last thing Dixie said before he went limp again and his breathing became so faint and shallow that Morgan could barely feel the rising and falling of his chest.

The rattle of the wagon coming towards them sounded far away.

CHAPTER TWENTY-FIVE

Doc Chillingsworth met Morgan outside the boxcar late the next morning with his doctor's bag in his hand. His sagging hound-dog eyes were bloodshot and his shirt wrinkled and untucked and showing bloody stains from his all-night vigil.

"How is he?" Morgan asked.

"He's been awake for an hour and asking for you."

"I take it he'll live."

"He's a fortunate man. The bullet entered five inches above his heart, and missed his backbone by a little less. He's got a big, wide hole in him and a shot-up lung, but I think he'll survive, barring any major setbacks," Chillingsworth said. "I, on the other hand, may not survive if I do not get some sleep."

"Thanks, Doc."

"Think nothing of it. You are a man with the reputation for a volatile temper and a propensity for pistol work, Mr. Clyde. I thought it perhaps conducive to my longevity to do my best to help your friend past his crucial hour."

"How's the girl doing? Ruby Ann."

"I had her moved to my tent yesterday for observation. She's going to be awhile healing, but she'll make it."

"Yeah."

"Had any luck finding the man who did that to her?"

"I'm working on it."

"And the man who did this to Dixie?"

Morgan shook his head.

"One thing about the Territory, there's no shortage of work for a medical man." Chillingsworth gave a goodbye tip of his hat brim and waddled his portly frame towards camp.

Morgan slid the door open and climbed up into the boxcar. Dixie was propped up on a set of pillows on his cot with his eyes closed as if he were sleeping. Morgan closed the door, and when he lit the lamp on the table he saw that Dixie was awake and watching him.

Morgan leaned his rifle in the corner and unslung the shot bag from over his shoulder. "Good to see you alive and kicking. Thought you were a goner when I found you."

Dixie looked down at the bandages on his chest, and then at the rifle Morgan had leaned in the corner. "When I asked about you this morning, Doc said you went out at daylight with your rifle. Said people in camp could hear you shooting for an hour like you were practicing. Hell, I could hear the boom of that rifle in here."

"I haven't shot the old gun in a long while, and thought I would check my sight in."

"You're intending on going after him on his own terms, aren't you?"

"Just felt like a little target practice."

"Fetch me a cup of water, won't you? I'm thirsty as all get-out."

Morgan poured a cup of water from a pitcher by the bed while Dixie watched him.

"The shot he made on me had to have been six hundred yards or better." Dixie's voice had faded, the exhaustion getting the best of him. "Had to have been up on that ridge across the river in the timber. He would have had a view of the whole river channel from there."

"You don't know it was him."

"How many men could make a shot like that? Six hundred

229

yards at least, and I was trotting my horse when he hit me."

Morgan handed him the tin cup of water and waited for him to finish it. Dixie's hand shook and slopped a little of the water over the rim of the cup. Morgan had to help him put it to his lips.

"Had to have been him, and you know it," Dixie said when he finished a sip of the water and coughed most of it back up.

"Did I ever tell you that you talk too much?" Morgan asked as he set the cup aside.

Dixie closed his eyes for an instant, but opened them again. "That's about the hundredth time you've said that."

"Well, you might listen for once and get some rest. That's a wicked hole you've got in you."

Dixie looked down at his bandages again. "I guess this is what I get for borrowing your red coat without asking. But maybe you can forgive me, since I took a bullet probably meant for you."

"You can have that coat. I'll see if Lottie Bickford can get the stains out of it," Morgan said. "You bled like a stuck pig."

Dixie sighed and his chest rattled slightly when he did. He waited as if gathering the effort to speak again. "You keep a watch on the skyline. He's out there waiting for a shot at you, and he doesn't miss."

Morgan snuffed the lamp out and went to the door. "Get some sleep."

He was outside and about had the door slid shut when Dixie spoke again, and his voice was barely a whisper. "What's it like to look down a set of rifle sights and pull the trigger on a man that far away? Must be an odd kind of bloodiness, that sport of hunting men and treating them like targets."

CHAPTER TWENTY-SIX

Morgan slept fitfully that night, and it wasn't only the sound of Dixie's raspy breathing and occasional groans of pain from the opposite end of the boxcar that caused his unrest. The old dream that had haunted him so long came again, and it was as vivid as if it were only yesterday.

He was lying on his belly at the crest of Little Round Top amidst the confusion of men shouting and rebel sharpshooters' bullets clipping through the trees above him. Over five hundred yards away and across the open ground at the foot of the hill lay a maze of scattered boulders called Devil's Den. It was from there that the enemy was pouring lead at the Union troops atop the hill.

The heavy target rifle was tucked to his shoulder with the barrel of it protruding through a small hole he had left in the pile of rocks he had stacked in front of him for a barricade. To either side of him the officers were pacing the lines trying to get everyone into position to repel a counterattack, lest the high ground be lost. He squirmed uncomfortably in his sweat-soaked uniform and wiped at his watery eyes. The afternoon sun caused a glare on the lenses of his scope so bad that what snatches of enemy snipers he caught appeared as nothing more than haloed phantoms flitting and floating through the boulders across the way.

And then he glimpsed a tiny cloud of black powder smoke rising from the boulders, and someone screamed that Colonel

Warren was down. The damned fool had skylined himself at the lip of the hill to scan the battlefield with a set of binoculars. Sharpshooters on both sides had long since made a practice of picking off officers, but the heat of battle had caused the colonel to forget hard-won lessons.

General Weed was the next to forget, pacing back and forth among his men and shouting orders and cursing at the top of his lungs to harangue them into fighting positions. A Rebel bullet tore through his chest with a sickening rip of flesh. From where Morgan lay, he could see the general down on his side, kicking and convulsing and spending his last breath. And just like Morgan, the rest of the men along the line watched him die, helpless and too afraid to break cover to drag the general back into the trees. Only one bold lieutenant summoned enough courage to crawl to him. He barely had time to lean an ear close enough to hear the last words of his commander before a second bullet took the top of his head off in a gush of blood spray. The shot that killed him came from so far away that the lieutenant's body was already sprawled atop the general's by the time the report of the Rebel sniper's rifle reached the Union line.

The frustrated soldiers fired randomly into the Devil's Den, some of them holding their guns above the barricades they had erected and pulling their triggers without even rising to aim, lest they expose themselves to more of the gunfire that had already taken the lives of so many of their officers. Those that were bold enough to take aim did little more good than those that didn't, coming no closer than to strike dust clouds from the boulders that hid the enemy. The sharp whine of ricochets echoed back to the hill, even above the roar of the rifles.

Another half hour passed, and General Vincent and Captain O'Rourke were the next to go, both dead at the hands of the same sharpshooter fire.

Morgan chanced a shot into Devil's Den, firing at no more

than a cloud of powder smoke and hoping to score a lucky hit. His own smoke must have given him away, for a bullet from the other side whined off the rocks before him and stung him with fragments that freckled his face with blood and tiny, stinging wounds.

He kept his position, lying deathly still for what seemed like an eternity. The blood from his wounds and the sour sweat soaking his uniform drew flies and a cloud of gnats, and they buzzed about his head and bit his face, tormenting him as if they knew he wouldn't dare wave a hand to chase them off. He kept his right eye to his riflescope, refusing to blink until tears coursed down his cheek. He could count his own heartbeats by the throb of his pulse in his temples.

Twice in that long wait, he thought he caught glimpses of a man with long, blond hair shifting positions among the boulders in the Den, but neither time could he find him long enough in his crosshairs to pull a trigger on him. There were too many hiding places down there, and each time he thought he located the shooter he was searching for, another shot cracked from somewhere else in the maze of rocks. Shrill, high war cries sounded from those boulders. That was an unusual thing for sharpshooters who prided themselves on stealth, but the Rebels had grown bold with success and couldn't resist taunting their enemy.

Long, blond hair. Already rumors had flown from battlefield camp to battlefield camp of a Rebel sniper with yellow hair as long as a woman's who never missed, and whom nobody could seem to hit to return the favor. Some of the Federals believed that one man was being unjustly credited with the kills of many, but others had started calling him Old Death. The boys in gray called him the Arkansas Traveler, supposedly after his native state and a popular fiddle tune of that same name.

Catching those glimpses of that blond-headed ghost flitting

through the rocks, Morgan knew the rumors were true. Old Death was down there, fiendishly accurate, and killing with every pull of his trigger. He caught another flash of movement among the boulders and shifted his aim slightly to the left. It took him several minutes of searching to find his target. A single eye and a patch of yellow hair were visible where the Rebel sniper peered around one side of a boulder and between the limbs of a fallen tree.

Morgan blinked hard, trying to squeeze away the sweat running into his eyes, and to focus on the mirage of a man aiming the dark eye of his own rifle up the hill. He engaged his set trigger, and the pad of his finger moved forward and caressed the other trigger, an ounce of pressure away from firing the rifle. He inhaled deeply and let out half the breath, watching his crosshairs rise and fall slowly to the beat of his heart.

It was in the instant that his crosshairs fell onto that eye peering around the boulder that the first canister round whistled overhead and landed in Devil's Den in a ball of fire and a scattering cloud of black smoke and shrapnel. More artillery rounds bombarded the enemy position, and Morgan could hear the Reb sharpshooters screaming and dying. The canister fire ceased as quickly as it had begun, and then a partial company of 1st U.S. Sharpshooters skirmished down the hill shouting war cries of their own to give them courage. Soon, the crack of their breechloading Sharps sporting rifles could be heard as they finished off the wounded. The problem in Devil's Den was removed by nightfall, and some twenty Rebel snipers were accounted for, either as dead or prisoners. But none of them had long yellow hair.

Morgan tossed and turned under his blanket, moaning sometimes, and his arms flailing and lashing out. The second dream was the worst.

Again it was a hot July afternoon, only it was the third day of fighting at Gettysburg. And again he was on his belly with the target rifle propped before him, this time rested across the side of a dead artillery horse with it gray guts spilled out of a wound between its flanks. The horse lay in a break in a low stone fence, and Morgan's rifle was aimed down Cemetery Ridge at the long line of Rebels charging at the Union line. The cannon smoke from the Rebel bombardment and the Union counterfire floated low across the battlefield. The enemy ran out of that smoke to their deaths like screaming madmen.

Three quarters of a mile of open ground separated the two lines at the start of the charge, and the advancing lines of Rebel infantry were targets too easy to miss. The Moore target rifle boomed in Morgan's hands again and again. The killing was so easy that it was sickening, and he looked forward to the punishing drive of the stock against his shoulder like penance to absolve him of the death he was dealing. The powder smoke and the smell of putrid horse guts was so bitter that Morgan could taste it.

Amidst the confusion of the battlefield he didn't notice the first bullet thump into the flesh of the dead horse beside him. He was running a cleaning patch down the bore of his fouled rifle when a second bullet passed over him and knocked a hole in the dirt beyond him. The roar of the guns had turned into a steady drone in his head, and he operated as if in a daze. It slowly dawned on him then that someone was shooting at him from his right, and not from the battlefield below him. He rolled onto his side and saw nothing but his comrades pouring fire down onto Pickett's Johnny Rebs coming up the hill. Looking beyond the far end of the line to his east, his eyes locked onto the houses and buildings at the southern edge of the town of Gettysburg. It was at least a half a mile or more to those buildings, but in the same instant that he decided it was time to move his position he saw a tiny cloud of powder smoke blossom in an upstairs window. Something like a hot iron ripped into his side, and he was on his back and praying that he would die—anything to stop the pain.

And Morgan's body trembled, and was still shaking when he awoke in the dark of the boxcar and sat bolt upright on his cot. Without thinking he groped for the wound in his side and was surprised to find a scar instead of the raw, bloody hole left by a Whitworth bullet.

It took him a long while to steady himself and to return to the present. It always did. And in that time he reflected on the shot made on him from that far building beyond Culp's Hill, and though he saw no yellow-haired sharpshooter in that window, he knew that it had been the same man he had seen in Devil's Den. He knew it with a certainty that he couldn't explain, exactly like he knew that the Arkansas Traveler with his little dun horse with the Whitworth rifle lashed to its saddle was the same one he thought of as Old Death, come to him after all those years to finish what he hadn't been able to on the battlefield. Nothing else could explain the note left for him, other than it was him. By chance or fate they had found each other again, and one of them must die.

The sound of Dixie's labored breathing from the far end of the boxcar steadied his mind, and a calm, cool practicality slowly replaced the anguish of old memories. He would have to be careful how he made his rounds or moved about camp, and to make sure to never take the same route twice or do things at regular times. Most men were creatures of habit, and the Traveler would look for such patterns to plan his shot.

Half the power of such a man lay in the fear he could cause. He could be anywhere, and there was nowhere in the camp that couldn't be reached from the distant hills with a far shooting rifle and a man who knew how to use it. No matter how hard Morgan worked to disguise his movements, there was no way he could totally avoid the risk of becoming a target. It was that thought that brought him to understand that he must do as the note said. There was no avoiding it. It was either go out and hunt down the Traveler on his own terms, or wait for a bullet from him when he least expected it. It would have to be soon, for Old Death wasn't one to be kept waiting.

CHAPTER TWENTY-SEVEN

Red Molly finished rubbing the beet juice into her cheeks, smacked her beeswax-coated lips together, and stared critically at her own reflection in the mirror. The lamp on her dressing table made her image flicker and waver before her, and the thin application of rice powder coating the skin of her face and the soot-black eye shadow gave her a ghostly appearance. She frowned and smiled and made other faces, watching the crow's-feet wrinkles form at the corners of her eyes, and the two creases to either side of her mouth that didn't use to be there. She put both hands to her temples and stretched back the skin of her face and neck, holding it that way, until she let go with a sigh.

She propped one foot on a chair beside her, hiked up her dress, and ran a hand over one bare leg. The bath man had charged her two dollars to bring a tub and hot water to her tent, and she had spent half the afternoon scrubbing herself and shaving her legs. It was a lot of trouble to go through for one customer, but a hundred dollars was a hundred dollars.

She rubbed talcum powder under her armpits, smoothed away the excess dust, and then took up the single perfume bottle before her. The dress she slipped into had once fit high on her neck, but she had personally altered it to a square-scooped neckline. She had gotten one of the Indian girls who brought her bathwater to help cinch her into her corset so tightly that she could barely breath, and so that both breasts were squeezed together until the tops of them rose up from that neckline in a most scandalous manner. She dabbed a little perfume behind each ear and then in the crease of her cleavage for good measure. Her long, red hair was washed and combed until it shone in the lamplight, and she gathered it and pinned it together with a silver comb at the crown of her head to accent her bare neck.

The sound of someone at her door came to her as she was draping the shawl about her shoulders, and she gave herself one last look in the mirror before she pulled back the door flap.

"What do you want?" she asked. "Make it quick. I have somewhere to be."

She had seen him before around camp. Many times. He had something to do with the railroad work—a loud little bald man with his pig eyes always leering. He smelled like stale beer and unwashed man stink, and though she couldn't see the details of him in the dark, she could hear him mouth breathing. He didn't step back, and she knew that he was enjoying being that close to her.

"Well?" she asked when the silence became too uncomfortable.

He grunted, and she felt his hand on her hip.

"I always did want to have a go at you," he said.

She shoved his hand away. "I wouldn't bed you for a king's ransom."

He snickered. "Uppity bitch, huh?"

He led her along the edge of camp, winding through a maze of tents and wagons and staying off the main street. The camp was quiet, and the only sound was the mud sucking at their feet. Somewhere a dog barked, and ahead of them she could see a light burning through a window and assumed that was where he was taking her. She had only met her soon to be customer for the first time that day in the mercantile, and his request for an "appointment" had been hurried and discreet, but to the point. A hundred dollars; be there at ten; not earlier or later; be clean. Show him a good time, and maybe this could be a regular thing.

She hesitated, and the one before her noticed and stopped and turned back to her.

"Come on," he said.

A hundred dollars. Oh, the things she had done for far less than that. Yet, she hesitated, although she couldn't say why.

"He doesn't like to be kept waiting," the man with her said in his strange accent.

She pushed away the fluttery feeling. She was Red Molly, the belle of the tracks, and not scared of anything. She had the little derringer tucked into her shoe top if it didn't feel right later on.

After what seemed like forever, they arrived at their destination, and her escort and henchman of the night held the door open for her as she climbed the steps slowly. The single lamp gave little light, and her customer was waiting for her on a couch in the shadows at the far end of the parlor. When he rose to meet her he was wearing some kind of silk robe, tied loosely at the waist and revealing that he wore nothing underneath it. Her eyes darted to the lavish furnishings surrounding her. What did she know of such men who wore silk robes? The price to outfit such a room was more money than she was liable to see in a lifetime.

He went to his desk and poured himself a glass of liquor from a crystal decanter, all the while studying her from head to toe like a side of beef he was considering buying in a butcher's market.

"Shut the door," he said to the man behind her.

She heard the door close, but didn't hear the henchman's retreating steps leaving the car platform. She wondered if he intended to watch through a crack in the window curtains.

"Care for a drink?" he asked.

She shook her head.

He took a seat back on the couch and crossed one leg over the other. "Take off that dress."

She had been naked before many men—filthy men, drunk men, and men that she had to squeeze her eyes closed tight and pretend she was somewhere else while they pawed and thrust at her. But somehow, this one was worse than all of them. It was the way he looked at her. The look on his face that she had taken as something urbane and polished that afternoon in the mercantile appeared different when alone with him in the shadows of the room.

"I said, take off that dress."

She slowly unbuttoned the dress, slipped out of the sleeves, and let it fall to the floor. She stood before him in nothing but her corset and bloomers, willing herself to give him a brief, naughty smile, and feeling her flesh crawl because of it. She was the one that was supposed to be in control of the turn. That was the rule.

"The rest of it."

She pointed at the decanter on the desk. "How about that drink?"

He made a circling motion with one finger, and she turned her back to him. *Tease him, but stay in control.*

She heard him rise again and come to her. He tugged so hard at her corset lacing that it staggered her. It dropped to the floor and her bloomers next. She could feel his breath on her bare shoulders and the press of his wanting against her buttocks.

What had she assumed? That he would be any different because he had money? That he would want to talk with her over dinner? Treat her like a lady? That they would chitchat over old times? Go for a walk about camp while she spun her parasol on one shoulder and he commented on the weather?

His arms reached under her shoulders and he placed his

hands on her breasts. At first he squeezed gently, and then more firmly, pinching.

"You're hurting me." She tried to shove away his hands without offending him. She was used to lustful impatience, and knew how to keep things from getting out of control. One of the first things a girl of her profession learned was that you drew a line somewhere as to what you would and wouldn't do.

He squeezed harder, his fingers digging into her flesh until a small cry escaped her. She tore from his grasp and whirled to face him. The look on his face told her that hurting her excited him.

"I think you picked the wrong girl." She raised a hand to gesture for him to keep his distance.

The sound of his open hand slapping her cracked like a gunshot in the confines of the car. She staggered back, fighting to keep on her feet, and fighting against the cobwebs that the opium and the punishing blow had left in her head. She bent at the waist and reached for the little pistol she kept tucked into her shoe top. His next blow wasn't open-handed. He struck her with his fist, not full force, but enough to clack her teeth together and enough to drop her to the floor. She was lying there trying to get her wits about her while he took up his drink again and threw it down in one toss, still watching her in that cold, calculating way.

She spit at him, and he kicked her in the side. She felt something in her ribcage give way, but she didn't make a sound other than the grunting rush of air from her lungs. She had learned as a child that there were those that enjoyed seeing your fear. They wanted to see you cry, to hear you whimper and scream and beg for mercy. That was why they hurt you. Maybe you couldn't stop them, but you could keep your fear from them; you could take that much away to spite them.

CHAPTER TWENTY-EIGHT

Bill Tuck wasn't normally an early riser, and he was grumpy and only half awake when he went to his saddled horse behind his saloon. It was still short of true daylight, but he could just make out the forms of a man and a woman walking his way. Walking wasn't exactly the word, for something was the matter with her and she leaned so heavily on him that he was all but propping her up.

Tuck tightened his cinch, about to write off what he saw as nothing but a drunken whore and her john returning after a late night tryst—a common enough sight—but then they got close enough to him for him to see that it was Red Molly. At the same time, he recognized the man. It took him a bit to place him, but it was that grading foreman. What was his name? Ah, Tubbs, that was it. He wouldn't have thought Molly would give that nasty little runt the time of day.

Something was wrong with her, and she seemed hurt or badly drunk. The two of them disappeared into Molly's tent, and Tubbs was a long time coming out. When he did once again appear in the doorway to the tent, he cast a furtive glance in each direction as if checking to make sure he hadn't been seen. Tuck remained unmoving on the off side of his horse. Tubbs left at a rapid walk, looking back at Molly's tent once.

Tuck waited until he was long gone and then went to Molly's tent. He found her on her bed. Her dress was hiked to her waist and the bodice of it torn down the front. He lit a lamp so that he could examine her more closely. She moaned and stared at him out of one eye, her other eye swollen almost shut. She was so out of it that he wasn't sure she recognized him.

"Somebody got a little rough, didn't they, sweet Molly?"

Tubbs, he hadn't seen the man around in a while. The rumor was that he had been fired by the Katy, but there was also a rumor that he was still hanging around camp waiting for work across the river to begin and somehow keeping himself in spending money, job or no job.

Tuck went back outside and tied the tent's door flaps shut. It took him half an hour to wake one of his whores and to send her to tend to Molly. She was called Peaches, and he gave her strict instructions not to leave Molly's side and not to tell anyone what had happened to her. Peaches wasn't overly bright, but she would do as he said.

The sun was already rising by the time he mounted his horse and headed out of camp. And when he crossed the railroad tracks he noticed Tubbs again. The man had a saddled horse of his own, and he was on the ground at the end of Duvall's private car and holding the horse at the end of one rein.

Tuck reached for his pistol, but before he could kick his horse forward he noticed Duvall, standing on the deck at one end of the car. The superintendent was looking down at Tubbs and holding some kind of conversation with him.

Tuck let go of his pistol and rubbed his chin thoughtfully. The word had gone out that Clyde was looking for Tubbs, and there the superintendent was talking to the twisted little runt.

Tuck stayed where he was until Tubbs mounted his horse and rode on, headed out of camp. Duvall disappeared inside his car.

Tuck contemplated following Tubbs and killing him, but something held him back. The man needed to be made an example of to show any other dumb, mean bastard what happened when you roughed up a whore or messed with the profits in Bill Tuck's camp. But information was a powerful thing, and Tuck felt that there was something here worth knowing, even if he didn't have all the pieces yet. He thought back to the dress Molly was wearing. He hadn't seen her wear it before—a fancy thing more suited to some high-toned New Orleans cathouse than for a two-dollar-a-throw dove working a railroad construction camp. She hadn't put that dress on for the likes of Tubbs.

He thought he had a handle on what had happened, but the trick was going to be in figuring out how to play it to his advantage. It might take awhile, but he was a patient man. He had a feeling that Tubbs wasn't going anywhere, and he could tend to that little bastard later.

He kicked his horse out of the timber and into the trail, headed east in the opposite direction Tubbs had gone. He was normally a man cautious of his surroundings, but he was so wrapped up in deciphering what he had seen that morning that he didn't notice the man sitting on the zebra dun horse in the tall grass on the far side of the little grassy glade that the trail ran through.

The three Kingman brothers were already at the bar nursing beers when Tuck stepped inside the saloon at North Fork. The saloonkeeper was at the far end of the bar making an effort not to look at anyone, and Tuck could only imagine how they had rousted him out of bed at that time of the morning to serve them.

Neither of the two younger, larger Kingmans said anything when Tuck walked in, seemingly content to hear out whatever it was he had gathered them for. Those two were always surly, scary-quiet sorts, but on the other hand, Texas George seemed in an especially spastic mood.

"I hope you had good reason to drag us out of our beds at

this time of the morning." George's mustache so covered his mouth that you couldn't see the workings of it when he spoke. His movements were always jerky and restless.

Tuck ignored him and glanced to the side of the room. Deacon Fischer had his back to the wall, sitting at a table alone with nothing but his Bible and a pistol laid before him. On the other side of the room were three other men. The one in the center of them had long hair combed back behind his ears. The butts of two pistols tucked behind his broad belt stuck above the edge of the table. The men to either side of him were two more of the same—Missouri border scum.

Another man sat alone on the same side of the room as the bushwhacker trio. He wore a derby hat and a suit coat, and seemed out of place in such a gathering.

"The Katy people and the government men will be in camp day after tomorrow," Tuck said.

"Is the money still in Duvall's safe?" the man with the long hair asked.

"It's there, minus what you boys already took from the Creeks."

Texas George jabbed the air with his bandaged hand. "I say we get the money tonight. Yank Duvall out of his swanky sleeping car and make him open the damned thing."

Tuck shook his head, and glanced at the man in the derby hat. "That's not the deal."

"Easy for you to say when you're not the one gonna risk your neck," George said. "All this talk, talk, talk, and I'm sick of it. We've got the guns now, and there's no sense mollycoddling around."

The man in the derby hat cleared his throat. "It will make more of an impact if you wait to make your move when Duvall's guests are in camp to see the christening of the new trestle."

"Railroad men," George scoffed. "You train barons make us

look like angels."

Tuck took a seat on the edge of a tabletop where he could see them all. "Mr. Huffman and his associates have offered us a nice bonus if we cause a stink while the Secretary of the Interior is here."

"And what good does that do you, railroad man?" Deacon's voice sounded strange in the room after he had sat so quietly for so long, and his words were aimed at the man in the derby hat, Huffman.

Huffman cleared his throat again. "Let us say that should the MK&T lose its right of way and permission to build across the Territory, then my company might be the one to fill the gap."

"Five thousand dollars on top of that Choctaw money sounds good," Tuck said.

"Sounds too complicated to me," George said. "Complicated plans always go south in a hurry."

"There are going to be a lot of people in camp with all the festivities," the bushwhacker with the long hair said. "And more soldiers."

"I take it your scouts are keeping an eye on Fort Gibson?" Tuck asked.

"I've got men watching the post. Those nigger horse soldiers ought to ride sometime today."

"How many?"

"It won't be a full company. Let's say thirty soldiers fit for duty and not tied up elsewhere."

"How do we know this fellow will come up with the five thousand extra he's promising us?" George jabbed his bandaged hand through the air again at Huffman.

Huffman squirmed in his chair.

"I'll see to that," Tuck said.

"And why should we trust you, or Huffman there, either one?" George asked.

"I trusted you for my cut of what you took off that Creek guard, didn't I?"

"That don't mean we got to trust you."

"George, you don't have to play if you don't want to." Tuck gave Deacon a look.

George noticed that and backed up between his brothers. "I wondered why you were here, Deacon. You never have been too fond of crowds."

"Deacon is working for me," Tuck said.

"Clyde," Deacon said.

"What?" George asked.

"Clyde is all I want."

The two younger Kingman brothers shifted at the bar, both of them eyeing Deacon and then looking a question at Tuck.

"Clyde's ours," George said. He held up his bandaged hand for all of them to see. "I owe that son of a bitch one."

"What do you care how he gets it, as long as he gets it?" Tuck asked.

"It matters to us," the biggest of the Kingmans said.

"Clyde will be attended to. If Deacon here doesn't get him, you three can handle it."

"When?"

"Soon."

"You're going to call him out, just like that?" George asked Deacon.

Deacon cracked his knuckles and pointed at George's bandaged hand. "You had your chance, George. How did that turn out for you?"

"We want to be there to watch it," George said. "We get him if the Deacon can't cut the mustard."

"The bridge," Huffman interjected. "Don't forget the bridge."

"We'll tend to the bridge." Tuck tipped his hat to the railroad man and then nodded at the rest of the men as if their meeting were over and he were going to leave.

"One more thing," Huffman said before Tuck could go.

"What's that?" Tuck asked.

"The more turmoil the better."

"How's that?" The bushwhacker with the long hair gave Huffman a hard look.

"Let's say that a good show is to my advantage. The MK&T might survive the financial hardship, but not a fiasco in the press. The bloodier the better."

"You'll get your money's worth," Tuck said.

The bushwhacker grunted. "Don't worry, Huffman. My boys specialize in bloody."

CHAPTER TWENTY-NINE

Morgan stopped on the edge of the street to stand with the Pinkerton who was watching the whiskey wagon being unloaded in front of the Bullhorn.

"Tuck must be planning on some celebration," the Pinkerton said.

Morgan could only nod. Already, the population of the camp had seemed to have grown overnight. Word had spread about the festivities to inaugurate the new trestle, and people were pouring in from all over to see the show. Wagon camps surrounded the main tent city, and an area to the south had been roped off for the Choctaw entourage that should arrive at any time. Across the tracks from the main camp was another roped-off area for the Washington guests. The great tent Duvall had ordered erected stood in the middle of it.

"How was your round this morning?" Morgan asked.

"Quiet so far." The Pinkerton patted his pick handle in his open palm. "No trouble for the other boys, either."

"You haven't seen Red Molly have you?"

"Haven't seen her since yesterday. How's that policeman of yours?"

"He's on the mend. Keep your eyes peeled."

"I'm on it, Chief."

Morgan crossed the street and skirted down the side of the Bullhorn until he was at the back of it. The door flaps to Red Molly's tent were tied closed, and he was about to give her a shout when a woman's eye peered outside at him through a slit in the flaps. It wasn't Molly's eye.

"I'm looking for Red Molly."

"She ain't here."

"Where is she?"

"She's gone." The woman hiding behind the tent flaps was a poor liar.

"Open up."

When she hesitated Morgan slid his knife from its sheath and sliced through the canvas thongs in one sweep. He shoved past the woman trying to block his entrance, but stopped short at the sight before him.

Molly was sitting on her bed, wrapped in a blanket like she had the chills. When she looked up at him it was to reveal one knotted cheek and the eye on that side so swollen as to be only a slit. She cocked her good eye to him and tried a feeble smile through her split and bruised lips.

"Now you know what I look like without my makeup." She tried to laugh, but winced and clutched her middle with one arm.

"What happened?"

"Thought I would take a ride around camp, and the damned rental horse threw me."

"I've never seen you on a horse."

"Now you know why."

"Don't lie to me, Molly. You never have. Tell me who did this to you."

"Leave it alone. I can handle it myself."

"Was it the same one who roughed up Ruby Ann?"

"I said, let it lie."

"You're going to tell me."

Molly sighed and lay on her side, drawing her knees gingerly to her chest.

"Leave her alone," the other woman in the room said. "Can't you see she's in no shape to talk?"

"This isn't like you, Molly."

Molly didn't answer him, and the other whore stepped between them. "Please leave."

"Tell me, Molly, and I'll make it right," he said over the woman's head.

Molly rolled over and put her back to him.

He turned on his heel and strode out of her tent, and he was standing outside it when the woman attending to Molly came out of the door with a bedpan in her hands. She sloshed the contents to one side of the doorway and went back inside. He glanced down at the pink tint of bloody urine pooled in the trampled mud. When he looked up, Bill Tuck was motioning to him from the back of the Bullhorn.

"How is she?" Tuck asked when Morgan made it over to him.

"Who did it?" Morgan asked.

"I don't know. I found her like that yesterday morning."

"She didn't talk?"

"She's not telling anyone anything."

"You sound like you're the one not telling me everything."

Tuck glanced both ways out the back of his saloon as if he expected eavesdroppers. "I saw that grading foreman bringing her back to her tent."

"Tubbs?"

"That's him."

"Know where he's at?"

Tuck shrugged. "I want him as badly as you do. Molly and I go way back."

Morgan could have said many things about that, but didn't. "You see him, you send someone to let me know."

"Do you think he's the same one that did for Ruby Ann?"

"That's my guess, but the thing that's bothering me is why

Molly won't talk. You do something like that to her, and she'll usually cut your heart out herself."

"We'll get him," Tuck said. "Molly's got the same problems most of these damn whores have, but she's better than most. And if word gets out that anyone can beat on my whores and get away with it, then I'm done in this camp."

"Molly said she was independent."

Tuck let out a gust of breath. "You can believe what you want to, and so can she. But regardless of the arrangement between us, she works out of my place and people are going to see it like she works for me."

"And that bothers you worse than somebody doing that to Molly, doesn't it? You're some piece of work."

"Do you know what your problem is, Clyde? You're quick with a gun and nervy enough, but you're soft in the middle." Tuck pointed towards the tent behind them. "Molly there, she isn't soft. She sees things how they are and knows her place, and she's never once complained. There are personal matters and then there's business, and you don't let the personal get in the way of business."

"You killed her husband. I know it, and everybody knows it."

"And she's still hanging around. Ever ask yourself about that? Want to know why? It's because she knows that I take care of what's mine. She shorts me, I tend to it. Some tinhorn gambler cheats me, I tend to it. One of my whores gets beat up, I tend to it. Maybe that's hard, but it's fair."

"You leave Tubbs to me, hear? Let the law handle it."

"Meaning you get to kill him and not me?"

CHAPTER THIRTY

Later that afternoon Morgan met four of the Pinkertons carrying Dixie on a stretcher. He rose up slightly when he saw Morgan approaching.

"You look like you're having a bad day," he said.

"I believe I'm supposed to be saying that to you. What are you doing out of bed?"

"Thought I would have these jaspers tote me down to the whorehouse." Dixie tried to laugh, but it brought on a fit of coughing.

"Doc said to move him to the hospital tent so he can watch him," one of the Pinkertons said. "He's afraid pneumonia is trying to set in."

Dixie clutched his chest with one hand and looked up at Morgan with watery eyes. "I'm fine."

A train whistle sounded up the tracks, and their attention turned that way. A locomotive pulling a short string of cars was smoking into the outskirts of camp. Two passenger cars were hitched at the rear of the line.

"I heard some of Duvall's guests were going to arrive early," Dixie said.

"Get him inside," Morgan said to one of the Pinkertons.

"No, I want to stay here for a bit and see who gets off the train," Dixie said. "I always did like to see folks get off the train. Seeing the comings and goings down at the depot house was about the only new thing that ever happened back where I come from."

Morgan was going to argue the point, but the train was already parked in front of the depot decking. Waiting a few moments for the passengers to get off the train shouldn't hurt Dixie too much, providing the Pinkertons didn't mind standing there and holding his stretcher up. They were all four stout men, and none of them complained, perhaps as interested in seeing who got off the train as Dixie was.

The first passenger off the train was a portly, well-dressed gentleman with long chin whiskers. He was somewhere on the south side of middle age, and carried himself with an air that said he thought himself important.

"That's J.J. McAlester," someone in Morgan's group said. "Indian trader south of here. Married him an Indian woman and now they say he has the Choctaw coal concessions locked up."

"He doesn't dress like any frontier trader I ever knew," Dixie said.

"He won't be a poor trader for long when this railroad gets to his trading post. Those mountains south of here are rich in timber, and that coal concession is going to be worth a fortune. McAlester's crafty, and he'll be figuring on how he can take advantage of the new tracks."

"Who are those other men with him?" Morgan asked.

"Who knows? One muckety-muck looks like the next one to me," Dixie said.

"That skinny little one coming over to shake McAlester's hand is Huffman. I worked around him up in Missouri," one of the Pinkertons said. "He's Jay Cooke's man."

Morgan looked a question at him. He recognized the name of Cooke, for he had seen mention of the Philadelphia banker in the newspapers, but that was all he knew. "Cooke with the

Northern Pacific?"

The Pinkerton nodded and continued. "The Northern Pacific and the Kansas Neosho Valley Railroad. The first company to build to the Kansas line won the grant from Congress to go on across the Territory. Cooke's money was backing the KNVR, and it got beat out by the Katy in the race down the Neosho Valley."

One of the other Pinkertons chuckled wryly. "That Duvall is a cagey one. I heard that a government man from Kansas had to put his stamp of approval on a section of track at the border to name a winner in the race for the contract. Duvall had a flying outfit put together to go forty miles ahead to build some track and try to fool that inspector into thinking his company was farther along than they were."

"Did Duvall get away with it?" Morgan asked.

"No, but he was gutsy enough to try it."

"And who's that?" Dixie rose up to a full sitting position, pointing in the direction of the depot. His tone said it all.

A most beautiful blond-haired woman in a dark green dress and a feathered hat gave her hand to one of the men on the depot and stepped down from the train. She was tall and slim, with a high-headed way about her.

Dixie let out one of his whistles between his teeth. "Now that one's a looker. And kind of a proud one, ain't she?"

The woman had the attention of all of Morgan's group, and of every man on the depot deck and those in the crowd who had come to watch the train's arrival. Her bearing made it seem as if she was well aware and used to the kind of attention she was receiving.

"I bet that's Duvall's woman," Dixie said. "They say that's who he goes to see when he takes the train up to Kansas City from time to time."

"Can't say as I blame him." One of the soldiers from the

Gatling guns had left his post and walked over to stand with the Pinkertons.

"All of us together couldn't afford her," one of the Pinkertons threw back at him. "She looks like she's high maintenance."

"Oh, quite expensive." Morgan had drifted off a little ways from his group without any of them realizing it.

They all looked to him, for there was something in the way he said it. At that time the crowd around the woman parted a little, and she turned her head and looked right at them. A funny expression came over her face, visible even at that distance. She seemed to hesitate for a moment while Morgan stared back at her. She carried a dainty wrist purse on one arm, and it dangled from its string when she lifted that hand tentatively to shield her eyes against the sun.

"You know her?" Dixie asked.

"I ought to," Morgan said. "She used to be my wife."

Chapter Thirty-One

"How are you, Helvina?"

The blond-haired woman looked Morgan up and down from head to toe. "Morgan, I barely recognized you. A bit rustic, but I'd say the look agrees with you."

"I wouldn't have expected to see you here."

"Nor did I expect to see you."

"How long has it been? Nine, ten years?"

Her chin lifted slightly. "You tell me."

How many times had he seen that chin lift exactly like that when she was about to get angry at him, or when she had her mind stubbornly set on something? He studied the dimple in her proud little chin. There had been a day when he found that dimple extremely attractive.

"How's Ben?"

"He's at West Point," she said. "But you already know that. He told me you wrote to him."

"He didn't write back."

"And you expected him to?"

"Why have you hardened him against me?"

Her chin lifted higher and her green eyes flashed. "Got some regrets, do you? You can't play father to him. That chance passed you by long ago."

"You took him and left without a word to me where you were."

Her nostrils flared as she inhaled deeply and her lips squeezed tightly together, as if composing herself. "You make such a simple thing sound so melodramatic, as if I have been on the run from you for all these years. For goodness sake, Morgan, let it go. We're done with each other."

"Melodramatic? Woman, what about those Pinkertons you sent to me in Chicago? What was it they called their little visit to me? A deterrent to my unwanted and amorous affections?" Morgan pointed to the hairline scar at the end of his right eyebrow.

The two of them stood facing each other with their eyes locked. Neither said anything.

"Helvina?" Superintendent Duvall's voice carried above the crowd.

She looked around, embarrassed that others might have overheard her conversation with Morgan. Her face transformed into a bright smile when she recognized Duvall coming to her out of the crowd of people on the depot platform.

Duvall's searching gaze passed from her to Morgan with the question he was about to ask written plainly on his face. "You two know each other?"

"We knew each other back in New York," she answered quickly.

Something about seeing her again made Morgan feel wicked, and he couldn't resist the urge. "We used to be married."

Duvall waited for her to verify the truth of that, and she shrugged as if it were nothing.

"Probably slipped her mind," Morgan threw in while she and Duvall shared an awkward moment.

She turned to Morgan with her mouth set in a firm line, thinning those lips formerly so plump and full. "Some things are easy to forget."

"I know you said you were married once, but I didn't think it was to . . ." Duvall started.

"To what?" Morgan asked.

"Excuse me." Duvall cleared his throat and straightened his cravat and gave the lapels of his sack coat a tug. "This is embarrassing for all of us."

"Those were the exact words my father said when I told him I was marrying Morgan." She waited for Duvall to gather himself, but when he was too slow she added, "Morgan was once seen as an up and coming commodities trader. I bet you didn't know that, either, did you?"

"I never would have guessed such." Duvall gave Morgan a playful grimace to take the sting out of his words. "No offense meant."

"None taken," Morgan said. "My climb up the financial ladder ended as quickly as it began. In fact, a storm and five sunken shiploads of Mississippi cotton was all that it took to bring me back to earth."

"I've taken a few hard licks in business myself. A man has to keep plugging away," Duvall said.

She snorted lightly, no more than a soft, ladylike hiss of disdain rushing out of her nose. "You must not know Morgan very well. His stubbornness is only surpassed by his pride. His plan to regain his stature was to accept a lowly policeman's job and work off his debts."

"I doubt the superintendent wants to hear us pick at old wounds," Morgan said. "I'm glad to see you hale and fit, Helvina."

She must have only then realized the increasing vitriol in her words and the flush of anger warming her cheeks. She cut off what else she was about to say and turned to her beau. "I'm famished, Willis, and Morgan is right for once. I'm sure you don't want to stand here and listen to an old feud."

Duvall wrapped an arm about her waist. "You'll please excuse us, Clyde."

Morgan listened to the rustle of her dress hissing across the deck boards, and watched the sway of her hips beneath the waspish narrowing of her corset-cinched waist, shifting her bustle right and left as Duvall led her away. She had always possessed a walk that could turn a man's head.

Helvina and Duvall were soon joined by the others from the train, and never once did she look back his way. He turned and caught up to the Pinkertons carrying Dixie towards Doc Chillingsworth's hospital tent.

Dixie looked up at him, and then twisted his neck to try and look back behind them. "You were married to her?"

"We all make mistakes."

"How come I never get to make a mistake like that?"

"If you don't shut up I'm going to have these men dump you in the mud."

"It bothers you that Duvall's with your ex-wife, doesn't it? It would me. Especially if my ex-wife looked like she does."

"Doesn't bother me at all. He and Helvina ought to be a fine match." Morgan veered away from Dixie and his porters.

"Where are you going?" Dixie called after Morgan.

"I'm going to have myself a drink at the Bullhorn. She always did have that effect on me."

CHAPTER THIRTY-TWO

The fifteen-man Choctaw delegation entered camp in a long, single-file procession, every one of them carrying a rifle draped across his saddlebows. Morgan, standing on the side of the street, was sure that there were tribal leaders among them, but couldn't tell them apart, for every man was dressed in plain working clothes and riding nondescript, shaggy little horses that looked no worse for their wear despite all the long miles they had come up from the south. The crowd on the street parted to make way for them, and the Choctaws rode into the roped-off campground awaiting them without a word to anyone.

Before long, Duvall and his entourage arrived, and several members of the Choctaw delegation were taken over to Duvall's private car. The Indians seemed especially intrigued with the Gatling gun at the corner of the railroad office.

Morgan drifted through the crowd, stopping occasionally to check with the Pinkertons he had posted throughout camp. His last stop before lunch was to pop into the telegraph office and send off another wire to Fort Gibson requesting the status of the cavalry force that should have arrived the day before. The reply stated that the soldiers would ride south that evening, and be in Ironhead on the morning of the secretary's arrival or sooner.

He was still frowning over that news when he met Saul at the mess tent. The cook was dressed in a white chef's smock and carrying a covered, sterling silver tray.

"Where you headed, Saul?"

Saul nodded in the direction of the VIP tent across the tracks. "The superintendent and his rich folks are about to run me ragged."

"That's quite an outfit you're wearing. Can't say that I ever saw a railroad mess cook wearing a chef's uniform."

Saul looked down at his white jacket. "They gots their own cook brought down from Kansas City. He's the one that made me wear this silly house outfit."

"I imagine Duvall is pulling out all the stops for them."

"You don't know the half of it," Saul said. "Who ever heard of drinkin' champagne in the morning. They's mixing it with orange juice. Havin' stuffed pheasant for dinner whilst the rest of the workin' fools is makin' do with beans and fatback."

Morgan pointed at the chuck line inside the tent. "Beans and fatback built this country. I believe it will suit me fine for lunch."

Saul grinned. "You make sure you get them other cooks to give you fresh cornbread, and I'll bring you some ice cream this evenin'. Them dudes over yonder brought ice with 'em packed in sawdust, and that Kansas City cook is going to have me turnin' on the crank of that ice cream bucket all afternoon."

Morgan parted with Saul and got the other mess cooks to make him two plates of beans. He carried the plates and a towel-wrapped bundle of cornbread to Red Molly's tent. Molly was seated in a rocking chair beside her bed, dressed only in a robe. Her bad eye had turned to a black plum. She sat aside some kind of poultice that she had been holding to the injury to take down the swelling.

"Where's your nursemaid?" Morgan asked as he looked around her tent.

"She went to get us some lunch."

"Well, I've beaten her to the punch." Morgan laid a plate of beans in her lap and then slowly unwrapped the cornbread.

"And now for the *pièce de résistance.*"

"I'm not hungry."

"You need to eat." He took a seat on a stool in front of her and spooned himself a mouthful of beans. "Mmm. I wonder what the poor people are eating?"

"You didn't come here for lunch." She sat the plate of beans on the dresser beside her and adjusted her position in the rocker, wincing slightly at the movement.

"I'll find Tubbs," he said. "He's around here somewhere. It's only a matter of time."

"I've made no charges against him."

"Tuck told me he saw Tubbs bring you back to your tent like this."

"This is not your problem."

"Anything that happens in this camp is my problem." He went to the coffee pot warming on her stove. "It wasn't too many days ago that you wanted me to kill the man who mistreated Ruby Ann. Now you're trying to protect what's most likely the same man."

"Protect him? Is that what you think?"

He saw the tears building in her eyes and he took a long time pouring himself a mug of coffee, stalling, and making no headway on how to proceed with questioning a woman who had been through what Molly had.

"You think I'm weak, and upset, and scared." He started to answer her, but she cut him off. "Well, I'm all of those things, and worse. But nothing you can do will make it any better. Nothing can take it back."

He poured her a cup of coffee, and noticed that her hands trembled when she took it from him. He settled back, knowing that he needed to listen rather than talk.

A sip of the coffee seemed to steady her, and her voice lost some of its quaver. "You think I can't deal with this? Pick myself up and keep on going? My daddy did worse to me from the time I was ten until I left his sorry ass when I was twelve. I've met worse than him since then. Worse by far. There's always going to be somebody that wants to take what little you've got. You can kill them until you melt the barrel off that pistol of yours, and you won't fix anything. You kill that man, and it still doesn't take back what was done."

"Letting him get away with it is the same as blessing it."

"You want to help me, you cuddle up in this bed with me," she said. "Just hold me until it's better."

The sound of running footsteps sounded outside the tent. "Chief Clyde?"

"What do you want?" Morgan answered. He didn't recognize the voice, and went to the tent flap with his hand on his pistol.

It was one of the Pinkertons, the one with the backwoods Kentucky accent and the checkered vest. "I looked all over for you."

"What is it?"

"Man came into camp and said he saw a dead body floating downriver from the new bridge."

"What man?"

"The dead one or the one that told me about it?"

Morgan suppressed the urge to comment on the Pinkerton's intelligence. "The man that told you about the body."

"It was one of the bridge crew. I think Scurlock is his name," the Pinkerton said. "He said he was gonna bring the body into camp, but thought you might want to look at it on the scene. Detective work, you know."

"Where's this Scurlock?"

"He's over at the Bullhorn."

Morgan twisted to look back at Molly. She started rocking slowly, not looking up at him.

"Duty calls," he said.

"A dead body?" she asked.

He gave her a regretful look. "A dead body."

"An easier thing for you, no doubt."

She rocked for a long while, listening to the creak of the chair's doweled joints and the bits of gravel crunching underneath the hardwood rockers. Morgan probably thought she was too scared to tell him who did it, no matter how long he had known her, and she couldn't tell him any different. It had to be that way. It was her pain, and hers alone, and if she could bear it, he damned well could.

The remembering was like suffering through it all over again. Him that hurt her so, that awful, diseased and spiteful thing— she hated him so badly that she could barely think his name. It was a numb, shaking kind of hate mixed with a sickening fear and loathing for her own body and his smug, leering smile that filled her until she felt like she needed to vomit. Nothing could fix that feeling. Not Morgan, nobody.

Untouchable, that's probably what that viper thought—too many connections in high places, too many lawyers, too much of a name. His kind always slithered out of whatever trouble caught up to them. Who was going to believe the word of a common whore or a two-bit frontier lawman of violent reputation over that of a man who commanded so much? Arresting him would only ensure that Morgan's name would be ruined, or worse, he would be outlawed if he killed him. No, it wasn't going to go that way. For once she was going to win.

Morgan was too good of a man to be drug down by a no-good whore and the likes of that one and his henchman. She knew her sins better than anyone excepting the Good Lord himself, slept with them every night, but she wouldn't go to the grave with that on her conscience Both the bastards needed once to suffer and beg and grovel. But it wasn't going to be

Morgan Clyde who did it. There was no justice in that, anyway, and least of all, no satisfaction, no closure.

Mr. high and mighty Superintendent, Willis Duvall, and that vile, snickering runt, Tubbs, one and the same. They didn't know her, not at all; didn't know that she would not let them win.

The tremble of her body grew until she stopped rocking the chair and clutched the arms of it until her knuckles turned white with the pressure, and she sobbed once, loudly, barely suppressing a scream.

Angrily, she let go of the chair arms and wiped at her tears. She took the pistol out of one of her dresser drawers. It was a seven-shot Manhattan .22, so dainty and feminine with its mother-of-pearl grips and engraved barrel. Not powerful, but easily concealed, and the kind of thing no one would expect you carried on your person—hidden power and shameful naughtiness, like wearing nothing under a dress, a tiny devil. Click, click, the cocking of it a song guiding her thoughts.

Twice since her ordeal she had considered taking the pistol out and killing herself, imagining sticking the barrel in her mouth, tasting the oily steel, and the blade of the front sight digging into her pallet. But something stopped her each time, and she felt ashamed because she couldn't do it. Maybe it was weakness, and she despised weakness in herself. Maybe it was fear. She had been afraid before and hated that, too.

They had no right, no right at all. Putting a bullet in her own brain would be the same as admitting they had won. Did those fools think she had never been raped before or they had taken what little dignity she had left? Did they think they could break her by making her crawl and beg? She had been crawling half her life, and pride was something only the rich and the sheltered could afford.

She broke the revolver open and spun the cylinder, lost in

thought and anguish, and mesmerized by the hypnotic blur of the tiny brass cartridge butts spinning and spinning. The sound of the pistol snapping closed sent a sharp pain to her chest down where the emptiness was.

Seven shots. More than enough to do what she had to do; more than enough to send the two of them straight to hell where they belonged.

CHAPTER THIRTY-THREE

Morgan and the Pinkerton who had retrieved him went in the back door to the Bullhorn. The crowd was heavier than ever, the entire confines of the tent were awash in the smell of unwashed bodies pressed together, and a thick cloud of tobacco smoke hovered like a fog. The clink of bottles and glasses and drunken banter, and the spin of the roulette wheel and the coins stacked and restacked on tabletops, rose like a din. They waded the crowd, searching and questioning, but no one had seen the man they sought. The whole while, Bill Tuck watched them from the bar, a scowl on his face.

"Who are you looking for?" he asked when Morgan neared.

"A man by the name of Scurlock." Morgan looked to the Pinkerton in the checkered vest for more details.

"Works with the bridge gang. Little fellow in pinstriped California pants. Smokes a pipe," the Pinkerton added.

"He was in here, but he left right before you came in," Tuck said while he wiped at the bar with a cut-off section of burlap sacking that served as a bar rag.

"Know where he went?" Morgan asked.

"Not a clue, but you might try his tent. He looked like he had too many and needed to sleep it off."

"Got any idea where he stays?"

Tuck motioned down the bar to one of his bouncers, and the man came over to them. "Pork Chop, you got any idea where Scurlock stays? You know, the little Welshman that always wants

269

someone to play the piano so he can sing."

"I think his tent is the one just past the Italians," the bouncer replied.

"Thanks," Morgan said to Tuck.

"How is it that I ended up doing you a favor?" Tuck stopped with the rag and rested both palms flat on the bar top, shifting his cigar from one side of his mouth to another.

"I doubt you'll make it a habit."

The sound from Tuck's throat was somewhere between a grunt and a laugh. "Not a chance."

Morgan went outside, followed by the Pinkerton.

"Go see if you can find us a wagon to bring back the body. I'm going to find Scurlock," Morgan said.

"Want me to get some help?"

"No, the guards at the bridge can help us load the body when we find it. We need all hands on deck here. Looks like it's going to be a wild one tonight."

Truly, the street was teeming with people. They stood in clusters on the edges of the street or gathered about their campfires to tell stories. The fact that they were killing time told that they were visitors rather than belonging to the construction camp. It was only early afternoon, and already both saloons were doing a full-out business.

The Italian members of the railroad work gangs were a close-knit bunch, residing in three tents staked out at the edge of the timber on the southeast edge of the camp. Morgan went beyond them to the single tent standing between two large water oak trees a few yards back in the woods. It wasn't a true tent, but instead Scurlock had draped a wagon sheet over a rope strung between the trees and weighted the two edges down with rocks and small logs to keep the wind from lifting them. He circled wide and went to one open end of the tent.

There was no one inside. He took study of the single pallet

on the ground made of two moth-eaten wool army blankets and one soiled patchwork quilt. A salvaged wooden crate sat in the far end of the tent. Morgan could tell from the beaten earth on one side of it that Scurlock used it as a chair and had it positioned where he could see the camp. A spare shirt and pair of socks hung from the tent rope at one end, but those were the only personal belongings other than the bedroll.

Morgan left and made a pass through camp, but failed to stumble across the man he sought. What's more, there was no body to be found when he and two of the Pinkertons later drove a wagon to the place on the river where it was supposed to be, even after they spent two hours searching both riverbanks. None of the Pinkertons guarding the bridge had actually seen the body, nor had any of the work gang or the ferryman downstream.

"None of us saw a body, nor did we know about it until you showed up," Hope McDaniels said. The construction foreman had his hands on both hips and his brow wrinkled in thought.

"It was one of your men that supposedly found the body," Morgan said.

"Scurlock wasn't even at work this morning."

"Maybe he came early and found the body, and went to tell someone instead of hanging around for the morning's work," Morgan said.

"Then where is he now, and how come he didn't tell your Pinkertons on guard here?"

Morgan didn't have an answer for that, and the two of them stood side by side on the new trestle, looking downriver at the Pinkertons and other men still searching the willows on the north bank of the river. The bridge now completely spanned the South Canadian, bank to bank, with it pylons and timbers rising high above the slow brown current.

"Looks like you got your bridge done in time," Morgan finally said. "I guess Duvall is happy."

McDaniels grunted at the understatement. "By dark or early morning we'll have the tracks tied to the rest of those across the river. He's going to drive his guests across the bridge to inaugurate it. They're supposed to think it's a big to-do, being the first ones over it, even though we've already had the work train across it twice this morning, and by the time they get here we'll already be building track again to the south."

"You got it built, that's what matters. Not many men can stand back and point at something like that and say 'I did that,' or 'I'm leaving that behind.' "

"Aye, she's a bonnie bridge." McDaniels looked around at his project, as if seeing it for the first time. "Duvall be damned; high water and outlaws be damned. We did it, didn't we? The whole thing can fall in the river next week, but we built it."

Several of the men within earshot stopped what they were doing and nodded to each other or patted each other on the back.

"Boys," McDaniels called to his crew. "The first round is on me tonight!"

Even the men down the river heard him that time and gave out a cheer.

"That's why I came to this country, you know," McDaniels said. "She's a growing land, and needs men to build things. Men with vision who aren't afraid to work."

"That she does," Morgan replied.

"Rome had that kind of men to build her, and ancient Egypt, and all the other great civilizations. There was a time when none of them were anything but an idea someone had, or a place they came to and said 'here we will build.' "

"I took you for an engineer and not a philosopher."

McDaniels looked embarrassed, but only for an instant. He pointed at the Remington on Morgan's hip. "And what about you, Mr. Clyde? Does that qualify as a tool of your trade?"

"At every place and in every time where there are men that want to build, there are also men that want to tear it down."

"And so you stand in the breach?"

"Something like that, or maybe this gun and this badge are the end of a long line of my bad decisions."

Morgan caught a ride back into camp on the work train with the men while a couple of the Pinkertons followed behind in the wagon-without-a-body. McDaniels pointed at the heart of the camp when the train rolled into Ironhead and the men were getting off.

"How about that drink I offered?" McDaniels asked.

"Maybe later," Morgan replied.

He watched the foremen and his men troop towards the Bucket of Blood, laughing, telling jokes, and sharing the rough camaraderie that was universal for men who sweated and toiled for their living. He took a different route through camp, passing along its edge. It was pitch dark by the time he neared Scurlock's tent again.

None of the Italians were at home, probably getting an early start on the morrow's coming celebration. The word was going all over camp that Duvall was granting everyone a day off except for a few men doing some tidying up and tending to some last-minute details on the bridge.

Morgan passed through the narrow gap between two of the Italians' tents, and he could see Scurlock's tent ahead. There was a lantern glowing from within it, and the shadow of a sitting man with a pipe in his hand was outlined on the pale tent wall. It looked like he had finally found his man.

As it was, his attention was on Scurlock's silhouette, or he might have heard the quick steps behind him sooner than he did. He stopped just before he came out from between the Italians' tents and whirled to face whoever was coming down the narrow passage after him, and in that same instant somebody

273

else came from his side and struck him a wicked blow to his temple. His head felt like it cracked asunder, and he tasted mud. Sometime later he realized he was down on the ground and that his hands were being tied. The rough grass rope bit painfully into the flesh of his wrists, and somebody kicked him in the back of the head when they realized he was still conscious and struggling against his bonds.

Chapter Thirty-Four

Bill Tuck was careful that no one noticed him going out of the back door of the Bullhorn—no small feat, for it was nearing midnight and the saloon was doing a booming business. He avoided the main street and made his way along the south edge of camp in the dark. The weather had warmed a bit, and a thick fog had rolled in from the river bottom. He walked slowly to keep from tripping over unseen obstacles and to give himself time to think.

Superintendent Duvall's private car was a mere shadow under the light of the half-moon slithering in and out of the fog, and Tuck paused short of it and resituated his nickel-plated .32 in the slitted vest pocket over his belly, then reached inside his coat on his left side to the Colt Army riding in a special leather pocket sewn there. The big cap-and-ball revolver was uncomfortable to carry like that, as the weight of it sagged the garment awkwardly, but the fact that the superintendent had sent for him was enough to make him cautious.

A voice from within the car beckoned him when he knocked on the door, and he went inside to find Duvall alone and seated in an upholstered, high-backed chair. The superintendent gestured to the other chairs facing him, and Tuck took a seat closest to one of the walls where he could keep an eye on the doors at both ends of the car. Duvall pointed at the decanter of whiskey before him, but Tuck shook his head.

"I imagine you're wondering why I called you here," Duvall

said with one leg cocked atop the other and his hands laced together on his lap. His usual suit coat and tie were gone, and his feet were encased in a pair of Chinese slippers made of some kind of velvet.

"I did ask myself a few questions to that point," Tuck replied. He could hear someone else rustling around behind the closed door leading to what he supposed was Tuck's bedroom on the far end of the car, and that made him nervous.

Duvall looked at the ceiling as if trying to recall some file stored in his head. "I understand you got your start in the logging camps on the St. Croix up in Minnesota."

"Know what a river pig is?" Tuck asked.

Duvall's expression told that he didn't.

"They put their logs in the river to float them downriver to the mills. Somebody has to walk those log rafts to keep them from jamming up. One wrong step and you're smashed to a pulp or under the water with those logs pressed tight over your head."

"Dangerous work."

"Yes, dangerous." It was Tuck's turn to smile. "Didn't take me long to figure out that entertaining folks was easier and more profitable."

"You set up shop outside of Memphis after Grant took it. Made a good living off the troops stationed there or passing through during the war." Duvall said it as a statement instead of a question.

"You seem to know a lot about me."

"I make it my business to be informed. Would you agree that next to me, you're the man who runs things in this camp?"

"I only run my saloon."

"Tsh. We are both strong men, Mr. Tuck. Let's not be humble when it is only the two of us. Everyone, including myself, knows that you run most of the gambling and whores in camp, sell most of the whiskey, and other than Irish Dave's little operation, you have managed to scare off or run out every other potential competitor who sought to open shop in Ironhead."

"I tend to business as I have to."

"I notice that your business requires you to keep a strong force of . . . let's say . . . violent types to ensure things run smoothly."

"I have a few men on the payroll to keep things quiet in my saloon."

Duvall smiled. "Bouncers, yes, but I've also noticed others paying you visits. You would be surprised at what I see from this car."

"What are you getting at?"

The jovial mask slipped from Duvall's face like water, and what replaced it was steady and coldly serious. "You have men who aren't above doing some nasty things for the right price. Men who know how to keep their mouths shut or they wouldn't work for you."

"You have an active imagination, Superintendent."

Duvall's eyes narrowed. "You disappoint me. I thought you were a businessman."

Tuck remained silent for a moment, but decided to take a chance. "For the sake of conversation, what is it that you want done?"

"I want a thorn in my side removed."

"Supposing I could make that happen. What would I get out of it?"

Duvall nodded. "Aw, now the businessman appears."

"If you want a man killed, it's going to cost you."

"The price is open to negotiation, within reason, of course."

"Who is it?"

"Not one, Mr. Tuck. I want two men killed."

Tuck didn't blink, but he did pause. "On top of my fees, I

want your promise that I get the saloon business locked down in the next construction camp, and that you'll do nothing to prevent that. And I want five percent of your company store."

"No to the share in the store, but your other request can be met."

"I want Clyde off my back."

"Done, but be discreet."

Somebody moved behind the door Tuck had entered through, and he turned to see Tubbs standing on the far side of the glass window in it. "Clyde's been looking for him."

"My man Tubbs has become a bit of a risk lately, and I don't like risks I can avoid."

"I take it that he's one of them you want gone." Tuck watched Tubbs through the window in the door. Tubbs had his back to them and had no clue that his boss was at that very instant hiring his murder. "Are you particular about how it's done?"

"There's no message to be sent, if that's what you're asking. Only, make sure that his body isn't found."

"The other man?"

Duvall bent over and poured himself a glass of whiskey, waiting until he had taken a sip before answering. "The other man is an entirely different matter. Let's say, that like you, I must keep an eye on the competition."

"Quit talking circles, Duvall. I need a name."

"Are you familiar with a man named Bert Huffman?"

"Huffman with the KNVR? Cooke's man?" Tuck kept his poker face, but wondered if he did a passable job of acting like he didn't know the man.

"The very same," Duvall said. "He's a nettlesome sort, and it's time that Cooke figures out to stay out of my business."

Tuck leaned back in his chair. "I'll handle Tubbs for free, providing you meet my other demands, but Huffman's going to cost you three thousand. There will be those that come looking if Huffman goes down, and that means risk for me. And the man I have in mind for this job doesn't come cheap."

"Done, only make it appear an accident if you can."

Tuck was only beginning to soak in the ramifications and possibilities of the deal he had made, still turning it over and over in his mind to see how he could make it pay to his advantage, when the door in the far end of the car opened and the most beautiful woman he had ever seen walked into the parlor. He immediately knew her kind, but knowing that in no way limited her effect on him.

"Talking business again, Willis?" she asked and gave Tuck a cool glance that said she thought him so far beneath her as not to be worth recognizing his presence.

"Railroad business, love," Duvall said, patting the couch beside him for her to sit down. "Mr. Tuck was just leaving."

The blond woman remained standing, twining on a lock of curled hair with a finger beside her temple, and giving Tuck a new appraisal.

"Tuck? Aren't you the saloonkeeper that had a brother-in-law killed by Morgan Clyde?" she asked.

Duvall started to interject, but Tuck rose with his hat in his hand before he could say anything. "I don't believe I've had the pleasure of introduction."

She gave him that same haughty, selfish look, as if whatever interest she had briefly held for him had passed.

"Forgive Helvina," Duvall said with a chuckle. "New Yorkers can be most abrupt and tactless at times. The only thing she loves more than gossip is to remind us all that we're little better than a pack of barbarians."

"What you said about Morgan Clyde and my brother, how did you know that?" Tuck asked her, hardly hearing what Duvall had said.

The woman poured her own glass of whiskey, and stared at

Tuck over the crystal rim of the glass with some kind of mischievousness that he couldn't place. "I do find you all to be boorish and most uncivilized, but that's what interests me about the West so much. It's all so scandalous."

"Who are you?" Tuck asked.

She examined a fingernail and let Duvall answer for her. "Helvina is my fiancée."

For the first time Tuck noticed the large diamond engagement ring on the same finger she was studying so intently. If the gem was real, it was worth a small fortune. But of course it was real. She was the kind that could get men to do anything and wouldn't settle for less.

"Goodnight, Mr. Tuck," Duvall said after he cleared his throat. "I trust you will attend to our agreement."

Tuck left them and went to the door. Tubbs opened it before he could, and closed it behind him. The two of them stood on the car's platform.

"Ever see a woman like that?" Tubbs asked. "Acts like her cunt don't stink. I'd like to . . ."

"Shut up," Tuck said, barely able to keep from striking the man.

"She caught your fancy, eh?" Tubbs chuckled, and then his voice changed. "What did the superintendent want with you?"

"Just wanted to talk a little railroad business, that's all," Tuck answered over his shoulder as he went down the steps.

"The boss is all right. Thinks he's smarter than the rest of us, but he pays good."

"Oh, he thinks a lot of you."

Tuck walked briskly back to the Bullhorn, and approached it by the rear door. Before entering, he lit a red railroad lantern and hung it from a sawed-off limb left on the unpeeled cedar tent post for that very reason.

He glanced at the dark forest at the edge of camp, thinking

and plotting. What Duvall had revealed shocked him not at all, and not only because he guessed other, darker things about the man. If life had taught Tuck one thing it was that all business-men were thieves at the core, and the only difference between a man like Duvall and a back-alley pickpocket artist was simply a different financial bracket.

And leverage. Leverage was everything, and he had just got-ten more leverage than he had ever hoped for. The trick was go-ing to be in playing it right. Very tricky, but it could be done.

The last of the Bullhorn's customers left the saloon at exactly two in the morning. Two of the Pinkertons stood at the front door with pick handles in their hands to see to it that the saloon closed down for the night according to Chief Clyde's rule. Tuck stood at the back of the saloon and watched them leave, estimat-ing the profit that Clyde was costing him.

When the last of his patrons had gone, he dismissed his help and tied the front door flaps shut and blew out the lamps. He was outside the back door and closing it when he realized that someone was standing nearby. The sound of breathing was all that gave the man away.

"Got another job for you," Tuck said.

It was eerie how the Traveler saw his signal so quickly, as if he were always hiding and watching, seeing everything.

"I'm here." The voice from the darkness was gravelly and high-pitched, and laced with backwoods, country twang.

"Do you know who Bert Huffman is?"

"Jay Cooke's heel hound?"

"That's him. I want him attended to tomorrow during the festivities."

"That Huffman made him a little ride over to North Fork the other morning, and there was lots of others moving on the trail," the Traveler said. "And then you come along behind him like there was some kind of meeting."

"And how do you know this?"

"I seen things. My guess is that you're double-crossing Huffman."

"That's my concern."

"Yore asking for trouble, cousin. Cooke will put the Pinkertons on you, and they won't quit until they bring you to bay."

"Cooke won't know I had anything to do with it. There's liable to be lots of noise when the Secretary of the Interior rolls into the station. That's the time to do it."

"Noise won't keep people from seeing Huffman was shot."

"I've got a plan for that."

"Your plannin' and schemin' is gonna get you in trouble one of these days."

"You tend to your specialties and I'll tend to mine."

There was a movement in the shadows and Tuck saw one side of the Traveler's face lit by the red railroad lantern. A cold eye stared at him under a hat brim.

"Yore g'ttin' too proud, cousin. Those fancy clothes and the money have made you forget where you come from, but I ain't forgot."

"Are you going to take the job, or not?"

"What about Clyde?"

"Don't worry about him. I'll take care of that."

"You done put me on him. I took your money."

"Keep it. Plans have changed, and I need you to tend to Huffman."

"Easy livin' has made you soft, and you've forgotten how this here kind of thing works. I finish what I start."

"You listen to me . . ."

"Soft, cousin." The Traveler faded back into the darkness and the next time he spoke it was from farther way. "I'm the one man you don't boss."

"What about Huffman?" Tuck asked.

"You have my money ready. As soon as I kill this railroad feller and Clyde, I'm gone."

CHAPTER THIRTY-FIVE

They heaved Morgan in the back of a wagon, bound hand and foot. He was still addled from the blows he had suffered, and the hard floor of the bouncing wagon and his throbbing head made it difficult for him to follow what was happening to him. He sensed that there were two men on the wagon seat, but that was only a guess, for his captors said nothing to give him a clue as to their numbers or who they were. Somewhere and sometime, maybe a long trip or maybe a short one, the wagon stopped. He heard those with him climb out of the wagon, leaving him alone except for the sound of their boots scuffing the ground somewhere not too far off.

He didn't have long to wait, for there came the sound of horses, and Irish Dave soon looked down in the wagon bed from his saddle with a pitch pine and burlap-wrapped torch held high. On the other side of the wagon, Fat Sally's face appeared above Morgan. The wavering, sooty flame of the torch made the grins on both of their faces an ugly thing.

"Look what we got here," she said. "Looks scared, don't he?"

Irish Dave dismounted and handed the torch to the others in the background. He opened the tailgate at Morgan's feet and slid a knife from his belt and held it up so Morgan could see it. Morgan was about to kick out, but the sound of a cocking pistol stopped him. He looked up into the bore of Fat Sally's Colt Dragoon.

"Don't you so much as twitch," she said. "I've waited long

enough for this, and you ain't about to spoil my fun."

Irish Dave cut the rope that secured Morgan's ankles and stepped back. "Come out of there."

Morgan took his time, stalling and waiting for the circulation to come back to his stinging, swollen legs. He rose to a sitting position and scooted out of the wagon with his bound hands crossed at his waist in front of him.

Irish Dave drew his own pistol. "I told you, Clyde. I told you I was going to get you."

Fat Sally was still on her horse. "Get on with it, Dave. This saddle's too small and hurting my ass."

Irish Dave motioned Morgan to move farther away from the wagon with a wave of his pistol barrel. When Morgan moved, two other men that he didn't recognize came from the dark and started dragging something from the wagon bed. The sound of it grating on the wooden floorboards made Morgan think it was heavy.

Irish Dave shoved Morgan towards the front of the wagon, marching him with the pistol in his back. They followed a narrow trail through a dense thicket and Morgan saw the faint gleam of starlight on the dark waters of the river below them. Fat Sally came behind them on her horse, and the other men brought up the rear of the procession.

"That's far enough, copper," Irish Dave said when they reached a spot beneath a huge sycamore tree leaning out over the water from the high riverbank. He turned and called behind him, "Bring that iron over here."

The men he called to came forth carrying a cut-off length of railroad iron and dropped it at Morgan's feet. The beam of steel was at least eight-feet long and the two men grunted when they heaved it to the ground.

"Know what that is?" Irish Dave asked. "That's thirty-six pounds to a foot rail."

Fat Sally dismounted and tied her horse to a bush. She walked up to Morgan and kicked him hard in the crotch. He dropped to his knees with a groan.

"Felt that, didn't ya?" She laughed at him. "That's for the knot on my head your deputy gave me."

Morgan was still wretching and gagging when the men who had brought the section of railroad iron began to tie it to his ankles. He kicked out feebly and blindly, but that only got him another kick in the ribs from Fat Sally's boot. In the end, he was bound hand and foot again. Irish Dave and the other men jerked him to his feet, and he stood precariously at the edge of the ten-foot drop from the lip of the riverbank to the oily water below.

"What kind of swimmer are you, Clyde?" Irish Dave asked with a hateful grin.

"I bet he's a regular tadpole," Fat Sally laughed.

Before Morgan could say anything the other men picked up the railroad iron and carried it to the edge of the drop. They looked back at Irish Dave for approval to go ahead. There were several feet of rope between the iron and Morgan's ankles.

"How deep would you say that hole of water is, Sally?" Irish Dave asked, obviously wanting to drag things out for his enjoyment.

"Deepest hole I know of," she said. "Must be twenty or thirty foot to bottom."

Irish Dave clucked his tongue. "Go ahead and beg if you want to. I wouldn't blame you."

"Go to hell," Morgan spat back at him.

Tuck nodded at the men holding the railroad iron, and in that instant Morgan watched helplessly as the men with the iron heaved it up to give it a pitch into the river below.

And then there was the roar of a gun and one of the men's head flopped forward and back limply, and he toppled over the riverbank with his end of the iron still clutched in his dead hands. Morgan dove towards the sycamore tree just as two more gunshots cracked out, and the man on the other end of the railroad iron fell over the bank. Irish Dave's pistol flamed, and he grunted with a bullet's impact and went to his knees, still firing.

Morgan pinned himself against the massive tree trunk, and braced against the coming jerk of the iron as it hit the end of the rope. There was a splash below and his legs felt as if they were ripped from his hip sockets. He groaned with the strain, and felt himself sliding around the tree and towards the lip of the riverbank.

Fat Sally's Dragoon bellowed twice, and she was facing the way they had left the wagon and cussing whoever was shooting at them. Irish Dave's torch fluttered on the ground where he had dropped it, and Morgan caught a glimpse of the shadowed form of the saloonkeeper lying dead on the ground beside it.

Morgan's body was sliding and sliding closer to the drop-off, and he clawed for a handhold. The fingers of his bound hands dug franticly into the ground, and he caught hold of a gnarled root at the base of the tree in the same instant that his legs slid over the lip of the riverbank. The railroad iron swung beneath him, and he knew that to let go was to send him down to the bottom of the cold, dark water, never to surface again.

"Show yourself, you son of a bitch!" Fat Sally screamed.

Morgan heard the bullet strike her like the sound of wet flesh being slapped, and saw her fall in a heap atop Irish Dave's body. She struggled for an instant to rise, but her chest finally gave a great heave and a sigh escaped her mouth before she moved no more.

Morgan's grip was slipping as he weakened, and he hung to the root with nothing more than the end of his clawed fingers. He knew that he was never going to be able to pull himself back up—knew it with terrifying certainty.

A shadow moved from out of the woods, stepping over the bodies and coming to a stop at the edge of the riverbank. Morgan could barely make out a pair of boots inches from his face, his focus narrowed to nothing but the root he clung to. Whoever it was knelt and reached over the riverbank and cut the rope tying him to the railroad iron. The heavy steel hit the river with a low-toned splash. Hands grabbed him roughly by the collar and drug him upwards.

Morgan rolled onto his back, his chest heaving and his body trembling. He still lay there when the light of a fire fell across his face and he heard the crackling of its flames. He rolled onto his side and saw a man nursing the campfire to life with Irish Dave's torch. He crouched over the flames with a rifle across his knees.

"They about had you there," the man said. "You was meat for the pot if I ever seen it."

Morgan scooted on his back until he could prop himself up against the sycamore trunk. He glanced at Irish Dave with the top of his head blown off, and the bloody hole in Fat Sally's belly still bubbling blood.

The man across the fire saw where Morgan was looking. "Gut-shot her. Never was much good with a pistol, and fast shootin' in the dark ain't no sure thing." He patted the stock of the rifle affectionately. "Give me one clean shot and my rifle gun every time. That's work for a real professional."

Morgan considered the two bodies, and the other two men shot and gone over into the river. The man's claims to the contrary, killing four people in a gunfight in the dark wasn't shoddy pistol work at all. But Morgan had a feeling he had never met a man like the one squatted across the fire from him.

He was a little man, tiny in every sense of the word. An outsized and floppy brimmed hat sat atop his head, and beneath it two long, blond braids of hair hung down in front of both shoulders, Indian style. When the man looked up, the fire made his eyes gleam to either side of a bent and hooked nose.

"Bet you're wonderin' why I pulled your fat out of the fire," the man said.

Morgan saw what rifle was lying across the man's thighs. It was a Whitworth, and the same one he had seen on that zebra dun horse.

"Who are you?" Morgan asked.

"Names don't matter, but you know me." The Arkansas Traveler spat a stream of tobacco juice into the fire and cocked one ear slightly to listen to his spit bubble and hiss in the flames. "Me and you started somethin' onest that we never got to finish. Surprised me some, findin' you, but I never forget a face that I've contemplated puttin' a bullet through."

"What are you talking about?"

"Don't play me the fool, lawman, or I'll leave you in the river for the catfish." The Traveler lunged to his feet and came around the fire and squatted down again over Morgan. "I had you in my sights up on Little Round Top all them years ago, but you was lucky. Same when I put a bullet in you from that farmhouse the next day. Ain't many walkin' around that have had a taste of my medicine and lived to tell about it."

"Those days are over. You did what you had to do, and so did I. Let it lie."

"Don't matter. Me and you is hunters. It fair boils my blood thinkin' about stalkin' a man again that knows what he's about."

"You're crazy."

"Maybe." The Traveler nodded his head in a curious fashion. "Time to time I get to thinkin' I'm a little tetched in the head, but a thing like that gets in a man's blood, like an itch that needs scratchin'. Don't tell me you don't miss it—Injunin' around after men that might ambush you back, and lookin' for

them in your rifle sights and a knowin' that they might already
be peekin' at you in their own and about to pull the trigger. Me
and you, we've made shots that most men wouldn't imagine
could be done."

When Morgan didn't reply, the Traveler prodded his ribs
with the barrel of the Whitworth. "My bullet took you about
right there, didn't it? Must have knocked a chunk of meat out
of you. Pound of flesh, huh?"

The Traveler cleared his throat before he continued. He
talked as if he didn't care if Morgan answered him, and as if he
were talking to no one but himself. "Makes me think of a
mornin' over in Virginia. I had me this hole dug under a burnt
wagon carcass, and a pretty good view down the valley toward
the Yankee line. There was about a half mile of the prettiest hay
meadows you ever did see, green as green gets, and belly high
to a tall horse. Come daylight, one of our patrols and one of
yours had them a little fracas in the middle of that meadow.
Our big guns opened up on the hill behind me, but they was
ranged too short and their first volley landed right amongst our
boys. By the time it was good and daylight there was dead men
lyin' in the grass every which way. I was glassin' that meadow a
thinkin' the Yankees might take advantage and push on up the
valley, and I seen this Southern boy sitting up not far from me.
One of his arms was blown off at the shoulder, and he was
holdin' it in his lap lookin' at it like he'd never seen it before.
His own arm, mind you, like it was somethin' new just handed
to him.

"That boy called out for help some, but they was all dead
and his voice was fadin'. He finally started belly crawling
towards me, a'draggin' that arm with him. Pitiful it was, I tell
you. Wormin' along like that, he left a swath of mashed grass
like a big ol' snake, and it was slick with the blood a pumpin'
out of him. I don't know how he made it as far as he did, but

he finally bled out not fifty or sixty yards from my hole. And he was still clutchin' that arm to him when he died, like a little girl child clutchin' a baby doll."

The Traveler poked Morgan in the ribs again with the gun barrel. "Must be hard leavin' your own flesh behind, or seeing it lyin' there on the ground and knowin' it isn't connected to you anymore. Probably feelin' like it's still there, but rightly knowin' you can't get it back. I reckon that was why that boy wouldn't let go of that arm. Thought he could hold on to what was missin' until it wasn't missin' no more.

"That's the same as you and me. Got that missin' feelin' yourself, don't you? Like that blood and bone my bullet busted out of you left you empty, no matter how hard the doctors stuffed it back in and sewed you up. I feel it, same as you. Nobody ever took their pound of flesh from me, but I feel what's gone, even though I can't find no name for it."

"You shot my deputy." Morgan's throat was so dry he could barely speak.

"That was a mistake. He was wearin' your red coat. Could have finished him if I wanted to, but he didn't interest me none. They was always wantin' me to shoot officers in the war, but it was huntin' other sharpshooters that I liked. There ain't nothin' to puttin' a bullet in a man like your deputy. Those like him ain't watchful. Don't take nothing to Injun up on them, and every one of them has that same dumb, surprised look on their faces when they go down, like bad things can't happen to them. Me and you know different, don't we?"

"I'm not like you."

The Traveler rose and pitched Morgan's gun belt at his feet, and then he leaned over the bodies of Irish Dave and Fat Sally, doing something that Morgan couldn't make out. Morgan had his Remington clutched in his bound hands and pointing right at the Traveler when he straightened and looked back.

"You ain't gonna shoot," the Traveler said. "That ain't the way it's meant to play out, and you know it."

Morgan cocked the pistol.

"Yore kind of shaky there. Take care that you don't miss."

Morgan fought the tremble of his spent muscles, and canted his head around so that his one eye that wasn't bloody could keep the Traveler in focus. "You hold right there."

"You think I'm fool enough to hand you a loaded gun?" the Traveler rasped. "I didn't have no pistol gun of my own, so I used yores on them. My Englisher rifle ain't much for close, fast work, and I didn't figure you would mind, seein's how things were."

"I don't owe you anything."

"Oh, but you do, and I'll have my price," the Traveler said. "You take up your rifle and come out of camp before too long. I'll be waitin' for you, Green Jacket, and don't you make me wait too long. Gonna be like old times, me and you. The ol' devil is gonna tune up his fiddle and we're gonna dance the way we was made to. Dance 'til one of us can't dance no more."

The Traveler stepped away into the darkness so quietly that it was almost as if he had never been there at all. Morgan fumbled his knife from his gun belt and managed to cut himself free. He crawled to the fire, stopping once to vomit, and then sat before the flames with his chin sagging on his chest until the sun was peeking over the mountain beyond the river. And when he finally summoned the strength to get up he noticed the little downy feathers that the Traveler had left stuck in one of Fat Sally's nostrils, and also in Irish Dave's.

He stumbled wearily to Fat Sally's horse and climbed into the saddle, feeling like he was being watched.

"I'll be waiting." That's what the Traveler had said.

He found the train tracks and rode on the edge of the roadbed towards Ironhead. Halfway back to camp he pulled up the horse and studied the black column of smoke pouring into the sky in the distance.

CHAPTER THIRTY-SIX

"Ain't that Fat Sally's horse?" One of the men in the crowd asked when Morgan rode up the street and stopped in front of what had once been the Bucket of Blood Saloon.

Whispers passed through the crowd, as one by one, they all noticed the hatless and battered form of the camp peace officer in their midst. Morgan ignored them and stared quietly at the smoldering, charred framework as if in a trance. The fire that had consumed the saloon had also caught amongst a couple of nearby tents. One of the Katy's water wagons was parked nearby, and a bucket brigade thirty-men long was passing water along its length and putting out the last of the hot spots.

Morgan spied Saul in the mass of soot-faced, sweaty men. The cook had his sleeves rolled up, and obviously had been helping with the fire earlier.

"What happened here?" Morgan asked.

Saul shook his head somberly. "It was a terrible thing, Chief. Irish Dave and Fat Sally kept their closed sign hung on their place and never did open back up for business last night. 'Long about midnight some of the boys from over at the Bullhorn got tanked up and talkin' about the Bullhorn's whiskey being too high and the place too crowded. Wasn't long before there was a gang of the drunken fools a marchin' over to the Bucket of Blood to help theyselves. The more they drank the worse it got, and somewhere in the ruckus the place caught on fire."

"Anybody hurt?" Morgan asked.

Saul made a show of looking over Morgan's battered and exhausted appearance and at the horse again before he answered. "They ain't found no bodies in there, yet. You didn't try to stop that shindig, did you Chief? You look like you been fighting fire yourself."

Morgan looked over the crowd and searched the street from one end to the other. He spied one of the Pinkertons in the bucket line, and another one standing a little distance away in front of the company store. Farther up the street at the depot, he could see the soldiers in their gun pit watching the crowd.

"If you's wonderin' about your Pinkertons, well, they made a try to stop it," Saul said. "Texas George took one of them's stick away and worked him over with it, and they sent the other one runnin' up the street to the depot while they peppered his heels with they pistols. The onliest thing that stopped them from hoorahin' the whole camp was them sodgers cranked off a few rounds from those big guns over they heads. That got the mob's attention in a hurry, but the saloon was already burnin' by then."

"Did the soldiers get George?"

"No, they never came out from behind their sandbags. I guess they was afraid to leave all that money everyone knows they're guardin'." Saul sighed and then clucked his tongue. "You ain't never seen growed men act so crazy. I reckon they would have put fire to the whole camp if they hadn't been afraid of them sodgers' big guns."

Morgan pushed his horse through the crowd, moving at a walk as the people around him slowly parted to make way for him. None of them said anything, but like Saul, they all recognized the horse he rode. Fat Sally had been a lover of horses, and everyone in camp knew the little black horse with the bald face and the two back stocking legs.

He turned the horse loose in the Katy's corrals, and was

leaning on the fence trying to get his legs under him when Superintendent Duvall and an escort of Pinkertons walked up. Morgan's head was still throbbing, and it was with great effort that he raised it to look between the corral rails.

"Where were you last night?" Duvall asked. "My camp about burned to the ground."

"I had a headache." Even the sound of his own voice was enough to make Morgan's head hurt worse.

Duvall turned and pointed to the camp. "By this evening there won't be more than a few good men left in Ironhead. Nothing but border trash and outlaw scum come here to raise Cain, because they can. And Secretary Cox will arrive tomorrow and this is what he's going to see. The Choctaws won't take their payment and leave until the army gets here to provide them an escort, because they fear they won't get two miles down the trail without being robbed. And now I'm stuck with a bunch of dumb, heathen Indians to embarrass me in front of my guests."

"They're hardly dumb, nor heathens either," Morgan replied.

"What about Irish Dave and Fat Sally?" Duvall asked. "They disappeared last night, and here you come into camp riding her horse. People are talking."

"Let them talk."

"Bill Tuck is telling that you had a personal grudge against Irish Dave—something that happened in New York."

"Bill Tuck is a damned liar. I'd heard of him, but I never met Irish Dave until I took this job."

"Well, there are those that might think you had something to do with Dave's disappearance, and that Fat Sally might have had the bad luck to have gotten thrown into the mix."

"You're the same man who wanted me to hide and heel every man in this camp that wasn't working for your railroad, and now you're worried about the likes of Irish Dave and Fat Sally, or what Tuck has to say?"

"I can't have questions being asked of my chief of police. Not now that there are so many around who would love to ask questions that might cause me a great deal of trouble or show me in a bad light. There's two reporters over in the VIP tent, and one of them is already penning an article about what he calls my 'private army of Pinkertons and gunman marshal.' "

"Did you ever ask yourself what Tuck might have to gain from spreading such rumors, or how it is that the Bucket of Blood conveniently burned the instant its owners weren't around?"

"Where are the soldiers you sent for?" Duvall spat back at him.

"They should have been here yesterday evening."

"Well, they aren't."

Morgan took a deep breath. "I'll take your Pinkertons into camp and bust up the rough ones before they have time to get any real trouble started. Buy us time until the army gets here."

"The Pinkertons don't leave my money until that cavalry company out of Fort Gibson gets here," Duvall said. "And you don't look in any shape to do anything."

Morgan looked through the corral rails toward the camp. "If we don't go down there and head this off now, it's liable to blow wide open. We'll bust a few heads on the mouthy ones, close Tuck's saloon, and lay down the law before the hangers-on and the usual riffraff get too drunk."

"Tuck's advertising that he's going to open early tomorrow," one of the Pinkertons beside Duvall observed.

"I don't like the bastard, but Tuck's abided by the business hours rule so far," Morgan answered.

"Maybe so, but his runners have been going through camp all morning telling everyone that at ten tomorrow he's going to serve an hour of free drinks to any man in camp in honor of the secretary's visit."

Morgan eyed the Pinkerton, and noticed the man's scabbed-over ear and the faint beginning of a black eye. He wondered if he was the Pinkerton that had his club taken away by Texas George, or the one that had been sent running back to the depot.

"What's camp look like right now?" Morgan asked.

The Pinkerton with the black eye gave that brief, careful thought. "Rough, is what it is. There's a mob with their horses tied up down at the meeting tree. Been here since last night, and they've got the outlaw look about them."

"Some of that bushwhacker bunch?"

"They're here for trouble. They aren't drinking enough to have come for nothing but the celebration, and the only kinds of callouses they have on their hands are gun callouses."

"How many?"

"Ten or twelve of them, most times, and one of them leaves every now and then like they're sending out outriders or messengers."

"What about Texas George and his brothers?"

"They're down there with them now."

Morgan looked back to Duvall. "What do you say? Let me take the Pinkertons and the soldiers down there and arrest those men, or run them out of camp. If we shut down the Bullhorn the normal rowdies will be harmless enough."

Duvall gave it some thought, but he finally shook his head. "Can't chance it. That might be what they want us to do."

"Wire the secretary right now, if you already haven't," Morgan said. "Stop him from coming here until we can get a handle on this. Make some excuse if you want to. Stall. Delay."

"I can't."

"You can't? You say you don't want to be embarrassed in front of the Washington sorts, well, it sounds like there are those in camp planning on embarrassing you badly."

"I said I can't," Duvall snapped back at Morgan. "The telegraph wires must be down somewhere."

"Cut, most likely," Morgan thought out loud, and from the look on the others' faces he could tell they were thinking the same thing. "Hook up one of your pony engines to your car, and load your guests already here and your money and send them back north."

Duvall started to argue, but the Pinkerton with the black eye beat him to the punch. "What the chief says makes sense. We're outnumbered two to one, and that bunch won't be cowed by the sight of a badge and us putting up a front."

"We keep our cool and wait things out," Duvall said.

Morgan hitched his gun belt to a more comfortable position and straightened himself. He winced when he took a few tentative steps towards the corral gate on his stiff and swollen ankles.

"Where are you going?" Duvall asked.

"I guess I'll do what I've always done."

"And what's that?" Duvall called after Morgan as the lawman hobbled out of the corral.

"I'll go down there and read them the Riot Act while you wait."

"By yourself?"

"That's the job, Superintendent. Always is when you get right down to it."

CHAPTER THIRTY-SEVEN

Morgan went first to his boxcar to take a whore's bath with a washcloth and an enamel basin full of cold water, and to change into a fresh set of clothes. He shaved gingerly around the pump knot on his right cheekbone where a boot had struck him, and studied the deep cut along the end of his eyebrow on that side of his face. After a while, he shrugged at his reflection with resignation, and slicked back his hair with a comb. He was overdue for a haircut, and his coal-black hair hung almost to his collar.

He had lost his hat somewhere during the night, and that caused him a momentary frown before he gave his black frock coat a methodical and meticulous brushing, and then took a seat on his cot and began scraping the mud from his boots. He sat there lost in thought for half an hour, dabbing a rag in a can of black polish and rubbing it into those boots.

When he emerged from the boxcar his high boots were polished to a mirror shine and he wore a fresh white shirt with the collar buttoned on and a blood-red cravat tied at his throat. His black frock coat was unbuttoned and the left side of it tucked back behind the Remington on his hip.

Nobody in Ironhead was doing anything that resembled work, and the entire population seemed to be on the street. Red, white, and blue bunting and streamers had been hung across it near the tracks, and the camp had the atmosphere of a holiday, despite the fire that had taken the Bucket of Blood.

As it was, a lot of people saw Morgan when he crossed the tracks and moved down the street, and those that met him gave way quickly. Many of them were regulars who would usually call out some friendly greeting or pass the time with comments about the weather, but nobody said anything to him that morning. The battered side of his face, the one squinting, bloodshot eye and drooping eyelid, and the grimace caused by the cigar clamped in his jaw teeth made him look meaner than any man ought to be, as if he were half snarling. Before he had gone fifty yards, the populace of Ironhead were whispering that Morgan Clyde was hunting someone.

His first stop was at the company store, and he made his way to a rack of hats. The storekeeper, always ready to make a sale, quickly joined him and took a narrow-brimmed, gray felt bowler from its stand.

"Care to try it? I think it our most dapper style, and quite popular." The storekeeper proffered the hat and pointed at a full-length dressing mirror nearby.

Morgan scowled at the bowler hat. "Give me something in black. I like black."

"Black, yes, indeed." The storekeeper nodded nervously. "On second look, I would say black is definitely your color."

Morgan looked at the storekeeper and grunted softly. When he emerged from the store he tipped his new hat down against the glare of the sun hitting him in the face, and he gave the broad, flat brim of it a snap, as if saluting the morning and what was to come.

He moved briskly down the north side of the street, and Doc Chillingsworth with Red Molly on his arm emerged from the flow of foot traffic and all but ran into him.

"You ought to have that cut over your eye sewed up," Chillingsworth said to Morgan.

From the look of the doctor's pupils and the flushed, dazed

301

look about him, Morgan assumed that he had already been at the whiskey, or in his laudanum bottle. Or both. Morgan frowned when he noticed the same glossy, dazed shine in Molly's eyes.

"How's Dixie?" Morgan asked.

"Doing better than I expected," Chillingsworth said. "Constitution of a horse. It's going to take that collapsed lung a while to totally heal, but he should be up and around in a week or so unless I miss my guess."

"Glad to hear that."

"He and Ruby Ann were playing checkers when I left."

"How's she?"

"Her body's healing, but she still isn't herself. Hasn't said more than a few words since they found her."

"She's got wounds worse than those on her body," Molly said. "You be patient with her."

Morgan tried to hide his surprise that she was out and about so soon after her ordeal. She was dressed finer than he had ever seen her, and the dress she wore must have cost her dearly. It was of maroon velvet, tucked tight at the waist and the hem of it brushed the ground. A matching maroon fox-hunting cap sat atop her pinned-up red hair with a long peacock feather tucked into it. She stared back at him with her chin lifted in the high lace collar, as if to challenge any questions she expected him to ask. The bruises on her face had already begun to fade to yellow, and she had put some effort into covering them with face powder. Despite the front she was putting on, Morgan could see how she favored her right side, and the line of her mouth tightened once when she moved wrong.

"And where are you two going, dressed so fine?" Morgan asked.

Molly gave him her old smile—the same smile that had won her the affection of many a booted and belted man in camps all along the line. "The doc is taking me down to the VIP tent to mingle with the high and mighty. I hear they've got champagne on ice, and a tent full of rich, horny businessmen too far from their wives."

"I would think you might want to take a break for a while. You know . . ."

She leaned close to him, and gave him a peck on the cheek. "You be careful, Morgan Clyde."

Morgan's ex-wife walked up to them at the very instant Molly straightened from kissing him on the cheek. The sight tightened the prim set of her cheeks and mouth, and her brows lowered for an instant.

"What are you doing down here alone, Helvina?" Morgan asked.

"Here? Why, I'm enjoying the sights." She spun the lace parasol she carried over one shoulder, and turned a half circle and looked around with feigned, innocent oblivion, as if lost to what he meant.

"You should go back."

She ignored him and gave Molly an appraising look. "I don't believe we've met. I'm Helvina Vanderwagen, of the New York Vanderwagens."

"Red Molly O'Flanagan." Red Molly's voice was short and clipped.

"Red Molly?" Helvina perched her eyebrows and her lips curled inward in a wry, cutting smirk. "No doubt of the upstate Red Mollys, or perhaps Boston?"

"County Kerry by way of Tralee across the Atlantic to Quebec, and my name is what I've made it."

"Of course." Helvina gave a patronizing smile and looked around her again. "It's all so rough and vibrant and magnificently filthy. I must say this camp reminds me of walking through the Five Points or the Bowery."

303

Morgan cleared his throat. "Helvina, it always bothered me how much you enjoyed your slumming."

"I could say the same about you. Why, you've practically made a career of it." She pursed her lips and made a show of taking in him and Red Molly standing side by side. "You look good together. Quite the matched pair, right down to the bruises. You aren't pimping on the side are you, Morgan? I know that money is hard to come by for a man of your profession, but really . . ."

Red Molly stiffened. "Bitch, I'll . . ."

Two of the Pinkertons appeared around a corner, and having spotted Helvina, they hurried to her.

"Ma'am, you shouldn't slip off from us like that," one of them said. "The superintendent gave us implicit orders to . . ."

"Oh, pish posh." Helvina waved a dismissive hand at him. "You let me handle Willis. He's all bark and no bite."

"Take her back," Morgan said.

Helvina's face took on a strained look. "Grown bossy, haven't we? Don't you have other business to attend to? Perhaps there is someone who needs to be shot or a dead dog to drag off the street?"

They watched her walk away with the Pinkertons following in her wake and the parasol spinning on her shoulder while she looked from left to right at the passersby as if she were window shopping.

"A most unpleasant woman," Doc Chillingsworth observed after she had left. "And I would venture to guess she really hates you."

"Helvina likes to have things to dwell on. It's sort of a hobby of hers, but I can't say I haven't given her a few reasons."

"I'd like to . . ." Red Molly didn't finish.

"It wouldn't do any good," Morgan said. "The voice of God himself couldn't convince Helvina that she isn't right."

"Watch yourself, Morgan," Molly said quietly. "There's new men in town, and they didn't come here to see the sights."

"Same to you." Morgan tipped his hat brim to them and headed into the street to meet the army.

He was only halfway across the street when a small boy ran up to him.

"Mister, I was told to come and fetch you," the boy said.

Morgan vaguely recognized the kid as one belonging to the storekeeper. "Who sent you?"

The boy rubbed at his snotty nose with the back of one hand, and seemed to give that some thought. "Don't know who he was, but he said to tell you that some man named Tubbs is passed out at a table in the back of the Bullhorn, and that you might want to talk to him."

Morgan gave the kid a handful of small change. "Thanks."

The boy ran off through the tents while Morgan made his way to the Bullhorn. A closed sign hung on the post in front of it, and one of Tuck's bouncers stood beside it watching Morgan come his way.

The bouncer jerked his head in the direction of the tent door. "He's in there. Passed out over his table last night, and Tuck said not to move him. Would have told you then, but you were gone."

"Are you the one that sent the boy?"

"I am. Tuck said you were looking for Tubbs," the bouncer answered. "Said you wanted to talk to him about that whore, Ruby Ann, and what was done to her."

The tent flaps were tied shut, blocking Morgan's view inside the saloon. The bouncer untied them and folded back one of them and stepped aside.

Morgan stepped through the door and the first thing he saw was a man seated in the shadows at the far corner of the tent. It took a moment for his eyes to adjust to the gloomy light, and by the time that he realized it was Deacon Fischer waiting there and not Tubbs it was too late. The sound of the bouncer's pistol cocking and the press of its barrel between his shoulder blades followed that realization. Morgan stepped farther into the saloon at the prodding of the pistol.

"Go back outside and make sure no one bothers us," Deacon said to the bouncer.

Morgan felt the pressure removed from his back, but Deacon already had his own pistol out and was pointing it at Morgan's gut.

CHAPTER THIRTY-EIGHT

"Have a seat." Deacon gestured at the chair across the table from him.

Morgan remained where he was, judging the pistol in Deacon's hand and knowing that his best chance might be to pull leather right then.

"What's this about?" Morgan asked, looking for Deacon's attention to waver for an instant—anything to give him an edge.

Deacon gave an odd shrug, more of a hiccup jerk of his shoulders. "Five hundred dollars, maybe that's it. A man has to make a living."

"Five hundred? I thought it was three." Morgan continued to stall and to look for any advantage, even if it was grasping at straws.

"The price has gone up. There's a little bonus if I put you down today," Deacon said. "I gave you fair warning, one shootist to another, but you didn't listen. Too proud. It's a failing of our profession, isn't it? Pride."

Any hope for whatever opportunity Morgan hoped might show itself ended when the three Kingman brothers came in through the back door.

"What do we have here?" Texas George said with a broad grin when he spotted Morgan. "Got us the big boar hog of Ironhead Station, the man everybody says is so damned deadly." George spun around to look at his brothers. "He don't look so dangerous, do he?"

The biggest of the brothers was carrying a brass-framed Henry rifle, and he gave Morgan a single, almost uninterested glance before he slapped the rifle down on the bar and went behind it and began pouring beers for himself and his brothers. Texas George paced back and forth watching Morgan while the other brother bellied up to the bar with one side turned to Deacon and Morgan and his hand resting on the pistol at his hip.

"Wouldn't have thought you would need help," Morgan said to Deacon.

Deacon glanced at the others with a frown. "I told you Clyde is mine."

"And we told you we wanted to watch him bleed," Texas George threw back at him.

Morgan expected Tuck to show up at any moment. He couldn't imagine the man he was sure was behind the situation not wanting to be there to gloat. But it would also be like Tuck to want to keep his hands clean. He was probably somewhere locking down an alibi.

"I came here for a killing," Texas George snarled, still pacing back and forth and glaring at Morgan. His movements were quick, and so nervous and twitchy as to be rabbit-like—that's what he reminded Morgan of, a vicious little rabbit. "Deacon, do your thing, and if you can't handle him, we will. Just shoot his sorry ass right now and get it over with."

"George, I'm only going to tell you once to step away." Deacon's pistol shifted slightly towards the outlaw.

"Do what he says, George." The brother behind the bar was holding a mug of beer with foam all over his mustache. He licked it away thoughtfully. "This ought to be interesting."

George stiffened, but backed off, stopping when he reached the bar with his brothers.

Deacon glanced at Morgan's holstered Remington. "Why

don't you set that on the tabletop, real easy-like."

Morgan had never given his gun up to anyone, and he waited a long count of three before he slid the Remington from its holster slowly and set it on the table. Deacon leaned forward and drug Morgan's pistol to him with his free hand, and nodded at the empty chair. Morgan sat down, turning his chair slightly so that he could watch the bar out of the corner of his left eye and not have the three Kingmans totally at his back.

There was a half-empty bottle of whiskey on the table in front of Deacon and he slid a spare glass across to Morgan. "Have a drink. Men like us shouldn't go down without a little ceremony and sacrament. Don't you think?"

"If you wanted me, I would have thought you would have called me out on the street where everyone could see."

"You think too much of your reputation." Deacon poured himself a glass and downed it before he continued. "Besides, you and I don't need an audience. Who out there would care, and who's going to remember us when we're gone? Men fear us, and we mistake that for respect. The vanity of the damned, I fear."

Deacon floated his pistol around in front of him, toying with it and watching Morgan's reaction to the threat of the weapon pointing from place to place on his body. Tired of the brief game, Deacon tilted the barrel upwards and put his nose to the bore of it and inhaled deeply.

"Ever notice how gunpowder smells like brimstone?" Deacon laughed weakly. "The smell of murder and wrath. Me and you got that smell all over us."

It was obvious that the Deacon had been drinking, and drinking heavily. There were dark bags under his eyes as if he hadn't slept for nights, and a slight slur to his speech. He was always crazy, but he seemed addled and rambling, as if the liquor had taken his wits or something had finally broken loose in his mind.

But drunk or not, crazy or not, the cocked pistol leveled over the tabletop at him was steady as a rock.

Deacon poured them both a drink.

"God forgive me, but I love that smell." Deacon inhaled deeply again, and then raised his glass to Morgan in toast. "One sinner to another, I always respected your work."

Morgan didn't raise his own glass, nor did he drink when Deacon tossed his down. Deacon's eyes narrowed at the full glass before Morgan.

"Drink," he commanded.

Morgan slowly picked up the glass and turned it over and let the whiskey pour out on the floor. The sound of it splattering was loud in the room, and one of the Kingman brothers chuckled.

Deacon flung his glass across the room and drew a knife from his waistband left-handed so fast that it was incredible. He stabbed the blade into the table between them and let it go. The two of them stared at each other over the deerhorn-handled, double-edged Arkansas toothpick still quivering in the hardwood tabletop.

Slowly, Deacon leaned forward and slid Morgan's pistol across to him, leaving it at the table's edge with its butt in reaching distance of Morgan. When he leaned back, he un-cocked his own pistol and lay it down before him in a similar fashion and lifted his right hand slightly above the tabletop, holding its fingers splayed wide and palm towards Morgan as he had that morning in the saloon at North Fork.

"Woe unto the wicked! It shall be ill with him: for the reward of his hands shall be given him," he said. Morgan's eyes flickered back and forth between his pistol and Deacon, shocked that Deacon was going to give him that much of a chance. Behind him, he could hear the scuff of boots as the Kingmans moved down the bar and closer to the back door out of the line of fire.

"Show me your hand, Clyde." Deacon's voice was a rough whisper, almost more of a hiss. "Show your sin to the Almighty."

Morgan raised his own right hand a little at a time, planning how he would grab his pistol when the time came. The Remington before him was turned awkwardly, and it was going to be tricky getting it cocked and bringing it to bear in time. And he knew Deacon was fast, had seen it in the way he drew the knife—unbelievably fast. He readied himself to take a bullet, maybe more than one. The Kingmans would get him in the back, but all he could hope for was to take Deacon with him— take the punishment and put one good one right through Deacon's chest and keep pumping them into him as long as the deacon left him standing. Take pain to give pain, every fight was like that.

"Blasphemous hands," Deacon said. "Black with sin and marked with murder like Cain himself. A quick way to hell as much as if Lucifer himself handed us the ticket to get on the train."

Morgan flexed his own fingers, wondering if Deacon was going to wait for him to make the play and thinking that was the way the man wanted it—mad with whatever drove a man like him, honorable in his own violent, twisted way, and confident in his skill to the point of fearlessness.

"You can't beat me, Clyde," Deacon hissed. "No matter how bad you want to, you can't."

Morgan glanced at the knife between them, and Deacon saw him.

"Ah, you see the other option. Feel it, don't you?" Deacon's voice began to quaver with some kind of fervor. "Save your soul, Clyde. It's not too late. Hear the Lord speaking to you, telling you to take up that knife and cut off that iniquitous hand and maybe you can live."

"Son of a bitch, you ever hear such!" Texas George cackled

from somewhere near the back door. "Deacon, you're crazy as a shithouse rat."

"Shut up, George," one of his brothers said.

"I'll be merciful. Take up the knife, Clyde. Cut your sin away." Deacon's chin trembled, but his gun was as steady as the mad light in his eyes. His voice grew louder, booming hell and damnation like a tent revival preacher from a pulpit. Spittle flew from his lips. "And if thy right hand offend thee, cut it off, and cast it from thee: for it is profitable for thee that one of thy members should perish, and not that thy whole body should be cast into hell."

Morgan took one last look at his pistol, and then he locked eyes with Deacon. When he finally spoke it was so quiet that Deacon barely heard him. "What do you want me to put on it?"

Deacon's face drew up in confusion, and inadvertently he leaned slightly closer over the table, breathing through his mouth. "What's that?"

"I said, what do you want me to put on your tombstone?" As soon as he said it, Morgan's right foot resting against one leg of the table kicked out, and his hand darted towards the tabletop.

CHAPTER THIRTY-NINE

Morgan kicked the table leg hard, driving it away from him and into Deacon's middle. Both their pistols skidded wildly as Morgan's hand found the handle of the knife. He jerked it free and made a backhanded slash at Deacon's throat in the same instant that the outlaw gunman's hand snatched his sliding Smith & Wesson on the move. Morgan followed with another wild swing of the knife and then thrust the blade deep into Deacon's side, feeling it grate on rib bones as it slid home.

Deacon groaned, and in a wild spasm, overturned the table and knocked Morgan away. His pistol lifted while the red line across his neck opened wider and wider as his head wobbled and tilted back until it was looking up at the ceiling. Blood poured from the wound and from his mouth, but his body wouldn't die, like a snake with its head chopped off still writhing and its muscles contracting under some strange compulsion and cursed will to live. His gun arm swung slowly, blindly, tracking toward Morgan as if the gun itself had a mind of its own and knew where Morgan stood. Deacon's other hand strained to pull the knife from his side.

Morgan staggered backwards as Deacon's pistol roared. The gun never made its way to him, and went off far short of its mark. Somebody at the end of the bar near the back door cursed and fell down with a crash, and Texas George was screaming and cursing.

Morgan charged Deacon again, sliding in behind him.

Deacon stared at him out of the side of one wild, dying eye as his body jerked with the impact of a bullet, and Morgan cocked the pistol in the Deacon's hand and clamped his trigger finger over Deacon's own. He aimed the deacon's gun hand, and the Smith .44 bucked and bellowed and the Kingman before them staggered back two steps and fell to one knee.

Another bullet knocked a chunk from the chair, and Morgan was faintly aware of someone firing at him from behind the cover of the bar. He ignored them and kept his attention on the Kingman brother directly in front of him. The outlaw had dropped his pistol when he was hit, but was cursing and clawing for his other pistol in its shoulder holster beneath one armpit. He never got it out for Morgan hunkered lower behind the shield of Deacon's body and thumbed the hammer and squeezed off another one that took the Kingman brother in the chin and flopped him over backwards.

Something hit Morgan hard and staggered him sideways, and spilled his and Deacon's bodies against the back wall of the tent. He managed to hang on to Deacon's pistol and sagged against the canvas wall and strained to see through the gunsmoke.

Texas George was behind the bar and fanning the lever on his brother's Henry rifle as fast as he could work it. And he was screaming something at Morgan as he fought. Fire leapt from its barrel and the whole room was one loud, numbing roar. Searing pain raked the flesh across the top of Morgan's collarbone, and threw his aim off. Glass shattered behind Texas George, and Morgan thumbed the Smith's hammer again and missed a second time. But it was enough to make George duck behind the bar.

Morgan staggered upright and hobbled towards the bar in the same instant that George's remaining brother fired from the back door. Morgan had a fleeting glimpse of that Kingman framed in the sunlight coming through that open door, and he snapped a shot at him and heard the man grunt with pain before he fell away to the outside.

George's head appeared above the bar, but when Morgan swung the Smith toward him, the outlaw let out a childish, high-pitched scream and ran after his brother. Morgan tracked him over the barrel of the Smith, but the hammer snapped on an empty chamber. He flung the pistol at George as he ran out the door.

And then there was nothing but the sound of Morgan's breath coming in ragged gasps, and gunsmoke floating through the dim light. Morgan scooped up his Remington from the floor and managed a few tottery steps towards the back door.

"Where are you going, George?" he shouted. "Here I am!"

He fell before he reached the door, and he could not seem to get his legs under him again. He was still lying there when he became vaguely aware of someone standing over him. Through slitted eyes he looked up at Bill Tuck, silhouetted in the open doorway. Tuck was watching him intently with his hand on the pistol in his vest pocket. Everything about the way he stood said he was contemplating murder. Tuck's pistol was halfway drawn when running footsteps sounded and then there were people coming through the doors at each end of the tent.

"It's all over, everyone." Tuck's voice rose above the murmur of voices. "Nothing to see here."

"Somebody get the chief a doctor," another voice sounded.

Tuck looked down at Morgan, and the expression on his face changed slowly and he let go of his pistol. "Yes, get this brave man a doctor."

CHAPTER FORTY

Red Molly stood under a shade tree a little distance from the VIP tent and sipped her champagne and looked over the small crowd before her. Some of the railroad cook staff was attending to a long buffet line of food set up under a canvas fly, and most of the men were gathered there. Cigar and pipe smoke rose in tiny clouds as those men swapped jokes and witty banter, and engaged in various political and business discussions. None of them had approached her so far, but she saw several of them looking her way.

And the women looked at her, too. There were only two of them: a short, stout redhead like herself that seemed to be the wife of some Arkansas judge in attendance, and Morgan's ex-wife. Twice, Molly had caught them whispering to each other while they nibbled daintily at the caviar and crackers and threw an occasional catty glance her way. She paid them little mind, gaining more enjoyment from their hateful antics than it angered her. Let the fish egg–eating bitches glare at her all they wanted.

Doc Chillingsworth came from the buffet carrying a mug of beer and a plate bearing some kind of hors d'oeuvres that she didn't recognize. He joined her under the tree and turned around where he could watch the crowd like she was.

"Better go easy on the booze," she said.

"I'm thirsty."

"Drink some water."

He mocked a fake shiver, and shook his head violently and

316

made a distasteful curling of his lips as if he wanted to spit. "Water? Oh, no, that stuff will kill you."

"Stay sober."

He cocked an eyebrow at her and straightened and sucked in his belly. "Wouldn't want to embarrass you in front of all our fine new friends, would I?"

She snorted and couldn't help but laugh. It felt good to laugh, even a little bit. Doc was always good for that.

"Who are all these men?" she asked.

"Who knows? Important sorts. Ask them if you don't believe me."

"The way they act, I've never seen people so confident and snooty."

"Most of these aren't even the rich ones. Those will come on the train tomorrow with the secretary. These are the second-tier, small businessmen looking for contracts and local politicians not connected enough to make the secretary's entourage." Doc gave her a questioning glance. "Why did you want to come down here, Molly? And don't tell me you're looking to turn a trick."

"I told you I came for the champagne."

"We've been here an hour and you're still holding the same glass."

Molly spied Superintendent Duvall walking her way with two other men. She quickly downed what was left of her champagne and handed the glass to Chillingsworth. Her fingers tugged at the drawstring of the wrist purse she wore. Duvall seemed to be in some kind of argument with the other two men, and he didn't notice her until he was almost within touching distance. He stopped with a look on his face she couldn't interpret, but one that quickly changed to some kind of challenge, as if he were daring her to say something. The purse wouldn't open, and she fumbled clumsily at it.

"What have we here?" Duvall asked, his words aimed at his cronies.

The other two men gave him knowing looks and appraised her head to toe boldly.

"Good morning, Superintendent," Chillingsworth said.

"Gentlemen, I'd like you to meet Doc Chillingsworth and his fair companion, Red Molly. She's one of the leading citizens of this construction camp," Duvall said. "Or should I say, one of its leading attractions."

One of the men cleared his throat and nodded at Molly with what he must have thought was a charming smile, but the other man, the one in the derby hat, paid her little mind and kept his attention on Duvall. There was something about the calculating way he looked at the superintendent, almost as if he were measuring him for a coffin.

"Like what you see, Huffman?" Duvall asked. "Perhaps I'll send her to you tonight if you'll promise me you and Cooke will quit needling me and let me build my railroad in peace."

Molly caught her breath and fought back the tears welling in her eyes, at the same time struggling to open her purse without drawing attention to it.

"Not a chance, Willis. I enjoy needling you too much," the one called Huffman said.

Duvall's eyes narrowed to almost a squint when he looked back at Huffman, and he didn't notice Molly's attempts to open the wrist purse. She had finally opened the top enough to squeeze her hand inside it, and took hold of the Manhattan pistol inside it.

"Such unpleasant games and political chicanery you speak of, Huffman. Especially with such as this before you." Duvall pointed to her. "You don't know what you're missing. Molly here is a real sweetheart, and such spirit, I tell you."

She tried to tug her hand free of the bag, but the drawstring was still too tight to pass through with her fist closed around the grips of the little .22 revolver. The three men before her seemed oblivious to her attempt to draw the weapon.

Duvall turned slightly towards Huffman. "Funny thing, I received a telegram two days ago that informed me the board of directors would be bringing their clerks along tomorrow to audit my ledgers. It seems someone has been spreading the vicious rumor that I'm skimming off the top. You wouldn't have anything to do with that, would you?"

"Why, Willis, I have no influence in your company. Your troubles here have turned you paranoid."

The third man with them stepped between them. "Now, gentlemen, there is no need to quarrel. Especially in front of the *lady.*" The way he said "lady" broke the tension between Duvall and Huffman, and caused all three men to laugh, Duvall the loudest.

Molly tugged harder at the pistol in her purse. *The twisted son of a bitch looking at her like that and laughing.* Her thumb found the hammer and she was about to cock it and simply raise the purse and fire through it into his chest.

Huffman noticed her efforts and took a step forward with a shake of his head. "Having difficulties there?"

Molly froze, still clutching the pistol. Huffman's movement had put him between her and Duvall.

"I said, are you having troubles?" Huffman asked a bit louder. "Perhaps you need a handkerchief to dab your eyes."

She was so startled that she took a step back when he reached to the lapel of his suit coat and pulled forth a white handkerchief and offered it to her.

"Use mine," he said.

It took her an awkward moment to realize what he meant; first to realize that she was crying, and secondly that he thought she was rummaging in her purse for something to wipe her eyes. She took the handkerchief in her left hand, and held it as if she had never seen one before.

"Yes, wipe your eyes, Molly," Duvall said. "Gentlemen, you'll have to forgive Molly. She's usually a bit high strung, a failing common to her gender I'm afraid."

Duvall gave her one last smug look, and pushed past her, followed by the other man with him. Huffman remained longer, as if he sensed something more to her distraught demeanor and to Duvall's words to her, and then tipped his hat and went after his companions. She turned as he passed, helpless to free her pistol or to raise it, for Huffman still blocked her view of Duvall's back.

"That Duvall doesn't know how close he came to getting a piece of my mind," Chillingsworth said when the superintendent was gone. "Whore or not, there's no sense in belittling you to impress his friends."

Molly watched Duvall disappear inside the VIP tent, and let out a sigh and relaxed her grip on the pistol. "No, he doesn't know how close he came."

"What's that?"

She pulled her empty hand from the bag, angry to see that it was shaking. She wiped at one eye with the handkerchief Huffman had given her. "I said you spilled beer on your shirt."

The doctor gave his shirt a once-over, and having found nothing but the ordinary food stains and the soiling of two days of continual wear, he gave her a confused look. He would have asked a question, but it was at that moment that gunshots sounded from camp—a lot of them, one after another, and to Molly it sounded like a war was going on inside the Bullhorn Palace.

"Morgan's somewhere down there," she said.

"That he is," Chillingsworth said. "And I'm not at all ashamed to admit that I never had the nerve to do what he does for a living."

CHAPTER FORTY-ONE

It was the pain that woke Morgan. Not pain in one particular place, but pain all over. It was as if every joint and muscle in his entire body had been beaten with a hammer and rubbed raw with a rasp. He groaned and tried to roll onto his side, but it felt like someone was digging a knife blade into his left leg and he quickly gave that up.

"It's about time you woke up." Dixie was seated in a chair beside the cot he lay on.

Morgan looked around the room to orient himself. It was a tent no different than many others in camp, but his mind was foggy and it took him several more moments to recognize it as belonging to Doc Chillingsworth. There were four cots in the front room of the tent serving as an infirmary, and a doorway leading to a back room made of poles and planks where the doctor slept.

"How'd I get here?" Morgan asked.

"The crowd picked you up off the floor of the Bullhorn and carried you down here on a wagon tailgate yesterday."

"Yesterday?"

"You've been asleep for better than eight hours."

Morgan lifted the blanket covering him and noticed the heavy bandage wrappings around his left thigh, and winced at the sight of his bruised, swollen ankles where the railroad iron had been tied to him. He twisted his head slightly, until his chin brushed against something atop his right shoulder above his collarbone. It was too high up for him to have a good look at it, but he could see the white of another bandage there, and trying to move his arm on that side almost made him cry out.

"How many times was I shot?" he asked.

Dixie rose and went to a coat tree made out of a peeled cedar log with stubs of limbs left on it near the stove, moving slowly with one hand held against his chest and a wheeze to his breathing.

"Twice. Once in the leg, and once there high up on your shoulder," Dixie said, short of breath after only taking a few steps to the stove. "Doc said that one in your leg got nothing but meat, but that one by your neck almost cut that big tendon in two."

Morgan tried to move his right arm again, but it didn't work right, no matter how he gritted his teeth and tried.

"Ah, don't look so scared. Doc stitched it back up, and said you ought to heal up in a few months, although you might not ever pitch in a Sunday baseball game again."

"What about . . . ?"

Dixie finished for him. "Grat Kingman's dead, and Fischer likely won't live out the day."

Morgan couldn't hide his surprise. "Deacon isn't dead?"

"He's cut and shot all to doll rags, but he's still hanging on," Dixie said. "Lottie Bickford has got him down at her tent. That's where Doc Chillingsworth's gone."

"What about Texas George and the other brother?"

"They lit out. I hear that Bennie Kingman was bleeding like a stuck pig, and George had to help him on his horse."

"They almost got me. I wouldn't have given you ten cents for my chances."

"Well, pardon me, but I think they got the worst end of it. You're the talk of camp. Everyone's telling how you turned the Bullhorn into a slaughterhouse. They say you couldn't take a step in that joint without putting your foot in blood. One of those reporters in camp came here this morning to see if you were awake so that he could interview you."

"My body doesn't feel like I won."

"No, I imagine not. I was helping Doc work on you, and it looked like those boys hung you up by your heels and tried to kick your ribs in."

"Wasn't them." Morgan gave a brief account of his encounter with Irish Dave and Fat Sally at the river.

"So you're telling me that the Traveler saved you so that he could have the pleasure of shooting you himself? I swear, it wouldn't pay to be your guardian angel. Poor thing probably has bullet holes in him, too." Dixie took Morgan's black frock coat from the coat tree and held it up where Morgan could see it. He stuck one of his fingers through a bullet hole in one side of it, wiggling the finger as if to prove his point.

Morgan didn't say anything while Dixie took down his hat from the same coat tree and pitched it on the cot with him. He wiggled his good left arm from under the covers and turned the hat in his hand, examining it. There was another bullet hole through the top of the crown.

"Shame. It was a new hat," was all that Morgan said.

"If that one had been a little lower it would have let some air into that hard head of yours," Dixie said. "Feel lucky now?"

"Lucky is the last thing I feel," Morgan replied. "How's camp?"

"Still standing. The Tenth Cavalry never has gotten here from Fort Gibson, but Duvall's hanging tight. His Pinkertons came down here last night and cracked a couple of heads and arrested three men to try and get a lid on things."

"Did he send the money back north like I asked him?"

"No."

"What's Tuck doing?"

"Doc said some of Duvall's guests came into camp last night to see the sights, and of course, they ended up in the Bullhorn. Tuck gave everyone a free round on the house in your name. Raised a toast to you and gave a little speech about what a staunch advocate for law and order he was."

Morgan tried to sit up, but winced and eased back down on his cot.

"Best you take it easy for a spell," Dixie said. "Killing yourself trying to get off that cot so you can go kill Tuck ain't going to help anything."

"What time is it?"

"Don't have a watch."

"There's one in my vest pocket."

Dixie found Morgan's blood-crusted vest, and when he pulled out the watch there was a wry smile on his face. He closed his hand around it, and went to the open doorway and looked out it and up at the sun. "Best guess is that it's about eight or nine o'clock in the morning."

"My watch wasn't in my pocket?" Morgan asked.

Dixie turned around and opened his palm so that Morgan could see the watch. The case was dented and blackened with a smear of lead, and when he opened the warped lid pieces of the busted lens tinkled to the floor. It was obvious that another bullet had struck the watch where it lay in Morgan's coat pocket.

"Want to rethink your luck?"

CHAPTER FORTY-TWO

The next time Morgan woke up, Ruby Ann was sitting on her cot on the far side of the tent from him and staring at him with a blank expression. Dixie sat in a chair in the doorway watching the street. He glanced at Morgan when he heard him moving in his blankets, but immediately his attention shifted back to whatever he was watching outside.

Morgan bent his good leg and used it and his good arm to shove himself up to a sitting position. The pain it caused made him groan, and Ruby Ann quickly rose and came to help him, doubling his pillow behind him and adding a folded blanket to give him a backrest. Without him asking, she brought him a pitcher of water.

He drank three glasses full before he paused to look up at her. "Thank you, Ruby Ann. That was nice of you."

She didn't reply, and returned to her seat on the cot and faced him with the same blank expression.

"She doesn't say much," Dixie said from the doorway.

"I wish she would quit staring at me," Morgan said. "What's so interesting out in the street? Sounds like there's a crowd out there."

"The secretary's train just rolled in, and everybody's going down to the tracks to see the show."

A band fired up outside, and the sound of the brass and a base drum startled Morgan. "There's a band in camp?"

"The Kansas City Hook and Ladder Company No. 3 sent

their band down on the train to toot some horns for the party," Dixie said with a grin. "And that Indian agent, Pickins, he brought over a choir of little Indian kids from the academy at North Fork. You ought to see them all dressed in their little white robes and carrying their Bibles."

Red Molly stumbled into the hospital tent carrying three precariously balanced plates of food. She steadied herself and spun around and cursed at someone outside. But her face changed when she saw Morgan awake and sitting up in bed. "Thought the three of you might be hungry."

"Famished," Morgan answered.

Molly threw one more heated look out the door at whoever she had been cursing while she handed out the food. "Those drunken fools almost made me spill this twice trying to cross the street. It's a madhouse out there."

She drug a chair close to Morgan's cot and seated herself and offered him a spoonful of beef stew.

"I can feed myself, Molly. I'm not an invalid."

"Sshh!" She shoved the spoon in his mouth before he could argue more.

"I want you to get one of the Pinkertons as soon as the secretary's speech is over. I need a favor done," Morgan said.

"What's that?"

"I need someone to round up a couple of men in the morning and go get two bodies down by the river."

She paused with another spoonful of beans halfway to him. "Bodies?"

"Irish Dave and Fat Sally. I was going to bring them in yesterday, but I was sidetracked."

"What happened?" she asked.

"They tried to kill me."

Molly passed a worried look at Dixie, and Morgan saw it.

"You keep that quiet for now, Morgan. Don't you tell

anybody," she said. "You tell me where they're at, and I'll go down there and roll them in the river myself after it gets dark."

"What's the matter? You're acting funny."

Molly gave Dixie another look before she answered Morgan. "Can you walk?"

"I won't run any foot races, but I imagine I can walk."

"It might not be a bad idea to move you to my tent before dark."

"That's enough, Molly. I'm in no mood for games, so tell me straight."

"Tuck opened up early today and he's been serving free booze for the last couple of hours. There must be fifty or sixty men inside his place, and more drinking in front of it."

"She's right. It's getting rough out there." Dixie leaned forward in his chair where he could better see out the door and down the street to the Bullhorn. "Hardly noon yet, and most of that crowd has already tied one on. And Tuck's egging them on. There's been a couple of times earlier when I could hear him all the way up here speechifying about low wages and carpetbag, tight-fisted Yankees and crooked politicians building their railroad where no one asked them to, and building it on the backs of better men."

"Tuck's a Yankee himself," Morgan replied.

"Doesn't matter," Dixie said. "Most men hear what they want to hear."

"Somebody has been spreading it around that you murdered Irish Dave and Fat Sally over an old grudge." Molly held up a hand and waved off the protest forming on Morgan's mouth so that she could finish. "Those two disappear, and then you ride into camp on Sally's horse."

"They're dead, but I didn't kill them."

"Doesn't matter. Somebody is stirring up that bunch of drunks, and talking about how no vigilante marshal ought to be allowed to hide behind a badge."

Morgan made a wry face. "I bet I can guess who got that talk started. Probably the same man that was toasting me the night before."

Molly put a gentle hand on his shoulder. "Morgan, I don't know who started the story, but I'm afraid somebody is trying to work up a lynch mob. You know how crazy men can get when they're drinking like that."

"How come that fool Duvall doesn't send the Pinkertons down to break it up?" Morgan asked.

Dixie spit a stream of tobacco juice out the door. "Secretary is about to give his speech, and Duvall's keeping his hired detectives at the train for a bodyguard."

"Where are my clothes?" Morgan moved as if to get up, a grimace of pain on his face.

Molly held him down with a hand on his chest. "You're not going anywhere. There's not a thing you can do in the condition you're in."

"Molly, I'm not going to argue with you."

She kept her hand on his chest and held up the spoon she had been feeding him with like it was a weapon. "Don't make me use this."

He took hold of her wrist, about to shove it away, but the sound of spurs in the doorway drew their attention. Sergeant Harjo, the Lighthorse sergeant, stood there.

"I heard you were dead," Harjo said.

"Heard the same about you," Morgan said. "How many men have you got with you?"

Whatever Harjo was about to say was cut off when Molly threw the spoon down in the bowl of stew, splashing Morgan. He slapped away the hot broth with his good arm while he gave her an incredulous look.

"What the hell has gotten into you?" he asked.

Molly rose and stormed to where Morgan's clothes lay folded over the back of a chair. She hurled the clothes at him. "You go ahead and get yourself killed and see if I care."

Sergeant Harjo barely ducked out of her way as she went out the door in a huff. He took a peek out the door to watch her go and then grinned at Morgan. "Women."

Morgan managed to swing his legs over the edge of the cot, setting his bad leg down gingerly. It dawned on him that he was naked and that Ruby Ann was still staring at him, but he was in no mood to care. It took him several attempts to pull his pants on, and he found that his feet and ankles were too swollen to get into his boots, especially trying to tug into them one-handed.

Dixie noticed and retrieved a pair of moccasins that he handed over. "Traded those off of one of those Choctaws who came in here wanting Doc to give them something for the croup. Maybe they'll fit you."

Morgan slipped his feet inside the buckskin shoes and stared at his swollen feet, dreading bending over and trying to tie the moccasins' laces. If anything, his headache had grown worse instead of better. As if reading his mind, Ruby Ann darted forward and knelt and tied the moccasins.

"Agent Pickins told us that most of your Creek party went under," Morgan said after he took a few deep breaths to steady himself.

"What would Pickins know? He ran off at the first shot," Harjo said, making no attempt to hide his disgust at the mention of the Indian agent.

"Who was it that hit your party?" Morgan asked.

"Didn't recognize any of them except for Texas George," Harjo said. "Him I got a good look at. The bastard rode right past me and killed my horse out from under me with a load of buckshot."

The pain was so bad Morgan almost cried out when he

slipped his game arm out of its sling so that he could put his shirt on. He threw a quick glance at Dixie and Sergeant Harjo to see if they were about to say something, but both men kept poker faces. Ruby Ann helped him into the shirt, and he couldn't help but notice the bloodstains across one side of it where he had been shot.

"You didn't say how many men you had with you," Morgan said while Ruby Ann helped him put his arm back in the sling.

"Just me and one other in camp," Harjo said. "But I've got fifteen more men waiting two miles from here."

"You better send the man with you to get them," Morgan said while Ruby Ann tucked his shirt in and helped him re-sling his arm. "For now, you and me and Dixie will have to do."

"Do for what?" Harjo asked.

"Yeah, what?" Dixie added.

"Keeping the peace," Morgan said. "Where's my gun?"

Harjo shook his head. "This is white man business."

"You mean to tell me that you didn't come here looking for the men that ambushed you?"

Harjo said nothing to that, only staring at Morgan.

Dixie handed Morgan his gun belt. "I don't know what you think you're going to do with that, the shape that you're in."

Morgan made a fumbling attempt to sling the belt around his hips and catch the other end of it one-handed.

"You can't even put your gun on," Dixie added.

"This camp is going to blow sky high if we don't get out there," Morgan said. "That fool Duvall doesn't have a clue."

"And what are two crippled lawmen going to do about it?"

Morgan nodded at Ruby Ann for her to buckle on his gun belt. "You don't have to come."

"Now that's a hell of a thing to say to your deputy." Dixie tried to look offended, but didn't quite manage it.

Morgan slipped his good arm into a sleeve of his frock coat

and draped the other side of it over his bum shoulder. "What about you, Sergeant? There are likely men out there that were in on the robbery of a Creek payroll."

Harjo nodded uncertainly. "Those bastards opened up on us from the brush, and we didn't stand a chance. We lost three good men that day, and five more wounded. Not to mention the money that belonged to my people."

"Then I'd say you owe them one."

Harjo said, "I've got no jurisdiction over white men."

"Jurisdiction?" Morgan jerked the badge off his coat lapel. "Hold up your right hand."

"What?"

"I said, hold up your right hand."

Harjo held it up.

"Do you solemnly swear to uphold the Constitution of the United States and any and all laws of this nation?"

"Better answer him, or we'll be here all day," Dixie said.

"I do," Harjo replied.

"And do you solemnly swear to shoot any son of a bitch who gets in the way of those laws," Morgan continued, "or any son of a bitch you need to shoot?"

Harjo's grin matched Dixie's. "I do."

Morgan pitched the badge at the Lighthorse sergeant. "Good. You're now a duly deputized member of the Katy railroad police, and that's all the jurisdiction you need."

"You make a habit of swearing in red Indians?" Harjo asked.

Morgan jerked a thumb at Dixie. "I deputized this unreconstructed Rebel, didn't I?"

"He has a hard time finding anyone to work for him, so he can't be too picky about his recruits," Dixie threw in.

"Where's your man?" Morgan asked Harjo. "We're going to need him."

"He's slipping around trying to spot Texas George."

"Go find him while I think on how to play this."

"Anybody ever tell you that you're one stubborn white man?" Sergeant Harjo never got to finish his observation about Ironhead's chief of police, for the band started up again outside.

Morgan gave one last critical look at the bullet hole in the crown of his hat before he sat it on his head and tugged the brim low down on his forehead. "Sounds like they're starting the party without us."

"Don't sound so let down." Dixie retrieved his Spencer carbine from where it learned in a corner. He moved too quick and had to stop to catch his breath. "You any good with your left hand?"

Morgan adjusted the Remington holstered on his hip to where it sat handier to a backhanded draw. "No, never was much good with it."

Dixie grimaced. "Figures, but you could have lied. Just this once you didn't have to tell the truth. Just once."

CHAPTER FORTY-THREE

The crowd moving towards the tracks was already past them by the time Morgan and Sergeant Harjo stepped outside. They remained in front of the hospital tent, as it was near the back of the crowd and afforded them a good view of the proceedings.

The crowd formed a line forty yards deep the width of the street, and the front of it stopped within ten yards of the train. Wagons had been parked on each side of the street, and many of the onlookers were standing in them to get a better vantage. The Gatling gun and its gun pit was no longer at the door of the railroad office, and in its place and parked alongside the depot decking was a wagon containing the choir of children that Agent Pickins had brought over from the nearby Indian academy. They stood stiffly in the bed of the wagon and stared straight ahead at nothing but the sky over the train top in their little white robes with red crosses sewn into the chests. A photographer had set up his camera on a tripod nearby and was aiming it at the crowd.

Morgan had no clue where the Gatling gun had gone, but Duvall had taken several of the soldiers and positioned them at the edge of the tracks with their rifles at port arms to keep the crowd at a respectful distance. A couple of the Pinkertons could be seen at the foot of the steps to the platforms on each end of the rear-most passenger car.

Morgan sensed movement at his side, and caught a glimpse of Sergeant Harjo fading into the crowd, probably gone to search for the other Lighthorse man. He scanned the crowd himself. It was restless and liquored up, but so far behaving. The band was giving its best effort at Stephen Foster's *Camptown Races,* and other than some clapping and a few joyous whoops and loud talk, the only disturbance was the two Indian girls from the bathhouse deciding they wanted to dance together. The crowd parted a little in its center to make room for the young women, and the mob of men around them cheered them on. The two Choctaw girls were sloppy drunk and staggered and stumbled through some wild mixture of a native war dance and frontier freestyle steps that in no way matched the beat or the flavor of the music.

The band finished with a fading gasp from the tuba, and Superintendent Duvall and the secretary appeared on the deck of the passenger car at the hind end of the train, both men waving to the crowd as if it were an election campaign stop they were making. A flagpole had been mounted to the roof of the train at an angle above them, and the American flag hanging from it draped down right above their heads. A Pinkerton bodyguard and a handful of dignitaries stood behind them on the platform, including Huffman, the KNVR man. Several faces looked upon the crowd from the open windows of the passenger car, and Morgan spotted his ex-wife's among them. She was laughing and sipping a drink and pointing out something in the crowd to another woman in the window beside her.

Agent Pickins stood on the ground before his children's choir in the wagon with his back to the crowd. At some signal from Duvall he lifted his hands to the choir, and they began to sing the National Anthem. The clear, high-pitched timber of their voices rose to the sky, and even the noisiest of the crowd went silent. Agent Pickins's hands waved back and forth, energetically and fervently directing the children in song like some symphony conductor.

". . . and the home of the brave," the children finished in high harmony.

A ragged cheer went up at the conclusion of the anthem, and Duvall held up his hands for silence. He began a lengthy speech about the construction challenges his railroad had overcome, and thanked his laborers for their hard work and the Katy's investors and board of directors for their vision and patience.

"That man does like to hear the sound of his own voice," Dixie said.

Duvall finished his speech to a mixed round of half-hearted cheers that, from the look on his face, was obviously not the response he had hoped for. Several of those on the platform patted him on the back, and he nodded to them and cleared his throat before he introduced the secretary and stepped aside for him. The secretary held his hands wide in a gesture of greeting.

"I can't tell you how proud I am to come here to inspect the latest accomplishment of this railroad, and to be a citizen of this great nation," the secretary said.

"Go back to Washington, you tin-plated son of a bitch!" somebody shouted, followed by drunken laughter.

The secretary ignored the heckler and continued. "One day a whole network of railroads will crisscross our land, making it easier to move goods and products and helping us all become more prosperous . . ."

"You mean making your kind richer!" another voice shouted.

Morgan and Dixie both tried to spot the latest heckler, but the voice seemed to come from some other place in the crowd from the first one.

The secretary held his hands at arm's length and pushed his palms downward through the air in a gesture of appeasement and a request for silence. A beer bottle came flying through the air and shattered on the tracks in front and below the secretary.

"You were a might low, Davy!" somebody shouted. "Throw

another one and see if you can do better."

Two of the soldiers started forward at a nod from Duvall, but the crowd was too tightly packed and made no effort to move out of their way. Morgan thought he spied the group of men in the crowd that was responsible for the jeering and the thrown bottle, but they were on the far side of the street from him. And by then, shouts and catcalls were going up from other places in the crowd. Agent Pickins was trying to get his children's choir down out of the wagon, while the more sober and civilized in the crowd were trying to make their way out of it as quickly as they could, as if they sensed the mood changing.

Bill Tuck appeared out of the masses and stepped up on the depot decking in front of the band where all could see him. He held up his hands to those gathered before him. "Calm now, calm, gentlemen. What are our guests going to think of our camp?"

He nodded at the band behind him and said something to them over his shoulder. To a man, the band looked nervous and about to break and run, but to their credit, they promptly burst into a rousing rendition of the *Battle Hymn of the Republic*. Perhaps it had been Tuck's intent that the music distract and soothe the drunken rowdies, or perhaps he had the opposite intention, but no matter, the Southern contingent in the crowd was strong and numerous, and the grumbling began immediately and quickly raised to shouts and threats. Someone flung a handful of fresh horse manure at the trumpet player, and a few rocks and other miscellaneous flying objects soon followed it. Many of the Irish tracklayers and the northern men in the crowd took offense at the disrespect shown such a popular anthem that many of them had sung during the late war, and threats and shaking fists were aimed at those so rudely protesting the band's efforts.

Either Tuck or the band made a quick poll of the crowd and

must have decided that the Southerners outnumbered those of the opposite persuasion, for they ceased their tune and broke into *Dixie Land* without so much as an off beat or a missed note, as if two such songs could be joined into a medley. In fact, if anything, they played it more loudly than they had the previous song. The new song brought on boisterous cheers and whoops from its fans, louder rumbling from the Northern contingent, and before it was halfway through, two different fistfights had broken ought amongst the tightly packed assembly of human flesh gathered alongside the train. Tuck shouted something, but the uproar had grown too loud for him to be heard. The last Morgan saw of him, he was making his way along the edge of the crowd towards the Bullhorn without casting a backward glance at what he was leaving behind.

"You go around and tell those soldiers to fix bayonets and disperse this mob. Get the Pinkertons to help them." Morgan had to raise his voice almost to a shout for Dixie to hear him over the din.

Dixie didn't have time to question him, for Morgan was already hobbling away. Dixie cut between the hospital tent and the company store, intending on circling around and approaching the train from the side opposite the crowd. He moved slower than he would have liked to, his breath coming in strained gasps, and cursing his poor health with every step and anyone who got in his way.

What had started as drunken men bickering and passing boisterous threats among the crowd was quickly turning into an all-out melee. Two men were slugging it out, fist and skull right in front of Morgan, and he backhanded his Remington out of its holster and hit the nearest one over the head with the barrel. The man fell like he was poleaxed, and before the other combatant could realize what had happened Morgan clipped him in the chin with the pistol. The hard steel clacked the man's teeth together and sent him staggering backwards. Someone bumped into Morgan's bad shoulder and by the time he had righted himself on his one good leg and shook off the pain he was separated from the two fighters and being jostled and pressed farther away.

The band cut short its rendition of *Dixie Land,* but did manage to give it a final flourish. Immediately, a wild round of cheers for the song went up from among the crowd, and somebody fired off their pistol into the air. The gunshot was taken as a signal by others that a full-fledged celebration was in order, and considering that there were no fireworks on hand, their revolvers would have to do. Soon pistols were going off everywhere.

For a brief instant a crack showed in the crowd, and Morgan had a clear view of the passenger car at the end of the train. Duvall put a hand on the secretary's shoulder and shoved him towards the door leading inside the car. The superintendent was almost through the door behind him, with Huffman and the others hot on his heels, when Morgan saw Huffman reel and stagger and fall against the handrail, clutching his chest. Already, there was a growing blot of blood on the light-gray suit coat he wore.

The wild gunfire continued and some tough howled like a wolf and was answered by some other drunk's poor imitation of a rooster's crowing. Finally, someone other than Morgan must have noticed that Huffman had fallen.

"He's been shot!" they shouted from the passenger car.

There was a woman's scream, and the crowd grew a little quieter, distracted momentarily from their mad revelry. The Pinkerton kneeling over the fallen Huffman had his pistol drawn and was glaring at the crowd and calling inside the passenger car for help.

"Some fool accidentally shot him," someone near Morgan observed.

Morgan turned away from the train and made a quick search of his surroundings. Amidst the pistol fire he had sworn he heard the deeper bellow of a rifle. His eyes locked on the low, timbered hill two hundred yards to the west of the camp, and he thought he detected a faint, dissipating cloud of gunsmoke floating there.

But no one else seemed to have noticed, although the pistol shots came to an end, whether by concern for the fallen KNVR man, or because their cylinders were empty. Morgan spied a group of four or five men brawling not far from him, but was having little luck shoving his way to them. Somebody took a swing at him that jostled his hat, but the confusion was so great that he couldn't locate who had tried to clip him.

A loose, saddled horse charged through the crowd at a run, knocking aside whoever didn't get out of its way. Morgan barely saw it before it slapped him in the side of the head with a flapping stirrup and staggered him. He looked back along the seam it had parted through the crowd and saw the soldiers forming up in a tighter line with their bayonets fixed to the end of their Long Tom Springfield rifles. Dixie was behind them waving and shouting something at the engineer in the locomotive who was leaning out of his cab.

Behind the stampeding horse came a stream of Indian children at a run, their short legs churning underneath their white choir robes as they tried to keep up with Agent Pickins running in front of them. They passed to either side of Morgan as he stood with his pistol upraised and looking beyond them for a way to join the soldiers.

The only way was to try and edge his way to the side of the street, but the whole world exploded before he could take one step. The roar of the explosion washed over him like a wave, and the air seemed to turn so thick that it was like he was submerged beneath water. Everything around him slowed to a crawl, and he was faintly aware of chunks of wood and other debris flying through the air past him. His eardrums expanded until they were too big for his skull, and then just as quickly they receded and he was falling and falling forever, through the wash and roar of sound and fury as if it would never end. And as the flames swept past and around him, he thought for the third time in less than the span of a day that he was dead.

Chapter Forty-Four

Morgan tasted dirt in his mouth and blood, and it took him several long moments to figure out that he was lying flat on his face. He rolled over to a sitting position and stared dumbly around him. Smoke was everywhere, and bits and pieces of burning debris rained down from the sky. Bodies lay around him like twigs or blades of grass scattered before some mighty wind. Some were perhaps dead, and others groaned and writhed in pain or struggled to their feet slowly and achingly like men drug back from the brink of hell. Soot and grime coated their faces and clothes, and trickles of blood oozed from the ears of some of them from the concussion of the explosion.

Morgan finally realized that what he was looking at across the street was the railroad office, or what had once been the railroad office. All that was left of it was the splintered, charred skeleton of two of the frame walls and a collapsed portion of the roof. A man in smoldering clothes and a piece of board piercing his arm staggered from it clutching his wound and with tears streaming down his cheeks.

Slowly, Morgan's hearing was returned to him, and he began to recognize the voices around him—at first no more than a blurred, dull drone, and finally a distinct mix of voices and specific sounds hitting him all at once. A horse nickered, someone was crying nearby, and another was calling pitifully for a doctor. He shifted to one hip and got his good leg and good arm under him and struggled to his feet, one of the few standing where there had once been at least three hundred people around him. It was all like a bad dream.

The side of the secretary's passenger car was on fire, and someone else rose up from the ground between Morgan and the flames. It was one of the soldiers, and he and Morgan shared dazed, confused looks.

The sound of hoofbeats pounding the street came from behind Morgan, and he was slow to turn around and face them. Four-wide the horsemen came, at a dead run, ten or twelve of them, all brandishing guns. They rode like men born to a horse, and Morgan noticed one of them with the reins in his teeth and a pistol in each fist, bushwhacker style.

Morgan clawed at his holster, but found it empty. It took his fogged brain too long to remember that he must have dropped his pistol when he was blasted from his feet, and he barely had time to glance at the ground in search of it before the riders were upon him. The first of them raced past him and jerked a boot from his stirrup and gave Morgan a hard kick in the chest.

Morgan fell backward, and by the time he got to his knees again half the horsemen were fanned out across the street amongst the shocked and scattered crowd. They fired their pistols into the air, or at the side of the secretary's passenger car. Glass shattered where the bullets struck the car, while the other half of the horsemen dismounted in front of the destroyed depot house. The men that remained mounted shouted threats to those around them, or pointed their pistols at anyone who didn't flee fast enough to suit them.

Morgan's coat was hanging from one arm and tangled about him, and he fought to shed it. At last free of it, he groped wildly for his pistol. He saw Duvall's safe sitting amongst the ruins of the shattered building, and watched as the dismounted men went straight to it. The door to the safe hung open and sagged on its hinges, as if the charge that had blown the depot to bits had been placed directly beneath that square of steel.

One of the men leaned over and looked into the safe, and gave a curse. "It ain't here. They must have moved it."

"What do you mean it ain't there?" the man beside him asked. He leaned over and had his own look in the safe.

Morgan's hand bumped against cold steel, and he looked down and saw his Remington half pinned under the body of a man moaning and groaning and coming to life in front of him. Around him, more people who had been knocked senseless and flattened by the explosion were getting to their feet.

Dynamite. That's where the dynamite McDaniels was missing had gone. It was the first clear thought Morgan's addled mind could form, and he clung to it like he was afraid to let it go.

A hiss of steam rolled out from under the locomotive, and the train lurched forward with a slow grind of its wheels and the clank of its pinned connectors between the cars jerking tight. The men by the safe climbed out of the maze of broken lumber and ran to where their comrades held their horses for them.

"Stop that train!" one of them shouted. "That's where they probably moved the money!"

Bullet holes stitched the wooden sides of the passenger car, showing pale white amidst the bright green coat of paint. The engineer must have been ducked down in his cab, for he was out of sight as bullets ricocheted off the steel sides below his window with an angry whine as the train slowly left the station under a hail of gunfire.

A rifle barrel popped out of one of the shattered windows in the passenger car and one of the outlaw horsemen was knocked from his saddle. At the same time, three of the soldiers were running for the tail end of the train. Two of them managed to grab hold of the handrail alongside the steps up to the deck, but the third of them fell with a bullet in the back, arms flung wide and falling forward as the car rolled past. One of the Pinkertons, the same one that had knelt over Huffman's body, rose up from the platform and provided covering fire while the other two soldiers climbed up beside him.

More gunshots came from the passenger car's broken windows, and another of the horsemen slumped in the saddle and his horse spun in a circle in the middle of the street, held by the dying outlaw's death clutch on the reins. The rest of the outlaws' horses were wild with the gunfire and the confusion, and the dismounted men of their party were having a hard time getting back into the saddle. Half the train was beyond the head of the street by the time they remounted, and they charged towards the tracks with pistols blazing. The two soldiers and the Pinkerton knelt on the rear deck of the passenger car and returned their fire.

Morgan holstered his Remington and lunged to his feet and went in a wobbling trot towards the circling horse with its dead rider. He lunged and managed to grab one of the reins on the first try, and shoved off the dead rider. The horse refused to still, and he could feel his broken ribs grind together as he heaved himself in the saddle on the fly.

The fleeing train and the outlaws had both disappeared around the corner of the smoldering depot house; Morgan gave the horse a one-legged kick and the animal bolted forward as if shot out of a cannon. He reined the horse around the depot at a dead run, and not fifty yards in front of him was the train, slowly building speed towards the river. Between the train and him was the line of outlaws fanned out to either side of the tracks, some of them already racing alongside the passenger car and firing into it.

The horse beneath him was running free and straight alongside the tracks, and Morgan gritted his teeth and shook free of the sling on his bad arm. He shifted his reins to that hand, and with his left, he fumbled at his holstered Remington. The gelding he rode clipped the end of a railroad tie and almost fell with him, its front feet scrambling and its nose almost plowing the ground in front of it. He checked the horse's speed long enough to let it get its legs back under it, and then raced forward again.

One of the soldiers on the end of the passenger car rose up with his rifle shouldered and aimed at one of the pursuing outlaws, but he never got to shoot. A bullet struck him before he could, and his head snapped back and his body went limp and he toppled over the edge of the handrail and hit the tracks in a lifeless heap. One of the outlaws coming behind spurred over the body, his horse leaping wildly and shying from the dead man beneath it. The rider was still in midair when either the Pinkerton or the remaining soldier on the rear of the train shot him from the saddle.

In the same instant, one of the other outlaws rode close beside the platform, and he shot the Pinkerton at point blank range. The Pinkerton fell on his side, but managed a blast from his shotgun back at the man who had shot him. Some of the shot must have struck the outlaw's horse, for it veered wide, fighting its rider's efforts to rein it back to the side of the train.

There were only four cars in the train, and it was rapidly gaining speed. Morgan was within twenty yards of it and closing when he rode up to the back of the outlaw nearest him. He thrust the Remington against the outlaw's ribcage and pulled the trigger. The outlaw cried out and slid over the opposite side of his saddle, grabbing desperately for his saddle horn, but slipping farther and farther down the horse's side and out of sight, until his body struck the ground speeding beneath him. His boot hung in the stirrup, and his body bounced and skidded limply beside the running horse like a flapping, limp flag.

Ahead of Morgan, two of the outlaws had ridden ahead of

the passenger car and rode their horses so close to it that they almost brushed against it. One of them put a foot in the saddle and braced against it and made a wild leap for the front deck of the car, catching hold of the ornate cast-iron banister and roof support and swinging himself onto the train. The other rider raced ahead, obviously aiming to do the same with the engine.

Morgan leapt his horse over the tracks and headed up the opposite side of the train. Barely had he done so when one of the outlaws on that side noticed him and reined up and rolled his horse back over its hocks to face him. Morgan pulled harder than he intended on his reins, and his horse jammed its hindquarters in the ground in a shower of chat and loose earth of the roadbed, and it reared high against the pain of the bit digging into its mouth. The horse's front end was still off the ground and its head lifted in his lap when Morgan snapped a shot at the outlaw blocking his way. The Remington felt awkward in his left hand, and he knew he had missed the man badly the instant he pulled the trigger.

The outlaw's pistol flamed, as Morgan rode the fall of his horse down like a felled tree. The instant its front feet hit the ground he kicked it forward, circling wide of the rider before him and resting his Remington across his saddle at hip level. He thumbed the hammer and touched off another round, and again he missed. The outlaw's horse was a fine broke animal, and he spun it effortlessly around on its hocks and brought his pistol to bear on Morgan once more. But another gun roared and the outlaw pitched forward over the neck of his horse.

Morgan glanced at the rear of the train and saw Dixie leaning against the open doorjamb as if it took that to hold his weary body up. But he held the smoking Spencer carbine still pressed to his shoulder and aimed at the outlaw he had just shot.

Morgan nodded to him in salute and reined his horse back

toward the train that had pulled away from him during his delay. A bullet ricocheted off a railroad iron beside him, and he spied four more outlaws ahead of him twisted around in their saddles and firing back his way. He snapped a shot at one of them and leapt his horse across the tracks and out of their line of sight. None of the outlaws were on that side of the train, except the single rider racing far ahead of him for the locomotive. Morgan had a free run for a while, but the train was working up to speed and he was hard-pressed to close on it.

He had almost caught up to the rear of the train when one of the outlaws on the other side faded back until the two of them were racing side by side on opposite sides of the tracks. The outlaw fired at him without effect, and then dropped off on the far side of his horse, Indian style, before Morgan could return the shot. Nothing but the outlaw's left calf and his hand on his saddle horn was visible to Morgan, so he held his fire and kicked his horse forward to once more put the train between the two of them. A gun barrel poked out of a shattered window right beside him, but the soldier looking back at him realized who he was before he fired. Morgan leaned low over his saddle and asked his horse for more speed.

Beside him, Dixie and one of the soldiers appeared on the rear deck of the passenger car carrying the Gatling gun. It had been removed from its artillery carriage, but someone had connected the gun to a kind of tripod stand. Once positioned, Dixie knelt with his shouldered Spencer while the trooper took hold of the rear of the battery gun and swiveled it towards the outlaw running his horse directly behind the passenger car. The Gatling's multi-barrels spun in a blur and a burp of sound, and the outlaw tipped over the back of his running horse like he had been hit in the chest with a giant sledgehammer.

The train had reached a speed that most horses weren't going to match, and one by one the outlaws fell back, and when they did so they came right into the path of the Gatling. The trooper manning it turned the firing crank and the gun roared and stitched a line of bullet furrows into the ground beside the tracks, slowly working its way towards the two outlaws who first appeared.

They tried to veer their horses wide at the sight of the Gatling and the bullet furrows working towards them, but it was already too late for that. The first of the .50-70 bullets spraying at them took a horse in the neck and flipped it end over end and sent its rider flying over its head as it crashed to the ground. The other outlaw managed to get off a shot that knocked splinters from the wall of the car beside Dixie's head, but the Gatling's barrels spun again and the next burst struck the outlaw in the chest at a range of less than ten yards. He jerked with the impact of the bullets shredding his flesh.

Dixie threw a quick glance at Morgan and waved him towards the front of the train. The single outlaw ahead of Morgan was riding a fast horse and somehow staying abreast of the locomotive. He fired repeatedly into the cab and shouted for the engineer to halt the train. Not far ahead of them, Morgan could see the trestle spanning the river.

The Gatling gun was roaring again behind him. The chase had taken them over a mile, and his horse was beginning to labor. No matter how hard he urged it on he couldn't close the last bit of distance between him and the outlaw ahead of him.

Something flew down at the outlaw from the rear of the locomotive. It barely missed the outlaw's head, and whatever it was bounced and rolled heavily and almost struck Morgan's horse. He looked up to see the tender in a pair of pinstriped overalls and a red cap standing atop the tall, mounded stack of firewood carried in the tender car. He already had another chunk of stove wood held above his head in both hands, and again he hurled the wood at the outlaw. The stick of firewood missed its mark as before, but the outlaw did have to check his horse to avoid being hit. That was enough for Morgan to close on him. He tried a shot at the outlaw's back, and another one when the man twisted in the saddle and saw him coming.

The outlaw had twisted around to his left to bring his gun to bear, and Morgan reined quickly the opposite way. The outlaw had to twist the other way in the saddle to find Morgan again, and by that time Morgan's horse had pulled alongside him. Morgan leveled the Remington at point blank range.

The pistol's hammer snapped on an empty chamber as the outlaw whirled in the saddle to face him. Morgan lashed out with his empty pistol, but the outlaw ducked the blow and was bringing his own pistol to bear. Morgan drew back the Remington and flung it backhanded as hard as he could. The flying gun struck the bushwhacker full in the face, and he dropped his reins and clutched his saddle horn with both hands to stay mounted.

Out of the corner of one eye Morgan saw the beginning of the trestle and the steep drop-off of the riverbank only a few yards ahead. The outlaw beside him seemed oblivious to the danger.

Morgan reined his horse against the outlaw's mount, pressing tight against him until they rubbed legs. He kept reining towards the train racing beside them. At the last instant possible, the outlaw recognized the precipice before them, but he had dropped his reins and his horse was in a blind runaway. Morgan pulled back on his own reins and steered hard to the left. The lathered gelding he rode barely managed to slow and turn, and so close to the drop-off did it come that its back hooves crumpled the sandy lip of the riverbank. Morgan watched wide-eyed as the outlaw and his horse sailed over the bluff and out of sight.

Morgan pulled his gelding to a stop as the train rattled onto the first of the trestle, and cast a look down over the riverbank below him. It was a twelve-foot dive to the next shelf of sand that sloped down to the edge of the water, and on that shelf the fallen horse was trying pitifully to get to its feet. Both front legs were broken, and the horse rolled over on the body of its rider, crushing him if he wasn't already dead.

But it was what lay beyond the fallen outlaw and his horse that startled Morgan most. The body of one of the Pinkertons he had left to guard the bridge lay there dead on the sand, and beyond it three men were standing in waist-deep water next to pylons that supported the bridge. Two of the men had rifles and were aiming them downriver. A bullet splashed the water near them, and Morgan saw gunsmoke lift from the willows farther downstream. Apparently, some of the Pinkerton bridge guards were putting up a fight.

The man without a rifle held a length of cannon fuse, and he hooked the end of it over a spike or bolt head on the support pylon he stood by. He was trying to strike a match on his belt buckle when Morgan's stamping horse sent a shower of loose sand and earth trickling down the embankment.

Texas George turned his surprised face up to Morgan, the lit match and the end of the cannon fuse in his hands only inches apart. Somewhere behind Morgan a bugle sounded.

Texas George's surprised look changed to a broad grin as he touched the match flame to the end of the fuse. Beside Morgan the train flew past, shaking and vibrating the wooden trestle. He caught a brief glimpse of Dixie hanging out over the handrail of the passenger car deck as it passed, and something flew through the air towards him. It was Dixie's Spencer carbine, and Morgan caught it with his good hand and slid from the back of his horse, all in one move.

The other two outlaws with Texas George didn't see Morgan until he was sliding down the steep riverbank towards them.

One of them swung his rifle towards Morgan, just as Morgan cocked the Spencer and pointed it one-handed like a pistol and fired while he was still sliding down the bank. By sheer luck or fate, the .52 caliber bullet struck the outlaw aiming at him in the forehead and he sunk into the river.

Morgan's bad leg jammed into the struggling and dying horse at the bottom of the bluff, braking his descent, but sending a shiver of pain all the way through his body. The other outlaw behind Texas George fired, and his shot kicked sand in Morgan's eyes. Morgan hunkered behind the struggling horse and cursed and jacked the lever of the Spencer to chamber another round. Another bullet struck the horse in the neck while he rose to a sitting position and cocked the carbine.

Before he could fire, one of the Pinkertons in the willows downstream made a good shot and left the remaining rifleman floating facedown in the river. Morgan willed his bad arm to work and took a two-hand hold on the Spencer and swung it towards Texas George. The little outlaw was already ducking and dodging amongst the bridge pylons, splashing among the shallows and working his way upstream. He paused and looked back once to snap a pistol shot at Morgan, but Morgan's bullet knocked a chunk from a bridge timber beside him and sent him fleeing once more.

Morgan fell back on the sand, his breath coming in ragged gasps and his heart thudding wildly in his chest. He could feel the warm stickiness of blood soaking his left pants leg, and his right shoulder ached to the point he could barely think. He lay there for a long moment until his mind registered the hissing sound coming from the bridge pylon in front of him.

He used the Spencer as a crutch and lunged to standing position. The cannon fuse George had lit was steadily burning up the pylon, and Morgan traced its sparking path as it climbed. He hobbled forward, his bad leg finally about to quit him, and taking most of the weight on his good leg and the butt of the Spencer as a crutch. The burning fuse was almost too high up the pylon for him to reach, and he splashed into the shallows at the edge of the river.

The fuse had burned out of his reach and he watched it turn where it was draped across a horizontal bridge timber connecting the first pylon to another. Ten feet above the water and up that second pylon, Morgan saw the bundle of dynamite tied there.

The river was waist-high to him by then, and he fought against the slow but strong current, lunging and pushing hard toward the pylon ahead of him. Railroad spikes had been driven into the pylon for a climbing ladder during the trestle's construction, and Morgan let go of the Spencer and took hold of the lowest spike. He reached for the next one and his right shoulder screamed and sent fire throughout his body that caused him to tremble and shake with the effort. Ignoring the pain, he found a foot purchase below the water and began to climb. The fuse above him had burnt to within three feet of the bundled sticks of dynamite.

Hand over hand, groaning and grunting with the strain, Morgan climbed, never taking his eyes off the burning cannon fuse. It seemed as if he climbed in slow motion, and as if he would never reach the fuse in time. He was still two feet below the crossbeam when the burning, hissing fuse was only inches away from the dynamite. His good arm took his weight on the next spike above him and he jerked himself upward in a last-ditch heave, and his bad arm reached out desperately for the fuse. He felt his body falling and feared his leap hadn't been high enough.

CHAPTER FORTY-FIVE

Morgan's outstretched arm and his straining fingers reached for the fuse in the moment his body started to fall back to the river below. He hit the river below flat on his back, and the murky water closed in above him. It was a long count of three before he rose to the surface, shaking the water free of him and gasping for air. He stared up at the dynamite above him for a long moment, and then looked down at the two-inch section of fuse clutched in his trembling right hand. He would have laughed had he not been so tired and beaten.

He waded out to the shore and flopped down on the sand at the edge of the water, still clutching the fuse in his hand and staring at it. He heard something above him at the top of the riverbank, but couldn't find the energy to turn and look up, or to care. Somebody shouted at him, and he finally craned his neck around to look behind him. A line of cavalrymen stared down at him, black men in uniform, and Tenth U.S. Cavalry flag flapped in the wind above them. Every one of the Buffalo Soldiers had a Springfield carbine pointing his way.

Morgan held up the tiny bit of cannon fuse, as if it explained everything. "I thought the cavalry always rode to the rescue, but I'd say you boys are more than a little late."

The Buffalo Soldiers didn't lower their weapons, but Morgan ignored them and fell back on the sand staring at the sun shining down from the clear blue sky. He was still lying like that when he heard the Pinkertons coming his way from downstream, and the sound of some of the soldiers coming down the steep riverbank on foot. He laughed out loud, and knew anyone that heard him was liable to think him crazy.

Two of the Buffalo Soldiers helped him up the riverbank, and he was standing at the north end of the trestle watching the train backing across it while the cavalry company's white lieutenant tried to interrogate him as to the afternoon's events. Morgan gave only brief, broad statements that in no way pleased the officer, and frustrated him even more when Morgan left him and walked towards the coming train.

Dixie was sitting on the handrail at the edge of the passenger car's rear deck, and he smiled broadly at Morgan.

"You look like you need a ride." He held down a hand to help Morgan up the steps.

The train was moving at a crawl, and Morgan caught the steps on the fly and managed his way up to Dixie with a little help.

"I trust I can find you in camp," the lieutenant called after him. "There are a lot of questions you haven't answered."

Morgan looked back at him. "You come find me about two days from now. I feel like catching up on some sleep."

Sergeant Harjo rode up with another Indian with him, as well as two other white men wearing badges that Morgan didn't recognize. They reined their horses in beside the train, keeping even with it. Harjo looked back at the bushwhacker bodies scattered along the train tracks in the distance towards camp, and then at Morgan's hatless, battered figure.

"You played hell, Chief," Harjo said.

Morgan looked at Dixie. "What is it you say? You ought to see the other guys?"

"That's right." Dixie laughed, and the laughing caused him to wheeze and cough.

"These men with me are deputy marshals from the federal court at Fort Smith," Harjo said.

One of the men beside Sergeant Harjo, a tall fellow with a dove-gray hat and a handlebar mustache waxed to needle-sharp points at the tips, nodded his head. "Judge Story sent us down here to look things over. We've heard half the bad element in the Territory is camped out here, and we've got warrants we'd like to serve on a bunch of them."

Morgan waved a hand around him. "Look all you want."

"We'd like to talk with you when we get a chance," the same deputy marshal said. "Folks in camp tell us that Fat Sally and Irish Dave have gone missing, and that you might know where they are."

Morgan sighed. "I'll tell you like I told the lieutenant here. You look me up after I've had time to take a good hot bath and get a few hours' sleep."

"You realize that you're bleeding, don't you?" The deputy pointed at Morgan's leg and at his shoulder.

"Yeah, I realize that." Morgan turned his attention back to Sergeant Harjo. "If you want Texas George, the last time I saw him he was running upriver."

"Thanks." Harjo and the other Lighthorsemen immediately turned their horses and rode away to the west.

Morgan turned his back on the deputy marshals and stepped through the open door of the passenger car. The inside was in shambles, and everywhere there was broken glass. A few of the men inside were in the process of turning the furniture right-side up from where they had used the chairs and sofas for barricades against the walls and windows. Morgan's eyes locked on the small safe along one wall.

Superintendent Duvall noticed him standing there and came the length of the car to meet him. "Where in the bloody hell have you been? Would you just look at this?"

"You moved the money to that little safe there, didn't you?" Morgan asked.

"And a good thing I did!"

Morgan looked past Duvall to where Helvina and another woman sat on a sofa clutching each other. Both women looked to have been crying, and Helvina's lower jaw was trembling when she looked up at him.

"How do you like the West now, Helvina?" Morgan asked. "It's all so scandalous, isn't it?"

He turned and went back out on the rear deck before she could answer him, his eyes on the whiteness of the tents of Ironhead in the distance. Dixie joined him at the railing.

"Sorry, I wasn't much help today," Dixie said. "This hole in one of my breathing sacks has taken the starch out of me and I ain't my usual self."

"You did fine."

"No, I let you down out there, Chief. I should have been riding with you instead of hunkering in here with the women and the dudes."

"I didn't hire you because I thought you could whip any man on the line."

"Then what did you hire me for?"

"I hired you because I thought you would fight when you were in the right. Win, lose, or draw, what matters is that you fought and that you didn't back down."

"That ain't much to say for a fighting man."

"That's the best thing you can say, and there's not many that I can say it about."

They stood silently until the train backed into the station. Besides the blown-up depot house, things looked better than Morgan expected. Instead of bodies lying everywhere, most seemed to have survived the explosion with no more than wounds or burst eardrums. The explosion had caused a fire in the nearby bathhouse, but volunteers had already managed to put it out and keep it from spreading to the rest of the camp. Doc Chillingsworth's hospital tent was busy, and men were helping the wounded there or carrying them on stretchers.

"Shit, ain't this something?" Dixie asked.

Morgan was already halfway down the steps.

"Where are you going?" Dixie called after him.

"I'm going to get some sleep. You get some men and round up anybody that needs rounding up and hand them over to those two deputy marshals."

Secretary Cox and Superintendent Duvall shoved through the door and past Dixie. Duvall waved his hand at Morgan trying to catch his attention, but Morgan kept on walking towards his boxcar bunkhouse on the west side of the tracks.

"You there," Secretary Cox called after him. "I think I owe you a debt of gratitude."

Morgan kept right on walking.

"Did you hear the secretary?" Duvall asked loudly.

"He heard you, Duvall," Dixie said. "He just ain't in the mood to listen."

CHAPTER FORTY-SIX

Torches had been lit and mounted on pole stands the length of the street, and the coal oil and pitch pine flames cast a weird orange glow over it, flickering and filled with sooty streaks of shadow that danced and weaved and crawled like wiggling worms over everything it touched. A patrol of dismounted cavalrymen marched along the row, the clank of the sabers at their hips and the scuff of their leather riding boots the only sound. Two federal deputy marshals walked at the head of their column, probably going to arrest someone else or to make sure they had left camp.

Ten corpses lay propped up on planks in front of the Katy store with a soldier to guard them, as if they might still be dangerous, even in death. All ten men lay with their arms crossed over their chests, locked in that pose by rigamortis and the ropes lashing them to the planks. A photographer had set up his camera late that afternoon and taken pictures of the deceased, and didn't seem bothered by the fact that no one had bothered to close their eyes. By nightfall, their complexion had already turned a chalky white, the face skin of several of them had drawn up until their teeth were revealed in ghastly grins, and the color had already faded from those sightless orbs until their milky pale stare was an eerie thing under the torch light.

Molly took one last look at them across the street from her before she shuddered and looked away. Ten dead men—nine bushwhackers that had fallen in the attempt to rob the Katy payroll and blow up the trestle, and another outlaw who had been foolish enough to stick around after the word went out that the army was going through the camp and removing its unwanted citizens with extreme prejudice. He hung around long enough to shout out that no, so-and-so colored soldiers were going to run him out of camp, and fired off an ill-advised and poorly aimed shot at them. Two of the buffalo soldiers took issue with his prejudice and rebellious remarks, and promptly riddled him with bullets from their .45-70 carbines. His death was more than enough to ensure the message went out loud and clear that Ironhead wasn't a healthy place anymore for outlaws and other deviants.

Molly ducked behind the corner of a tent and stayed out of sight until the patrol had passed. The army had placed a curfew on the camp, and not a soul could be seen moving about other than the guards scattered throughout the camp or one of the patrols. The Bullhorn Palace was closed for business for the first time since Ironhead came into being. The sound of its piano and the spin of its roulette wheel, a nightly regularity in camp, had gone silent, and not a single lamplight glowed from inside it.

She kept off the main street and moved quietly through the tents, trusting to the little bit of moonlight to guide her. She knew she was getting close when she smelled it, and soon she was working her way along the timber at the edge of camp. Ahead of her, she could make out the row of plank and tin-roofed little buildings before her. Stopping behind those structures, she sat down at the foot of a large tree and unfolded the blanket she carried. It was four hours until daylight. Stretching her legs before her, she covered herself with the blanket, laid the little Manhattan pistol in her lap, and settled in for a long wait.

CHAPTER FORTY-SEVEN

Bill Tuck double-checked the street to make sure he was in the clear before he crossed it in a few long, running strides. It was only a short distance up the far side to Doc Chillingsworth's hospital tent, and he took one last look behind him before he ducked inside the front flaps. A lantern hung from the tent's ridgepole lit up the dozen men and one woman lying on the cots in the front room. He made a quick survey of them, but the man he sought wasn't amongst the wounded.

He eased to the entrance of the back room and peered through the doorway. Doc Chillingsworth was asleep in a chair beside a single bed, his head propped against the iron headboard. The kerosene lamp beside the bed had been turned down to a tiny flame behind the glass globe. Beside the doctor, nestled deep in the feather mattress and swaddled to his chin in a white sheet, was Bert Huffman.

Huffman's eyes were open and he watched Tuck enter. That unnerved Tuck a little, as if the man had been waiting for him.

"I heard you were shot," Tuck said in a whisper. "Thought I would come check on you."

"Who did it?" Huffman managed after a convulsion of his throat and a deep swallow.

Tuck shook his head. "The drunken fools were firing off their pistols. Could have been any one of their bullets that hit you."

Huffman started to say something else, but grimaced as if a wave of pain had struck him. He closed his eyes and clenched his teeth, and Tuck could see that he held his breath to wait out whatever hurt had come over him.

"You shouldn't have been on that train deck," Tuck said.

"Your men did this," Huffman finally managed.

"Not my men." Tuck threw a worried glance at Doc Chillingsworth, but the doctor was still snoring. "It was a bad accident. Nothing more. Some fool fired off a pistol and happened to hit you."

Tuck started to leave, but the intensity of Huffman's stare held him in place.

"I want to believe you." Huffman's voice had grown so weak Tuck could barely hear him.

"Why would I want you dead? We had a deal," Tuck hissed.

"Why, indeed?" Huffman clenched against the pain again, and then continued, "I better never find out anything to the contrary."

Tuck's eyes locked on the feather tick pillow Huffman's head rested on. It would be relatively easy to jerk it out and press it into Huffman's face and smother him. Nobody would ever think anything but that the man had died of his grievous bullet wound in his sleep. But there was the doctor, sleeping right beside him.

As if on cue, Doc Chillingsworth snorted and jerked himself awake. It took him a moment to register Tuck standing there, and he rubbed at his face and tried to blink the sleep from his eyes.

"How long have you been there?" he asked.

"I came to check on him," Tuck answered.

Chillingsworth glanced at his patient and then at Tuck. "You two are friends?"

Tuck shook his head. "Business associates."

Chillingsworth looked back at Huffman, but the KNVR man's eyes were closed. For a second, Tuck held out hope that he had died, but the doctor placed his hand under his nostrils and then laid an ear to his chest.

"Just sleeping," he said when he straightened.

"How badly is he hurt?"

"Very badly. Frankly, I'm quite shocked that he has lasted this long, and even more shocked that he has remained lucid." Chillingsworth rose and went over to a table nearby littered with bloody rags and surgical tools. He reached inside a washbasin and pulled something out that he held in the lamplight for Tuck to see. It was an oddly shaped bullet, hexagonal and twice as long as most bullets.

"Funny thing," Chillingsworth added. "Everyone is saying it was a stray pistol bullet that hit him, but that is no pistol bullet. As many bullets as I've cut from the flesh of my patients over the years, I've never seen its like."

"Strange," Tuck said when Chillingsworth handed him the bullet.

"I'd best go check on my other patients." Chillingsworth scuttled past him and disappeared into the front room.

Tuck glanced at Huffman's pillow again, and then at the Whitworth bullet he held in his open palm.

"Care for a cup of coffee?" Chillingsworth called to him.

Tuck stepped into the front room. "I believe I'll pass. Goodnight, Doc."

He stepped outside so quickly that Chillingsworth didn't have time to say anything else, nor did the doctor notice him pocket the Whitworth bullet.

CHAPTER FORTY-EIGHT

The little bald man and former grading foreman called Tubbs was the third man to the latrines that morning, arriving at the second outhouse from the end barely after sunup. He was apparently in a hurry, for he came at a shambling trot and never looked around him before he entered and slammed the plank door shut behind him. He was long about his business, and was still seated in the outhouse after the other two patrons had finished their business and left.

She waited until those other two were gone, and made sure that nobody else was coming before she stepped from the woods. The blanket she had covered herself with the night before was wrapped about her hand, and she held it before her as she walked quickly to the front of the outhouse he had chosen. She only took a single deep breath to steady herself before she laid hand to the door.

"What the hell?" he said when she jerked open the door.

"Remember me?" she asked as she cocked the pistol wrapped within the blanket.

The little .22 caliber rounds made only harmless, muffled pops within the blanket, but he grunted with every shot she fired into him, holding up the newspaper he had been reading as if it might protect him. The bullets gnawed a ragged hole through the paper before they gnawed into his guts.

Seven times she shot him, and then she closed the door and walked back to camp. Never once did she look backward, and she didn't let go of the pistol until she was back inside her tent. She laid it beside her on her dresser, and took a seat in her rocker. It was still dark inside the confines of the canvas walls, yet she did not light her lamp. Instead, she sat there, rocking and occasionally glancing at where she had laid the pistol, feeling it even though she could not see it. Seven more cartridges for one more man.

CHAPTER FORTY-NINE

Morgan and Dixie sat in chairs on what remained of the depot decking, soaking in the afternoon sun and doing their best to ignore the sound of the construction crew demolishing what remained of the railroad office behind them. Morgan's bandaged leg was propped on a shipping crate before him, and he took a puff of his cigar and then thumped the ash from the end of it with a flick of his finger against it.

"Pretty morning," Dixie said beside him.

"Yeah."

"How come every time we get some peace and quiet somebody comes along and ruins it?" Dixie pointed down the street.

The two newly arrived federal deputy marshals were riding their way leading two horses behind them. Both horses carried a tarp-wrapped body draped across their backs. The deputy marshals ignored the stares they were getting from the people in camp, and made their way to the depot where they pulled up in front of Morgan and Dixie.

One of the lawmen dismounted, and one at a time he lifted the canvas tarp on the bodies and lifted their heads for Morgan to see their faces. The buzzards had been at Irish Dave and Fat Sally and what remained of their features was bloated and discolored, but Morgan recognized them all the same.

"I guess you found them where I told you they would be," Morgan said.

The lawman on foot nodded. "We've got men trolling the river right now for the bodies of the two you said went over the bank."

"I don't know if you'll find them, but they're there."

The dismounted lawman nodded again, and then looked to his partner before he spoke again. "You said the Traveler carries a big bore rifle, but both these victims look to have died from pistol rounds, if I don't miss my guess. There's not an exit wound on either of them."

"I told you, he used my pistol."

"Uh huh." The two lawmen shared another look between them.

"And you never knew Irish Dave before he came here?" the deputy marshal still on his horse asked. "Not back in New York?"

"Never laid eyes on him until I came to Ironhead," Morgan said with a hint of impatience beginning to show in his voice.

"What about this trouble between you and him in the Bucket of Blood?"

"I've already told you about that." Morgan's word were clipped and concise, as if it was taking a tremendous effort for him to continue. "I arrested Dave and my deputy here had to subdue Fat Sally when she tried to interfere with the arrest. There's nothing more to it. We let Dave go the next morning."

The deputy marshals seemed to be trying to think of another question, but one of the Pinkertons came along the boardwalk and interrupted the conversation.

"I think you all should follow me to the latrines and have a look at something," he said.

"What is it?" Dixie asked. "Or do I want to ask?"

"I'm not trying to be funny," the Pinkerton said. "You need to go down there. One of the soldiers found him and asked for me to come get you."

Superintendent Duvall came around the corner of the

burned-out depot with Helvina on his arm. Secretary of the Interior Cox and a small group of dignitaries were with him.

"What's this about?" Duvall asked, apparently having overheard much of the conversation on his approach.

"I was just telling these peace officers that a soldier found a body down at the latrines," the Pinkerton said.

"I trust these federal men can handle that," the secretary said, and laid a hand on Morgan's shoulder. "The chief here must be given time to recuperate from his wounds. This camp and this construction project owe a great deal to his heroic efforts yesterday."

Morgan clenched his jaws and looked at the hand on his shoulder, but said nothing.

"Yes, leave Chief Clyde alone while he convalesces," Duvall threw in.

"I'm not your chief anymore," Morgan said.

"What's that?" Duvall asked.

Morgan shrugged out from under the secretary's overly friendly hand and unpinned the badge from his vest. He pitched the tin shield to Duvall.

"I resign, as of now," he said.

"You can't . . ."

"I can't what?"

"There now." The secretary stepped between them. "Can't you see this man is stressed from recent events?"

Morgan glanced at Helvina and caught her watching him. "You look in fine feather this morning. Much better than when I saw you last."

She lifted that dimpled chin slightly. "I would be lying if I said the same about you."

"We'll go see about that body," one of the deputies said.

"If I might dare, whose body is it we speak of?" Duvall asked. "I take it this is a victim of yesterday's attempted robbery, or is it the results of military marshal law?"

The Pinkerton shook his head. "No, he said the body isn't even cold yet."

"Anybody we might know?" Duvall asked.

"Said his name was Tubbs. Somebody caught him on the john and pumped him full of bullet holes."

"Tubbs?" Duvall repeated, and he turned to Morgan at the same time the deputy marshals did.

"Wasn't Tubbs the man you were looking for in regards to the beaten whores?" one of the deputy marshals asked Morgan.

Morgan saw where that question was leading. "He was."

Dixie leaned forward in his chair and spit a stream of tobacco that barely went wide of the deputy marshals. "Morgan and me were in our boxcar all night, and the only place we've been since we got up was to breakfast and here. Ask anyone who was in the mess tent at daylight, and they'll tell you they saw us."

"We'll ask around," the dismounted deputy marshal said. "Curious, though, how all your enemies keep ending up shot."

"You wouldn't wonder about that if you knew the kind of people that decide they want to be our enemies," Dixie said, squinting at the two federal lawmen and working his chew around in his cheek.

"I understand one of those whores who got roughed up is a friend of yours, Clyde," the same deputy marshal added.

"I don't like what you're implying." Morgan straightened in his chair and leaned slightly forward. "In fact, I don't like what you've been implying since the instant you came into camp."

"Gentlemen," Duvall said. "I'll remind you there is a lady present."

Helvina gave them all a demure and coy smile and then waved a dismissive hand. "By all means, don't mind me. Please continue to interrogate him."

The dismounted marshal climbed back on his horse. "I take

it that you will be around here for further questioning, Clyde, should we deem it necessary."

Morgan looked down at his bandaged leg. "I doubt I'm a flight risk."

The deputy marshals turned their horses and headed back into camp with the Pinkerton leading them towards the latrines on foot. They left the two horses bearing the bodies standing in front of the depot.

"Who do they intend to take care of these bodies?" Duvall asked indignantly.

"Not my concern," Morgan said. "I told you I quit."

"I advanced you a month's pay," Duvall said. "I'll expect you to settle the overpayment."

Helvina took Duvall by the arm before Morgan could answer. "Speaking of money, I think you have a meeting with your directors to attend. We wouldn't want to keep them waiting, would we?"

Duvall looked at the VIP tent across the tracks with displeasure. "They have no right to question me. I've built this railroad this far, and I'm the man to see it to Texas."

She patted his arm. "I know, Willis, I know, but you'll have to keep your cool. You have nothing to hide, but it's perfectly normal for your directors and shareholders to want a look at the ledgers, and to ask difficult questions."

"Pencil pushers and legal whiners," Duvall said again as the group started across the tracks.

Dixie watched them go and then said to Morgan, "You really quit?"

"Yes. What about you?"

"I don't know. Do you think it was Tuck that got Tubbs?"

"Maybe."

"What about Molly?"

"Maybe."

"What do you intend to do about that?"

"I intend to sit right here for a spell. Those federals or whoever is the next chief of police can worry about it." Morgan leaned back in his chair and closed his eyes against the pale white sun shining down on him.

Dixie watched him for a long while, expecting him to say something else, but he didn't.

CHAPTER FIFTY

Two mornings later the bay horse Morgan had purchased was tied to the side of the boxcar. Dixie sat in the open door of the car and watched Morgan hobble to the horse on his game leg and swing his saddlebags across the back of the saddle one-handed.

"You're in no shape to ride," Dixie said as he handed Morgan his leather-cased sharpshooter rifle.

Morgan kept his back to Dixie and said nothing while he hung the rifle case beside the swells with the saddle strings. His leather valise containing his meager belongings already hung from the saddle horn, and a blanket roll was tied on behind.

"Those deputy marshals won't be happy to find out you're gone," Dixie said. "They still aren't convinced you aren't a murderer."

Morgan leaned against the saddle and twisted his head around to look at Dixie. "What am I, Dixie?"

"You're a hundred and seventy-five-dollar-a-month peace officer, unemployed with damned few prospects, fewer friends, and two bullet holes in you. Other than that, you're perfectly normal," Dixie said. "You cleaned up this God-awful excuse for a railroad camp, and nobody's ever going to say thanks."

Morgan untied the bridle rein and led the horse close to the open door of the boxcar. With a little effort he managed to get himself to a sitting position in the doorway and coaxed the horse close enough to put his good foot in the stirrup.

"Look at you," Dixie said. "You can't even get on your horse regular, and you're telling me that you're riding out of here."

Morgan swung himself up on the horse and settled in the saddle gingerly. He reached in his pocket and retrieved a cigar that he stabbed in one corner of his mouth. He struck a match on his saddle horn and cupped the flame to the end of the cigar.

"I can't handle this camp alone," Dixie said.

Morgan shook his head. "You can. Things are quiet now, and the camp will be moving on down the line before it has time to get rowdy again."

"What about the next camp?"

"Are you saying you're going to keep working for Duvall?"

Dixie shrugged. "Call me a fool, but I've worked at worse jobs than this peace officer bit."

"Well, if Duvall's smart, he'll make you chief."

"You're the chief, and besides, we work better as a pair."

"You'll do fine."

"Where was it that you said you were going?" Dixie asked.

"I heard there is a big salt flat three days' ride west of here up on the Arkansas, and they claim that the buffalo are as thick as flies there in the spring." Morgan shook out the match and looked to the west. "I've never seen a buffalo. Thought I might do a little hunting."

"Want some company? Like you said, things are quiet here for now, and I could use a little peace time myself."

"I guess I'll ride alone."

Dixie looked to the west himself. "You ain't going buffalo hunting. You're going out to meet the Traveler, aren't you?"

Morgan nudged the horse forward.

"Are you coming back?" Dixie asked after him. "You know, if . . ."

Morgan didn't answer him.

"What do I tell Molly?" Dixie called after him. "She cares about you, and she's in trouble if those deputy marshals think she killed Tubbs."

Morgan rode his horse along the railroad tracks headed north without looking back. Dixie continued to watch him until he was nothing but a speck in the distance.

Dixie adjusted the bandage on his chest and leaned against the doorjamb after Morgan was gone. He was still leaning there when a group of men crossed the tracks and came his way. He recognized all of the men as Pinkerton detectives that he and Morgan had worked with in camp, but the man walking in the lead was new to him.

That man stopped the group a few feet in front of Dixie, and cleared his throat to get his attention as if he thought him sleeping. He was young, perhaps in his mid-twenties, hatless, and with a dark mass of wavy hair and a heavy mustache. He was also immaculately dressed and carried a silver-handled walking cane in one hand.

"Are you Deputy Rayburn?" the man asked.

"I am. And who might you be?"

"William Pinkerton."

"The last name I'm familiar with, but your first name doesn't ring a bell."

The young man grounded his walking cane. "Unfortunately, my father, Allan, suffered a stroke a few years ago. The running of the agency has since been left to my brother and I."

"What brings you to these parts, young Pinkerton?" Dixie at first dismissed the dapperly dressed young man as no more than some rich, spoiled dude, but it slowly dawned on him that there was something about the set to his face and the glint in his eyes that hinted of danger. Dixie could see no gun on him, but somehow he was sure that the young William Pinkerton was armed.

"I've come all the way from Chicago . . ."

"Chicago?"

"Yes, Chicago. As I was saying, I've come a long ways in search of a man, and I'm told you might be of some assistance in that regard."

"What man?"

"Morgan Clyde."

"What do you want Chief Clyde for?"

The young man glanced at one of his detectives before answering. "Morgan Clyde was involved in a . . . hmm, difficulty, let us say, with some of my agents in New York a few years past."

"What kind of difficulty?"

"Morgan Clyde shot and killed one of my detectives and grievously wounded two others with a knife."

"And you're only now looking for him? Something tastes sour here."

"As I said, there were some, perhaps, extenuating circumstances and misunderstandings that leaned my father toward leniency on Clyde's behalf. However, I am not my father, and now I have received a telegraph a few days past informing me that he threw another of my detectives out of a moving train."

"That Pinkerton Morgan threw out of the train got what he deserved, and I imagine Morgan had his reasons for whatever kind of fracas he got into with your men back in New York. He ain't one to pick a fight, but he'll damned sure finish one."

"That is your opinion, sir. However, we at the Pinkerton National Detective Agency look after our own, and it would seem that your friend, Clyde, needs to be taught some proper respect. Would you happen to know his whereabouts?"

"I wouldn't tell you if I knew."

"I find your attitude to be most unpleasant, and bordering on insult if not criminality." Pinkerton pointed his cane at Dixie to give emphasis to his accusation, and a couple of the detectives behind him started forward as if to lay hands on Dixie.

Dixie reached around the corner of the boxcar door and brought out his Spencer carbine and cocked it and leveled it on the men before him, all in one smooth, almost nonchalant motion. "What was that you were saying, Mr. Pinkerton?"

The detectives backed up a step, with their boss among them.

"Very well, Deputy Rayburn. I'm confident that we can find Clyde with or without your help, or my men and I would pursue this discussion farther."

"You get along." Dixie jabbed at them with the barrel of the Spencer. "I've had my fill of you."

Pinkerton spun on his heel stiffly and led his men away, leaving Dixie alone once more. He sat the carbine aside, and leaned his shoulder against the doorjamb again. He was drowsy and half asleep, and almost didn't notice Texas George and his brother Bennie riding up the railroad tracks at the far edge of camp, the same way Morgan had gone.

Dixie straightened. "Morgan Clyde, you've got more trouble than any man I ever knew. First the Traveler, then the Pinkertons, and now Texas George and that brother of his, all after your scalp. And I'll be damned if I don't almost pity those fools when they catch up to you."

Dixie watched the Kingmans disappear the same as Morgan had, and when they were gone he began to sing.

"O, I'm a good old Rebel, now that's just what I am . . ."

HISTORICAL NOTES

1. Perhaps no more lawless stretch of country ever existed than the Indian Territory, the very same geography that would form the state of Oklahoma in 1907. Famous for its Indians, infamous for its outlaws, and often known as the "Indian Nations," "Indian Country," or simply "the Territory," it was the stomping grounds of such outlaws as the Dalton Gang, Bill Doolin, Cole Younger, and Henry Starr, and would later become the jurisdiction of the notorious Hanging Judge Parker.

2. The MK&T construction camp of Ironhead Station later became the town of Eufaula when merchants from nearby North Fork Town moved their holdings to the camp to take advantage of the new railroad. During a portion of 1872, Ironhead Station might have been the wildest hellhole on the American frontier.

3. North Fork Town, also at times known as Micco, now lies under the waters of Eufaula Lake, one of the largest man-made lakes in the world. Standing Rock, once rising up in the middle of the Canadian River with its strange pictographs and carven symbols, many supposedly leading to treasure, and once a famous landmark for travelers and explorers, also lies beneath those waters. The grave of the famous female outlaw, Belle Starr, lies on the side of a little mountain overlooking one of the lake's dams on the Canadian River.

4. Although I have taken slight historical liberties for the sake of fiction and the plot of this novel, in 1872, a drunken mob of

Indian Territory toughs and outlaws did surround the Secretary of Interior and his entourage in a private railcar when they came to inaugurate the trestle at Ironhead. Shots were fired at the secretary's train car, and an attempt was also made to blow up the trestle with explosives. The secretary was so shocked and angered by the lawlessness and rampant drunkenness that he sent in the Buffalo Soldiers of the 10th U.S. Cavalry to clean up the camp, just as I have portrayed in the novel.

5. The Whitworth rifle, such as the Arkansas Traveler carries in the novel, is a story in itself. The Confederacy, always strapped for cash and in short supply of arms, purchased a limited number of the rifles from the British Whitworth Rifle Co. While different barrel lengths and sight variations were offered, what made it unique was its one-of-a-kind hexagonal bore, superb accuracy, and its light weight in comparison to other target rifles of its day. Confederate sharpshooters armed with these rifles executed some of the most legendary long-range shots of the war and made life dangerous for Union officers foolish enough to skyline themselves in the belief that they were too far out of the accurate range of small arms fire.

Non-students of firearms history often erroneously assume that Civil War era rifles, especially muzzleloaders, weren't accurate. If you are one such, then consider that when tested in the presence of the British Minister of War, the Whitworth rifle shot a 4.44-inch group at 500 yards, and a 12-inch group at 800 yards, and later scored confirmed kills beyond one mile during the Civil War. Rifle targets preserved at West Point and other target shooting documents of the day record shooters achieving sub-minute-of-angle accuracy with .45 caliber muzzle-loading target rifles such as the Whitworth or the R.R. Moore rifle that Morgan Clyde owns in the novel. In 1859, custom rifle builder and marksman, Morgan James, demonstrated the phenomenal accuracy of his target rifle to a crowd of observers by firing a nine-shot group at 110 yards that measured .38 inches, roughly putting all his bullets in the same hole. During the same year at the first annual competition held by the National Rifle Club, Colonel Hiram Berdan, the founder of Berdan's Sharpshooters of which the fictional Morgan Clyde was a member, took a scoped Morgan James muzzleloading target rifle and put five consecutive shots into a 10-inch circle from 600 yards away.

ABOUT THE AUTHOR

Some folks are just born to tell tall tales. **Brett Cogburn** was reared in Texas and the mountains of southeastern Oklahoma. He had the fortune for many years to make his living from the back of a horse, where cowboys still step on frisky broncs on cold mornings, and drag calves to the branding fire on the end of a rope from their saddle horn. Growing up around ranches, livestock auctions, and backwoods hunting camps filled his head with stories, and he never forgot a one. In his own words, "My grandfather taught me to ride a bucking horse, my mother gave me a love of reading, and my father taught me how to shoot straight. Cowboys are just as wild as they ever were, and I've been fortunate enough to know more than a few."

Somewhere during his knockabout years of cowboying, training horses, and working in the oilfield, he managed to earn a BA in English and a minor in history. Brett lives with his family on a small ranch in Oklahoma. The West is still teaching him how to write.

The employees of Five Star Publishing hope you have enjoyed this book.

Our Five Star novels explore little-known chapters from America's history, stories told from unique perspectives that will entertain a broad range of readers.

Other Five Star books are available at your local library, bookstore, all major book distributors, and directly from Five Star/Gale.

Connect with Five Star Publishing

Visit us on Facebook:
  https://www.facebook.com/FiveStarCengage

Email:
  FiveStar@cengage.com

For information about titles and placing orders:
  (800) 223-1244
  gale.orders@cengage.com

To share your comments, write to us:
  Five Star Publishing
  Attn: Publisher
  10 Water St., Suite 310
  Waterville, ME 04901